# The Kielder Strain

## The Kielder Experiment, Volume 1

Rebecca Fernfield

Published by Redbegga Publishing, 2022.

# Copyright

# CHAPTER ONE

*Kielder Forest*
*Thursday, November 18th, 9.15 pm*

The urge to run drove Anita deeper into the forest. With no idea of direction, and no sense of time, all she could hear was her own rasping breath and the pounding thump of her pulse. A cloud of white breath billowed in the torchlight as she cast it around for direction. Surrounded by trees, she searched for a path, for any clue of a way out.

Nearby, a branch cracked. *Stay still. Stay calm.* She flicked the torch off, hoping that if she remained still, *he* wouldn't find her. Heart hammering, she waited, and listened, regretting with every passing second that she hadn't gone with the others.

Something moved overhead and, with a flap of beating wings, a bird, black against the dark blue sky, erupted from the branches. It disappeared beyond the canopy where the stars, without the pollution of light, filled the sky with sprays and pinpricks of brilliant silver.

Anita listened, maintaining her stillness, willing her breathing to slow. Nothing moved, at least nothing large moved. Perhaps *he* had finally stopped following her. Flicking the torch back on, she stepped out into a clearing where a fallen tree lay, its roots enormous tentacles hanging above ground.

*If only she had gone to the Institute with the others, she would be safe in bed by now, tucked up in the sleeping bag with Jamie.* She gritted her teeth. *Jamie. It was all his fault. Why had she ever listened to him? Because you're an idiot, Nita. That's why.*

Torchlight revealed the clearing but there was no evidence of a path, or a trail back to the campsite and without a path she would remain lost, trapped in the woods until morning. *Her mother had been right, she was an idiot. An idiot who had no idea about what it took to make it in the real world. An idiot who got herself thrown out of university because she was too easily led and was now on a slippery slope to exactly nowhere.* She clenched her jaws and forced her mother's nagging voice out of her head.

Pulling the zipper of her jacket to beneath her chin, she sat on the fallen trunk, the roots a wall against the woods. Yesterday, when they'd trekked through the forest so that Nate could make a map of routes to the *Institute*, she'd looked through the trees. The forest floor had seemed ancient with its massive, upturned roots and wind-blown trees hidden beneath thick blankets of emerald-green moss. Nothing moved among the ferns growing in the dappled light. Nothing crept among the moss-covered and rotting trunks. That had seemed odd to Anita. She had expected birds of prey to be perched in the branches, squirrels running up and down trunks, launching themselves from tree to tree, and deer jumping from behind the undergrowth startled by walkers invading their home. But there had been nothing; a dead place. Perhaps it was because the trees were pines? It was a man-made forest after all. She huffed; *Man poisoned everything.*

Close by a branch snapped.

Swinging the torchlight in the direction of the noise, she scanned the trees, but nothing moved. Wind blew cold against her face and another branch fell with a crack somewhere in the forest. She wiped at her nose with her sleeve as the tip began to sting with cold and her teeth to chatter. Spots of rain tapped against her jacket and wet her lashes, and she moved to the overhang created by the upturned root where she could sit and get some protection from the coming storm. As the wind picked up, the rain came sharp. She hugged her knees and waited.

The torchlight flickered, its batteries waning. "Shit!" she whispered and tapped the torch against her palm. It brightened, dimmed, then brightened again and she switched it off to save the battery in case *he* came close again. *He must be a lunatic. Who, in their right mind, would chase her through the forest and torture her likes this?* As her eyes adjusted, the outline of the trees grew visible against the night sky. Everything was grey, or black. Only the sky was an expanse of midnight blue speckled silver. As the minutes then hours passed, her eyes grew heavy and, despite her fear, she fell into a fitful sleep.

She woke to the crack of rotten wood.

Instantly alert, heart pounding, her eyes flew open to a clearing washed a dark grey as the shadows of night began to recede.

Snap!

Scrabbling against the root, Anita searched the grey space for the source of the noise. At the edge of the clearing a figure moved between the trees.

A flash of light, flickering as it moved, dragged her attention from the figure to the other side of the clearing. She scrambled towards the light.

"Hey!" The call was barely audible, her throat dry.

The light moved deeper into the woods and then disappeared.

"Hey!" she called again and began to run. "Stop!"

Sprinting away from the root, she caught glimpses of the light. A dark figure appeared at the periphery of her vision, running parallel. She pushed harder, her thighs burning.

"Hey! Stop. I'm here," she called as she reached the far edge of the clearing and crashed back into the woods.

Footsteps pounded behind her.

Branches scratched her face and caught at her hair. Running blindly into the forest, she raised an arm as protection. The dark figure drew parallel, a single tree between them. Darting to the left, she stumbled, thrashing her arms to force the branches to part. Catching her foot, she tripped then fell. Her hands slammed flat against the cold dirt, pain shooting through her knees as they knocked against worming roots.

As she scrabbled against the earth, pushing up on all fours, sour breath, hot and moist, brushed the skin of her cheek.

# CHAPTER TWO

*Eighteen hours earlier*
*Kielder Village, 9.16 am*

Javeen swung the patrol car into the station's car park and cursed; PC Stangton's bicycle was already in its stand. She'd hoped to get in before him. 'Late again, Latimer?' he would say with that self-satisfied smirk and glint in his eyes that told her he knew exactly why she'd been shunted to this backwater. She had lost count of the number of times she had wanted to slap his smug face. *If he gave her that wink again!* She breathed out the tension with a huff and her shoulders sagged with resignation. *She only had herself to blame.* They all knew about it—exactly why she'd been transferred; she was an embarrassing faux pas that needed sweeping under the carpet, or rather, 'disappeared' to Kielder.

"Note to self," she muttered. "Do not bed a Superintendent with aspirations of climbing up the greasy pole to became Chief Super, particularly if he's already married." She pulled the handbrake up with a vindictive yank and stared at the tiny Police Station. Tucked away at the end of the village, the last building before the road disappeared back into the forest, it seemed to cower beneath the trees; its slate roof mottled with lichen, its white-washed walls crawling with green algae.

She had to admit - although it was a secret she hugged to herself - she liked the place. Was it boring? Compared to Grimsby, her last placement, yes it was. She shuddered at the memory. Hell, the women there were worse than the men, and you could bet, nine times out of ten, the females were the perpetrators when the neighbours called to complain about a fight next door. Take Aileen Ricks for instance. Now, there was a woman you didn't want to cross. Built like the proverbial outhouse, at forty-one she was as wide as she was tall, a cigarette permanently on the go, and more than happy to lob an ashtray, remote control, plate, or kettle – all of which she had done – at her husband. Mr Ricks wasn't exactly small himself, but no match for Aileen's abusive temper and abhorrence of his 'habits', as she used to call the irritations that set it off. You couldn't fault her work ethic though; sixty hours a week at the local fish processing plant whilst juggling kids, a husband (when he wasn't on the docks), and a house, was no easy feat.

Javeen sighed. Grimsby. The town that had made her wonder if she had chosen the right career and driven her into the arms of the very married Superintendent Nigel 'bloody' Parker. Policing there was certainly gritty, just like the weekly police procedurals she'd been glued to as a teenager. If she was honest, despite the tantrums, and angry, bordering on abusive, phone call to Nigel after she'd realised it was him that had organised her move, Javeen was relieved when she'd been banished to the sleepy backwater that was Kielder.

As she entered the office, she wished for the second time that she had beaten Stangton into work. He looked up from his desk as she walked through the door. A gust of cold

November wind blew dead leaves across the threshold with her.

"Aye, aye. Look what the wind's blown in!"

Javeen stifled a groan as he looked at her with interest bordering on contempt.

"Late again, Latimer?" Light shone on his scalp where his hair was thinning to bald. His cheeks were ruddy. "Up too late, were you? Walk of shame, ay?"

She dropped her handbag on the table a little too hard. *Oh, shut up, Stangton!* Her sex life, or lack of it, was nothing to do with him, but confronting PC Stuart Stangton, village bobby and nosey parker extraordinaire, just wasn't worth it.

"Ay?" His eyes gleamed with mirth, enjoying watching her squirm.

Javeen swallowed down her irritation as she slid her handbag inside the desk drawer and threw him a tight smile. "Oh, you know ..." If she couldn't bite back, she would tease.

He raised his brows, a smile breaking across his lips, a glimmer of greedy interest in his eyes. "Oh, aye?" He waited.

Ignoring him, Javeen walked through to the tiny kitchen and switched on the kettle. *Let him stew.*

"Two sugars," he called from his desk.

*Make your own coffee.*

"Spill the beans then, Latimer. Who was it?"

She dropped an overlarge spoonful of coffee into her mug and drowned it with milk. His eyes bored into her back.

"Blackwell from the garage?"

Again, she ignored him. However, Andy Blackwell from the garage would be a contender. At six foot three with broad shoulders and muscles that over-filled his t-shirt he was certainly a bloke you wouldn't kick out of bed. But no, her bed mate last night, as it had been every night since she'd arrived in Kielder had been a hot water bottle, a cup of tea, and a copy of the next Stephen King on her TBR pile. Since she'd arrived, she'd made pretty good headway through that list.

"Maybe it was Jack from the *Hound and Stars*? He's got the hots for you."

This was news to her. Jack, landlord of the village pub, was pushing seventy and didn't look as if he'd had the hots for anyone since 1979.

"Give me a break!" she retorted.

"Pah! Don't tell me then. I'm not that bothered. Who you shag is your own business."

*Chance would be a fine thing!* "Too bloody right!" She gave the coffee an extra stir, knowing the scraping of metal against the hard surface of the mug grated on his nerves.

"As long as he wasn't married, Latimer, ay?" Stangton muttered his petty vengeance.

Javeen bit back her words. One of these days she wouldn't be able to hold back and then he'd know about it. *Nosey sod.* She sauntered back to the office and placed her mug on the coaster. Milky coffee spilled over the sides.

"Watch it!" Stangton remonstrated moving a pile of papers away from the mess. "Anyway, you haven't got time to drink that. We've just had a call from the *Institute*. There's been an incident up there."

"Incident?"

"Vegan extremists."

Javeen snorted. "Vegan extremists?"

"Don't laugh, Latimer. It can come harsh when they whip you with their celery sticks."

"Right. So, what exactly have they been up to?"

"Lobbing avocadoes. Waving placards. All very scary stuff."

Javeen sighed. Chaos seemed to have followed her to the village.

# CHAPTER THREE

*Kielder Institute, 9.36 am*

The door to the lab opened and Max tensed as the lock clicked. *It was her—again!* His heart tapped in time to the tack, tack of her heels as she made her way across the floor. The noise seemed to fill the small room.

"Dr Anderson, how's it coming on?" For a moment Dr Marta Steward stood at his shoulder then stepped to the window and closed the slatted blinds, shutting out the grey morning light. "That's better."

The bank of trees across the car park disappeared from his peripheral vision along with the straggle of scruffy activists with placards at the gates. He gritted his teeth remembering the smeared mess across his windscreen from the flour bombs they'd thrown at the car that morning. *Stupid, ungrateful fools!* They had no idea just how important their work at the *Institute* was; it didn't seem to matter to them that it would save lives.

The protesters' appearance at the *Institute* had given Max heartburn. He'd thought the location, deep in the forest, only two miles from the most remote village in England, would have given him, and his colleagues, some protection. He'd been wrong, and now the petty anarchists were here lobbing stones and flour paste-filled balloons as he passed through the gates. At least the protests weren't like those in the city; there he had become frightened. The lab had come under frequent attack, and he'd feared for his life on more than one occasion. This lot, thankfully, seemed to lack the edge and cohesion of the other terrorist group. That they had been terrorists was certain, the death threats, break-ins and, finally, the incendiary device detonated at the front doors, had proven that beyond doubt.

A familiar scent seeped into his nose and Max glanced at the director as she slipped behind him. With blonde hair freshly brushed to fall seductively at her shoulders, she stood with hands on hips and smiled down at him. His heartbeat tripped against his ribs and his hands trembled. Vegans with a passion for animals weren't the only thing that struck a chord of terror in Max's heart. Marta's shirt was buttoned low, and the lipstick looked newly applied. He tensed - *be polite—no encouragement* - gave her a tight smile in return, then turned back to his microscope, peering down into the lens, and watched the virus as it infected the healthy cells on the slide he had prepared minutes earlier.

"Max?" she prodded, pushing his arm with her hip. "Aren't you talking to me?" Her voice was light and breathy. He clenched his jaw. "Well?" she asked and leant down over his shoulder.

*No!* "Of course," he replied. "Just observing the cells from the sample Barnard sent up."

Warm breath, laden with coffee and cigarettes was hot on Max's cheek. *Didn't the woman have any respect for personal space?* He sat upright.

"The outbreak?"

"Yes."

"Well, what's the verdict?"

"Take a look." Max gestured to the microscope.

Catching the back of his chair, Marta leant over, brushing against his shoulder, her too blonde hair tickled his cheek. Max twirled his wedding ring with his thumb. Her smell was familiar. He breathed it in. *Yes! Chanel No. 5, the perfume he'd mentioned he was buying Laura for her birthday.*

Max pulled to the side, but Marta leant in closer, her breast soft against his neck, her ribcage pressing along his back. He had hoped that after his wedding her 'attentions' would stop but his marriage seemed to have made them worse. She placed a hand on his shoulder and squeezed. Heart racing, and a knot growing in his stomach, he covered his startled reflex with a cough.

"Hmm," she said peering down into the microscope whilst rubbing at his shoulder. "So that's the lyssavirus?"

"Yes, rabies." Suddenly animated, he forgot about the breast pushing against his shoulder. "But not a form we've seen before." He twirled the chair to face her.

"So, it *has* mutated." She stepped back and straightened.

Max took a breath, relieved at the space between them. "Yes, and very aggressively. The human victims died within three days of being bitten. Marta ... I think we're looking at gain of function here."

"Anyway, what were the victims bitten by?"

With his concerns about the origins of the virus ignored, he said, "Infected dogs at a campsite near Whitby."

She laughed. "Vampires?"

"Hah! No. Nothing supernatural, but there is a colony of bats nearby."

"Have they been tested?"

"The bats? Yes, the sample's here." Max slid the report across to her.

"There hasn't been an indigenous case of rabies since the 1920s and no deaths since 1902. To have three in one week is ... unusual. I do think gain-"

"Four more cases were reported yesterday."

"Hell!"

"Adults this time though."

"Same area?"

"Yes, both rock climbers. Two of them presented at the hospital after a couple of hours. The others were picked up three hours after infection."

"The children—what symptoms did they display?"

"Typical of post-infection rabies: high temperature, confusion followed by aggression, the classic frothing at the mouth, then paralysis and death."

"Death? All of them?"

"Yes, and all within seventy-two hours."

She shook her head and sighed. "And the adults?

"At least this time the team were able to quarantine the victims and monitor them."

"And?"

"So far it doesn't look good. Twelve ..." He looked at his watch. "Ten hours after infection and they're already showing late-stage symptoms."

"Ugh!"

He sighed and nodded in agreement. "Once the rabies virus gets to that stage there's no helping them; all the staff can do is make them comfortable."

"So, the incubation period has been catalysed?"

"Yes, it looks like the usual eight weeks has been shortened to eight hours."

"Have the dogs been destroyed?"

"Yes."

"And the colony?"

"Protected, but I think under the circumstances ..."

"It needs eradicating"

"If the tests come back positive and it's deemed a reservoir, then yes, but I do think that-"

"The Department has agreed to our terms, so we need to start work on a vaccine for the mutated virus."

"I've already started."

Marta sucked in her breath.

"I ... you were out of the country—we couldn't reach you, so I took the initiative and began trials."

"Overriding protocol ..."

He hated the red tape that accompanied the *Institute*'s decision-making. At least when he'd worked for the Department there had been no question of delaying finding a vaccine for such an outbreak. Another wave of guilt washed over him. Marta's offer of employment had just been too good to refuse, even if it did drain the Department of his skills. "Yes, but in the circumstances-"

A knock on the lab door's glass panel interrupted him. Marta ignored the knock but Max stood to unlock the door, embarrassment staining his cheeks as Sally, his assistant, gave him a quizzical frown; the door was never locked.

"Doctor Anderson ... the dog ... Shep—I mean subject 24B, is ready for you."

Max sighed with relief. "Excuse me, Doctor Steward-"

"Shep?"

"The transplant patient."

"Ah. Yes. Incredible work, Doctor Anderson. The results are more than we could have hoped for."

"Well ... there's still work to do and-"

"The interim report suggests-"

With Sally in the room he frowned a warning.

She bit her lip. "You're right. We should wait for the trial to end before celebrating. The outbreak has to take priority now."

"It does."

"I want a report on my desk by the end of the day, Doctor Anderson."

Max stepped out into the corridor, moving away from the confined space of the door frame before Marta had a chance to slide her body past him. "Certainly." With a poker face he strode down the corridor, Sally at his side. Marta's office door shut with an irritated bang.

"I've taken all Shep's vitals."

"Thank you, Sally.

"And the beagle? Is he prepped for the vaccine trials?"

"It's a she, and yes, she is prepped, but I didn't want to mention that in front of the old cougar."

Max snorted. "Sally, you really must-"

"I know, I know—disrespectful and all that, but she really does need reining in. Laura would have her guts for garters if she knew what was going on."

Max stopped. "Going on? I love my wife, Sally."

"No! I didn't mean that. I meant that Steward is making a nuisance of herself—it's sexual harassment you should-"

"I can handle it, Sally."

"Sure, Max, but-"

"Let's not talk about it, please. I'm going to deal with it."

"When?"

"Soon. I'll be in a stronger position once the final trials are completed, and I've submitted my report."

"You're not kidding—it could make you rich."

Max sighed and pulled gently at Sally's elbow. "Sal, you've got to keep your voice down. You know that's not the way it works."

She shook her head and rolled her eyes as they passed through the double doors and stepped into the lab.

"Are you going to publish?"

*No.* "If the *Institute* agrees."

BLAKE DALTON CHECKED his inbox. There were five new messages but only one that piqued his interest.

**From:** Marta.Steward@KielderInstitute.org

**Date:** Tuesday, 15th November, 1:14pm

**To:** B.Dalton@TBTech.com

**Subject:** Regenerative capabilities of ZF Stem Cell Slicing – mid-trial results

Blake

The outcomes of Dr Anderson's trials are quite astounding. I've attached my report on the interim results. It is as we hoped.

Regards

Marta

He picked up his phone and dialled. "Morgan. I'm sending you an email." He waited. "Got it? Good. Read it, then call Jobe. Tell him we're leaving for Newcastle. Get packed. Joan will arrange everything."

# CHAPTER FOUR

Max strode to the row of cages at the back of the lab. Despite the air-conditioning, there was the definite smell of dog in the room along with something fusty, if not a little rotten. He checked the cages as he moved towards them. Only two had inhabitants, the rest of the test subjects having already been taken down to the incinerator. "So, Sally, how is Shep doing?"

"Good! All his vitals are good. His heart rate is completely normal and the scar ... well, I think you need to take a look for yourself. It is healing amazingly well."

"Can I see the notes please?" Sally retrieved the clipboard from the desk, her black ponytail swinging behind her shoulders, and handed it to him with a smile of green eyes beneath a vibrant pink fringe. He liked the way she asserted the uniqueness of her personality with self-assurance, he'd like his daughter to have that same confidence—if he ever had one.

"Thanks." He scrutinized the data. "You took his bloods?"

"Yes, this morning. Max, the oxygen levels are just what you'd expect of a young dog."

"Hmm."

"It's like a miracle."

"I think you may be right," he replied, although getting the funding for the research project in the first place had been the real miracle. It had taken more than he wanted to give to get the go ahead for the study—and way more than he could stomach now. He thought of Marta up in her office and the numerous times she had propositioned him since she had agreed to help with his bid for funding. Sure, he'd given in once, well, more than once, but now ... he forced the memory aside and scrutinized the data. "The heart has responded exceptionally well to the stem cells. You're right, Sally. These readings are what we'd expect of a very young dog, not one of Shep's age." The dog looked full of energy which was extraordinary considering its own heart had been replaced with a diseased one. Making that transplant had felt horribly wrong, but here Shep was, as good as new, if not better.

"It's amazing! So, do you think that the cells of the heart are *actually* younger?"

"Well, it's too early to say, but they do *appear* to have regenerated, and there's no sign of the disease."

Max passed the clipboard back to Sally and unlocked the glass door behind which the thirteen-year-old beagle sat. He stared down at the dog. It didn't look quite the same.

"Sally, didn't Shep have grey on his muzzle?"

"He did."

"Well, this dog doesn't. Are you sure this is the same dog?" He knew that it was. He had a soft-spot for the mutt and recognised his markings, and besides, the ring stapled through his ear had '1989 - Anderson - ZFS' printed on it, Laura's birth year. He called. "Shep!" The dog looked up, its deep brown eyes alert and wide with expectation as Max stood in front of the glass panel. He unlocked the door and let the dog walk out. There was no sign of the arthritis that had plagued him last week. It licked his hand and a wave of guilt washed over him. "There now, boy." The dog nuzzled at his knee and sat. Max reached into his pocket and offered him a chicken-flavoured treat. "Shh!" he whispered. "Don't tell anyone." Stroking the dog, he felt along its sternum and belly where the surgeon had made his incision. There was no trace of a scar.

"Max ... Doctor Anderson. I know it's not my place to say this, but if the stem cells are regenerating, and making him younger, this could be massive. I mean, my mum would kill for younger looking skin. You'll make a fortune if you sell this to the cosmetics industry."

The intellectual rights to the research were not something Max was willing to discuss with his assistant, even if she had become indispensable. "I've not considered the research for that kind of thing, Sally, but with this breakthrough, it could end the need for organ transplants. Anyway, the results remain the property of the *Institute* and not myself. I can't profit from it—not in the way you're suggesting."

"Doctor Steward seemed to think it would be of commercial value."

Max frowned. "What do you mean, Sally?"

"Well, she was in here earlier, asking me all about the research, and the results. She noticed how Shep was ... regenerating too."

Max bridled. Marta was being careless. "I've already spoken to her. She'll get a full report as soon as the trials are complete."

"Well ..." Sally tapped the open lid of the laptop. "I think she already knows. She's been accessing your notes."

A LOW MIST ROLLED THROUGH the forest as Stangton swung the car around yet another bend. Moss-covered shapes seemed to loom from the white mist between the trees.

"Always gives me the willies seeing those things." Javeen muttered as Stangton accelerated up the hill then braked to go around yet another corner. Anything that fell to the forest floor rotted and overgrew with moss and lichen. The stumps of broken trees loitered beneath the canopy. She had expected more life in the place, but even up at Kielder Castle where you could get a decent full English during the summer months, the displays, set up for the visitors to read, only mentioned the reintroduction of water voles and ospreys. The animals must be there, you just never saw them. Her belly swished with a growing nausea. No doubt Stangton thought he was a good driver, but she could tell him, with total conviction, that he was not. Her belly lurched as he accelerated again and swung around the bend as the road wound its way through the forest to the hillside *Institute. If she barfed!* She took a breath to quell the nausea and opened the window.

"Something wrong, Latimer?"

"Nope."

Gravel sprayed from beneath tyres, as he swung the car round another bend, and he laughed. "Can't take a bit of action, eh?"

"You call this action?" she spat. "You're throwing me about like a ragdoll and I'm about to lose my breakfast."

"And there's me thinking you'd be a great navigator." He snorted as he accelerated once more.

"This is not a rally!"

"Nope, but I've got to get my kicks from somewhere. Sure as hell not going to have much fun with you around."

*Where the hell had that come from?* An edge of malice had crept into his voice. If moving here had been a relief, Stangton was the fly puking on the cream of her cake.

The narrow road opened up to a clearing and the gates of the *Institute*. Circled by massive pine trees, the *Institute* rose out of the mist overwhelming the forest. With its wide steps obscured, the door seemed to hang in the air. Built by a Victorian industrialist as a retreat away from the factories and harsh streets of his Midlands hometown, it was a Goth's wet dream of spires, carved stone lintels, and decorative brickwork. It sat behind wrought iron gates with elaborate finials of alternating spikes and sharply pointed fleur-de-lis, both of which could impale a foolish protester if they made the error of climbing over.

"There's your excitement," Javeen snapped back.

The four individuals that made up the crisis at the *Institute*'s gates turned to look as the car made its entrance. A tall boy, barely a man, poked a placard at Javeen as their eyes met. 'Kielder Killers!' was written in thick red marker pen across the top. Beneath, it read, 'STOP the MURDER'.

"They do animal testing here, right?"

"Yep. The *Institute* bought this place last year to get away from activists in the city."

"Guess they didn't find somewhere hidden enough."

"There's no place to hide, not even in Kielder."

From her vantage point on the hillside, the vast blanket of trees that made up the forest stretched to the horizon. "I don't know about that."

"Fascist pig!" a girl shouted as they waited outside the gate. "Murderer."

Javeen sighed. The girl couldn't be more than eighteen years old and, with her gamine frame, blonde, wispy plaits falling onto her shoulders from beneath a thick woollen hat, purple paisley harem trousers complete with black Doc Martins and khaki parka, she looked every inch the radical, vegan, wannabe-anarchist. In other words, a student having a strop against the establishment.

"Shouldn't you be at school?" Javeen threw back.

The girl stared, obviously searching for a suitable retort. "Fascist!"

"Anita!" A boy, with overly long and tousled dark hair, grabbed the girl's arm. "We haven't got a beef with the pigs."

The girl yanked her arm away and twisted to the boy. "They're here to stop us. They're fascist pigs!"

Javeen rolled her eyes. The girl was a stuck record, bleating the same line over and over. The protest was a damp squib, nothing for the *Institute* to get het up about.

The guard, not much older than the girl, and gangly in his ill-fitting uniform, opened the gate to let her through. It closed with a clank of rusting iron behind the car, a welcome barrier between them and the heckling students.

Stangton parked the car between a new blue Lexus and a black Range Rover, also immaculate. Both cars put her own scratched and battered little blue Volkswagen Polo to shame as well as the 1.5 ltr Vauxhall Ford Fiesta police car that was now sitting between them like a poor relation. The police car rattled as it reached sixty, not that going sixty was achievable along the windy lanes through the forest, although Stangton had tried his best.

She stepped out of the car, thankful for a lungful of fresh, moist air to quell the rising nausea from Stangton's stop-start driving only to be hit by the smell. Something was burning, or had been burned, and the air was full of the stench of singed hair. Stangton noticed her wrinkling nose. "Incinerator." He said baldly.

"Incinerator," she repeated.

"For the dead animals."

"There must be a fair few bodies in there then." She cast a glance at the four protestors still punching their placards skywards. "It stinks."

"Beagles, apparently. Tilly works here. She's seen them brought in. They're all sworn to secrecy—part of their contract is to keep quiet about it all or they lose their jobs."

"But she told you?"

"She's my wife. She tells me everything."

"Still—if she's signed a non-disclosure agreement as part of her employment then ..."

Stangton scowled. "Then nothing, Latimer."

The steps appeared from the mist as they approached, and the door opened without a knock. A security guard, a man Javeen recognised as Billy Oldfield, took their details, and accompanied them through to the director's office. With dark wooden panels lining the walls the building felt more like an old-fashioned school than a modern laboratory. The doors along the main corridor were closed, and a single light brightened the space. The only nod to modernity was the camera fixed in the direction of the entrance. Presumably, somewhere in the building, was a room with monitors complete with guard swivelling on his chair in boredom; *Kielder Institute* was hardly a hotbed of activity.

Wide and winding stairs complete with heavily carved oak balustrade, led them to the director's office. Flanked by three men with sombre faces and dark suits, the director, Dr. Marta Steward sat behind a massive desk. She made no effort to introduce them. "Our location appears to have been discovered, PC Stangton. I know that you're familiar with our history—the persecution of my staff in Leeds and the attacks that forced us to come to Kielder."

Stangton agreed that he was aware of the situation.

"I take this current breach very seriously," Marta said. "The protest outside can't be allowed to continue. I've already had one member of staff, an essential member who is crucial to our work, threaten to leave."

"They don't seem to be a real threat," Javeen offered. "They're just students protesting against your use of animals in testing."

"PC Latimer. It was only last year that one of my staff members was hospitalised after an attack by one of these 'students' and our laboratory was bombed. If you're not going to take this seriously then we will." The men at her side stood a little closer.

It would be better if they did act, the police presence at Kielder was made up of exactly three people. Javeen, Stangton, and Amy Brice their administrative assistant, and she only worked two mornings a week—hardly a force to be reckoned with. If things turned sour, then reinforcements would have to be drafted in.

"If you have your own security team then you have the right to protect your own property, Doctor Steward," Stangton replied. "We'll have a word with the youngsters. They do have the right to protest and, so far, they don't appear to have committed any crime. Until that happens there's not much we can do, I'm afraid."

Dr. Steward's lips set to a hard line. "Until they do something?" Her voice was entirely scathing. "We have to wait until they attack us before you'll enforce the law?"

"That's correct. They haven't broken the law, so there's nothing to enforce."

The same tone of contempt that Stangton aimed at Javeen was now directed at Steward. She sensed a lack of empathy with Steward's dilemma and remembered the photograph on his desk of his wife Tilly with her arm around their black Labrador, smiling happily from a hillside. Another depicted the dog romping across the hills, white breath billowing as it lolloped. She remembered also the narrowing of his eyes and the way he'd spat 'incinerator' when she'd wrinkled her nose at the stench around the *Institute*. Couple that with his love of 'excitement', his yawning dissatisfaction with the boring nature of policing at Kielder, and she wouldn't put it past him to actually stir up a bit of trouble.

"We'll talk to them, Doctor Steward. Explain exactly what they can and cannot do," he said laconically.

"Exactly how much of the land around here belongs to the *Institute*?" Javeen asked. "How much further than the gates does the land extend?"

"Almost to the bottom of the hill. We've got four acres in total."

"So, the protesters are actually trespassing?"

"That is correct and you, as Police Officers, under the Criminal Justice & Public Order Act 1994, Section 61, subsection 2, are duty-bound to remove them."

Stangton coughed—his giveaway nervous tick.

"If you're not willing to do that, then I am more than happy to have our solicitors contact your superiors."

"We'll have words," Stangton relented.

"I want more than words, PC Stangton. I want action. These people are a menace and have proven to be a threat to the staff working for the *Institute* on previous occasions."

Another cough. From her cold eyes, pursed lips, and steely voice, Steward was not a woman that would accept being ignored or patronised. Javeen took an instant dislike to her but couldn't help admiring her strength.

"Now, if you could go downstairs and deal with them, we can all get back to work."

Dismissed, Javeen followed Stangton out into the corridor. He remained silent until they reached the bottom of the stairs. "Bloody woman!" He took a quick glance around. "Who the hell does she think she is?"

*Only the Director of the Institute, Stangton.* "She's right though. We do need to do something about the protestors."

"Just a bunch of scruffy kids."

"We both know that, but-"

"Listen, we'll have a word, give them a choice - leave private land or be prosecuted - then give them a lift down the hill. They can protest, they just need to stay off the *Institute*'s property." Stangton opened the heavy door and strode towards the gates and the protestors.

Ten minutes later, with the protestors squeezed into the back seat, the car made its way down the hill to the boundary of the *Institute*'s property. Pulling over to a stop, Stangton held the car door open and the four stepped out. "Right. See that sign." He pointed to the sign at the side of the narrow track. "It says trespassers will be prosecuted. That's you. You will be prosecuted if you trespass on the *Institute*'s land again."

"It's a free country!"

"That's just where you're wrong. This land belongs to *Kielder Institute*, and they've made it very clear that they will prosecute anyone who steps foot on their land without permission. Do you want to be tied up in court for the next few years with blood-sucking solicitors and barristers putting you into debt?"

"But they're testing on animals!"

Stangton sighed. "You can stand here with your protest, but don't step beyond that sign. Got it?"

The girl with the paisley harem trousers nodded and only one of the boys seemed at all belligerent.

"What they're doing in there is wrong. They should be shut down."

"That's a matter of opinion. There are ways and means to change the world, lad, and this isn't one of them. Now, are you sure you don't want a lift back to the village?"

"No, we're staying."

The girl stepped forward. "Could you take me back, please?"

# CHAPTER FIVE

*Kielder Institute, 2:30 PM*

With her break over, Lois stubbed out her cigarette on the metal rim of the ashtray and made her way back to serving the murdering monsters inside. Mind you, the air still reeked with the stench of burning dog hair so it would be a relief to go back. She had gagged when Mel, the other server who worked afternoons, told her what the smell was, and silently raged; she couldn't let them know how much she objected to it. Nate said she had to keep a low profile, and besides, her mother had got her the job and she didn't want to let her down. Her phone pinged. Anita this time.

She felt like piggy-in-the-middle between those two. The police had moved them on from outside the gates and Nate was roaring about it and having a go at Nita because she went back to the campsite and wouldn't stand at the boundary protesting. Nita was upset because Nate had shouted at her and called her a 'snowflake', but she was knackered and cold and just wanted to go back home, and could she stop with Lois at her house tonight, please?

Lois could feel another 'talk' coming on and if Nita and her mum got together talking about Nate then her evening would be ruined. She sighed, stuffed the phone back in her pocket, and went back into the canteen.

Lunchtime was over and only a few of the staff were at the tables or waiting in line to be served. She smiled at Dr. Patrick although inside she wanted to shout at her about how cruel it was to test on animals. Jamie had said they were using dogs, and Nate said it was beagles. Lois hadn't seen any, but if she did, there was no way she'd be able to stop herself from ripping the cages open and running home with them in her arms. She positioned herself behind the counter and tied the long apron around her waist then reached for the slip of paper holding the next order; a flat white. She took the bag of ground coffee from the side and glanced down the queue of staff waiting to be served.

*She was here again! The girl with the fur coat. Real fur!*

Lois turned back to the coffee machine and pulled the handle, expertly mixing the coffee with steaming and frothing milk, then sat it on the waiting tray.

"I asked for a flat white!"

"Huh?" The woman's voice sat on the edge of her awareness as Lois stared at the girl, certain the fur was real. Her stomach knotted; the woman was a monster for wearing the skin of an animal. It was barbaric!

"I asked for a flat white!" the customer repeated with a tone of irritation.

Lois huffed and the crease deepened between the woman's overly plucked and crayoned-in brows.

"Excuse me?" The customer pursed her lips in disapproval and Lois noticed how the gaudy lipstick smeared across her lips was bleeding into the crevices of her ageing skin. Lois snorted; her mouth looked like the wrinkled flesh of a dog's bum-hole.

"Well?" she asked, her frown deepening.

A tap on Lois' shoulder broke into her thoughts as Mel sniggered.

"Can I help?" Sheila asked from behind.

"Yes! Get better staff for a start," the woman replied.

"I do apologise," Sheila said still hovering over Lois' shoulder.

Sheila's breath was moist on her cheek and the sourness of cigarettes made it stink.

"Lois, can you serve this lady please?" Sheila's voice was tart—overly polite but carrying the 'you're-going-to-know-about-it' threat that Lois recognised too well.

"Certainly." Lois pushed the tray towards the woman. Coffee spilled onto the saucer, froth leaking over the rim to the tray.

"Right!" The woman huffed. "I asked for a flat white and this is a frothy mess of I don't know what."

"It's a Caffe Misto," Lois replied, ignoring the woman's glare, her attention trained on the woman with the fur collar as she moved along in the queue. Their eyes met momentarily, and Fur Collar smirked, turned to the chiller, and reached for a plated cake.

*Monster!*

Fur Collar turned to her friend, snickered, then moved forward in the queue. The sneering laugh grated on Lois. How could she stand there and laugh when she was wearing the pelt of a tortured animal?

*Monstrous! She was disgusting, repulsive. She was a murderer!*

Fur Collar noticed Lois' stare, turned to her friend, laughed, then made belligerent eye contact once more. There was no doubt about it—they were talking about her.

"Lois!"

*That's it!*

"Can I have the flat white?" The customer's voice was terse.

"Lois! Take a break-"

"There's no need to be so aggressive!" Lois shot back at the customer, ignoring Sheila's pestering voice.

"Pardon?"

"Oh, just shut up," Lois muttered.

"What did you say?"

*Damn! She'd said it aloud.*

"Lois Maybank, leave the counter immediately and-"

Sheila's voice faded as Fur Collar cackled, an over-large leather bag swinging on her arm. Lois' cheeks stung with rising mortification.

Ignoring the woman demanding her coffee and Sheila pulling at her shoulder, Lois pushed past Mel to the front of the coffee shop, striding past the tables and the staff drinking their coffee. Lois' eyes didn't leave the girl, her orange face shiny in the lights.

"Murderer!" Lois shouted.

"What?" Fur Collar reacted with an incredulous laugh.

"Murderer!" Lois repeated. "How many animals were tortured and slaughtered so that you could wear that coat?"

"It's fake!" the girl returned with indignation.

Lois stopped in her tracks, doubting herself for one second, then bore down on the smirking girl. Grabbing the collar of the coat, she felt the pelt beneath.

*It was real!*

Vindicated, she continued her attack and yanked at the collar.

"Lois!" Sheila called.

Consumed by anger, Lois yanked at the coat again. The girl screamed, tottering on her too-high heels, then crashing against Lois' shoulder where she left a smear of pink grease on the white cotton shirt.

"Lois!"

With Sheila's steel grip around her arm Lois was yanked back. The woman with the coat lurched forward, falling to the floor with a scream.

"Lois! What the hell are you doing? Marcy! Call security."

"Her coat! It's real!"

Sheila's grip tightened around her bicep. "You silly little cow!" she hissed.

# CHAPTER SIX

Max scratched at Shep's ear as the dog sat by his side and yawned. It was completely unorthodox of course, against protocol as Marta would insist, to have the dog out of its cage, but they owed Shep big time. The animal had endured a heart transplant on humanity's behalf, been instrumental in ground-breaking research, and helped change the future for thousands of critically ill patients waiting for organ transplantation. That was the official line, and, to an extent, it was true.

It had been worth it of course, all the testing, to prove that the regenerative capabilities of zebra fish cells could be transferred to stem cells. To date, five patients had been taken off the organ donation register, not because they'd died, the most usual explanation for their removal, but because their own hearts, livers, kidneys, and in one case a cancerous spleen, had regenerated, become whole, and cancer free. How much it had cost the *Institute* to 'employ' these patients wasn't Max's business and was something he chose to ignore. Max stroked the dog's head—his very young-looking head, without the tell-tale grey hairs of age. Perhaps Sal had a point. The regenerative properties of the spliced cells were outstanding. Perhaps it *could* have wider, and very lucrative, implications. Perhaps he'd pass it by the 'old cougar' later. He smiled down at the dog as he remembered watching the video of the first patient, the joy shining in his eyes, as he was told he no longer needed a transplant. "You did good, Shep." He turned to the assistant. "Sal," he called. "Could you prepare subject 354 please."

"She likes to be called Molly."

He sighed as he walked Shep back to his cage. Sal really needed to distance herself from the pups, especially for this trial. So far none of the subjects injected with WLV1, the mutated lyssa virus, and administered with the trial vaccines, had survived. "Sally, don't name it. You know it's likely to die."

"I know. It's just they're so damned cute. Why the hell can't we use rats?"

"Dogs are the carriers. These pups are ... dispensable."

"Ugh. I love my job, but some days ..."

"I get it," he replied with a glance at Shep curled up in his cage. "It'll be worth it though—once we get the vaccine right."

"When do we start human trials?"

"As soon as we get this to work." He gestured to the small glass bottles of vaccine sat neat and tidy in the cooler.

"Barnard said there's been another death."

"He's correct. So far, no one who has been bitten has survived, and the last two dog attacks were twenty miles from Whitby."

"It's spreading then."

"Yes." Tension tightened across Max's shoulders, and a dull ache spread heavy fingers across the back of his head. "It's up to us, Sal. We've got to figure this out." He'll also be more than happy to deposit the generous bonus into his bank account once the vaccine was created and found effective. He pulled on a pair of thin rubber gloves, reached into the glass-fronted chiller, removed a bottle of the live virus, and moved across to the tray of syringes Sal had set out.

"Perhaps this one will work?" Sal opened the cage labelled Beagle X 354.

"We need it to, Sal. If the spread continues ..."

Taking the pup by the collar, one hand under its back end, Sally lifted the dog across to the table and waited as Max prepared the virus. He took the glass vial, inserted the syringe with a practiced hand then withdrew 10ml.

"Hold him still."

Sally soothed the pup with kind words as Max felt for a suitable spot.

"This won't hurt, fella."

"It's a girl."

"OK. This won't hurt ..." He searched for a suitable diminutive, gave up, and gently pinched a fold of skin, slipping the needle under the top layer between the pup's shoulder blades. The dog showed no evidence of discomfort. Max retrieved the needle and rubbed at the injection site. *Poison administered.* "There you go, all done." He disposed of the syringe and empty vial in the hazardous waste bin.

"That wasn't so bad, was it." Sally stroked the pup's head, hands protected by plastic gloves. "I don't think she even noticed."

"No, Sal. I don't think she did. Sadly, she will notice its effects. As soon as I inject the vaccine put it back in the cage. No extra cuddles. Got it?"

"Yes." She held the pup a little tighter.

"And under no circumstances are you to re-open the cage door!"

"I know, Max!"

"I don't care how cute he-"

"She."

"She is. This particular strand of the rabies virus is quick to take control of the subjects and they exhibit extreme aggression within the first two hours."

"I know. This is the seventh time we've done this.

"I just need to make sure you understand—there's no cure if you're bitten."

"I've been reading the reports; the symptoms are terrifying."

"Doesn't bear thinking about, but they've caught this early, the damage will be limited. The original colony has been destroyed so they're hopeful that they've curtailed the spread in that way."

"How many human fatalities have there been so far?"

"Counting the five people reported as having been bitten yesterday, that would be a grand total of twenty."

"Yes, but the five aren't dead yet."

"Sadly, once they've been infected there's no hope. It's not like the ordinary lyssavirus. With that we could offer treatment before the symptoms presented, with this mutated version there's nothing we can do—even if we do intervene at the earliest stage our medicine doesn't work, and once the symptoms do present, it's a fait accompli, which is why what we're doing here is so important, and why this little fella," he took the pup in his arms, "is doing us a tremendous service." The dog strained against his hold and Max's heart began to race. "Best not tarry any longer, Sally. Pass me the vaccine." He gestured to the pre-prepared syringe on the table. With the virus administered to the dog, along with a strong sedative, he carried it to the cage.

Max returned to his desk and began to enter the details of the trial into his research notes. Keeping an accurate record of each trial was crucial. Each time they went through this process was a step closer to finding the right mix. His hopes were high with this latest batch.

"How long will it take ... before we know?"

"A couple of hours," he said staring at his monitor. He typed in more data.

"May I take a break now, Dr Anderson?" Sally asked.

He leant back and turned to her. "Yes, of course. I'm sorry—I get so involved that time slips away."

She smiled with relief. "Can I bring you a coffee? They do a nice flat white in the café?"

He looked at his watch—six-thirty pm. "I didn't realise it was so late. You should have gone home hours ago. Are they still open this late?"

"Till seven."

"Hmm. No, it's ok. I've got my supplies here," he said nodding to the kettle at the end of the counter. "Why don't you call it a day? I work late, but I don't expect you to."

"If you're sure!"

"Yes, of course. Get off home and I'll see you first thing."

MARTA TURNED THE CAMERA feed off. The girl was on her way home and Max was obviously going to work late again. Once she'd finished her meeting, she would show him exactly why he belonged to her and why the silly ring on his stupid finger meant exactly nothing. She walked to the sideboard.

"Drink?"

Blake Dalton grunted a yes without taking his eyes off the computer screen and the text displayed there.

"As you can see, Blake, the dog shows no signs whatsoever of the arthritis that was crippling it before." She picked up the bottle of wine from the sideboard and poured another glass for Blake and some for herself.

"I agree, the change is marked, and the regeneration of the organs and scar tissue is remarkable."

Marta slid close beside him as he scrolled through the data, her hips level with his face, and slipped her hand across his shoulder. She passed him the glass of wine. "Now, where were we ..."

"IDIOT!" NATE'S SHOUT reverberated against the camper van's walls. His angry face reflecting back at Lois from the surrounding windows. Outside the dark was complete, a small lamp hanging from the back of the driver's seat the only light.

Lois ducked, her head sinking into her shoulders as spittle landed on her face. "Don't' shout! They'll hear." She leant back against the cushion, the sourness of the decades old fabric leaking its years of accumulated sweat in the damp. *Whose idea was it anyway to camp out in the forest in November? His!* She shifted uncomfortably on the seat, cold, hungry, and now with a lump rising in her throat, her heart beating too fast, and her cheeks burning as she thought of the others outside. The walls of the van were thin and the fabric of their tents thinner.

Nate peered at her, searching her eyes. "What the hell did you think you were doing?"

She broke his gaze. "Shut up! I know."

Nate ran his hands through his hair, pushing his fringe back. It stood to attention then a single clump of greasy hair wilted back down, the tip touching his forehead. *He really needed to wash his hair.* Nate turned to the window, his scowl reflecting back to Lois in the glass.

"It won't make any difference."

"That job was perfect. You could come and go without a problem at the *Institute*. You were our mole."

*What the hell was he talking about?* "Mole?"

"Yes. A plant."

"Plant?" She was completely lost now.

Her response seemed to ignite his ire. "For Christ's sake, Lois. You were in the perfect position to find out exactly what they're doing in there and now the police have got you on their radar too."

"We already know what they're doing!" She countered, ignoring his comment about the police though her stomach twisted at the memory of PC Latimer's scathing questioning. *Damned meat eaters—they were all the same; no understanding of just how cruel they all were.* "They're testing on animals."

"Yes, but we needed intelligence: where the animals are kept, what security details are in place, when the place will be empty so that we can get in."

Lois cowered as Nate's anger seemed to balloon. "We could go in tonight?" she suggested.

"We don't have all the information we need and not likely to, thanks to you!"

"I couldn't help it, Nate. She was just standing there and all I could think of was how many animals had been killed in that video we watched."

"Video?"

"Yes, you know—the one with all those coyotes laid out—the one where the trappers had killed them, and their paws were caught in those steel traps. It was horrific. Don't you remember?"

"She wouldn't have been wearing coyote! We're in England, not Canada!"

"I overheard the lab assistant talking to her boyfriend."

"And?"

"She was complaining about the dogs—said they were all dying, and they should use rats instead, but the director won't allow it."

Nate growled. "This is exactly why we need to get into that place and destroy their work."

"What about the dogs?"

"The dogs?"

"Yes, the dogs. We need to go in and rescue them. That's the whole point, isn't it?"

She flinched as Nate narrowed his eyes. Contempt leaked from him. "Listen. You've got to see the bigger picture, Lois. Attacking one woman in the street isn't going to help."

"It was the canteen."

"Sure, the canteen."

"What about the dogs?"

"Listen, we hit them where it hurts: cost them money, destroy their research—that's the bigger picture."

"And take away their animals—that's what'll hurt too."

"Sure." Nate replied, staring beyond her. He snapped back to awareness and narrowed his eyes. "Right. There's no point in wasting any more time freezing our arses off in this forest. We go in tonight."

# CHAPTER SEVEN

A bang jolted Max from sleep and the sickness of being shunted from unconscious to awareness washed over him. His arm, which had been laid across his belly, flipped involuntarily and knocked the mug of coffee on his desk. Cold, dark liquid pooled next to the laptop and spattered over its keyboard.

"Damn!"

He tipped the keyboard upside down. The screen flashed, illuminating the desk, and he reached for the roll of paper towels at the end of the lab table. After pulling off a handful of sheets, he mopped up the mess, relieved that it had only been the dregs that were left in the mug. If he was lucky no harm done. If not, having to admit to Marta that he'd wrecked another laptop would be embarrassing.

The lab was silent apart from Shep's snores. The test subjects that had died earlier in the day had all been cleared and taken for incineration in the basement furnace and only Subject 354, or Molly as Sally had named her, remained.

He checked his watch. Eleven twenty-six; more than three hours later than he'd promised to be home. He called home, and Laura answered after the fifth ring.

"Hi," was her sleepy response.

"Sorry, babe. I fell asleep."

"Uhuh. Well, come on home now."

"Just going to do some final checks, then I'll be there."

"I'll be waiting." Her reply was lazy and sensual, and tugged at his groin.

"Get some sleep. I'll kiss you awake when I get there."

"Hmm. But which lips will you kiss?"

"Whichever you want me to."

"You know which. Don't be long." The phone clicked to dead.

Getting home became urgent and he spent the next minute checking the laptop but his relief when the screen flashed, and his research notes reappeared, was short-lived when he heard the familiar tack of heels in the corridor. He ducked beneath the table as Marta walked into the room.

"Max!" She walked further into the room. "Max?"

He rose from his crouch before she realised he was hiding. "Marta?"

Startled, she took a step backwards. "Max! You scared me."

"Sorry. Just dropped a pen." He held up a pen retrieved from his pocket as evidence.

"I'm glad I found you."

*Here we go!* "I was just about to go home. Laura's waiting for me."

"Hmm. I bet she is," she responded with a smirk and took a step closer.

*Distract her.* "I was just about to check on Subject 354. I think we may be close to a breakthrough; the latest vaccine has got us further than any of the others. The dog was injected with the new formula this afternoon and, so far, isn't showing the usual symptoms."

"Show me."

With relief, Max walked across to the cage where Molly/ Subject 354 lay curled in sleep. "Her vitals aren't exactly normal. She has a raised temperature but so far has not shown the deterioration and aggression that is usual at this stage."

"And she's not dead, so that's a plus."

"It is," he agreed. "Some of the others have lived a little longer, though not by much, and by this time they would be showing the classic signs of the infection."

"And she's not. In fact, she looks normal."

"Yes, which is why I stayed on tonight, but I really must go home now."

Marta placed a hand upon his shoulder. "So soon? Can't you stay a while with me—share a coffee? I have some news you may be interested in."

"No, I really-"

"No? But you might when you hear what I have to tell you." Her hand slid down his chest. "Come on now, Maximillian. We've had fun in the past."

"Yes, but-" He held up his left hand, and the ring of gold on his wedding finger.

"That didn't stop you before, did it, Maxi? Hmm? Not when you wanted the funding for your zebra fish."

"No, but-" He grabbed her hand as it slid below his belt.

"But?" Their eyes locked. "I helped you, Max. Don't forget who it was that got you the position in the first place. And don't forget, if it wasn't for me convincing the board - and believe me I had to work hard to get their approval - then you wouldn't have made the breakthroughs that you have. All those patients would have died—if it weren't for me. Don't I deserve a little respect for that? Hmm? Don't I deserve a little love and affection for that, Max?"

She pushed her body closer to his. The ache that he'd felt for Laura had no sense of morality and it rose again as Marta's hand reached to stroke between his legs. "Don't tell me that you don't want to, because I can tell that you do." She leant into him. Her lips were gentle on the sensitive skin of his neck as she kneaded at him. A groan of desire escaped his lips. "What happens in the office, Maxi, stays in the office."

He gasped as she cupped his balls. "Tell me the news," he said through a groan.

The light in the lab flickered.

She kneaded him and kissed his neck as she whispered. "*Titan Blane Industries*." She squeezed. "They're very interested in our research."

He groaned as his excitement grew and made a last, weak, effort to pull away.

"They're offering millions, Max, millions ..."

All thoughts of Laura lost, he tugged at Marta's skirt, pulling it up her thighs. Forcing his mouth on hers, he pulled her panties down. She reached for his zipper and slipped her hand inside. Her fingers were cool against his skin. Running fingers through her hair, he pressed his tongue hard inside her mouth, and they stood locked together, stroking, kneading, making the ache desperate. She pulled away.

"Yes ... and if we play it right, we could be rich beyo-"

The lights blacked out.

"What the?"

"Just a power cut." Too aroused to care, Max lifted Marta to the desk. She wrapped her legs around his hips.

The door slammed open.

"What the hell?"

"Get off, Max," Marta hissed and pushed at his chest, long nails digging into his flesh as she forced him away.

Max pulled at his trousers as chaos broke out and torchlight swept the room.

"You said it would be empty!" a man shouted.

"It should have been," a woman's voice shouted back.

Torchlight filled the room, casting light along the lab tables.

Max fumbled at his zipper as Marta scuttled behind the table. Someone sniggered.

A snort. "It's Doctor Anderson and the Director, Doctor Steward."

"Looks like they were up to more than paperwork."

Max recognised the voice. Marjory Maybank's daughter. Sally had told him about the scuffle in the canteen. The police had to be called to the fighting women and Lois had been given a telling off. He'd scoffed at that. She'd have been arrested for assault if it had happened in the city, but here, in the rarefied, and obviously lawless, atmosphere of Kielder and its secretive *Institute*, the local 'elites' were protected. As usual, it was who you knew rather than what you knew; but wasn't he evidence of that? A surge of guilt. No doubt, the girl's uncle or aunt worked here. Marjory had all her fingers in all the pies around the village and it was well known she'd made generous contributions on more than one occasion to the pot of funding for their research. Not that she wasn't well rewarded for it. He'd seen the photos of her villa in Spain and the yacht she kept down at Henley.

Steel hands grabbed Max's arms as he fumbled with his zipper. "Destroy the laptop and the other computers."

"No!"

AS NATE, JAMIE AND Errol dealt with Dr Anderson and the director, Lois strode to the bank of cages and swung her torchlight across them. "There's only two dogs." Her voice, with its note of disappointment, was drowned out by Dr. Anderson's. Lois ignored the chaos behind her and shone light into the cages. The first dog, Subject 24B, according to the sign, was the older of the two. The beagle looked at her with interest as the light woke him. The younger one, just a puppy, opened its eyes, jumped up, and trotted to the front of the cage. "Hey, little one. Don't worry. I'm here to set you free." It bared its teeth, then ran around the cage in a circle. Odd behaviour for a puppy but being kept in a cage wasn't normal—it was bound to make the dog a bit weird. A bit of love and attention would solve that problem. "Don't worry, I'll get you out." Perhaps her mum would let her keep this one? Perhaps she could keep them both? They were beautiful dogs. "How come there's only two? We were told there were eight."

"Incinerated." The director's voice had a nasty edge.

Lois swung around and shone the light directly into her face. *Bitch!* "You've murdered them all?"

Marta scoffed. "They were test subjects."

"They're vital for our research," Anderson added.

"What you're doing is cruel! Why do you have to use animals? They have rights too!"

Nate lifted the laptop and smashed it against the table.

"No!" Anderson shouted as Nate lifted it again. "No! My work."

"Calm down, Max. It's all saved on the cloud."

The man quietened and dragged his eyes from the broken laptop to Lois. "We're doing research that can save people's lives. You have no idea how important our work is."

"I don't care how important your work is, mate," Nate countered. "Testing on animals is barbaric. Now, just how do we get into the cloud?"

"You're not." The director's voice was steel.

Nate stared back at the woman. "We are. And," he held up the hammer, "I'm prepared to break bones to get in."

Anderson's eyes widened with fear. Lois turned back to the cages; watching Nate intimidate them churned her stomach. She opened the cage of the older beagle. He licked her hand and she crouched to stroke his head. "Good boy. Do you want to come home with me?"

Behind her Anderson shouted about 'disease' and 'outbreaks'. Something about 'Whitby' and 'dogs' and 'rabies' and 'one hundred percent mortality'.

"Come on, boy! Come on out," she crooned to the beagle. The label clipped through its ear made her stomach churn. She'd take that out straightaway.

Anderson's voice broke into her thoughts. "That's my dog!"

Lois swung around to the doctor. "Your dog? Then why's he in a cage?"

"He belongs to the *Institute*. Put him back!" Marta demanded.

"Marta!"

"So, he's been tested on then?"

"No, he's just my-"

"He's crucial to our research. As you can see, he's perfectly healthy."

"But what about the others—the eight puppies that were in the pen outside? You tested on those didn't you! And now they're all dead. He's coming with me. I'm going to set him free."

"No!"

"Why don't you test on humans and leave the animals alone?"

"That can be arranged," Marta muttered.

Dr Anderson pulled away from the hand that gripped him, and Lois noticed with satisfaction that Nate's efforts at intimidation didn't seem to be working as well as he thought; she was not the only one who was incompetent.

"Tell me why you don't use humans. At least they could give their consent. Huh?" The beagle took a step out of the cage and Lois turned her attention back to the younger puppy. It sat at the back of the cage, its eyes watchful.

"Yeah, why not use humans?" Jamie asked.

Anderson patted his leg, and the older beagle ran across the lab. When it turned, it began to growl at Nate, Jamie, and Errol.

"Well, the ethical implications-"

The dog snarled and Nate took another step back.

"For crying out loud, Nate, that's not a Staffie or a rottweiler it's a bloody beagle. It won't hurt you." Jamie shouted as the dog began to bark. "Get him to tell you how to get into the cloud!"

Lois smiled as Jamie took the lead. Now they would get somewhere; the last time he'd been riled a policeman had lost a tooth

Nate trained his torch on Anderson, raised the hammer, and slammed it down on the desk next to him. The dog growled but cowered.

"See! The dog won't bite."

Anderson took the opportunity to grab the hammer. Jamie jumped too. With a satisfied grin as chaos broke out across the lab, Lois unclipped the latch holding the second cage closed. "Come on boy."

The hammer slammed against the table and Marta screamed and began to claw at Jamie.

"Leave the dog!" Anderson shouted as Lois opened the door of its cage.

Chaos filled the small room but startled by the anxiety in Anderson's voice, Lois closed the door. The dog sat at the front of its cage, its large brown eyes questioning. "You want to come home with me, don't you," she crooned. The dog cocked its head as though listening. "Yes, you do!"

"No! Don't let him out."

"I'm going to set him free. What you're doing here is despicable."

"Grab his arm, Nate!"

Anderson grunted as Jamie pushed him face down on the desk, right arm slammed across its surface. "Give me the access code or I'll smash your fingers!"

Ignoring the men, Anderson continued to shout. "Leave him inside. He's part of our trial. The Lyssavirus-"

"Leave her!" Marta hissed. "Take the dog. We've finished with it anyway."

"Marta!"

"She wants him as a pet, let her take the dog.

"Marta. You know-"

"Take it!" the woman shouted as the cage door swung open.

"Marta! No!"

"Shut up, Max. I'm not about to let a bunch of scruffy, smelly tree-huggers ruin our work."

"Hey! I'm not a smelly tree-hugger."

Anderson was screaming now. "Leave the dog inside the cage." The pup trotted forward and sat in the doorway. Lois stroked its head.

"The Lyssa virus—if it bites you there's no-"

Nate punched Anderson in the belly. "Shut it!"

The pup bared its teeth.

Anderson staggered against the desk, winded.

Spittle frothed along its gums.

It growled and Lois retrieved her hand as it snapped.

The pup had morphed from adorable to vicious in two seconds flat. Heart tapping a rapid beat of fear, Lois tried to close the door, but the dog sprung forward, teeth snapping. Lois stepped back, and the dog flew past her in a rage of snapping teeth and frothing spittle. Its snarls filled the room as it turned to face her. Hackles raised, the dog snapped at her like a demented beast.

"Get out of here." Anderson shouted. "The dog has rabies. If it bites you then you'll be infected. There's no cure."

"What the hell have you done, you stupid bitch?" Nate hissed.

Typical of him to call her names! The evening was turning into a shambles. First, Anita had refused to come along, and the dog she was trying to save had become a demented beast, and now Nate was turning into Mr. Nasty.

"Just walk to the door," Anderson shouted as the pup continued to snap and snarl.

It twirled in the light, as though chasing its tail, and Lois watched mesmerised as it went round in a circle.

"To the door!"

Torchlight illuminated the door as Nate swung it open. Trust him to be the first out—he was spineless when it came down to it, a spineless bully. The Director followed him and then Jamie and Errol.

As Lois made a move to follow, the pup stopped its psychotic roundabout. Red and glistening eyes locked on her. Jaws snapping, hackles raised, froth dripped to the floor. She froze as it lowered its head, ready to attack. Anderson grabbed her arm. "Run!"

Lights flickered, the room brightened, and the dog pounced.

Pushed by Anderson, she crashed against the desk, and the dog scuttled past, hurtling into the far wall.

Snarling from the older dog added to the cacophony of guttural sound. The young dog turned and launched itself at

Anderson. The older beagle jumped, its teeth snapping as it launched across Anderson's body. Spittle flew, teeth gnashed, and Lois screamed as the younger dog sank its teeth into the older beagle.

"No!" Anderson screamed, his voice ringing with pain.

The demented dog tore at the beagle's flesh, red froth filling its mouth.

Desperate to stop the horror, Lois searched the lab for a weapon, settling on a fire extinguisher hanging on the wall. As she stepped to it, the pup withdrew its teeth from Shep, and watched. As she reached a hand to take the cylinder from the wall, it scuttled across the floor. Teeth bared, blood-red froth sliding over its canines, eyes wide and staring, it pounced. She swung the cannister. Cold and heavy in her hands, it thwacked against the dog's head. *If it bites, there's no cure.* Before it had chance to right itself, she followed through with another blow. Lois screamed as fear turned to rage and she smashed again and again until the dog stopped snarling and lay still. Blood pooled around its body. Arms suddenly weary, hands trembling, she dropped the extinguisher to the floor.

Crouching over the older dog, Anderson sobbed. The dog whined and pulled itself towards the man.

# CHAPTER EIGHT

**B**lood soaked the fur around Shep's neck, the flesh around his muzzle was torn, its teeth bared to the light. "Shep!" Max said in a broken whisper.

The girl stepped close. "I'm sorry!"

He ignored her as the dying dog licked at his hand.

"This dog is a hero! You have no idea what you've done. You stupid, stupid girl."

"I ... I said I was sorry."

"Sorry?"

"Yes, I-"

"Just shut up. Just shut the hell up. You've destroyed this dog's life. Do you know that?" He rounded on her. "He'll die now. The other dog ... he was infected with a virus that we have no way of treating. It has a one hundred percent mortality rate. Do you understand? A one hundred percent death rate."

She remained silent and he turned again to Shep, his brown eyes pleading. At the perimeter of his iris the white had turned pink. The speed with which the virus was taking over startled Max and he moved back. There was only one choice; to destroy the dog himself. Watching Shep descend into a raging and violent madness would be more than he could bear.

"Step away from the dog. The virus is quick to act and if it bites you ..."

The girl backed away and Max retrieved a vial of pentobarbital and phenytoin from the cupboard. Shep's death would be painless. A sob caught in his throat as he pierced the vial with the needle and filled the syringe. He had wanted this to be Shep's last week at the *Institute*, but not this way. At home he'd already placed a basket with a comfortable cushion next to the log burner, ready for Shep to make it his home. He sniffed back tears. *Get a grip, Max. This has to be done.*

"I'm sorry," the girl repeated as she cowered behind a table, the bravery she'd shown when the pup had attacked gone.

Syringe in hand, he knelt to Shep. The dog eyed him. Though ringed with red, a glimmer of their soulfulness remained. Max frowned. The flesh on Shep's nose, which had been gaping and pink only minutes before, was healing, the torn and gaping streaks of pink flesh were narrowing. *Incredible.* Mesmerized as the flesh knitted together before his eyes, the syringe was forgotten.

"What is it?" the girl asked.

"It's a miracle." The last of the pink disappeared. "His body is healing." Shep's eyes darted from Max to the girl as she stepped forward.

"Is he going to be ok, then?"

Shep was already a miracle, but this ... if his body could repair like this, then perhaps it could destroy the virus.

"I think he should be put back in his cage. I can monitor him then."

"I thought you said the virus was deadly."

"It is, but Shep ..." Max didn't want to divulge any sensitive information, and the results of their research were not for public knowledge. "Shep is different. I'm hopeful he can fight it."

The girl remained quiet as Max lay the syringe on the desk then slipped his arm beneath Shep's head. The dog closed his eyes, accepting the stroking hand and they sat together. As the minutes ticked by, and the dog remained still, Max felt encouraged; perhaps there really would be a miracle here tonight.

"Is it working then?"

"It's too early to tell."

"But you said it would change, and it hasn't."

"Not yet."

"Don't you think you should put it in a cage—just in case?"

The girl was right. "Yes, I should. Come on Shep."

The dog's eyes snapped open, and Max caught his breath as Shep jumped to his feet; something in the dog had changed.

Max jumped back, but the dog pounced, jaws wide, and bit down hard on his arm. Shep released his arm and turned his attention on the girl as she screamed. Before Max had a chance to shout a warning, Shep attacked. Launching himself into the air with a powerful jump, he sank his teeth into her throat. She fell to the floor with the beagle straddling her. Gurgling screams filled the air as she batted at the dog's sides. Max grabbed the syringe and stabbed it into the dog's haunches then grabbed at the scruff of its neck.

Its jaws remained locked but as blood leaked from the girl's throat, Shep's power waned, and he slumped beside her. As the euthanising drugs coursed through the beagle's veins and its life drained away, the girl gasped for breath. There was no point in trying to stem the flow of her blood; she was already dead. They both were.

# CHAPTER NINE

Marta sat down with a slump in her chair and tapped the keyboard to reanimate the live feed from the lab. As the infected dog had hurled itself at that stupid little bitch and started to snap and snarl, Marta had sprinted out of the lab. She shivered. The dog had looked hideous with its red eyes bulging from their sockets. Of course, she'd seen the videos of the infected dogs at Whitby with their frothing mouths and snapping jaws, but seeing one that close, it was obvious the thing was insane. The pup had seemed so docile when she'd seen it earlier and Max had been so hopeful that the vaccine had worked this time – she'd been hopeful too as there was a very lucrative bonus tied up with finding a vaccine quickly, one that she and Max would benefit from.

The screen flickered back to life and Marta watched with rage waning to frustration as Max sat with Shep across his lap. The dog was lifeless. She slammed her hand on the desk. All that work! She ran a hand through her hair. Never mind; they had the trial results, and enough data to keep the project progressing forward without too much of an issue. Thankfully, Blake had seen the dog for himself and agreed to commence with human trials.

Marta noticed the girl's legs, cut-off by the edge of the monitor. She manoeuvred the camera with a click of the keyboard and swallowed hard then reached a trembling hand for her phone. Calling an ambulance was what she should do, but that would raise too many questions. She zoomed in on the girl recognising her as Lois Maybank, the daughter of Marjory Maybank, one of their trustees. She'd noticed her in the canteen the other day. Billy hadn't said anything about her being an animal right's activist and there was no mention of her being involved in this morning's ruckus outside the gates, although the fracas in the canteen later in the morning was perhaps an indicator that she was.

The camera focused on her upper body. She was grasping her neck as blood seeped through her fingers. Marta pulled the camera back. On the floor the crazed puppy lay with its head a mess of blood and gore, a large fire extinguisher at its side. The girl pulled her hand away and Marta gasped. The front of the girl's throat had been torn out to leave a gaping wound. She could almost hear her gasps of air as blood pooled around her. Marta fingered her phone. *She really should phone the police, or an ambulance at the very least.*

Max entered the frame, crawling on hands and knees. He had a bitemark too. If they had both been infected the authorities would close the *Institute* down, at least whilst they investigated, and they could lose Blake Dalton and she was not prepared to do that. Max crawled to the girl. Eyes wide with fear, her skin waxen, she gasped for breath and he placed a hand on her shoulder and began to speak. No doubt trying to assure her that all would be well. *Another lie, Max, but you're good at those, aren't you!* She zoomed in on the pair. She had never seen anyone die before, on the television and in films, yes, but not in real life. The girl jerked against the wall, eyes rolling to white, lips drawing back from her teeth. Marta clamped a hand to her mouth and sat back in the chair, unable to break her attention from the scene. The girl was dying, and in the most painful way. She should call an ambulance ... but they would hold her accountable for the accident and besides, the girl would be dead before they arrived so it would be a wasted effort. She mulled the problem over for several seconds before deciding to dispose of the girl's body in the furnace, once she'd died of course. Her belly knotted; dragging the body to the furnace wasn't something she could do on her own.

The girl's skin faded to a greyish white as blue veins appeared on her chin and across her cheeks. Max had disappeared from the screen. The girl opened her mouth in a rictus of pain. Marta heard the scream through the walls as the girl tipped her head back. The wound at her throat gaped, but ... Marta zoomed in again ... it was no longer bleeding. The wound should be pouring with blood, but it had clotted and now the wound no longer gaped. Marta zoomed in to a close-up of her face. As the girl continued to jerk, froth bubbled and slid down her chin. A down of dark hair covered her top lip and the sides of her cheeks, something that Marta certainly hadn't noticed when Lois had served her the choca mocha latte with extra sprinkles on Tuesday.

She focused on the wound. At its base, where the skin had flapped, the tissue had knitted together. The girl's breath was coming hard, and the torn skin was vibrating with each lung-full pulled through the gash, but it appeared to be healing, and healing very rapidly, not unlike Shep. She scanned back across the room. Shep lay completely still, a syringe in its neck. Blood covered its muzzle.

With his eyes rolled back in his head, blood seeping across the whites, Max began to jerk and spasm. Marta took in the scene. The girl's wound was mending, the cells regenerating, her body though wracked with pain was changing. It was impossible, but it was happening in front of her eyes. If the rabid dog bit Shep as he tried to protect Max, and then went on to attack Lois and Max, then somehow, they too were regenerating.

Marta picked up her mobile and dialled the last number called. It rang twice.

"Blake. I'm sending you the live feed from the lab. Max and a girl have been attacked. She should be dead, but she's not. Her wound is healing as I watch."

She waited for him to click the link, and they watched the feed together.

"Did you see that?"

"Zoom in. I need to know what the hell I just saw."

The camera zoomed in on Max's mouth.

"His teeth have grown. How is that possible? Check the girl."

Marta panned back across to the girl.

"She has them too, and the wound has almost completely healed. What the hell should we do? They'll close the *Institute* down."

"Calm down, Marta. I'm on my way. Go down and lock the lab. I'll meet you there."

"Be quick!"

"Marta, this is something we can deal with. Calm down and see it as the opportunity it is. Whatever Max has created in that laboratory is going to be very lucrative for us, very lucrative indeed."

The phone call disconnected, and Marta took a final look at the screen before running back down to the laboratory to lock the door.

THE DOOR OF THE *Hound and Stars* swinging shut after Blake Dalton, brought with it a waft of the cold November air. Javeen checked her watch. She really needed to go home and get some sleep. She had determined to be early for work tomorrow and be sat at her desk, fresh-eyed and with a coffee already half-drunk, before Stangton got to work. She could give him the supercilious greeting he loved to throw at her. The problem was Andy.

After finishing her shift, going home to a cold and lonely cottage with her meal for one ready to bung in the oven, even if it was a cooked-from-scratch casserole, wasn't something she could face that night. The day had been frustrating, Stangton's goading had irked her and, as she'd driven past the pub, Andy Blackwell had walked along the path and stepped up through its doors. She had driven almost to the last house along the road, resisting the urge to park up and follow him in, before giving in.

Her attraction to him first hit her at his garage when she had taken her car to get a tyre changed. He'd made her a coffee whilst she waited, and she had sat on the cold faux leather and chrome chair watching him work. He oozed masculinity in his dark blue, oil-covered overalls. Combine that with his height, she guessed he must be a good foot taller than her five-foot-three, broad chest and slim waist, and Javeen was hooked. He'd handed her the invoice with oil-stained hands along with a bright smile, and she'd wanted to feel his arms wrapped around her. Her head would only reach his chest, and she'd have to stand on tip toes to kiss him. *Calm it, Latimer!* He'd given her a wink as she'd thanked him and turned to leave and her heart tripping a quicker beat. Stangton's mention of his name earlier in the morning had given her a quick shock, and thoughts of the mechanic with his large workman's hands, had whispered to her throughout the day. Seeing him walking towards her as she drove home, and then going into the pub, had been the last straw.

She decided to go in, order an evening meal, and sit by the open fire, secretly hoping that he would take the opportunity to join her. It had taken precisely eleven minutes before he'd asked if he could sit in the seat opposite with the excuse of enjoying the warmth of the fire. They hadn't stopped laughing and talking since.

The logs burned low, and the flames flickered with the draft that rode across the floor as the door closed behind Blake Dalton.

"He was in a hurry!"

"Hmm, I heard him talking about 'staying calm' and 'seeing it as an opportunity'.

"Did you see his face when he got that phone call?"

"Yeah, looked like he'd been slapped with a wet fish."

Javeen laughed as Andy mimicked the shock and then deep frown that had passed over Blake Dalton's face. Until that moment he had been exchanging crude banter with the landlord and Billy who was doing his best to keep the pub's finances in the black by drinking much of its wares.

"I'd really better be getting home."

Andy looked at her with disappointment. "I'll walk you to your car."

"I'll be alright."

"No, it's ok. I'd like to."

Javeen waved goodnight to Jack and then gave a nod to Billy and left. Behind her a muffled shout was followed by a fist banging on the bar and one of the men chuckled.

She turned to Andy as the door shut behind him. "What was that about?"

"I think they had a bet on!"

Javeen's stomach sank. "A bet?"

"I overheard old Jack tell Billy there's no way a classy bird like you would go home with me."

"They had bets on that? Cheeky buggers!"

Andy laughed. "Well, they were wrong. You're not coming home with me. I'm walking you to your car."

"Thanks."

"Although, perhaps you'd like to come back to mine for a coffee? I've enjoyed talking tonight and ... it's still early ... and-"

"I'd like that," Javeen answered though bit her lip; she'd been too quick to reply.

"Great!" He sighed the words. "I mean ... great. It's just up here, next to the church."

# CHAPTER TEN

The figure of Lois, or what had been Lois, disappeared into the trees, and the dark engulfed her. Another wave of pain surged through Max's arms, back and legs, as a chill made him shudder. White breath billowed before him. He could feel the virus working through his body. It wouldn't take long for it to kill him.

*What did he have left? Eight hours of life, most spent in an agony of pain and violence.*

The rage had already had its first outburst. Marta shouldn't have locked the lab. He would have left voluntarily. His teeth gnashed as pain ripped through his back. Her slumped figure had been the last thing he'd seen as he'd swung on the bannister to throw himself out of the way of the second bullet. It had splintered the balustrade as he'd taken the stairs in two agonising leaps, a bullet hole already ripped into his shoulder.

He shuddered at the memory of subject 213; the youngest of the beagles they'd tested. That particular trial vaccine had been a disaster, seemed to enhance the virus, and the pup had become a vortex of rage. For three hours it had thrown itself at the bars of the cage, snapping and snarling as Max took notes. It was the hardest trial he'd had to endure. The dog had run round and round the cage, frothing at the mouth, until its aggression had turned in on itself and the dog had begun to tear at its own flesh. It had died with massive wounds to its haunches, paws chewed, tail missing, and teeth broken. Max had desperately wished he could shoot the pup to put it out of its misery. Its death still haunted Max's nightmares.

Headlights flooded the driveway as a car swung through the gates. Max drew back. He may only have a few hours of lucidity left and, at the end, death would be on *his* terms. Running along the back of the *Institute*, he kept to the shadows, and ran out through the gates. The moon was a perfect orb of brilliance, its light silvering the frost growing on the grasses along the verge. From the hillside, he could see above the trees to the lake on his right, its surface shining like black glass. To his left was Kielder village and at its edge the castle. He could make out the bellcote of the church and the row of houses opposite. Laura would be asleep in the third house. He had to see her one last time.

Powering forward, stones skittled, kicked by his pounding feet, and trees sped past as a blur. Pain wracked him again and he stumbled before regaining his balance. His arms pumped methodically as he ran faster than he had ever run before, his breathing effortless. As he sped down the hill, air whistled past his ears, and the undergrowth crackled as small creatures scurried within.

Minutes later he reached the village. It was deathly still. Sparse streetlights cast an orange haze across the street, though the moonlight made them redundant. As Max saw through the dark to the end of the street where the sign for the garage sat at the bend in the road, he realised his vision was blurred and removed his glasses. The large print on the sign became clear, 'Blackwell Autos. MOTs £39." He discarded the glasses.

He reached the church. Built of stone in the early thirteenth century, replacing an earlier one from the eighth, it sat nestled against a backdrop of tall pines, and was set back from the road, surrounded by lichen-covered and weathered gravestones. Laura had thrilled at living so close to the quaint church and had been in raptures about the tall lancet window with its stained glass, apparently by Kempe, a Gothic Revival artist. She attended it regularly on Sunday mornings, helped arrange the flowers, and did her stint of keeping it clean. Above the lancet window of slatted stone and stained glass was a bellcote and it had become her job to ring the bell to call the faithful—all fifteen of them.

Max had been surprised by the outpouring of religious fervour that had taken his wife once they'd moved, but after they'd lost Amy, he realised it gave her solace. He remembered the child in her mother's arms—a perfect tiny angel swaddled in a soft white blanket but for the blue lips and complete lack of movement. Their child had been stillborn, and Laura hadn't been quite the same since. For that matter, neither had Max. Life had taken on quite another meaning and he'd come to realise what a miracle it was.

As he reached the church's entrance, he stopped and stared at the squat building with its short bellcote and grasped the wooden gate. Its grey stone blocks shimmered, and he was overwhelmed by an urge to kneel in front of the carved figure of Christ hanging from the crossbeam in his agony, and pray for help, for safe passage, for succour as he headed into the oblivion of death. For the first time, Max was overcome with fear for his soul. Pain wracked him again, an agony ripping down his spine as though the vertebrae were bursting through his skin. He fell against the gate and growled, biting his jaws together to keep the noise inside. He buckled. The pain ebbed as sweat trickled at his temples and his shirt clung to his back and chest. Cold waved over him and the urge to gnash his teeth and scream was like another pain shooting through his body. He had to get to Laura. Pushing away from the gate, he ran to their home. A single light brightened the window of the house opposite as Max jumped over his garden wall and landed with a thud on the lawn. He turned, caught a glimpse through the partially closed curtains of Emily Carmichael being attended to by her carer - the final visit of the night - then crouched low beneath the wall.

The house sat in darkness. Laura would be in bed, sound asleep, expecting him to return and make love to her. He pulled keys from his trouser pocket and unlocked the side door. The house was warm after the cold of the November night. He closed the door with a soft click and wiped his feet. He may be dying, but the last thing he wanted was to be remembered for making a mess on the newly sanded and waxed floorboards of the cottage. He trod gently up the stairs enjoying the aroma of their home; cinnamon and orange lingered in the hallway, a small bowl of liquid with spice sticks and citrus zest sat on the hall table—one of Laura's simmer pots. She hated chemical fresheners, said they were carcinogenic, full of benzene and formaldehyde. After Amy's stillbirth, in a flying and gut-wrenching rage, she'd thrown out every aerosol in the house and it had taken Max hours to calm her and convince her their child's death wasn't because the sprays had contained phthalates. As he passed the bathroom, he picked up the scent of oatmeal soap and toothpaste, and, as he reached the bedroom the waft of Laura's Chanel No. 5 was softly powerful, but, above all of that, was her body odour mingled with his own. The bedroom carried the scent of sweat, breath, and sex. He had never noticed it before. Laura always kept the bedroom linen fresh and the windows ajar to let in the fresh air, but the smell was intense.

He pushed the bedroom door to reveal the room. As usual, the curtains were open; both of them loved to wake to the dark skies of early morning in the winter and let the moonlight brighten the room. Silver light reached across the white duvet to the golden curls of Laura's hair. His breath rasped, catching in a throat sore from running in the cold. He could smell her, really smell her. Taking another step into the bedroom, he peeled the duvet back. Aroused, he licked his lips at the sweet, salty scent rising from between her legs. An urge, deep from within his groin pulled him towards her. He wanted to lunge down and take her. He leant in, his nose close to her thighs and inhaled; she was ovulating. *How the hell could he tell that?* Need pulsed hard between his legs. She stirred and his mouth watered, dripping saliva onto her nightgown. The patch became translucent, showing the dark patch of pubic hair below. The virus pulsed through his blood and sweat trickled down his temples, landing as droplets on Laura's nightdress. He pushed down the urge to bite into her flesh. He clamped his jaws together. To gnash, bite, and rip at her would be an ecstasy. She muttered in her sleep and turned. He staggered back, pulled at his hair, punishing his desires, and ran back down the stairs.

Outside, he jumped over the wall and ran until he was back in the woods. In a tearing rage, he screamed at the night, and threw himself at the trees. Bark, jagged and harsh, scratched at his skin. He gritted his teeth and forced himself to run through branches, enjoying the pain the harsh needles and twigs brought. Let them whip his body and torment his flesh. *Monster! He was a monster!*

EMILY CARMICHAEL LAY back on her pillows, her hand cupping the plastic mouthpiece and took a deep suck of oxygen, as deep as she could these days. Her heart tripped a little harder than usual, a fluttery beat that she tried to ignore; listening to her heart struggling each night seemed to make it worse. Tonight, this rapid beat hadn't been tripped by anxiety, but by the sight of a man leaping over Laura Anderson's wall. He'd practically flown over, as though he had springs on his feet, then galloped off into the night. She sucked again at the oxygen. Perhaps she should call PC Stangton and let him know there had been an intruder at number three. She glanced at her clock. No, he'd be tucked up in bed fast asleep now, and she didn't want to bother him, or that lovely new lady Constable although she still hadn't come out of Andy Blackwell's house so couldn't be the one on call tonight. Besides, she couldn't be sure that it wasn't Max Anderson himself vaulting over the wall, though quite why he'd be running from his own house was hard to fathom. She coughed, pulled the oxygen mask from her face, and dropped it to her side. Her lungs were tight, and, despite the extra help, she just couldn't catch her breath.

'I'm waiting, Emm'. Cyril's voice carried across the room, it seemed to be somewhere and everywhere and nowhere.

"I know, love. But I'm not ready."

'Don't be long. I miss you.'

A sob stuck in her throat - *No, Cyril, I won't be long* – she leant back on the pillow and gazed out of the window. Seeing the moon, watching clouds float over its brilliant silver glow, was her one pleasure on these long and sleepless nights. There were nights when she couldn't sleep; insomnia had grasped her in her early sixties, and now, in her nineties, it had become a raddled old companion. Newer, was the fear of sleep, or rather of not waking. There were times when she'd jolt awake to the feeling of sinking. 'This is it', she'd think, knowing that if she allowed it to take her down, she'd certainly die. She'd struggle then, to pull herself to consciousness. The Grim Reaper wouldn't take her yet, though, not until she was ready, and even Cyril's whispered encouragement couldn't budge her; there were more moons she wanted to gaze at, more sunrises she wanted to delight in. *Just another lilac, let me see just another lilac bloom over the peonies in the spring, then I'll come.*

An ungodly, and guttural, scream from outside startled Emily from her thoughts and she instantly wished the curtains were closed. She crossed herself quickly and grasped for the oxygen mask. *God help them! Whoever that was, God help them.*

# CHAPTER ELEVEN

B illy took a final swig of beer, draining the pint glass and sat it back on the table.

"Time now, Billy."

Billy gave a wobbly thumbs up to Jack. The old bloke was alright. He'd been a party animal back in the day—if any of the landlord's stories were half true. Billy staggered to the door where Jack waited to let him out and a waft of cold air blasted his alcohol-warmed cheeks as he tripped down the step to the pavement.

"Steady there, Billy."

"I'm alright, mate." He reached up to slap a hand on Jack's shoulder. "Thanks for the lock-in, mate." He was a good bloke, that Jack, letting him drink till after hours. Kathy would kill him though, but what was he supposed to do whilst she was doing her shift looking after Mrs. Carmichael or the Reverend? She'd be home now though, so likely to give him the cold shoulder and nag him about being late for work tomorrow. He would get it from Steward then too. *Wouldn't be the first time, wouldn't be the last.*

"See you tomorrow, Billy."

"Yeah, if she lets me out."

"Night."

The door closed and Billy was left alone to stagger back home. One good thing about living in this village, it wasn't far from pub door to home. He'd catch it when he got back though, he'd promised Kathy he was just going for a couple of pints, not five with whiskey chasers. It had been that Andy Blackwell's fault. Billy had planned on going home after a couple, but when that tasty bit had walked in – wasn't she the new policewoman Stangton had been laughing about? – and Andy had started to chat her up, he had to see how it all panned out. They'd left together and Billy could tell Andy was on a promise. He'd laughed and handed his five quid over to Jack then ordered another beer as solace for losing the bet. He'd thought she would have better taste than that grease monkey; he'd been wrong.

The cold air brought some clarity to Billy's sozzled brain but with it came a queasy stomach. Suddenly bilious, Billy burped. Gas rumbled from his stomach and belched as white clouds in the November air. "'Scuse me." He continued his stumbling walk whilst footsteps pounded in the near distance. Billy's brain lagged, and the figure at the other end of the street, though running towards him, didn't register.

Nausea covered him like a wave, and he lurched against the corner of Mrs Belasis' cottage and swung into her drive, bending before retching and spewing the last three pints onto her gravelled drive. "Sorry," he muttered to the wall as he retched again. As more beer sloshed to the ground, the footsteps grew loud. He took a lurching step onto the drive, stepping through the beery vomit, and retched once more. This time the vomit was a morass of carrots, though he could have sworn Kathy had cooked sweetcorn for tea. Finally aware, Billy turned as he wiped at his mouth, a trail of saliva linking his coat sleeve with his lips; someone was running down the path, only a few feet away. In his stupor, Billy stood stock-still, then rocked on his heels as the - *what in God's name was it?* - thing ran past.

The thing locked eyes then sprinted past. Billy sagged to his knees, his eyes staring wildly into the now empty space. The thing had looked like a bloke from the village or the *Institute*, he couldn't place him, but he could have sworn ... no, his mind was playing tricks. The thing had fangs and its face had been dark with long hairs. His mind searched for understanding. And ... *Jesus! It's eyes. Hallowe'en. Was it Hallowe'en? It was a dog. Too big. A wolf.* As he crashed to the path, the man's wolf-like face with its hideous blood-red eyes filled his mind.

AS BILLY STAGGERED into his own hallway, alcohol finally sending him into oblivion, Anita crouched behind the toilet block where the longer grass at the treeline met the mown grass of the campsite. She sighed with relief as her bladder emptied. The toilet-cum-shower-cum-laundry-cum-washing-up block sat at the head of the campsite, near the shop and the squat reception building. Not that their proximity mattered to Anita; the whole place was locked up for the winter months and was now dark and desolate in the night. She clutched the torch as urine soaked into the grass, some splashing back onto her buttocks, and shivered. Left alone - *the others can go and wreck the Institute by themselves!* - the place was bloody creepy. Shining the torch to cast light over the grass and illuminate the blocky silhouettes of empty barbecue stands and slatted picnic tables didn't help. Instead, she trained light on their tents and the camper van. Wind whipped through the tranche of camping space between the trees; hair blew into Anita's face, and the tent fabric dented as though punched.

A gravel road ran from the camp's entrance down past a stream and out to the village, flanked either side by mown strips of grass for at least a kilometre. The pub, with its homecooked meals, was the only good thing about this place and Nate wouldn't let them go to the pub. Jamie had even called her 'stupid' when she'd suggested it. They were supposed to be keeping a low profile, he'd snapped. She'd snorted at that. *Keep a low profile!* Yeah, they were really doing that with their placards stamping around outside the *Institute*, and the tents and camper van parked unofficially at the campsite weren't exactly hidden. The owner was turning a blind eye that was all.

This wasn't her first visit to Kielder. She'd come regularly with her parents before she'd started university and had seen Ken, the campsite's owner, give them the evils as they'd walked through the village on their way to the *Institute*. He knew they were on his site, so don't give her 'we've got to keep a low profile'. She was starving, and Jamie calling her an 'idiot' had been the last straw. They could protest all they liked up at the *Institute*, she was going home. She shivered again as the stream of urine became a trickle, waited for the last droplets to fall, then pulled up her jeans.

A rustle and the sound of crashing erupted from the woods. Startled, she swung the torch into the trees. There was nothing to see of course, the trees were too thick. *Must be a deer.* A howl split the air, and she froze as the eerie noise wove through the trees and gripped her. The wind whipped at her face as a gust swept over the campsite and buffeted against the tents. The rustle of leaves and snapping of twigs repeated, but it didn't sound as close. She zipped up her jeans and trained torchlight on her destination—the two flapping tents and the locked camper van. They were at least fifty feet away. Movement to the left caught at the edge of the light and something jumped back into the dark. She stopped in her tracks and shone the torch where it had been standing revealing nothing but an empty space. She took another step towards the tents. Gravel crunched. Something was on the track ... behind her.

*How could it move so quickly? Was there more than one?*

She darted forward, racing to the tents. Footsteps followed, scuttling the gravel. She caught at her breath as her heart tripped with an unsteady beat. Dismissing the tents, she headed for the camper van and yanked at the door.

*Locked. Damn!*

It had been unkind of Nate to lock it, but what else did she expect. He was an arrogant, selfish sod, and cruel with it. They'd all heard him shouting at Lois tonight. That had really decided it for her. This trip had become something far more than she'd ever signed up for. Yes, she was up for waving placards and even shouting, but breaking in and destroying property? No. Plus, she didn't trust him to stop there. There was an edge to his temper that she really didn't like. She'd had her suspicions before, but tonight confirmed it, Lois was in some sort of dysfunctional, abusive relationship, and she, her best friend, had decided an intervention was necessary.

Something knocked against the van and Anita screamed.

As she swung the torch along the van a figure pulled out of the light. It snorted and then sniggered. If this was Jamie pulling one of his stunts, she'd kill him.

"Jamie?"

Heart pounding, she listened as he snorted with laughter.

"If that's you Jamie, I'm going to kill you!"

The laughter stopped and was replaced by the screech of metal as though a knife were being scratched along the door. He was going too far, and Nate would be furious if the paintwork on his precious van was damaged.

A hideous figure stepped out from behind the van.

It was not Jamie.

For a second, Anita thought that the man had some horrible deformity, but then she realised the hair-covered face with its elongated and fang-filled jaw, and burning red eyes, had to be a mask.

She screamed as he took a step towards her. He flinched and then thrashed against the van's side, hiding his face, and growled but then reached a hand towards her, fingers splayed. *Was he on drugs? An escaped lunatic? A serial killer hunting his next victim?* She screamed again as she noticed his talon-like nails. *Run!* With the tents offering no protection and the other buildings on the campsite being locked she had only one option—to head for the trees. But, as she ran for the safety of the forest, the hideous man followed.

THE STENCH OF THE GIRL'S urine had carried in tiny particles and rooted themselves in Max's nose. That and the aroma of her pussy. *How had he never smelt it before? It was intoxicating.* She wasn't ovulating like Laura, but she was ripe. He sniffed at the air ... *pussy!* ... licked it with his tongue ... *need it!* ... he gnashed his teeth ... *God help me! Go back to the Institute Max. Kill yourself. Euthanise!* He cackled. *Just a dead dog, like the others, like Shep.* He'd watched as the girl had done up her zip, the smell of her genitalia sticky on his lips, and his mouth had watered. The urge to fornicate was immense, a powerful urge ripping through his body, but behind it was something else, something that made his teeth gnash, a need to bite and tear at her flesh. *Hannibal ... Hannibal Lecter ... Hannibal the Cannibal.* He snorted. *No!* He smashed his head against the side panel of the van and scratched long, thick nails down it. *A hand of blades.* He cackled. The blades left streaks of bare grey metal in the green paintwork.

The girl disappeared into the forest, and Max followed.

# CHAPTER TWELVE

In the dark, in the morning's earliest hours, Javeen breathed in Andy's scent; he smelled of warm musk, engine oil, and sex. The night had been a revelation to her. *How had he learned to do that with his hands? She didn't want to know, wouldn't ask.* He murmured in sleep, and she turned to watch him. Curtains open, a silvery light played with his dark hair, it seemed almost white where the light touched it. Dark lashes brushed his cheeks, the stubble already covering his chin; he would look even more beautiful with a beard. She ached for him again. She'd definitely be back for more ... *if he wanted her.* Her confidence slipped. Perhaps he wouldn't? What if he didn't want to see her again? *Damn it, Javeen. Why the hell didn't you keep your legs closed, you're a bloody stupid little slut.* She'd done it again! Let a man touch her heart. *Stupid!* She stroked his chest. He really was quite beautiful. He murmured and his arm slipped across her belly. *She shouldn't have gone into the pub. Too much wine and she was anybody's. Come on, that is not fair! He seemed to like you.* She sighed, bit at her bottom lip, and wished she had gone straight home to the usual cup of tea and the next chapter of 'Pet Sematary'. Tonight, she would. He wouldn't want her, not after she'd shown just how easy she was—*spreads like butter, does our Jav!* She sank back into the pillow. Another hour and she'd leave. Stangton's beady, laughing eyes, mocked her. She really couldn't be late for work.

From the near distance the noise came again but the odd howl, or bark, of what must be a fox or a dog, was instantly forgotten as Andy woke and began to caress her breast and the desire to take him again made her ache.

A scream broke into the room, high pitched and laced with terror.

Javeen sat up, pushing Andy's hand from her breast, and listened.

"What the hell was that?"

Swinging her legs to the floor, she strode to the window. Moonlight reflected on her skin as Andy joined her, his naked flesh pressed up against hers, all thoughts of carnal pleasures gone.

"It sounded like a woman!" He reached to the floor for his jeans.

She stared out of the window, fumbled for the latch, and swung it open. Cold air blew over warm skin and goosebumps rose over her belly. She shivered. Ignoring the cold, she leant out. Wind whipped her hair.

"I can't hear anything now, but-"

"We're going to look. That wasn't natural, that wasn't."

"Could it have been a dog or a fox?"

"No. Not any dog or fox I've ever heard. Sometimes the deer make a racket, but not at this time of year, and not like that."

He pulled on his t-shirt as Javeen reached for her own clothes. "I'll be downstairs."

"Andy!" she called as he left. "Wait!"

A ringing thud sounded in the distance, and metal clanked against metal. Another shrill scream split the air and the light in the neighbour's bedroom switched on. Anita closed the window, locked it, then dressed.

Andy sat with boots in hand as she entered the kitchen. "Someone's in trouble, Javeen." He pulled on the first boot.

"You can't just go out into the night and-"

"We look out for each other around here, Jav. It's a small village. No strangers. Whoever is out there is one of ours."

Shame pricked at her cheeks. "I didn't mean that we shouldn't go, just that ... - *admit it, Javeen, you're scared!* - just that we should be prepared." Her first instinct hadn't been to go out and help; she'd thought of calling the Force in town. Next to Andy's fervent need to be out there rescuing whoever was in trouble, her own response had been inadequate. She was the one they had to turn to in an emergency. She was the Police, but Andy was the one leading the fray. *Man up, twinkle!* She took a breath. "Do you have a torch?"

RAGE TORE AT MAX AS he followed the girl through the woods. Every second was a torture. He wanted to leap, sprint between the trees, wrestle her to the floor and bite deep into her throat. His mouth watered, and cold dribbles of saliva glistened on his chin. She stopped, shone her torch around, then continued. He waited, digging claws into tree bark, slicing through its fibres. Hooked nails dug deep into the greenwood as he forced thoughts of carnage away. In lucid moments, the brutality of his need sickened him. He focused on his hand - the hairs had grown coarse and dark - and wrapped his other arm around the trunk, anchoring himself to the tree.

*Let her go, let her run free.*

*Save yourself!*

He wanted to warn her, scream at her to run, run for her life, but the instinct to hunt, the instinct to rip her flesh and devour her innards, choked back the words. He tried. "Run!" he shouted but only a long, hoarse grunt escaped his throat. A tear slipped from his eye, travelled in rivulets to his nose, and caught in the hairs that had spread across his cheek.

He slid down the trunk, sharp talons slicing through the bark, and squatted. He took rapid breaths, calming his body. His mind scratched through memories of the past hours. Pictures flashed in his mind, images of men in dark suits, Lois clasping her neck, pushing away from him, her eyes filled with terror.

*Shep ... Oh Shep.*

Shep dead on the floor, a syringe sticking from his fur, the younger beagle slain, its head caved in, an extinguisher at its side, Marta staring at him, her mouth slack, eyes darting from him to Lois to the man with the gun. Pain had ripped through his shoulder as he'd lurched forward, and the pop of the gun had tapped against his ear drums. He'd knocked the man to the side, barged past Marta, taken the stairs in two jumps and thrown himself through the door and into the night.

*Laura ... Laura.*

He longed for her warmth.

*When he was finished here—when he'd had his fill* – he cackled – *oh, sweet pussy, be mine.*

He slammed his forehead at the trunk then snorted.

*O lovely Pussy! O Pussy, my love.*

Again, he knocked against the trunk.

*What a beautiful Pussy you are.*

Pain rocked through his skull as his head collided with the uneven wood.

*You are. You are! What a beautiful Pussy you are!*

He hit it again, harder this time. The tree shivered. Max sobbed. "O Pu-." His chest heaved. Snot dribbled to his top lip. He sagged. "Oh, my love." He turned his head to the moon and howled, "Lauraaaa!"

The girl crashed through the woods in her efforts to put distance between herself and Max's snapping, snarling, howling grief. He let her run. She wouldn't get far, and even if she did – his lips curled back from his teeth in a smirk – even if she did, he'd easily, *oh, so easily*, catch up. He continued to squat and, as the minutes passed, his heartbeat slowed to a gentler rhythm, and the first snort of sleep caught him unawares. He jerked at the noise then lay down at the base of the tree, curling, head to knees, and slipped into oblivion and dreams.

His sleep was light, flirting with the edges of a deeper unconsciousness. As it dipped into the trough of nightmares, Max was running. The forest ricocheted with the sound of barking and behind him the pack ran. Sweat trickled from every pore as he sprinted through trees and jumped over fallen trunks. Caught in torchlight, dogs closed in, surrounded him, and bayed for his blood. They leapt as guns blasted and Max danced as bullets tore into his flesh.

He woke with a start and cold seeping through to his bones.

Standing, he shook leaves from his torn shirt, then tipped his nose upwards and sniffed, picking up the scent of her fear. It wafted in the air like a band of smoke, and he followed it to the clearing. A tree with its massive root lay fallen, stretching out across the grass. Crouched at the base of the upturned root, the girl sheltered beneath its bone white fingers. Running along the treeline, he approached from her blindside. He crept along the trunk and crouched, salivating. Asleep, she leant into the root, her arms tight to her body, a torch grasped in her hand. He shuffled forward reaching out a clawed hand to her face. Warm breath brushed the coarse hairs that covered his hand. *No!* She was beautiful as she slept, so young, her skin pale and unblemished, a blonde plait fell across her cheek from beneath her woollen hat. If he had a daughter - pain stabbed at his heart - he would want her to be this beautiful. She murmured in sleep. He snatched his hand away and jumped back behind the trunk. Saliva pooled in his mouth.

He pulled at his hair and turned, galloping away from the girl to the forest. Then squatted at the treeline, staring to the root, clawing at his face, digging claws into his own belly.

*You can't eat her, Max! That makes you a monster.*

He squatted and waited. Time passed and the charcoal of night faded to grey. In the distance, in the lower woods closer to the village, he heard voices. Two—a man and a woman. His heart picked up a beat. Movement at the root claimed his attention and the girl stood. He stepped out from the treeline. She saw him. He darted back behind the tree as the weak light of her torch shone in his direction.

The voices from the forest grew louder. If he hadn't slept, he could have slashed and sliced them too. Torchlight beamed into the trees and the girl searched the forest as light flickered among the trunks.

"Hey!" She stepped out from the root. "Hey!" She waved her arm as the light moved between the trees then ran to follow.

Max made his move. As she reached the treeline, he ran parallel. The urge to dig his claws into her flesh consumed him. He could hear the pounding of her heart, its beat irregular, like a tone-deaf drummer. Her yellow plaits bounced against her jacket. She raised an arm to protect her face against the branches as she ran through the trees. Max galloped beside her. Keeping her pace was easy – *she was slow, so slow* – he snickered and licked his lips in anticipation. There were no thoughts, only the need to sink his teeth into her ripe flesh. She glanced across to him as she pushed another branch from her face, stumbled as her eyes widened, then darted to the left. An ache of desire spread through his groin. Her foot caught and she fell, grunting in pain as her knee knocked against the worming root, hands slamming to the ground. Within a second, as she scrabbled to her feet, he was so close he could lick her cheek. Max knocked her back to the forest floor and straddled her. Aroused to the point of ecstasy, he sank sharp incisors into her neck and tore. In the distance the voices faded and left the forest.

# CHAPTER THIRTEEN

Their efforts had been fruitless and Javeen had returned to Andy's house, cold and weary, unable to find whatever had made that soul-scraping noise in the night. The dark of the forest had given her chills and there was no way on God's earth that she'd go back in there at night.

She flicked the kettle on and spooned in a heaped teaspoon of coffee to her mug, then added a few more grains – she needed the caffeine – and drowned it with milk, full-fat thank you very much. She may even eat the chocolate bar stashed in her drawer this morning. Lack of sleep made her grouchy and hungry. She rubbed at her eye with the palm of her hand. It stung with tiredness, but she gloated that this morning she had beaten Stangton into the office. She stirred the coffee with a clink of the spoon and took it back to the desk, sinking into her chair and closing her eyes. She could go to sleep right now; she was that tired. A flash of movement outside caught her attention and then Stangton strode in through the door, his cheeks flushed from the cold.

"Morning, Latimer," he nodded as he unclipped his bicycle helmet. "You beat me to it today, then."

"Yep," she said sitting forward and taking a slurp of coffee knowing that it would irk him.

"Looked like someone didn't get much sleep." He raised his brows. "Aye?"

Javeen kept her groan of irritation inside. "You're correct. I didn't. I-"

"No need to go into details, Latimer. I've been filled in on proceedings." He gave her a wink.

"What?"

"You and Blackwell."

"What the-"

"It's a small village, Latimer. The whole place knows if you so much as fart, and what it smells like."

How the very hell did Stangton already know that she'd bedded Blackwell? "We shared a few drinks in the pub after work."

"At ten fifteen of the preceding evening, PC Javeen Latimer was seen walking with the accused from the *Hound and Stars* to number four Church Lane. PC Javeen Latimer did not leave the premises until six-thirty am of the following morning."

Burning stung her cheeks. Who the hell had seen her? She remembered the neighbour's twitching curtains. Nosey old bag! "And just how the hell do you know that?"

He tapped the side of his nose. "Sorry, m'lud, but I can't divulge the source of my information." He cackled.

She threw him a look of scorn and swung the chair to face her monitor giving her coffee a more enthusiastic slurp.

"To serious business though, Latimer. There's been a report of an intruder at number three Church Lane. Mrs Carmichael reported a man vaulting the garden wall. He was last seen running in the direction of Main Street."

"Vaulting a five-foot wall?"

"... at approximately four-thirty am-"

"She called you at four-thirty am." Javeen was hopeful; it had been Stangton's turn to be on call last night. Normally, the 'on-call' shift was as silent as the grave.

"No, she waited until a decent hour. Didn't want to wake me she said."

"I heard screams from the woods last night, Stangton. I ... we ... went to investigate but couldn't find anything. Number three ... isn't that Doctor Anderson's house?"

"It is."

The phone rang and Stangton answered. His face instantly dropped to serious, all mirth gone. He pulled his pad forward and grabbed his pen, asked the required questions, replied, mumbled, then finished with, "We'll be there in ten minutes."

"And?"

"That was Billy Oldfield. There's been a break-in at the *Institute*."

"The vegan anarchists?" she asked with a roll of her eyes.

"No ... maybe, but whoever broke in trashed Dr Anderson's lab and two dogs are dead. It's like a slaughterhouse up there apparently."

"Doctor Anderson? The owner of the house where Mrs Carmichael said she saw a man vault over the five-foot wall and disappear up the road?"

"Yep." Stangton buttoned his coat as Javeen grabbed hers. She slipped the chocolate bar into her pocket—she had a feeling she would need it.

Twenty minutes later they stood in 'Laboratory 2' at *Kielder Institute*. A mess of blood and gore was smeared across the floor and two beagles lay dead. It was not quite the slaughterhouse that Stangton had described, but the smaller beagle's head was almost flat, and a large and bloodied fire extinguisher butted up against the cages on the other side of the room. The lab stunk of faeces and the metallic scent of blood. The room was muggy, and she gagged at the stench.

Marta Steward had her back turned and stared out to the thick bank of trees that stretched across the hills. Javeen squatted and rested her hand on the larger dog's neck avoiding the syringe sticking out at a right angle. The animal felt stiff. Had she expected a pulse? A small glass vial had rolled under the desk. She picked it up with gloved hands and rolled it between her fingers to read the sticker. "Beuthanasia D-Special. Contains pentobarbital and phenytoin. Warning: for canine euthanasia only."

Marta turned from the window, her face much paler than yesterday and her eyes puffy. She looked as though sleep had been rough last night, or non-existent. "It's what we use to euthanise the test subjects with."

Stangton rose from examining the smaller dog. "It may have been used on the larger dog, but this one died from blunt force trauma." Javeen held back a smirk, knowing just how much he had itched to say that phrase. "From the evidence, it would appear that the fire extinguisher has been used to kill the smaller dog."

Marta nodded and clasped a hand to her mouth.

"Do you have any witnesses to what happened here last night?" Javeen asked.

Marta shook her head. "We have CCTV installed, but it's only trained on the entrance gates and the front door, not the labs."

"We'll need to see the recordings."

"Of course. You'll need to talk to the Head of Security, Billy Oldfield."

"Are any of your staff missing?"

"All staff are usually here before nine-thirty, but we're fairly flexible in terms of time—as long as the hours are put in during the day, people can arrive and leave any time between seven-thirty and eight-thirty. Doctor Anderson often works later though."

"And where is Doctor Anderson?"

"I haven't seen him this morning. He'll be devastated when he discovers that Shep has died." She pointed to the larger beagle. "He was one of our successes. Doctor Anderson-"

The lab door swung open, and a young woman strode in, her morning greeting halted as she glanced from Javeen and Stangton to Marta. As she noticed the dogs on the floor her face crumpled.

"Shep!" She gasped. "Molly!"

"Step back please, miss." Stangton stepped in front of the dogs. "This is a crime scene."

The woman halted behind Stangton's outstretched arm. "Where's Max?"

"He hasn't come in yet, Sally," Marta stated.

"But his car's in the car park."

Javeen and Stangton exchanged a glance.

"So, he *is* here?" Javeen asked.

"If his car is, then he must be. He sometimes bikes to work, but it's too cold now for that and too dark to cycle home when he finishes."

"Doctor Steward, I think we'd better see the CCTV footage now."

She nodded. "Follow me."

JAVEEN DREW BACK WITH frustration and stared again at the blank screen, moving away from the waft of alcohol on Billy Oldfield's breath. "So, you're saying that there was a blackout last night and it wiped out all of the security footage from yesterday."

"Yep. And last week's. I've had to re-tune it all. In the old days it would all be there on the video tape, but this lot is digital. Technology! Knows how to screw you up."

*Was the man incompetent?* "Isn't it on the cloud somewhere?"

His voice waivered. "No, we've not got that."

Javeen noticed the tremble in Billy's hand. He wasn't known as an alcoholic. Sure, he'd had a few pints in the pub last night, and a couple of whiskey chasers, but unless he'd downed numerous pints after Javeen left with Andy (her cheeks stung as she remembered the twinkle in Billy's eyes as she'd caught him watching them talk) then there was something else wrong with him. He seemed nervous. What did he have to hide?

"Anything else you'd like to tell me, Billy?"

"Eh?"

"Well, I can tell that you're nervous." She gestured to his shaking hand. "Now, unless you've got some form of Parkinson's, which I doubt, because you had no problem lifting your pint glass last night, or you got totally blasted after I left, then something else is making you quake in your boots. Am I making you nervous, Billy?" She was pushing a bit too hard, he was not being interviewed after all, but she knew if she just prodded a little more, he may tell her why the CCTV footage had been wiped. She didn't believe the blackout story one bit.

"I ..." He faltered and tapped at the keyboard again.

"You can tell me, it will be confidential," she urged. *Come on! Spill the beans on Steward, Billy.*

"Last night ... after the pub ..." He stopped again and the tremble in his hand increased. He pulled it from the keyboard and stuffed it inside his trouser pocket.

"What did she ask you to do, Billy?"

"Eh?"

He gave her a blank look. She pushed again. "What happened?" Javeen searched his eyes. He seemed afraid—perhaps Steward and her heavies had nobbled him.

"A beast. There was this man ... this wolf-thing ... creature ... I know how crazy this sounds ... It ran past me, not on all fours, on two legs, but it had fangs and the most ... it's eyes ... its eyes were filled with blood and ..." He stopped but this time didn't resume. The words had flown out of his mouth in a jumble.

Javeen sighed. Perhaps he was an alcoholic after all.

"And then that scream." He pulled his fingers through his hair. Sweat marked the underarms of his sleeve, and its sourness wafted to her nose. The hair on Javeen's neck crept as he continued his story of how the thing had run past him as he'd puked into Mrs Belasis' drive, locked eyes for a second, then sprinted past and jumped over the wooden fence on the other side of the road and disappeared into the woods. The scream was perhaps the first one Javeen had heard as she'd lain with Andy. Billy's eyes searched hers as he finished his story then flitted to the wall beyond her shoulder before focusing back on the screen. Whatever he'd seen, fantastical as that was, he believed it was real.

"How much did you have to drink last night, Billy?"

He huffed. "I was drunk, I admit it. I'm a lightweight when it comes to drinking and Jack was egging me on."

Javeen grunted, the old codger knew how to get the locals to open their wallets.

"But ... that thing was real."

Javeen stood back, arms crossed, her fingers digging into her upper arms. It couldn't be true, not really, but perhaps someone did run past him and into the woods. Perhaps there was a nutter loose. Perhaps he was the thing that had screamed in the woods—probably some stupid prank.

"Could it have been a mask, Billy?"

He sagged. "I told you ... it was real. No mask has eyes like that."

"Alright, Billy. I'll make a note of your ... sighting." She didn't tell him that she'd heard the scream too and spent the early morning searching through the woods. She thanked him for his help then met Stangton in the entrance lobby.

# CHAPTER FOURTEEN

Max woke with a start. Light filtered through the criss-cross of branches. A bird cooed in the distance. A scurry of tiny paws tapped at his eardrum, and he held his hands to his ears to soften the noise. He shuffled to a squat, pushing away the branches he'd ripped from the tree to cover his body as he slept, and sniffed. Close by, very close, something moved. He sat deathly still.

From a cluster of bowing ferns, a large cat stepped forward. It seemed wary. Max salivated. The lynx, one of the five pairs that had controversially been reintroduced to the forest earlier in the year, lifted a paw, stared with amber eyes in his direction, and stood completely still. Max closed his eyes, each breath slow and silent, waiting for the cat to make its move. The paw descended and the lynx moved away. Max pounced, his claws digging deep through the amber fur penetrating the soft belly beneath. He growled with delight as he ripped at its flesh and devoured the innards.

With a mouth full of warm offal, he tucked the corpse beneath his arm and made his way to the clearing and the wooden cabin. Smoke curled in tendrils from its chimney. He took another bite of the lynx's liver, blood dripping at the side of his mouth, then ran behind the trees to the shed tucked away to the left of the house. A car crunched over gravel and disappeared down the track as he reached the shelter. He yawned, spittle dangled between his jaws, and he snapped them shut. Baring his teeth as a man appeared at the cabin door, Max watched from the cover of branches until he left the property.

Hooking the lynx over a bough, anchoring it between dividing branches, he moved to the door of the shed. Once inside, he ripped at the fabric covering his body and threw it to the floor. Removing shoes that no longer fit, he stepped onto the tattered remains of his shirt and trousers, curled beneath the workbench, and fell into a light sleep until his belly ached again and his mouth salivated at the urge to gnash, and rip, and gnaw.

AS THE SUN BEGAN ITS descent into late afternoon, Marta blew smoke out through dry lips. It mingled with the cold air as she leant out of the window, and she shivered. She shivered again as she glanced across the open space to where the grass met the treeline. Max and Lois, or rather the hideous and deformed monsters that had fled the laboratory last night, were still in there.

Blake hung his binoculars by his side.

"Was it them?"

"I'm not sure. I thought I saw movement."

"What the hell are we going to do, Blake?"

He returned her question with a gaze that made her squirm. "We are going to hold it together, Marta. I thought you were tougher than this—a real ball-breaker."

"I am, but those things-"

"They're part of the programme now. From our point of view, things couldn't have gone any better. This development is astounding. The power Max and the girl had! He barely flinched when the bullet hit his shoulder-"

"They were monstrous! The change in them was so quick-"

"I agree, they looked-"

"They weren't human."

"You could tell it was Max and the girl. Somehow, the dog's bite changed them."

"If *they* find out what has happened—they'll shut us down."

"Don't be so sure about that. Corbeur is very interested in the latest developments."

"This wasn't part of the original plan."

"No, but we need to go with the flow, Steward. What we have to do right now is bring Anderson and the girl back in. And hold our nerve." Blake looked towards the computer where a live feed played. "Walton is out there tracking them. If anyone can find them it's him."

From the desk, the computer screen flickered with movement and a man's voice could be heard.

"Turn up the sound. I can barely hear him."

"Blake. Do you copy?"

Apart from the flash of a boot or arm as he walked through the forest, the man was unseen.

"We're here, Walton. Go ahead."

"I think I've found him."

Marta's heart beat a rapid tattoo against her ribs. "Tell him to turn around soon. It's getting dark."

"Shh! Marta. Watch."

Walton walked slowly forward, a trunk loomed, filling the screen, and then a small clearing came into view. Ahead, a figure squatted on the forest floor. Its arms moved rhythmically backwards and forwards in a pulling motion.

Marta bent forward, peering at the screen. "What is it?"

Blake clicked the keyboard, and the camera zoomed in to focus. "Max!"

Crouched over the still body of a roe deer was Max Anderson, or something that still had the features of Max Anderson.

"He's ripping it apart ... with his bare hands."

Marta watched with disgusted fascination as the creature ripped at the flesh, moist, warm air rising in the cold, and pulled at the deer's innards.

"What's it eating?"

"Looked like a heart."

Marta gagged as the creature opened its jaws and took an enormous bite of the steaming offal. Spiked fangs sliced into the red flesh. Blood dripped at the side of its jaws.

"Max didn't have a beard. That thing has hairs all across its face."

"The girl did too. I noticed as she ran past me. It must be part of the transmogrification. That thing has fangs too, and I'm pretty damned sure Max didn't have those either."

"He didn't."

"You'll have to head this project now, Marta. Unless we can get another research-"

Blake grew quiet as the thing stopped and twisted its head in the direction of the camera, seeming to stare straight at them.

"He's seen us."

"Don't be stupid. We're in your office."

"Seen Walton, then. Look! He's sniffing at the air."

The office fell silent, and Marta heard only the in-out of Blake's breath and her own pounding pulse. She gripped Blake's arm as the creature moved towards the camera.

The camera held still for less than five seconds. Suddenly airborne, the creature sprung from the carcass to less than six feet from the camera, its blood-filled eyes almost black in the light. The camera jerked and the screen filled with trees, ferns and forest floor as Walton ran. His breath was heavy, and the office filled with its noise. The screen went dark as he thudded to the ground. Light suddenly reappeared and the creature's face filled the screen. Walton screamed as its teeth gnashed and became huge, its mouth widening as it descended. The camera rolled to the floor, and the screen went black as it was pressed into the earth. Walton's scream filled the room and Blake jabbed at the keyboard to reduce the volume.

"Shit!"

As Martha turned and vomited into the wastepaper bin, Blake reached for his phone.

# CHAPTER FIFTEEN

M ax ripped at the man's throat and quietly returned to the forest. In his peripheral vision, movement caught his eye. He could smell her again—the woman from the laboratory—Lois. She stepped out from behind the tree, sniffing at the air. He crouched low over the dying man, the warmth of his body brushing against his own. Lois took another step out from the shadow of the tree towards his kill.

His lips pulled back against his teeth. *Mine. It's mine.* She stepped next to the deer's carcass and crouched, her hand reaching out to take the innards, her eyes checking the spaces around her. But before she had time to lift the intestines to her mouth Max crashed into her, sending her smashing into a tree. She stood, snarled, then darted to the left. He gnashed his teeth, lunging close to her face, and stepped back to the deer.

Reaching for the liver he took a bite. Lois watched from the tree, a dark welt of blood running down her temple where the force of landing against the rough bark had torn at her skin. She scurried back between the trees. Max ate until his belly was full, then moved from the carcass and into the forest before turning to watch from behind a tall and nodding fern. Leaves rustled and the girl reappeared, the torn flesh now mended, and crouched over the carcass before reaching into its sliced belly and taking the remaining kidney.

AS LOIS FINISHES TEARING at the roe deer and made her way through the woods, Javeen replaced the phone's receiver. Her hand ached with taking down yet another report of noises coming from the woodlands. The door opened and a man stamped in, his boots leaving a muddy print on the mat. His hand rested on the door handle.

"Where's Stangton?"

Javeen forced a smile. Thomas Burdon's frustration leaked from him. To diffuse the situation, she would need to stay calm and be non-confrontational. "He's out on a call. Can I help?"

"Come out and see." He stepped out of the station and disappeared back into the gathering gloom. The sun was sinking rapidly, and a mist had rolled in from the forest to settle across the village. As she stepped outside, he was already at his Land Rover. Coupled to it was a low-sided trailer. Javeen could tell from his pursed lips and grim demeanour that he wanted her to look inside.

As she approached, the smell of sheep rose to her nostrils, and she made her best effort not to make it obvious that the stench was offensive. At the side of the trailer, she realised why the reek was so bad. Lying on its bed were three full-grown sheep. Blood had soaked into their wool, clotted and crimson in places, in others a dark pink. The stench of their ruptured intestines, which rolled like thick, grey worms from their bellies, clung to Javeen's nostrils. She moved her head to the side in an effort to suck in clean air.

"Aye, it's a sorry sight."

"Are these your sheep, Mr. Burdon?" Thomas Burdon was one of three hill farmers that had farmed the land for generations in the immediate vicinity of Kielder village.

"Aye. You can see from them markings," he stabbed a finger at the nearly luminous green splodges of dye on the animal's fleece, "that they're mine. The ear tags'll prove it. They're identified with DEFRA."

"Have you any idea what did this to them?"

"Have I any idea? Damned right I do. It's them lynx that were introduced back into the forest. I said this would happen. I told them," he raged. "I even told them about the one that escaped from the zoo in Wales and went on a killing spree, but did they listen? No, they did not, and this," he stabbed a finger at the sheep, "is what happens. I even went to the National Parks meeting they set up about it and told them. Didn't listen though, did they. Now look!"

The next half an hour was spent with Thomas Burdon taking his statement, making him a coffee, reassuring him that the matter would be taken seriously, and photographing the sheep, before the farmer went back up to his hillside farm, muttering about compensation, and the 'bloody idiots at the Lynx Trust putting a bloody bunch of cats' before his livestock and his family.

Javeen had listened as he'd made his complaints, nodded in the right places, taken notes, and wondered if a lynx could really do that type of damage to a sheep. Each of the animals had been gutted with a great tear from sternum to lower abdomen, and one had its throat ripped out. Mention had been made of the lynx perhaps being the source of the noise in some of the complaints already received, and she'd done some research. Her findings were uncomfortable if not unsurprising; although there was no confirmation of the release, controversy had been aroused by the Lynx Trust claiming they had overwhelming support and approval to release six Eurasian Lynx into the forest. Their opponents had argued that the lynx would prey on livestock, particularly sheep, and were efficient killers that preyed on animals up to four times their size, so perhaps a lynx could be the killer. She'd called the Trust for confirmation of the release, but the receptionist had been evasive and mumbled something about 'fake news'. She was waiting for the Trust's Director to return her call.

As the sun set, she checked her watch. Only an hour and a half remained before Andy would be at hers expecting the meal she had promised. Memories of last night sparked unexpected excitement and she smiled despite the stress of the day.

As early evening darkened, and Javeen stood at her bedroom window with newly washed hair wrapped in a towel, the howling in the woods started again. She closed the curtains with a shiver. She loved the rented cottage and had even considered buying it if she could convince the landlord to sell but sitting at the edge of the village without a neighbour in shouting distance, with the howling in the background, was making her reconsider. She switched the television on to drown out the noise and frowned in frustration as the screen brightened and fizzled with white noise. No picture appeared. She stabbed the controls at the screen. Each time she flicked over 'No signal' appeared. The howl repeated, and she drew her dressing gown tight.

After dressing, she made her way downstairs to the warmth of the kitchen and the aroma of the beef casserole cooking in the oven. After uncorking the bottle of a newly discovered favourite red wine, she poured herself a small glass, took a sip and waited for Andy to arrive.

He turned up freshly showered, fingers scrubbed of oil, and with a huge grin on his face. His eyes glinted as they caught the light from the hallway. He looked as happy to see her as she was of him. The tension that had been rising all day, making her jittery on top of all the odd events, receded and she ushered him into the warm kitchen before pouring him a glass of wine.

"Smells great in here."

"It's beef casserole, my mum's recipe."

"She a good cook?"

"Not really, but she has a few dishes that taste great."

The chatter continued through the evening and the day disappeared as they ate the meal, then sat side by side on the sofa. Completely at ease, Javeen relaxed in the warmth of Andy's arms, amazed that she could feel so at home with someone in such a short space of time. Another howl broke into the room as Javeen reached for the bottle of wine.

"Those howls are seriously creeping me out. Has anyone figured out what it is yet?"

"I'm not sure, but I think it could be a lynx."

"A lynx? I thought they'd decided not to go ahead with that. There was uproar among the farmers and landowners about it earlier in the year."

"I've been reading up about it. I think it may have gone ahead on the quiet. Thomas Burdon came to the station this afternoon with a trailer full of mutilated sheep."

"Nice!"

"They'd been disembowelled. I did some research and lynxes do prey on sheep, so it may solve the mystery."

"I can't forget that scream, Jav. That wasn't a lynx. It was human. Did you go back into the woods to check?"

"No, I haven't had time, and without anyone reporting a missing person I won't be able to get Stangton to agree to a search."

Andy was silent for a moment then added, "I had to drag Topsy out of the house this morning, which isn't like her. Usually, I can just open the back door and she's off. She's never been fearful of going into the woods."

A chill ran through Javeen as she remembered Andy's affectionate English Springer Spaniel. Dogs had a much better sense of smell, and perhaps danger, than humans. If the dog was wary of going into the woods, then there could be a predator out there. "She must be able to smell the lynxes. Anyway," she moved closer to Andy, "let's change the subject."

As they drank the wine and talked, the evening became night, and they drifted to sleep on the sofa until she led him upstairs to make love and block out the howling from the woods.

# CHAPTER SIXTEEN

As Javeen and Andy lay entwined in her bed, their energy spent from a night of lovemaking, Max uncurled from beneath the workbench to the opening shed door. A figure stood in silhouette against the grey light of morning. He couldn't see the face, but he could smell her—the woman from the laboratory—the one Shep took a bite out of—Lois. She stumbled forward, pulled the door closed behind her and limped across to join him. She sat on haunches, her eyes averted beneath dark brows that spread to her temples, her breasts visible beneath a torn shirt, the nipples erect. There was no sign of the damage Shep had wrought on her neck. Her lower body was naked.

Max slapped her face. She flinched and snarled. He slapped it again and pushed at her shoulder. She gnashed her teeth. He scuffled closer and circled her, sniffing at her hair. She smelled of pine and sweat and woman. He crouched behind her, leant in, and took in a deep breath through his nose. Particles of her scent clung to the hairs of his nostrils. Aroused, he licked the skin of her neck. She didn't flinch. Encouraged, he bit at her shoulder. She growled and pulled away, turned, and stood. This time she met his eyes, a challenge. He rose, erect, and stepped forward. She snarled and moved to the right. Max followed her movements, and they circled one another, fists clenching, unclenching, teeth bared. He snarled, the noise erupting from his belly, deep and guttural. She responded with a snap of her jaws, the elongated incisors bone white against dark red lips. He pounced, biting down hard on her neck, and licked at the blood seeping from the wound.

They continued to circle with his incisors sunk into her flesh. Her yelps of pain were followed by grunts of desire, the scent rising from between her legs, musky and sweet. *He would take her. She would be his.* She pulled away, pushing her claws against his chest, digging them into his flesh. The pain was exquisite, and the ache of his hard-on pulsed as she turned, dropped on all fours, and leant into the floor—an open invitation. Her pussy bulged between the dark hairs of her arse. Pink and glistening, he took it. Thrusting hard, digging sharp claws into her buttocks, he burst inside her warmth, tilting his head to howl as ecstasy rode him with enormous spasms. She was his now.

"WHAT IN THE HELL WAS that?"

*Something ungodly.* Reverend Baxter crossed himself. "Language, my child."

"Sorry, Reverend, but by hell—sorry! ... But that noise sent shivers through me. It sounded like a wolf but kind of screamy with it. It's made my flesh creep." Kathy rubbed at her forearm.

The Church gate clacked shut behind Reverend Baxter as Kathy led him up the path, hand at his elbow, to the Church. The huge key of the door rattled on its iron ring as he leant forward on his walking stick. He poked at the massive keyhole and missed. His hand trembled as he tried again.

"Shall I do it for you, Reverend?"

"No, Kathy, let me try, but thank you." He held the long iron key to the keyhole. It scraped backwards and forwards as he took aim. He grunted with frustration, and it scraped across the ancient metal then slotted into place. "Ah. There we have it." He turned the lock and Kathy twisted the massive iron door handle. Cold seeped out from the unlit interior.

"I'll get the heater going, shall I?"

The Reverend nodded and shuffled forward. His time was nearing, he could feel it in his bones, and, if he could, he would like to be kneeling before the altar, praying for the Lord to take his soul, praying for the villagers, and for God to make his passing easy. He made his way slowly down to the chancel and knelt.

# CHAPTER SEVENTEEN

J aveen uncurled, taking Andy's arm from her waist, and lay it on the bed. She swung her legs to the floor, rose, then bent to kiss his lips. He groped for her, eyes still closed, a smile breaking across his face.

"C'mere. I could do with a bit more of you," he chuckled.

"Got to get to work, otherwise I'd take you up on that."

He grabbed her backside and pulled her back down to the bed. "I'll make it quick."

She giggled as she fell onto him and then submitted to his need with her own passion. After, she showered and made coffee as he took his turn in the bathroom. The noise of the shower running had never sounded so good.

As he entered the kitchen, she slid an omelette onto his plate and dropped toast into the rack.

"I could get used to this."

She laughed. "Your turn next time."

"Deal. I'm a dab hand at pouring milk onto cereal."

"Cheat!"

As he ate, Javeen glanced at the clock.

"Shit!"

"What's up?"

"Work. I'm going to be late for work."

"Stangton won't mind."

"Ugh! Stangton will mind, and if he knows I've been with you, I'll never hear the end of it."

"Let him talk. He's just jealous."

"Why would he be jealous?"

"Well, word is he can't get it u-"

"Stop!" Javeen laughed with mock horror. "I do not want to know anything about Stangton's sex life."

"Or lack of it."

"Right. Or lack of it."

The next minutes were spent in a flurry as Javeen wolfed down the remainder of her breakfast, pulled on her shoes, double checked she had put on deodorant, then left, kissing Andy on the doorstep as she locked the door.

"Love 'em and leave 'em, ay?"

She grabbed his jacket and pulled him close. "I'll love 'em later." She dabbed a kiss on his lips.

To Javeen's relief, Stangton arrived at the station ten minutes after she had made a coffee and started on her 'to do' list. His cheeks were ruddier than usual, and he seemed tense. She resisted the urge to ask what was wrong and instead made a start on the list of calls she needed to make. First on the list was Nature England and then Lynx UK to ask again for confirmation about the lynx trials. Second was Marta Steward and then Laura Anderson to see if Dr Max Anderson had reappeared. The phone rang. The voice on the other end was clipped, and a little breathy, and it took a moment for Javeen to realise that the woman was holding back emotion. "It's Mrs Maybank. I want to report a missing person."

The ache across the back of Javeen's head deepened. "What's the missing person's name?"

"It's my daughter, Lois. She didn't come back last night. Or the one before that. I keep ringing her phone, but it just rings and then goes to the answer phone. Even when we argue she always answers my call. It's that Nate Cruickshank, he's abducted her or done something." The words came out in a jumbled rush, some falling over the others. "He's got a terrible temper, her friend Anita, was-"

"Mrs Maybank, could you slow down, please?" Javeen interrupted the flow of emotion. "When was the last time you saw Lois?"

"It was after the fracas at the *Institute*. I was livid and I'm afraid I tore her off a strip when we got home. It's my fault isn't it!"

As the conversation progressed, Javeen gleaned the information she needed. Lois had been sacked after attacking one of the *Institute*'s employees - Javeen had spoken to the girl herself - had argued with her mother, then left with her boyfriend who'd muttered something darkly about 'getting them back' and 'putting them out of business'. The man in Dr. Steward's office with the ill-concealed piece strapped to his side, came into mind. "Was Lois' boyfriend staying in your home?"

She was indignant. "Certainly not! They were stopping at the campsite with friends from university according to Lois."

Javeen realised that Lois' friends were the protestors who had caused a fuss at the *Institute*. The campsite was closed, if they were staying there, then the owner was turning a blind eye or had given them permission to stop. He'd be the first person on her list of enquiries. "I've logged Lois as a missing person, Mrs Maybank. I'll do my best to find her, but it may be that she's just gone away for a few days. She's-"

"She'd asked to borrow five hundred pounds. The money's still in an envelope propped up next to the kettle. She wouldn't have left without it. She doesn't have any other money, and her bags, and all her clothes and make-up, are still in her bedroom."

That settled it for Javeen. No young adult left home without money and toiletries. "I'll start my enquiries now, Mrs Maybank."

The phone clicked to dead and Javeen swung to Stangton. "Looks like we have two mysteries to solve now. Lois Maybank is missing, and it's possible she was at the *Institute* last night." Stangton's face remained grim and the scream Javeen had heard in the forest nagged in her ears. Something bad was happening in the sleepy village. "I want to talk to Ken Dixon. He owns the campsite, doesn't he?"

Ten minutes later Javeen stood beside Stangton in Ken Dixon's garden. Flat cap perched on his head, he leant up against his spade, the tines spiked into the rich loam, earthworms wriggling in the newly turned earth. White breath billowed dragon-like as he talked.

"Well, I was keeping an eye on them. The campsite's closed, but they paid me fifty pounds to stay a few nights. I can't afford to say no to money. There weren't no leccy nor water." Javeen listened, enjoying the sound of his ancient pronunciations, water had come through as 'wahtur', though it was not a local dialect. "I told 'em that, but the leader,"

Javeen raised her eyebrows, "lad's name was Nate, which I reckon must be short for Nathaniel, which if you ask me is a bit noncy for a lad-."

"Big Daddy's real name was Shirley," Stangton butted in.

"Aye, reckon it was. Well-"

"And John Wayne's was Marion."

"Aye, so it was. Well, Nate ..." he stared at Stangton as though waiting to be interrupted again, "the lad insisted that was fine. He had an edge to him, that one. When he talked, the others just listened, or nodded, like a bunch of brainless sheep. It's the schools you know, they just spoon-feed 'em these days. My daughter's a teacher down in Grimsby and she can turn the air 'lectric with her rants against the Department of Education."

A sharp twist in Javeen's guts had accompanied Ken's mention of 'Grimsby' and the face of Nigel 'bloody' Parker, whose name was now forever welded to the expletive, had arisen in her memory.

"Mr Dixon, could you tell me when you last saw them?"

"Aye, it was yesterday morning - real early - not much past dawn."

The morning after the break-in at the *Institute*.

"I wake early and—did *you* hear that ungodly racket in the woods that night?" Javeen nodded. "It was unearthly, made my skin crawl and my ring-piece shriv-" He gave Javeen a quick glance, "well, it gave me the willies. I was in the kitchen making a drink. I don't sleep too well and needing a piss every couple of hours doesn't help—something for you to look forward to Stuart. You do have your prostrate checked regular, don't you?"

Stangton mumbled something Javeen couldn't quite catch and cast his eyes down the garden and across to Dixon's greenhouse.

"Mr Dixon," Javeen continued, "you said you'd seen the students?"

"That's what they are, is it? Thought as much. Well, I didn't dare go out when I heard that scream, but when it came light, I drove down to the campsite. They was all packed up and just about to leave. Nate was in a right strop. I would have been too if it had been me." He looked at Javeen for her reaction.

"What was it, Mr Dixon?"

"Well," he paused for his dramatic expose, "the van had been battered."

"Battered? How'd you mean, Mr Dixon?"

"The panels were beaten in like someone had taken a hammer to it and there were scratches down to the bare metal." He swiped a clawed hand through the air to demonstrate.

"Had the van been broken into?"

"I don't know. None of the windows were broken. I reminded Nathaniel he'd agreed to park at his own risk, but he didn't take no notice, he was warbling on about Anita getting it in the neck when he found her."

Dread dropped like a stone in Javeen's belly. "Anita? How many students were here that morning Mr. Dixon?"

He remained silent for a moment. "Well, when they first turned up there was three lads and two lasses, but that includes Lois, Marjory's lass."

"And how many did you see leave, Mr. Dixon?" Stangton.

"Just the three lads."

Stangton remained tight-lipped as he caught Javeen's eye. They thanked Ken Dixon for his help then took quick steps to the car. "I've got a bad feeling about this, Latimer." He turned the ignition and the engine hummed. "A really bad feeling."

# CHAPTER EIGHTEEN

Back at the station, Javeen stirred coffee into two cups, drowned it with milk and boiling water and handed one to Stangton. Neither had taken off their coats or sat down.

"We should go into the woods to search." Javeen said.

Stangton wanted to wait and follow procedure. "You heard what Bill Elliot said. They're undermanned as it is and there's an Antifa march going on in town."

Javeen snorted. "Fascists raging against fascists! Too bad the irony is lost on them."

"There'll be more officers available to help but not until tomorrow at the earliest, and because the missing persons aren't children, it's not a priority."

She took a swig of coffee, glad the milk had cooled it. "But there's something rotten going on, Stangton. Max Anderson, Lois Maybank, and now this Anita girl are missing. The thing that links them all is the *Institute*."

"I'm glad you didn't mention the reports of wolfmen roaming the village. I'm starting to feel like Basil Rathbone in 'Hound of the Baskervilles.'"

Javeen laughed. "Farmer Burdon's sheep were possibly killed by a lynx. Maybe that's what is making the awful noise?"

"Do Lynx howl? I thought they were cats."

"Maybe that's why it sounds so odd. It's not like a dog's howl-"

"Or a werewolf's?" He made a dramatic swipe with a clawed hand through the air.

"Could be a yowl."

"Doesn't explain Billy Oldfield's sighting."

"Billy was drunk. We can hardly take his word for it. It's more likely a local playing a prank, or he had some kind of hallucination. I have to admit, though, that damned scream from the woods chilled me."

"And Mrs Carmichael is old and probably going senile." Stangton continued. His eyes looked beyond Javeen's shoulder to the window, and beyond that to the small carpark and the thick bank of trees.

"Two girls are missing, Stangton, and I don't think we should wait for the team to start searching for them."

"But-"

"I'm going in, Stangton. I'm not waiting for them to send us reinforcements. Max Anderson and those girls could be hurt ... or dead. I don't know what's going on in those woods, but I'm going to find out."

Stangton searched her eyes. "Finally found your balls, then?"

She held her tongue as her eyes searched his. He was right. Her attitude had stunk before yesterday; she'd been wallowing in her own self-pity, lost sight of why she'd joined the Force in the first place and become a victim of her own mistakes. She nodded. "Yes, Stangton. Yes, I have."

His smile broadened. "Good, then let's go and see if we can find them."

Her own smile broadened with relief.

"I'll fill up the travel mugs with coffee," he continued, "If you check we've got torches and plenty of batteries."

*Thank you.* "Got it."

An hour later, with one rucksack packed with equipment, and the other with food and drinks, they were back at the campsite beside the patch of flattened grass left by the tents. She hadn't noticed before, hadn't thought to look, but a track was visible in the grass leading from the tents to the trees.

"She may have gone into the forest this way."

"Could be, but I'm not sure how fresh this track is."

Stangton took the lead, and they stepped out of the thin morning sunshine and into the dappled light of the forest.

After nearly half an hour of walking through the woods, they stopped to drink from the flask of coffee. Javeen couldn't shake the feeling of being watched. She remembered reading about it; the sense of being watched was an instinct—something about the amygdala in the brain responding to an external gaze that the person wasn't aware of. The knowledge that she was subconsciously picking up on someone watching her was unnerving, and, given the circumstances, deeply worrying. She took a breath to ease the tension. Despite Stangton at her side, a shiver ran down Javeen's spine; they should have waited until a unit had arrived from the main town. The sun had already begun to dip in the sky. She checked her watch, 2:52 pm.

Stangton caught her eye. "We should turn back soon. It'll be dark before we get back to the campsite at this rate."

Javeen agreed with a nod. "Just ten more minutes, I'm coming back tomorrow though."

"In the afternoon, Latimer. The team should be here by then. We need to make enquiries in the morning. I want to speak to Steward again. I've had a few thoughts about the *Institute*."

"Agreed. Something's not right there."

Ahead the trees thinned out and beyond them was a clearing where a tree, felled by the wind, lay uprooted. Its trunk stretched out into the open space. A low mist rolled in across the grass.

"It's the roots and stumps that give me the creeps." She took another step forward. "They sit between the trees, rotting away, covered in moss. They look like monsters coming out from the mist."

Stangton laughed. "It's the feeling of being watched that's giving me the shivers."

Javeen bit her bottom lip. That he felt it too, made it worse. "Let's turn back."

"OK. Let's get to the clearing and-"

Alerted by his sudden silence, and the jolting stop of his step, Javeen followed his eyes to the forest floor.

Stangton gagged. "I think we've found one of the missing girls. Oh, God! I think I'm going to hurl." He retched and turned away from the sight.

Javeen groaned as she gazed on the body. She recognised the purple harem trousers. It was the girl from the *Institute*, the one they'd taken back to the campsite—Anita.

Before this, the only corpse Javeen had seen in the field had been a drug addict overdosed and dead, sprawled on her settee. Apart from the syringe still grasped in her hand, she could have been asleep. This death was completely different. The girl's blonde plaits were stained red, her clothes tattered across her chest and belly. The girl's lower body was intact, her paisley patterned harem pants though riding low, and showing the jutting bones of her hips, remained tied and undamaged so sexual assault was ruled out as a motive, but her torso was shredded, a bloody mess of skin, flesh, and torn innards. The ribcage was almost hollow, and her throat had been ripped out.

Javeen took a step back, a hand covering her gasp of horror, and gagged. The stench of faeces was strong, no doubt emanating from the entrails that had slithered from the girl's torn belly. The blood was dark, her skin grey, her death wasn't recent.

"God in heaven!"

"Jesus Christ have Mercy!"

Stangton crossed himself as Javeen did the same.

"Stangton," Javeen croaked.

"Yes," his voice rasped.

"She's been eaten."

"Yes."

"Maybe Mrs Carmichael isn't senile."

"I hope not."

She found his answer strange. "You want it to be a wolfman?"

"No, of course not. It must be an escaped wolf or rabid dog—there's a problem down in Whitby remember. No, what I mean is, if a human has done this, then we've got a maniac loose in the forest, someone utterly depraved."

UNABLE TO SHIFT THE feeling of being watched, and with the grotesque image of the slain girl biting at her, Javeen strode back to the car, barely keeping up with Stangton. A howl pierced the air as they reached the campsite and Stangton picked up his pace. "Come on!'" he called, now at a run, unlocking the car with the fob as soon as they were in range. Javeen followed his lead, running to keep up, and slid into her seat with a heaving chest and hammering heart.

Stangton locked the doors.

"You too?"

"Yes. Let's get the hell out of here." The engine burst into life as he spoke.

Javeen clicked her seat belt into place and Stangton manoeuvred the car around with swift precision and began the descent down the track to the main road. Javeen made no complaint of his driving this time.

"Sorry, Latimer. I had to get out of that forest. The girl ... hell, that poor girl."

"I'll call it in." Javeen reached for the receiver.

"Victor X-ray this is Charlie Foxtrot 3-1. Do you copy."

White noise returned. She tried again. Nothing. "How the hell can it not be working?"

"Try your mobile."

She reached for her phone and waited for the screen to come to life. "No signal."

"We'll call it back in at the station."

They spent the next minutes discussing the girl; what could have taken her into the woods, and what kind of animal, wild, or perhaps even human, could have eviscerated her?

On arrival, Stangton strode into the Station and grabbed the landline, listened then replaced the receiver.

"Dead?"

"As a dodo."

"What the hell is going on?"

"I have no idea, but we've got to report the girl's death. We need a forensics team up here pronto."

"And a search team. Max Anderson and Lois Maybank are still missing."

"Marksmen too. If a wild animal did that to the poor girl, then it needs tracking down and destroying."

"Man or beast," Javeen added.

Stangton muttered a response, hands on hips, and ran his hands through his thinning hair. His ruddy cheeks were almost florid.

"I'll drive into town and report it in person."

"Now?"

"Yes, now. The situation here is getting out of hand." He coughed then turned to the door, car keys in hand.

"I'll wait for you here."

"Sure," he replied. "I should be back before ..." he checked his watch, "seven."

"I'll be here."

As the door closed behind him, Javeen strode to the door and locked it.

MAX SAT AT THE EDGE of the clearing, staring across the car park to the tiny building with its spread of green algae on white walls. Inside, a woman moved about. He curled up next to a tree, hidden by the undergrowth, and let sleep take him. When he woke, twilight offered its purple haze, and the burning need to gnash and tear and bite had returned.

His attention returned to the building. Inside, he could see the woman clearly as she moved about the lit room, goading him as she passed the window, teasing him as she disappeared then reappeared. Saliva drooled into the hairs of his chin, collecting particles of dried blood as it slid among them. Behind him, he could smell the others, and hear the snapping of twigs as they shuffled beside him. Twilight shifted to black, and the woman opened the door.

# CHAPTER NINETEEN

Javeen opened the door to the orange haze of the single overhead light. A blast of cold swept across her face. She shivered and pulled her jacket tighter as she turned to lock the Station door. Stangton hadn't returned and it was now nearly eight o'clock. She'd spent the late afternoon going over her notes: the break-in at the *Institute*, the numerous reports of noises, sightings, missing persons, and now the girl savaged in the woods. Everything had kicked off after the break-in at Anderson's lab. That was the link, it had to be, and she suspected that although Marta Steward was insistent that nothing had escaped from the lab, that it had, and was most likely a rabid dog. Before the phones had gone down, she'd managed to confirm that *Kielder Institute* was indeed working on behalf of the UK Health Security Agency to create a vaccine for the mutated rabies virus that had broken out down in Whitby. It all added up: the dead sheep, the savaged girl, the missing scientist.

A howl pierced the night, stopping her thoughts in their tracks. She swallowed, reached into her pocket for her car keys, and checked the area. Nothing was visible beyond the orange haze that hung over her car. The howl came again as she strode forward. It didn't sound as loud this time and yes, it could be a dog, a rabid dog that could come charging out of the trees and bite her, savage her as it had done that 'poor,

poor girl'. She ran the last steps to her car and unlocked the door.

Her heart thudded a hard beat as the trees rustled.

*Calm it. It's just the wind ... What if it's not?*

She swung the door open and slid in, slamming the door shut with one swift movement and sighed, suddenly safe.

*For crying out loud, Jav. Calm down.*

As she passed the pub, considering for a second stopping off and sitting beside its warm and glowing fire before rejecting the idea, she checked in the rear-view mirror. Movement on the road caught her eye but when she checked again, the road was clear.

*Silly cow! Now you're imagining things.*

HUGGING THE SHADOWS, Max ran with the others through the dark street, following the car. They watched as the woman pulled into a driveway and stepped out. Lois moved forward. Max dug his claws into her shoulder then growled. The woman stopped, eyes darting to where they crouched, then disappeared to the side of the house.

Laughing voices carried from the village. The door to the house opened and slammed shut, metal scraped across metal as the woman locked herself inside. As the voices grew louder, Lois turned her back on the house and headed to the village.

# CHAPTER TWENTY

Anya drew another almond shape on the paper, glancing at her mobile as the drawing tutorial progressed. She paused the button to catch up, filling the almond with a circle and shading it as the woman on the video had. The artist's work was amazing: snakes that looked as though they would pounce from the page, apples that looked as though they were sitting on the table, and kittens you could pick up and cuddle. Anya's efforts at realising a 3D eye in its socket had so far failed, but each time she tried they were improving. As her dad had drilled into her, 'If at first you don't succeed, try, try, and try again.' She grumbled when he stopped her complaints in their tracks but, secretly, she knew he was right. She'd kept her first efforts, like he suggested—to see the improvements. The music playing in her ears stopped. She shaded in another section of iris and re-started the video. It buffered. She sighed with impatience and pressed refresh. Still it buffered. In the corner, the bars had dropped to zero. The phone had disconnected from the Wi-Fi and she had no roaming data left. She threw down the pencil.

"Mum!" No reply. "Mum!"

"Anya!" her father called up the stairs. "If you want your mother, come downstairs."

She huffed. "There's no Wi-Fi!"

"If you want to talk," he bellowed, "come downstairs like a civilised human being!"

*Yeah, right. Like shouting at her was civilised!* She yanked the earbuds a little too hard and pain scratched at her ear. *God, she hated parents!* She pulled her hoodie up and sulked downstairs.

"There's no Wi-Fi," she said as she entered the kitchen. Both parents sat at the table, coffee in hand. Its aroma a permanent fixture in the house.

"Hello to you too," her mum quipped.

"Well, I tell you what ..."

*Trust Dad to be difficult.* "Yeah?"

"If you take the rubbish out, then I'll see if I can fix it."

She needed her mobile on—and now! Ryan might snapchat her later. She returned a gruff 'OK' and took the bag of rubbish from beneath the sink.

"Put your shoes on. I don't want wet socks all over the carpets."

She grunted again but slipped her trainers on, stuffing feet inside, her heels squashing down the backs. She switched the outside light on and shuffled out into the yard.

Cold pinched at her cheeks and fingers, the wind blowing through her thin top. The bins were at the side of the outbuildings, three narrow rooms that housed a collection of cardboard stuffed in there when Dad couldn't be bothered to recycle it in one, a load of rusted tools in another, and a damp, spider-infested toilet in the third. Using the outside loo was a torture, but it was better than going in the bathroom after Dad had been for one.

She swung the gate that divided the back garden from the house and flipped open the lid of the grey bin. The outside light didn't reach that far, and a shiver ran over Anya's shoulders as she peered down the garden to the meadow that ended where the forest started. A rotten stench wafted into her nostrils from the bin and the feeling of being watched crept over her. She dropped the bag into the bin with disgust then tapped the lid to closed, stepped back, and knocked over a collection of tools her father had left out. She grunted as a metal rod thwacked her calf. *Why the hell couldn't he put them away like other dads? It wasn't like Mum didn't tell him. But no, he had to leave them out to go rusty and for her to trip up on.* It wouldn't be the first time one of his misplaced tools had caused her injury. Only last week she'd stood on a nail he'd left in the grass after working on another shambolic DIY project. Mum had done her nut when he'd used the picnic table as a workbench and cut through the seat.

She reached down to grasp the metal implements and prop them up against the side of the brick shed.

Something moved behind her.

She could hear its rasping breath. Heart hammering, she gripped the metal bar tighter. Raising the bar, she swivelled. Pain ripped through her shoulder, and a stench that reminded her of wet dog and shit, filled her nostrils. She thwacked the metal bar against the creature as it sank its teeth into her shoulder. The pain was immense and the creature heavy. She hit it again, ramming it back against the wall. Its bite released. She raised the bar again and thwacked it down. The creature yelped and Anya lurched forward, sprinting through the gate, all sense of pain gone in her need to get to the door. As the gate clacked the rasping breath returned. She lunged across the concrete pad outside the house and crashed through the door, slamming it shut behind her. The door rattled in its frame as the creature thudded against it. Frantically, she locked the door and stood back. The door remained still, and she listened to the tack, tack of the creature's footsteps across the concrete and the gate clack shut as the thing disappeared back down the garden.

AS ANYA STUMBLED BACK into the kitchen screaming in terror at her horrified parents, Javeen filled the kettle with water and flicked on the remaining downstairs lights, unable to shake the feeling of being spooked. It was irrational, but the sensation of being watched had clung to her since the trek through the woods. To make it worse the image of the girl, torn and gutted, flung against the tree, kept intruding into her thoughts. She decided to have a cup of tea, then take ten minutes to process the day and work on the mindfulness techniques she had been reading about; she needed to be fully present in the moment to get some relief from the haunting images of the girl.

Tea made, she made her way into the living room and sat down. She took a sip and leant back in the armchair, letting its soft velvet soothe her. It was her favourite chair, the place she always gravitated to when she wanted to curl up and feel soothed. She took another sip and reached for the remote. The screen flickered and the room filled with the buzzing of white noise. She tried another channel and then another. Nothing worked. She switched it back off and took another sip of tea, searching the pile of DVDs in her mind's eye. Perhaps a good film would take her mind off things, if she could settle enough to watch it.

In the distance, a car's doors slammed, and an engine started. It was followed by the scatter of stones in her driveway. Startled at the noise so close to her window, she spilled her tea. The hot water soaked through her trousers, and she jumped up, pulling the fabric away from her thigh whilst putting the mug down on the coffee table. She hobbled to the window and peered through the glass, blocking the light with her cupped hand, and watched as a dark figure disappeared around the bush at the end of her drive.

AS MAX LEFT THE HOUSE and the woman, and sprinted back towards the village, Jim Kendrick slipped a loaf of bread into the 'forever' canvas bag his wife had forced him to carry and handed five pounds to Sid. The old fashioned till tinkled with change as the drawer slid open. A howl scratched at Jim's eardrums and made the hair on his neck and scalp prickle. Sid held the drawer half shut.

"What in God's name was that?"

"Reckon there's a wolf loose in the forest. I heard they were fencing it off to try and catch it."

"Fencing off the forest?"

"Aye. Melvin Stubbs came in this morning on his way back from Falstone and said there's lorries erecting barriers along the road. Could just be roadworks though. You know how these things get twisted."

"Chinese whispers," Jim agreed. "The road to Stannersburn has got plenty of potholes so maybe Mrs Maybank's efforts haven't fallen on deaf ears this time?"

"Mayhap." Sid shut the money-drawer with a bang. "Cold's coming in," he said as he returned the change. "I heard that wolf howling last night. Sent shivers down my spine it did. I put the bolt across the door too and gave my rifle a clean—just in case. Mrs Blanchard said she saw something that looked like a wolf in the churchyard—she said it looked like half wolf, half man. But I reckon she's going senile."

Jim couldn't help a wry grin. Beatrice Blanchard, the village's oldest resident, definitely was a little odd these days, but then she was ninety-five years old.

"Having that fall last year did for her I reckon. She was as sharp as a knife until then. She's not been the same since. Shame."

"It is. Maybe there is an escaped wolf then?"

"Could be. There's no wolves in this area, and no sanctuaries like down south, but there is one up in Scotland."

"Could be deliberate. Like that one in Berkshire earlier in the year. Some nutter let it loose and they had to lock down the schools."

"Oh, aye. What happened there then?"

"They called out police marksmen, but they managed to coax the wolf into a trailer—no harm done."

"Maybe they'll send in a team here then, but don't bank on it. Out of sight, out of mind."

Jim nodded. The village was out of the way and with it being out of season and the tourists warm and cosy at home, unlikely to be a priority. A shudder ran through Jim as another howl pierced the night. Both men looked to the glass door, their reflections and that of the shop, blocked any view to the outside.

"Dark outside." Was Sid's flat statement.

Jim interpreted this as meaning 'rather you than me'. "Aye, nights are really drawing in." Jim shivered at the thought of leaving the small shop with its glowing log-burner in the corner to face the dark night with its unsettling howls. Comfortable chairs sat in a circle around it with a small coffee table at their centre. Rachel, his daughter, sat herself before the fire warming her hands.

"Rachel," he called, "time to go." The girl stood immediately, and Jim was thankful that she hadn't thrown one of her too frequent strops and turned around with a rude 'No!'. He dreaded taking his daughter out. For an eleven-year-old she had been very slow to learn the niceties of polite behaviour. He handed her the bar of chocolate picked up as he paid for the bread, and her face lit up. A sliver of guilt passed over him. He wouldn't have done the same for Lennie, but then Lennie didn't strike the same level of fear into him as Rachel did; he was a good boy, a joy to be around.

"Thanks!" She snatched the bar from his hands, and he resisted the reprimand that sat on his lips as she tore into the metallic wrapper.

"Don't eat it all at once," he said with forced joviality.

"You calling me greedy!" she snapped back.

Sid raised his brows and Jim's cheeks stung. It wasn't the first, or even the second time that Sid had cast a frown at Rachel. Embarrassed, Jim raised his brows in the universal sign of the long-suffering parent. "No, love." It took enormous effort to keep his voice calm and the biting words back, "it's just that you've got to eat your tea soon."

Sid shook his head, and the sense of failure that Jim too often felt when dealing with this difficult child, made him step quickly out of the cosy atmosphere of the village shop and out into the biting wind of the early November night.

"Wait!" Rachel's wheedling voice demanded. "Dad! Wait."

Irked, Jim turned. "Rachel, I'm two steps ahead of you. I'm not exactly about to disappear from view!" Exasperated at her rudeness, and disappointed that his resolve to stay calm had cracked, he turned back to face the road with a downturn in his mouth and despair eating at his heart. Every day she touched their life with a scratching unhappiness. Her behaviour bordered sometimes on disturbing, though Melissa wouldn't hear about getting help. 'She'll grow out of it,' she would say, or 'it's just a phase' though he could see the fear in her eyes, a fear that there was something wrong with their firstborn, fear that it was somehow their fault, and that they had failed their own child.

She caught up with him, slid her arm through the crook of his, and wheedled once more. "Wait will you!"

Spending time with her was a chore and, that he felt like that about his own child, added just another layer of shit to the whole damned shit-show. *They are your monkeys, and it is your circus.* He bit back his retort, looked to the moon, took a deep breath, and patted her fingers in an effort to be caring. "Let's get home. The beans will be done by now and your mum will be frothing at the mouth waiting for the bread." This made Rachel laugh, and a smile cracked across Jim's face though his jaws remained clenched.

A scratching, rustling noise caught his attention, and the creature that jumped out in front of him and ran across the road startled him more than he cared to admit. "Shitty cat!"

"Dad!"

"Well, the bloody thing scared me." The cat seemed scared too.

"It's just a cat."

Jim quickened his stride. The orange light from the streetlights cast its glow over the stone cottages along the street and the air was thick with the smell of burning wood. One good thing about living out here, getting wood for log burners was easy. Most houses had one, some were completely reliant on them for heating their houses and water, there being no gas mains to the village. He tightened Rachel's hand against his arm and took quicker steps. A clack in the near distance was the familiar closing of the Church gate.

"Dad!" she whined. "Slow down. I can't keep up."

He slowed his pace a little. She was right, she'd have to run to keep up soon if he didn't slow down. Behind him footsteps tacked. He turned to look. The road had been deserted when they left the shop and the noise of those footsteps was odd, unless the person was wearing a pair of tap shoes, or stilettoes, and those were just as unlikely in this village. As he swivelled, a figure jumped back into the shadows. His heart thumped against his ribs. He narrowed his eyes and shook his head as though to clear his vision; the figure had seemed naked, though covered in thick hair, and oddly stooped. Sid's talk of wolfmen added to an already overactive imagination fed by Jim's keen interest in the occult. Despite his interest, and, at one time, dabbling in the dark magic of Ouija boards, even staying overnight in a haunted house, Jim only flirted with a belief in the supernatural. What he'd just seen had been a figment of his imagination, a prank by one of the other villagers at best. He turned back to look again with a quick jerk of his head. Nothing. Absolutely nothing, and if there had been something lurking in the shadows, he'd have seen it right then.

"Come on, Dad. I'm cold."

"I'm coming, Rachel." Jim regretted his curt response. "Come on, love. Let's get home to that warm fire. Do you want a hot chocolate when you get in?"

Tack. Tack. Tack.

"Yes! Of course I dooooo-." Rachel's unsolicited terseness was cut short as a figure hurled itself from the bushes and threw her to the ground. As Jim realised that something had grabbed her, she was gone, carried into the woods by a galloping figure, a naked and very hairy woman, with snarling incisors. As Jim's brain desperately tried to process the scene, Rachel's scream came to an abrupt stop, and he was thrown to the floor. Above him, a creature that used to be his friend Max Anderson, snarled whilst gnashing its teeth before tearing out his throat.

# CHAPTER TWENTY-ONE

Max pulled the body out of the orange glow of the overhead light. The head knocked against the stone blocks.

*Jim ... his name was Jim.*

He snickered.

*James. Captain James T. Beam me up, Scotty!*

A flash of grief washed through him and he groaned.

*Jim. Jimbob. No! No! No!*

He dug sharp claws into his own temple and rocked, pressing claws through the thin layers of skin. Blood trickled into thick sideburns. Max crouched, resting on his haunches, alert to any movement, the spark of horror, and then regret, that had pricked his soul gone in an instant. The man was silent though his heart gave its final beat as Max ripped it from its bony cage. With claws piercing the hot flesh, he rammed it into his mouth, chewing and swallowing with greed. Warm blood trickled down his chin, glistening black in the orange glow. He grabbed for the liver and tore it from its mooring. The offal slipped in his hands, and he pierced it with sharp claws and took a deep bite. Aroused, he salivated as the flesh tore between his teeth, slid over his tongue, and into his throat. The blood, and the silky warmth of the meat, was an ecstasy as he swallowed. He grunted and shuffled as he reached for the innards but stopped as movement caught his attention.

In the distance metal clacked. Looking up, he stared at a face peering out from behind a curtain. The eyes were wide. Max snarled as he stared back. Terror flickered in the woman's eyes and the curtains dropped back into place. He took a chunk of membrane and coiled intestine in his mouth and tore. The tap, tap of footsteps sounded again. More food. He stood, dragged the body off the path and hid it behind a low wall, then crouched behind a thick shrub. He jumped back to the path, ran along the shadows, and checked from behind a parked car. A figure walked slowly up the path to the church. Lois ran to join him. He snarled as she reached his side and they both watched as the man took another slow step towards the church.

REVEREND BAXTER SENSED the animal's presence behind him before he had a chance to realise something had jumped over the wall and into the churchyard. He froze. The ungodly howling of this morning had reoccurred this evening, and he had been overcome with a need to pray. His need had driven him to walk to the church unaided by Kathy. It had been a slow and painful walk, and his heart was pumping hard with the effort, but it would be worth it.

He stopped as hot breath brushed against his neck. *Our Father ...* The breath was moist, sour, and laced with the unmistakable metallic scent of blood. His feet became stones. Unable to move, he waited as the thing behind him stepped to his side. It sniffed at his neck, withdrew, then moved to face him. At his other side, only slightly further away, another figure circled him. As a pair of eyes scowled into his, he felt the urge to urinate, and stumbled against his walking stick. The creature put out a hand and steadied his fall without breaking its gaze. The eyes were black at their centre, ringed with red, and only small areas of white remained. Its hair was dishevelled and greasy, and covered much of its face, though thinner across its cheeks. Bizarrely, memories of the village fete came to mind along with the face of Doctor Maximillian Anderson smiling at him from the stocks, his face flushed red, and his hair dripping with water as another child grabbed a wet sponge from the bucket and lobbed it at him. *Who art in heaven ...* He stared again at the creature.

"Max?"

It snickered and claws dug into the Reverend's shoulder from behind. He grimaced with pain and the creature gnashed its teeth then flew at its companion. The other beast was knocked back, its breasts moving freely beneath shredded cloth. The reverend looked away quickly as its legs splayed and he was reminded of Courbet's 'L'Origine du monde', a copy of which he'd been shown by a cheeky, if not irreverent, member of the congregation who'd pushed his mobile phone's screen at him. The Reverend had taken a good look at the painting and made a comment about that particular depiction of labia being an accurate representation of a woman's genitalia, then thanked the boy for showing it to him. The boy's cheeks had turned puce, and he'd shown up at church the following Sunday without being able to meet his eyes but with an extra pound for the collection tray.

The female cowered as the male snapped at her, but she wasn't completely subservient and offered him an angry snarl as she stood. The male turned again to the Reverend, took a step closer, put out its hand, then turned and sprinted across the grass, vaulting over gravestones and then the wall before disappearing into the dark. The female followed.

The Reverend slowly dropped to his knees on the grass, offered a prayer of thanks, and asked for mercy for the soul of the man who was now barely human.

THE MAN—*Reverend ... the Reverend ... sorry Father, for I have sinned*. Max chuckled. The man in the churchyard had been rotten. Max could smell the poison that laced through his body as keenly as if it had been shit trapped between his toes. Memories had floated too, but they were hazy, just faces and smells. He ran back to the body tucked behind the wall and dragged it across the road and into the forest. Closer to his lair he dragged the body into the tree where it would keep - *keep like a pig, hanging from a hook*. Max snickered. *Away from greedy scavengers*. In the village an engine thrummed into life.

AS JIM'S BODY HUNG safely over the bough, and Max turned his attention to the engine, Anya's father pulled the car out onto the road, quickly flicking on the car's headlights, hoping his wife hadn't noticed he'd started down the road without them to light the way. He checked the rear-view mirror. Anya was slumped in the back, her damaged shoulder hidden against the car's seat. It had taken every ounce of his fatherly authority to get her into the car. Apart from her teenage stubbornness, Anya was morbidly afraid of anything to do with hospitals; the mere mention of A&E had sent her spiralling into hysterics. She'd only grown calm when he'd laid it on thick about the bite getting infected and the possibility of the dog being rabid. His belly clenched—it probably was. Why else would a dog attack someone? It was not as if Anya was the intruder.

Michael had ridden Anya's tantrum with the weary stoicism that only a long-suffering parent could manage. The hardest part was seeing how ill she was becoming, and he was now convinced that the dog had given her an infection, even though he knew, in rational thought, that an infection – surely? - wouldn't take effect so quickly. Nevertheless, her face had drained of colour to such an extent that a network of blue veins could be tracked across her face, neck, and shoulders. When the whites of her eyes had begun to fill with blood, he had decided to get medical help. Karen had turned to him in horrified panic as the first blood vessels had burst. Ignoring Anya's protestations, he'd grabbed the keys from the counter, picked her up in his arms, and carried her to the car.

He shifted the gear into third and pressed the accelerator. The needle climbed to twenty-five. *Sod it!* Whatever the speed limit was, he didn't care, he had to get his baby to a doctor. As the car left the village boundary, and the road swerved into the woods, he checked the back seat. Her greyed-out figure hadn't moved.

"She alright?"

"She's asleep."

"Good."

Movement caught his attention from the back window. Something was moving behind the car. Something that the red lights picked out, then lost. An animal from the forest, perhaps a deer. He accelerated and it disappeared. Michael focused on the road ahead, headlights on full beam, and drove as fast as he dared, his wife's silence, an indicator of her own concern. Usually, she'd make a quip about his terrible driving. It was their little joke; both of them knew that he was a good driver.

Anya stirred then groaned.

"It's alright, honey," Karen crooned. "Go back to sleep."

The girl shifted again. Michael checked in the rear-view mirror. It was difficult to see, but she was facing the front, and from the glint of reflected light had her eyes open. She yawned, and the white of her teeth caught the moonlight. With a sense of relief, he noticed the fangs; if she was messing about with fake teeth, she must be feeling better.

"Look out, Karen!" he joked. "There's a vampire sitting next to you." Although relieved that Anya seemed to be recovering, it struck him as odd that she would be messing around with a pair of fake vampire teeth after feeling so shoddy only half an hour ago.

"Hungry," she rasped.

He made a bad attempt at a vampire's laugh and added, "Vor your blod." He snorted. His accent was terrible.

"I've got some crisps in my bag if you want so- ... agg!"

His wife's voice came to a suffocating stop. He checked the rear-view mirror again. Anya was leaning over her mother as Karen bucked and kicked, her arms battering against the girl's back.

"Hey! Quit it Anya, that's enough. You're hurting your mother!"

Karen jerked then flung and arm to the window. It landed with a thud.

"Quit it!" he shouted and pressed the brakes hard enough to jolt their bodies forward.

Anya's head bounced against the back of his seat. He twisted to the pair. Karen writhed on the back seat, gasping for breath, sucking air through the gaping wound in her throat and his daughter's blood-filled eyes glared back at him. He screamed as he reached for the door's handle and fell out of the car. In the distance were lights. As he scrambled to his feet and lurched onto the verge, the back door opened, and Anya staggered out. Behind her, two figures burst into view. Michael screamed as three monsters sprung through the air, jaws snapping, claws outstretched, and pinned him to the wet grass.

# CHAPTER TWENTY-TWO

The man had screamed until the girl had ripped his throat. Max had knocked her back, making her wait until his belly was full.

*Always first. He was always first. They had to wait. Know their place.*

He sat and watched as they fed, their faces smeared with his blood. The girl was greedy, and Lois slapped her, snarling with teeth bared. Max sat on his haunches and turned to leave. The body was heavy, too far from their place to take back. His mind flitted again to the woman in the house.

*Wait for me, little mouse.*

He snickered and the girl twisted her head to stare. Her eyes shone black, liquid pools caught in the moonlight. She snickered and turned back to the carcass.

*Eat your fill, little one. Eat.*

He gnashed his teeth, turned, and sprinted back towards the village.

A memory dug at him. She, floating in white, he waiting, She smiling, She crying, naked baby held to her breast. He gasped at the pain. Laura! He slowed, fell to his knees, tipped his head back and howled. "Lauuuurraaaaa!"

One more time, just one more time. Mouth watering as he remembered her smell, her taste, her breasts, her belly, her thighs, her lips, he sprinted. The urge to hold She, take She, eat She, overwhelming.

At their house ... his home ... their loving nest ... lair, the door opened with a click and Max stepped into the warm hallway. Lucidity returned. He was home. The scent of Laura was thick in the air. Her coat hung on its peg, her shoes beneath the hall table. He trod softly, the fibre of the runner caught on roughened feet, muffling each step. The house was silent, the downstairs rooms dark. Through the kitchen doorway at the end of the hall the red light of the kitchen clock glowed. He trod through to the kitchen, took a glass, filled it with water, and drank. The glass clinked against elongated canines and cracked. Thirst quenched, he returned to the hallway and stood at the base of the stairs. She was up there, lying in bed, waiting for him to come home.

Laura's breath came slow and steady from the bedroom, he could hear the gentle rise and fall of the bedclothes as she slept. Her scent intoxicated him, and he yearned for her warmth, to be in her arms. He stalled. Waited on the stairs, then turned.

*He couldn't go to her like this. Not as this monster.*

He took a step down. But - his heart hammered - he had to see her again. Just one last time, whilst he still has moments where he could think straight, where he was Max again. She moaned in her sleep, turned in the bed. He pounced to the landing and then he was at the open door of their bedroom. Just one last look.

As he stepped inside, she turned her face to him, and he watched her sleep. She looked the same as the first day they'd met. He'd never forget their eyes meeting across the room.

She was with a bloke with a long beard, he with a couple of mates from the university. The next evening he'd returned to the pub, and she'd walked in and smiled when she caught him looking at her. That had been the start. The day she became his wife was the best in his life, and his only regret was that their union had produced no children—no living children—*poor, poor Amy*. She murmured. Her lips parted and the white of her teeth glistened. The smell of her sex rose as she twisted again, her legs splayed. He had to touch her, hold her in his arms. He closed the door then drew the curtains until they were almost closed. Clouds shifted across the moon and the room became darker still. He stepped to his side of the bed. She was ovulating and he could smell the sweet saltiness of her pussy.

The ache of need warmed through his hips and began to pulse. Erect, and burning with the need to fornicate, he peeled the bedclothes back, uncovering her torso. She was wearing a thin cotton nightgown. Her nipples were dark against white skin beneath the thin fabric. She remained still and he pulled the cover down past her belly. The nightgown had ridden up to her waist. He ached for her. Fully aroused, he peeled the cover to expose her flesh and the dark mound of hair between her legs. He leant forward and took a long breath through his nose, slow and gentle, filling his nostrils with her scent, then parted her legs.

"Max, you're home," she said through her half-sleep.

Lowering himself, he grunted softly, pushing against her. She gasped then moaned as he slipped between her legs. Ravenous, he plunged inside, thrusting hard, grunting with effort. She moaned with pleasure.

*She belonged to him, no one else.*

As clouds shifted from the moon and a shaft of silvery light fell across the bed, he threw his head back and howled her name.

She screamed as he flooded her with his seed and deep within, where new life formed, the hybrids found their prey.

STARTLED FROM SLEEP, Emily looked across the road through the half-opened curtains. The moon was still in the sky though the night was fading. Stars twinkled in the midnight blue. How many more times would she see them? Her life was fading too, at ninety-three years old, she was grateful for each new day and woke to the sunlight with a smile.

Sudden movement over the Anderson's wall caught her attention and she watched with shallow breaths as a figure vaulted over again. The same man-thing as the other night. Its body arced with ease over the wall and landed with steady feet on the path. For a moment it passed through the orange haze of the streetlight. The man, though the poor creature must be deformed, was naked. For a second it seemed to stare right through her window, and she held her breath until it turned and galloped away.

In the Anderson's house a bedroom light switched on, and Laura's face appeared at the window. Even from this distance, Emily could sense her terror.

AS MAX RETURNED TO the forest, full of pain for She, yearning for the warmth of the Others, to curl up with them under the workbench, the window of the woodsman's cottage was bright and yellow in the early morning dark. He jumped down from the tree and landed with a soft thud among the pile of brittle needles. A figure walked across the window. The scent of burning oil lingered in the air and, as he passed the car parked beside the door, warmth brushed his legs. The engine was still hot, the woman just home. He could see no one else.

*Not that they would stop him taking what he wanted.*

He crept to the window and watched.

# CHAPTER TWENTY-THREE

A fitful night of dreadful dreams has left Javeen tired and edgy. She'd woken on more than one occasion with a start, sure that something was scratching at her back door, and even gone down to check that all her doors and windows were locked, and the curtains fully drawn. She'd taken a knife from the block on the kitchen counter to bed with her and laid it under her pillow. Now, sitting across from Emily Carmichael, listening to her tale of a 'wolfman' leaping over Laura Anderson's wall in the small hours, was doing nothing for her nerves. Javeen sat across from the elderly lady and waited. The woman was slow to talk, her words slurred, though she was determined to tell her story. She took another gasp of oxygen then reached a shaky hand to the bedside table for the glass of water. Javeen watched the hand, long and bony with skin that looked as though it would tear if touched, reach out with agonising slowness. She took the glass and handed it to Emily. The woman took a sip, leant back, and nursed the glass on her lap. This was the third report of a strange creature marauding through the village they'd had this morning. Javeen held her pencil aloft until she realised her hand was trembling.

"It jumped over the wall." Emily pointed a crooked finger to the neighbour's house. "That wall is five-foot tall, but it jumped over it like a high jumper at the Olympics."

"Could you tell me what it looked like?"

"Yes. It was naked, but hairy, and it was a man." Emily cackled. "Oh, my. It's been a long time since I saw a bit of tackle that big." She leant forward and whispered in conspiratorial tones. "That's the one thing I regret, lass; not having more sex when I was young enough." She sighed and leant back into her pillow. "It's too late now though. I'll be off up there soon." She poked her bent finger to the ceiling. "Cyril's waiting for me, you know. He's been to tell me not to be long."

A shiver of cold ran across Javeen's back; wolfmen and the dead visiting the living were not what she had signed up for. Emily leant back and closed her eyes. Kathy, the frail lady's carer, stepped forward to take her pulse.

"You're tired," Javeen said taking the opportunity to leave. Emily snorted, already asleep. Javeen backed out, whispering her thanks to Kathy. "I'll see myself out."

Kathy took hold of her arm. "She's not batty, you know. My Billy saw it too."

The penny dropped. Kathy was Billy Oldfield's wife. "He did mention it to me."

"Perhaps now you'll believe him," she said with undisguised triumph.

Javeen nodded and pulled her arm from Kathy's grip. "I know he believed what he saw. We believe there's an escaped wolf, or a particularly large dog on the loose, or someone perhaps in costume-"

Kathy snorted. "That has superhuman agility and speed?"

"Well-"

"There's something evil in those woods. The whole village knows it. The howls and screams are scaring the old folk half to death. My Eunice won't even play outside in the garden anymore."

"I'm sorry to hear-"

"No point being sorry, Constable. Get someone up to the village to deal with it. I don't want to be rude, but there's just you and PC Stangton here. You need to get more coppers in to hunt it down; dog, wolf, or psycho, it wants shooting dead."

"We do have a team coming up from the main town, Kathy. Rest assured, we'll do our best to keep the community safe."

"They can't come quick enough for me."

Javeen took her leave and crossed the road to talk to Laura Anderson. The house remained silent, and Laura didn't answer the door although Javeen was sure that a curtain twitched as she walked back through the garden gate. With tension pulling across her shoulders, and a pounding headache that she needed several mugs of coffee to help dissipate, she returned to the station.

She was relieved to see Amy Brice sat at her desk, but there was no sign of Stangton.

WHAT HAD BEEN MAX ANDERSON, curled beneath the workbench, falling asleep amongst the warmth of the others, and Kelly woke with a start to a buzzing in her head. She took a gasping breath as memory grabbed her. *A monster*

*had been in her kitchen and* ... her heart palpitated at speed, a quick hammering against her ribs ... *it had* ... she struggled for coherence ... *it had bitten her*. Suddenly aware of the stiffness in her neck and shoulder, she dabbed a hand there. Blood stained her fingers as she pulled the hand away. It had been real ... not a dream, or a nightmare. As she reached for the sink to help pull herself from the floor, the only sound was the scratching of the metal clasp of her shoes on the tiles. It rang in her ears, adding to the disorientation of the buzzing.

At the sink, she hung over the bowl to vomit. Her head pounded. Her reflection stared back from the kitchen window, the cupboards and door to the hallway filling the scene. Blood had soaked across her t-shirt and there were puncture wounds through the cloth. The sourness of the creature's stench was on her clothes and in her hair. An image of the attack appeared in her memory, as clear as though watching TV, but it couldn't be right. She must be misremembering. The thing in her memory looked wolfish, but human too. Sparse hair covered its face, and its incisors were long, but ... No. Whatever had attacked her must have been an escaped wolf or a mad dog.

She staggered from the kitchen to the bathroom and reached for the wall cabinet. The face reflected in the mirror made her gasp. Her skin seemed to have lost all colour and blue veins were threaded across her face and down her neck. Bite marks sat on her shoulder, their centres black with clotted blood, each puncture wound a hillock of red and swollen flesh. She opened the cabinet door quickly to block the sight then closed it slowly. Her eyes were heavily bloodshot, and the iris had darkened from their usual light hazel to a darker brown. The pupils were pinprick small. At her temples, across her forehead, and over her top lip, the hairs seemed darker. *It must be because her skin seemed so wan. She looked like death! Or, as though the Grim Reaper was waiting at her shoulder ready to drag her down to hell.* Pain seared her belly and beads of sweat trickled at her temples. The room grew dark then brightened and she vomited again. *Bed—she had to lie down. Call for help. Call Alwyn and lie down.* The floor rose and she swayed, lurched to the mirror, and crashed to the floor as her legs buckled.

Dreams haunted her sleep. Bloodied eyes and gnashing teeth loomed from the dark, the stench of death clung to her nose and blocked her throat, she choked, coughing, and spluttering as a muffled voice called her name.

She woke in her own bed beneath her favourite soft fleece blanket. A glass bowl sat on the bedside table, its contents red. Pulled up close, in her velvet chair, sat her husband, Alwyn. Slumped at an awkward angle, eyes closed, he rested in sleep. Each breath he took rumbled in her ears. She champed her teeth. *Hungry. Eat.* Her belly growled and her gaze fell to the jogging pulse of his throat.

"Kelly!" He sat forward, suddenly awake. His eyes widened as their eyes met, then he broke away and she pulled at the blanket to cover her shoulder.

"I've cleaned the wound and been to fetch the doctor. He's coming up to see you."

She reached out her hand. He flinched then took it. "Just lay still. Does it hurt?"

She grunted her response, her voice low and rasping, her throat sore.

"You look hot. I'll get some cool water and a flannel for your forehead. OK? Just wait there." His fear hung in the air and as he disappeared from the room her belly growled. The need to eat, stuff her mouth with raw meat, feel it slide down her throat, became overwhelming.

# CHAPTER TWENTY-FOUR

As Javeen returned from Emily Carmichael's house to the station, the car park was nearly full, and a small group of people waited at the door. They turned and watched as she walked. Intensely aware of each step, she waved then called an awkward 'hello'. The crowd parted to let her through then swarmed in behind, filling the small room. It erupted with voices grabbing for her attention.

"There were two of them."

"... looked like wolves ..."

" ... pulled the body across the road ..."

" ... monsters ..."

"Kelly Gray has been bitten."

"Please." She raised her hands as a barrier. "I can't hear what you're saying." The room grew quiet. "Janice, did I hear you say that a body had been dragged across the road?" The room fell silent.

"Beryl Taylor at number fifteen on Main Street said she saw one of the wolfmen attack Jim Kendrick right in front of her house. She said it jumped on him and then a few minutes later she saw it drag the body across the road. I went round to Jim's as soon as she told me. His wife said he's been missing since last night. She's been going mental with worry and not been able to get any help. No one will go out, what with the attacks, and there's no phones working so we can't call out for help." Janice Bainbridge's words tumbled out in a desperate rush.

Javeen remained calm, desperate to be logical, the face of calm authority. "When was this?"

"Mrs Taylor said it was before seven."

"And nobody reported it?"

"Beryl was too afraid, she said, and Jim's wife went out looking but got spooked when she heard the howling. The phones aren't working either so she couldn't call. Their daughter Rachel's missing too. They went to the shops together. Her mum's frantic with worry."

The room erupted with voices, the tension and anxiety in the room palpable.

"We need the police from the main town up here."

"Or the military. It must be a wolf to drag off a grown man, or a lunatic."

"Mrs Taylor said it looked like a wolfman."

"Billy Oldfield's seen it too."

Javeen caught Kathy Oldfield's sharp frown as Janice shouted about Billy. "Shh! I told you not to say-"

Someone snorted. "He was drunk!"

"Not that drunk!" Kathy Oldfield snapped from the back of the room.

Someone sniggered. Other voices rose in pitch.

"It was dark," Janice said in Mrs Taylor's defence. "She's old. But she said she saw what she saw. Said it was naked, and she could tell it was a man because she could see its ... well, she said she could see its 'dangler'. Her words, not mine." Janice blushed.

"What are you going to do about it?"

"I say we hunt them down."

"No, that's-"

"Someone's got to do something!"

The room was about to descend into panic and that would only spread to the rest of the village. "I can assure you that we have the situation under control."

A muffled snort.

"People are being attacked and you've got it 'under control'!"

Sensing the rising panic, she lied. "PC Stangton and I have arranged for a team of police marksmen and specialist trackers to come and search for the dog, or wolf-"

"What if it's a serial killer?"

"Max Anderson hasn't been seen since the *Institute* was broken into."

*Take control Javeen.* "Now, please! Let's not get ahead of ourselves. If it is a serial killer, which is highly unlikely, ..." she made eye contact with the most vocal villagers in the room, "if it is a man that is carrying out these attacks, we'll be carrying out a thorough investigation. In the meantime, I can assure you that PC Stangton and I will be doing our best to keep this community safe." *If she could find him!*

Her efforts were followed by a snort of derision.

"There's only the two of you."

"That's correct, but we are committed to helping the people of this village and surrounding areas." She was beginning to sound like one of the dry emails from her superiors. *Where was Stangton? Things were getting out of hand, and they needed a plan of action, pronto.* "And we have called for extra personnel-"

"We should go into the forest and kill it ourselves."

"If there's an animal loose, perhaps we should all stay inside until it's caught?"

This suggestion was met with approval from some of the villagers.

"That may be a good idea," Javeen agreed. "Staying inside, that is. Not going out to hunt it down. It's up to the authorities to deal with the situation. Staying at home, at least until we know just exactly what we're dealing with, is perhaps the best solution."

"What if it is a werewolf?"

"Don't be stupid!"

"I'm not. Mrs Taylor said it was a man, but it looked like a wolf. Said it was on two legs. What else would have the strength to drag a man's body across the road like that?"

"Beryl Taylor's going senile, Janice. She's eighty-four years old and last week she was talking to her mother in the park. Her mother's been dead for ten years."

*Are Billy Oldfield and Emily Carmichael senile too?* All three were unreliable witnesses: a drunk, an elderly lady with dementia, and another who talked to her dead husband. Even so, their stories were unnerving. Javeen listened as the villagers as they chattered among themselves.

"It'll be one of them rabies dogs from Whitby."

"Or a killer dressed up as a wolf."

More murmurs of agreement.

"Kelly Gray has been bitten by it. I went up to the cottage with Alwyn. We found her on the floor."

"Is she alright?"

"Yes, but she was out cold. Alwyn's taking care of her. I'm going back up to take some antiseptic-"

"She should go to hospital—for a bite."

Another murmur of assent.

"What if it's one of us?"

The room fell to silence and the tension became palpable. Then Janice laughed and the others join in, though the sound was tinny and fake.

*Take control, Javeen.* "Iain, I'll take your statement in a minute. Janice, could you repeat for me exactly what Mrs Taylor told you this morning."

Javeen took her statement and then spoke to the others individually. Most had come to report the strange noises that had marred the night, and only one had actually seen something that could be useful. Tension at the back of Javeen's head throbbed as she closed the door behind the last 'witness'. *Coffee—she needed another coffee.*

AFTER THE UNSETTLING meeting at the police station Iain was determined to check on Kelly and suggest that Alwyn took her to the hospital. If she had been bitten by a rabid dog, then time was of the essence. He had heard that the new strain of the virus was deadly, and someone had mentioned that none of the victims had survived so far. At the cottage, Alwyn's Land Rover was still parked beside Kelly's Volkswagen but when he knocked at the cottage door, his urgent rap received no answer.

"Hello!" he called as he stepped through the door.

No answer.

"Hellooo!" he shouted just a little louder and longer.

Uncomfortable at walking in uninvited, he stepped inside then walked through to the kitchen. Morning sun filtered through the kitchen window. Dressed with cream fabric woven with pink rosebuds and twining green tendrils, it made a pretty frame for the forest outside. The painted yellow cabinets and honey-coloured kitchen tops added to the feeling of warmth and comfort, although the bloody smears beneath the sink marred the scene.

More blood smeared the tiled floor although nothing else in the room looked out of place. *Perhaps Alwyn had already taken her to hospital—but both cars were still outside. An ambulance then?*

Iain stepped out of the kitchen and checked the other rooms. The cabin was arranged on ground level. A short corridor led to the living room and opposite were two doors which he presumed were the bedroom and bathroom. He took a tentative step forward, noticed a flicker of movement through the living room door as he passed, dismissed it as a bird seen through the window, and walked to the bedroom. The door was open. His gut wrenched as he scanned the room. The fleece blanket Alwyn had laid across Kelly that morning, lay strewn across the bed. A bowl lay empty on the carpet, a pinkish flannel at its side, but the chair was what caused him to start. Large patches of dark red were spattered across its light blue velvet and, as he skimmed the area, other splashes of blood became obvious. At the edge of the rug something lay drying in a repulsive lump. He took a step forward to see it clearly, gasped, and pulled back. By the curved shape of its edge, he could tell it was a section of kidney.

Back in the thin sunshine, he reached for his phone and scrolled through his list of contacts whilst nervously checking the area for movement. At 'S' he clicked on 'Stangton' and dialled. Holding the phone to his ear, he turned in a circle, checking into the trees, and again to the house. The phone didn't ring. No signal. His hands trembled as he slipped the phone back into his pocket.

The voice of a woman called out as though in pain. It called again and he was sure he could hear his name.

"Kelly!" he called back. "Kelly? Is that you?" *If it was Kelly shouting, did that mean the kidney was Alwyn's?* His sphincter contracted.

The noise repeated and was followed by a knocking that seemed to come from the shed. With tentative steps he stood before the shed and unlatched the door.

Four pairs of blood-filled eyes opened from sleep and turned to stare. As the creatures uncurled, Iain only had time to register that three of the four were naked before they pounced.

# CHAPTER TWENTY-FIVE

Javeen took another sip of coffee then sighed with undisguised relief as two white Ford Transit vans with a wide stripe of yellow and blue squares, drove into the Station's car park. The second had 'POLICE DOGS' in large blue print across its side. Her relief that Stangton had made it and sent in the cavalry was short lived as the first officer jumped from the van. Dressed in the typical police uniform of black trousers and white shirt, he was just a PC. She bit her lip, holding back her disappointment as he walked to the side of the van and opened the door. Three other police officers stepped out and among them she recognised PC Jenny Osborne. It was not the team she had expected, and she grew increasingly concerned that Stangton hadn't made it to town.

She recognised the form of Ted McDermot in the dog handler's van. He jumped out with a heavy step, the white flesh and dark hairs of his overhanging belly visible through the gap in his shirt. *Men really should go back to wearing vests.* He waved as he caught her watching. She returned his wave and strode forward, pushing down her disappointment.

"Morning, Ted."

"Latimer." He returned her greeting with a wink.

Javeen groaned inwardly. Would she ever get away from her past mistake? She ignored his overfamiliarity. "Glad to see you here. We certainly need your help. Have you seen PC Stangton?"

"No, Latimer. I've not, but I have heard about your problems. Head Office said you've got a wild dog on the loose, perhaps one with rabies, and a missing girl?"

He doesn't know! "We found one of the missing girls-"

"Ah. Good. One?"

"We have - had - two missing girls as well as a missing adult male. Unfortunately, it's not good news. One of the young women was savaged in the woods. She died of her injuries before we found her."

He searched her eyes with confusion. "Why ... Sorry, Latimer, no one mentioned an attack or a death. Forensics should be here."

"Yes, they should. Stangton drove through to town yesterday to call it in, but he hasn't been back."

"So Stangton's missing too?"

"Yes."

"How come he drove into town to report the incident?"

"We've got no radio, mobile, or digital signals. Communications are down."

"Odd." He pulled out his phone. "Yep, no signal." He held up the mobile for her to see the screen.

"Stangton was supposed to report the death and the sightings."

"They've got a similar problem down in Whitby."

"Wolfmen?"

"What? No, rabies. 'Wolfmen' Latimer? What's that about?"

She flinched from his derision. "Well, probably not, but it is what the villagers are talking about. Several sightings have been reported-"

"Mass hysteria, Latimer. That's what that is. There's no such thing as wolfmen, but when people get scared, and things start to go bump in the night, it's the kind of story that gets passed around and people start imagining all sorts of horrors. It's happened before."

"Oh?"

"Down in Dartmoor. 1996. A couple of dogs were attacked by what their owner said was a creature like a wolf. Suddenly there was a flurry of reported sightings. A child went missing and all hell broke loose."

"What happened?"

"It turned out a local farmer's dog had gone nuts and attacked the woman's dogs. Someone had overheard her exaggerating the story and then it got out of hand. She corrected the story pretty quickly, but the truth didn't stop people 'seeing' the werewolf."

"And the child?"

"Found safe with her older, married sister watching a film, but it was weeks before people stopped passing on the false stories. Mass hysteria is what it is, Latimer. Rest assured."

He opened the back of the van as the other officers joined them and clipped a lead to the large Alsatian sitting patiently in the back. "Anyway, whatever is in that woods, Cass will find it."

The dog jumped down and licked at Javeen's hand. She stroked its head and rubbed behind its ears. "I hope so, Ted. We need sanity restoring around here."

As the other officers gathered round, she led them into the tiny Police Station and recounted the incidents of the past days. The men and woman listened in silence, but with deepening concern.

PC Callum Banks, the senior officer, took centre stage as she finished. "Thank you, PC Latimer. That puts a different complexion on our job here today. Obviously, the situation has escalated since it was first reported. It's very possible that a very dangerous animal is at large in the woods. We haven't come prepared for that."

"Yes, but-"

"Let me finish, Latimer."

"Sorry."

"However, PC McDermot is armed-"

"With a tranquiliser gun."

"And we have Cass," he made a gesture towards the German Shepherd stood at PC McDermot's side. "Doctor Max Anderson and Lois Maybank are still missing."

"There's no evidence they're in the forest though."

"That's correct. However, Anderson's car is still parked at the *Institute* and Lois Maybank hasn't taken any of her personal belongings and doesn't have any money. The likelihood of either of them being anywhere other than in the vicinity is small."

"What are you suggesting?"

"That we proceed with the search."

"We don't have protection."

"Sod that. I didn't join up to be stifled by Health & Safety."

The officers nodded in agreement.

"All agreed then?"

A general consensus was agreed that they should proceed.

"Right, Latimer. You've got your search team."

Javeen kept her sigh of relief locked down. "Good."

# CHAPTER TWENTY-SIX

It took ten minutes to drive to the location where Javeen and Stangton had found the body. As she jumped from the van, her pulse throbbed at her temples. Finding Anita's body, and the continuing eerie howls that accompanied the nights, had taken their toll on her nerves, and she had become fearful of the woods. The sky shifted to drab, and a light drizzle spattered her face, the cold nipping at her cheeks. She pulled on her gloves and led the team into the forest towards the clearing and stopped at the tree where the girl's body had lain.

"Where is it then, Latimer?"

She stared incredulously at the trunk. Anita was no longer there. "She's gone!"

Ted McDermot led Cass forward and scanned the ground. "There's blood, some gore, and scuff marks. It was here." He turned to Javeen. "Something's dragged her off." He crouched to inspect the dark earth. "From the look of these marks, the body was dragged to this point then lifted. There are possibly some footprints here too, but I can't be sure."

Javeen considered the area. Certainly, there were drag marks and they stopped abruptly. She couldn't see the footprints as clearly as Ted did though.

"It would have to be something big to lift her up," Ted continued.

Uneasy murmurs rippled through the officers and PC Callum Banks took charge. "We're going to start the search from here. Spread out. Ten feet apart."

"If there's a killer on the loose up here, we should call for back up. We're not armed. We just came to help search for a missing girl." PC Jerry Sykes was losing his nerve.

PC Banks looked thoughtful. "We'll work until two o'clock."

Callum Banks also seemed to be losing his nerve. Two o'clock was only an hour away. The others nodded, though looks of apprehension spread between them.

As they began the search, Javeen stepped in time with the only other woman in the small group, Jenny Osborne, a short and stocky woman who could pin a perp to the floor with one swift twist of her chunky wrist.

"You settling in well, Latimer?" Jenny asked as she scoured the ferns.

"Yes, Kielder's a great place to work."

"Place to forget about the outside world, eh?"

Jenny's words were jarring. "If you're referring to what happened in Grimsby, I've put that behind me."

"Scandalous what they did to you though. The Super was as much to blame, from what I heard."

"I'd rather not talk about it, to be honest."

"Sure. If you ever do though ..."

"Thanks." Javeen was unsure whether Jenny was just interested in hearing the lurid details of her fall from grace, or whether she was offering a genuine hand of friendship.

She hoped friendship; it would be good to have another friend up here, it did get a little lonely, although Andy was filling that gap quite well. She drifted into memories of their night together and then remembered their last conversation. He wanted to go places with her. He'd suggested a bike ride through the forest once it was safe again, or, when the weather warmed up, sailing on the lake and perhaps in the summer, a trip to Seahouses and the Farne Islands. Warmth spread through her at the memory of his words; he was making plans for the future which meant she wasn't just a bit of fluff he'd bed every now and then. Things were coming right in Kielder, even if they were in the midst of a crisis.

Cass pulled at her lead and Ted was yanked forward. The dog's sudden excitement startled Javeen and she berated herself for being so jumpy and letting her concentration drift.

"Halt!" PC Banks raised his hand at the end of the line; he had found something. The line stopped moving forward and Javeen followed his pointing finger. Her heart made a heavy thud in her chest as her eyes focused on something hanging in the tree. The arm of a man dangled from the branch. She took several steps forward, forcing herself to look into the tree and block out the excited chatter of the other officers. Javeen recognised Jim Kendrick, the man Beryl Taylor had said she'd seen attacked by the wolfman and dragged off into the forest. His body hung over a branch, one arm shoved tight against the trunk, the other dangling down, the fingers already black. Blood had soaked his jeans and from the thinness of his torso as it hung over the bough, his innards appeared to be missing—just like Anita's.

Jenny jabbed her arm at another tree. A blackening face with long blonde plaits at its cheeks stared blankly at the officers Anita! One of the men turned from the scene and retched. Javeen's stomach rolled, and she vomited, bile spattering her shoes and trousers but with a quick wipe of her mouth she turned back to the officers. Sykes, a younger officer, turned away, hands on knees, his body heaving.

In the near distance a guttural scream-like bark joined the low grumblings of the officers and the commanding voice of PC Drake. He stopped to listen for a moment then continued. She could almost see the hair on his scalp creeping back from his forehead. He swallowed and pointed to Anita. "Is this the missing body, Latimer?"

"Yes." Her voice was barely audible.

He pointed a finger at Jim. "And is this your missing man?"

Javeen took a breath. *Stay calm. Stay in control.* "It's one of them. Jim Kendrick. We have a witness who said she saw him being attacked outside her house and dragged off into the forest."

"Dragged all this way?"

"It's too far. The attacker must have driven him here and somehow winched him into the tree."

"There's no sign of a rope-"

"The witness said she saw a ... wolfman attack him."

PC Drake's eyes rolled with contempt before he collected himself. "No such thing as wolfmen, Latimer."

"No, I'm not saying there are ... I'm just saying what the witness said-"

"Mass hysteria, Sir. I've already told her about that," Ted added.

"There must be more than one of them. One man-"

"Or woman.

"Sorry, Pilkington. Or woman,"

"Can't be sexist, Osborne."

Jenny's eyes rolled and she shook her head. "OK, Pilkington. One man, or one woman, couldn't have done this on their own."

The voices of Eric Idle and John Cleese instantly filled Javeen's thoughts, and she repressed a giggle. The moment was surreal. *For crying out loud, Latimer! Don't, for God's sake, laugh. The giggle wanted to burst out of her mouth as hysteria.* She took a breath, hoping the others didn't notice her discomfort.

"Agreed. We're looking at a couple of people at least."

The momentary terror of becoming a shambolic, giggling wreck, passed, but in the near distance the shiver of a branch caught in Javeen's peripheral vision, and she swivelled, her senses on high alert. Leaves shivered and then grew still. She turned back to focus on the conversation.

"What do we do now? We can't leave them here."

"That's exactly what we do, Sykes. We need to make a note of the location and inform forensics. They'll set up an investigation around the site. Osborne, pass me the bag."

# CHAPTER TWENTY-SEVEN

Jenny Osborne shuffled off the rucksack and passed it to PC Drake. Within a few minutes the area had been encircled with yellow 'police aware' tape held taut by metal stakes.

Drake took out his phone. Pressed the buttons then stared at the screen.

"Phone lines are dead, Sir," Javeen explained.

"It was working on the way up here."

"We haven't had internet access or mobile phone communications for the past couple of days, Sir."

"Odd." He replaced the phone in his pocket.

"It's patchy up here anyway, though."

A branch snapped among the trees. This time Jenny twisted to look.

"Gets to you, doesn't it—the forest, I mean."

Osborne took a deep breath as she turned back. "Yep, that and finding two mutilated bodies hanging in a tree. I think we've got a very depraved serial killer on our hands, Latimer. And, if I'm honest, I think we should get back to HQ and come back with an armed team—we're too vulnerable here." She shivered as she scanned the trees.

Javeen nodded quietly in agreement and was about to speak when she noticed something move next to one of the moss-covered tree stumps that sat like gargoyles between the trees. To make things even more dramatic, mist crept over the ground.

"It's like something out of a horror film here."

Javeen didn't reply. Her attention was targeted on the trees about fifty feet to their right. Something had moved among them.

Another branch snapped and she swivelled to the noise. A tree juddered to the left. There could be no more than twenty feet between the group of police officers and whatever was in those trees. She waited, not taking her eyes off the quivering tree, expecting a bird to flutter from its branches. Nothing escaped the evergreen. She swallowed, and her hands trembled as the realisation struck her that the team was completely unarmed and had no defence against whatever was lurking in the trees, be it depraved serial killer or crazed dog.

"Osborne ..."

"Yes."

"I think something is following us."

A tiny mewl sounded from Osborne's throat and her eyes flitted across the forest. "Don't piss around, Latimer. I'm on edge already."

"I'm not. Two o'clock in the shrubs and ten o'clock in that pine with the tree trunk fallen against it. Watch them."

"Jesus! Them?" Osborne shifted her gaze from right and then to left. "There's nothing there."

"Keep watching. I saw something move."

Osborne remained silent as she followed Javeen's instructions. Another rustle of leaves and then a thud made her hair stand on end. Heart beating hard against her sternum, she scanned the trees. If she was correct, something was circling them. From the movement of the branches and undergrowth, it was either one very fast creature, or perhaps even three. She felt an urgent need to urinate. *Calm it, Latimer! Calm it.*

Movement caught in her peripheral vision again and the snap of twigs ricocheted. The others were too involved in their discussions to notice. She had to warn them. *But what if she was wrong? She'd look stupid.* If she didn't, and they were being watched – *hunted more like* – then she could perhaps save some lives. If she was right, and from everything she had seen over the past few days, it would be a miracle if anyone survived.

"Sir." She took a few tentative steps forward and swallowed down the fear that she was going to look like a muppet and tapped PC Drake on the shoulder. He stared at her. She had broken protocol by touching him but, in the moment, that was irrelevant, all that mattered was warning him.

Cass pulled against her lead.

"Down, girl!" Ted instructed. The dog ignored his command and continued to pull towards the shivering tree.

"Latimer?" Searching her eyes, they exchanged an unspoken understanding, and he checked beyond her shoulder to the deeper forest, taking in the now agitated dog.

"I think we may be surrounded, Sir."

His eyes locked back on hers. "I think you may be right." Colour drained from his face and his eyes flitted to the hanging corpses of Jim Kendrick and Anita, then back to the trees.

"I think there may be three of them."

Wood snapped among the trees, somewhere very close. Drake's Adam's apple bobbed. "We should make our way back to the vehicles."

The dog pulled against its lead, growling at the trees. Ted followed the dog's line of vision and scoured the trees then loosened the lead and followed him. The shiver of leaves ahead was barely discernible. The dog barked and strained against its lead, pulling Ted forward with a lurch. He stumbled.

"Steady, Cass."

A branch bounced, spraying pine needles onto the forest floor. The dog growled, its teeth bared. The officers watched the trees with growing concern. The heavy-set German Shepherd jumped forward, straining at its lead, pulling Ted with it.

Thud!

Behind the tree something dropped to the floor.

"Ted!" Javeen shouted. "Ted, come back."

The dog barked, snarled, and leapt forward dragging Ted along the forest floor. PC Drake grabbed for the lead. With the extra weight, the dog slowed but continued to pull at the lead.

In a moment of hyper-awareness, Javeen experienced the chaos surrounding her: the trees and undergrowth moved, the flashes of something between the branches, Osborne pointing, Ted struggling to stand again, Callum pulling on the dog's lead, and the creature half hidden behind the tree.

A guttural howl sent a shiver of fear deep into Javeen's bones and the creature bounded forward.

Bowels suddenly weightless, she had the urge to defecate. *Run! Just fucking run!*

Branches snapped, shuddered, and divided as the creatures that had tracked them down made their final move.

Clawed hands sliced through the air and the dog jumped, teeth bared, snapping at the attacker. Ted stumbled, the lead still tightly wound around his hand, trapped beneath the dog as the creature pinned it down. In a single, decisive, and fatal movement, the 'thing' clamped its jaws around the dog's throat and tore. Ted pushed at the writhing dog, desperate to get from beneath it as the beast turned its attention to him.

As Ted screamed, sharp claws sliced across Callum's belly, and another figure darted from behind a clump of tall ferns. The scene took place at the periphery of Javeen's vision as she watched PC Drake's bowels slither from the gaping wound. Screams filled the space as another beast hurtled towards Sykes. Within a second, the young recruit was snatched up and carried off into the trees.

Osborne grabbed her arm. "Run!"

Another creature jumped from a tree and landed beside Harry Pilkington. As Javeen turned to follow Osborne, Ted's legs jittered as the creature reached into his abdomen. To her right, next to a clump of ferns, Harry bucked against the thing that straddled his hips. The thing was naked, and the light covering of dark hairs couldn't disguise that it was female. She held Harry's flailing arms by the wrist, gazing into his screaming face. As Javeen ran, the female rocked her hips over his, tipped her head back, and howled.

Javeen ran, powering herself away from the horror, every ounce of her being focused on running. She jumped the writhing worms of roots, knowing tripping would mean death. She barged past trees, pushing their branches out of her way, following the path they'd trodden minutes before. Her breath came hard. Behind her Osborne's breath rasped. With each second, she expected the branches beside her to bounce, and one of those hideous creatures to jump out and gut her too.

*Jesus, what had she seen?*

Her pulse thumped in her head.

*Focus! Focus on getting out of here.*

Behind her, Osborne's pounding footsteps matched her own. The woman grunted. Javeen looked back, saw her stumble, right herself, and continue running. In the distance she spotted the white, blue, and yellow of the police van.

*The keys. Who had the keys?*

Her mind raced, fumbled, she couldn't think straight.

*Osborne was driving. She would have the keys.*

"Osborne! The van ..." she turned to speak and caught the movement of a figure running between the trees. "The keys, Osborne. Get the keys ready."

Osborne glanced at the running figure and, eyes alive with terror, pumped her arms harder, jumped another root, and gained pace with Javeen.

"The keys!"

The van was fully visible now. The creature gone, playing with them the way a cat does with a mouse before it goes in for the kill.

*Would they paw her body before tearing it apart?*

Her arms pumped harder. Metal jangled. The lights on the van flashed.

Something that looked like a man ran parallel to Javeen. It ran with powerful strides and pumping arms. Naked, it kept pace, smiled as their eyes met, then disappeared. Behind her Osborne grunted.

Javeen turned. Osborne was on the floor, her foot hooked beneath a root, the keys next to her outstretched hand.

A creature appeared behind Osborne, a female, its face covered with a soft down of dark hair. Long incisors snapped in an elongated chin, its eyes black. Like the other it was naked. Its hair, though straggled, was plaited and tied to the side, and a pink flower, like the one Lois Maybank's mother had described her daughter as wearing, was clipped at the temple.

To the right, the male that had kept pace with Javeen, waited in the shadows, and watched. The female – *Lois* – took a step forward. Javeen grabbed Osborne's hand. "Get up."

Osborne scrabbled to her feet, face flushed, chest heaving. Javeen took a step back, her hand touching metal as she reached for the door.

Hope suddenly returned, and she grabbed for Osborne. "Get in the van," she hissed. "We can make it."

As Javeen turned to pull the handle, Lois pounced, and slammed against the open door as Javeen yanked Osborne out of reach.

"Get in!" Javeen screamed as she pulled Osborne into the cab.

The creature snarled and gnashed its teeth as it stared wildly through bloodied eyes. Lois, or whatever she had become, was insane. Jumping forward, Lois sank her teeth into Osborne's shoulder, and bit down. Osborne screamed, her eyes wide with shock. Instead of pulling, Javeen waited. Lois stared with crazed eyes, and a low moan leaked from her throat. As it withdrew its incisors from Osborne's shoulder Javeen gave a mighty yank on her arm whilst simultaneously kicking the creature in the belly. The thing screeched as it staggered back and the male sprinted from the trees, and Javeen screamed "Go! Go! Go!" as she handed Osborne the keys.

The male pounded on the window, teeth gnashing, saliva smearing across the glass.

The engine started.

"Go!" Javeen screamed as the male continued to pound the glass. "Go!"

Tyres screeched as Osborne floored the accelerator. The thing that had been Lois Maybank jumped in front of the van, teeth gnashing, eyes staring, saliva hanging between her teeth. Without flinching, Osborne slammed the van into gear and powered forward, hitting Lois with a thud.

Checking through the rearview mirror as they pulled away, Javeen caught a glimpse of Lois as she staggered to a stand then limped to the male and crouched at his feet, curling her arms around his legs. Oblivious to her, he watched the van move away.

# CHAPTER TWENTY-EIGHT

The van gained speed, swerving along the forest track, screeching around corners. Osborne drove with a grim determination, totally focused on the road ahead. Javeen clicked her seatbelt into place. "Jesus! Jesus! Jesus!"

Checking the side mirror Javeen could see only trees, ferns, and the road behind them. "I don't think they've followed us."

Osborne grunted. Her back seeped blood where long gashes had been scratched along the skin. At her shoulder, puncture marks were already swelling.

"Pull over, Jenny. You're hurt. Let me drive."

"In a minute. Once we get out of the forest, then you can drive. It's not safe yet."

They drove until they reached the turn-off they'd taken from the main road into the forest. Jenny turned in the direction of the village, then pulled over. She sagged against the wheel.

"You OK?" Dumb question. "I mean ... I know you're not OK, but ... how much pain are you in?"

Jenny sat back against the seat and flinched, pulling her torn flesh away from the fabric. Small fibres stuck to her skin and a damp patch of blood remained on the grey seat.

"Agony!"

"It looks bad, Jenny." The blood trickled freely down her back, the scratches angry and littered with dirt. "Swap over. I'll drive."

Jenny's skin was pallid, all blood seemed to have drained and, where minutes before her cheeks had been flushed, now they were pale and threaded with veins. Her pulse throbbed at her temple and her eyes drooped. Shocked at how quickly her colleague was deteriorating, Javeen swung the van to face the opposite direction and began the journey to the nearest hospital. She picked up the receiver of the police radio and pressed the button. Static crackled from the handset.

"Victor X-ray this is Charlie Foxtrot 3-1. Do you copy?" She listened. Only static returned. She tried again. Again, only static returned.

As Jenny groaned and slumped against the door, Javeen took the van from forty miles an hour to fifty, then sixty. The roads were empty and straight along this stretch, and she determined to make headway where possible. Further ahead, where the roads began to climb the last hill before the forest gave way to moorland, then farmland, she would have to slow down.

The sun had reached its highest point and was beginning its return to earth. Javeen glanced at the van's dashboard, 3:45pm. It would soon be dusk, and dark would quickly follow, but at least, by then, Jenny would be in hospital.

Movement caught her attention through the side window. Her belly flipped as a figure ran beside the van. It was him. The male 'thing' from the forest, arms pumping as he glanced into the van. The speedometer read forty-five miles per hour. She floored the accelerator. Fifty and it still kept pace. Sixty. Its head disappeared. For a millisecond she sensed relief, then the dark, glaring eyes reappeared, closer to the window this time. Sixty-five, seventy. He was gone. Ninety, one hundred. In the rear view the figure was visible, but the distance grew between them and then it stopped, turned, and disappeared into the trees.

The road ahead stretched out to a clearing then disappeared back into the forest. Beyond that was the end of Kielder Forest, and open road.

Jenny groaned.

"It's OK, Jenny. We'll soon be there. We're nearly out of Kielder. The hospital isn't far." The hospital was at least another thirty miles, but once they were beyond the forest, once they were safe, she would pull over and check in the first aid kit for anything that could make Jenny more comfortable.

The van sped around the corner and the road darkened as trees overhung the road once more but ahead, at the very edge of the forest, three vehicles blocked the road. In front of the cars steel barriers had been erected.

As she neared the blockade, she slowed the van. Five bulky men, all wearing bright orange hi-viz vests, complete with hard hats, stepped out from behind the cars. Something wasn't right. Since when did highway maintenance engineers use Range Rovers with tinted windows?

She pulled the car to a stop and stepped out. Jenny groaned.

"I need to pass," she called. "I have an injured officer on board who needs immediate hospital treatment."

A stocky man with extremely well-toned biceps, triceps, and squared, muscular shoulders stepped forward. He didn't resemble the heavy-set, slightly overweight roadworkers she'd become familiar with during her travels along the motorways of Lincolnshire and Yorkshire. None of them did.

"I'm sorry miss-"

"PC Latimer," she corrected.

"PC Latimer, the road is closed. You'll have to find an alternative route."

"There isn't an alternative route."

"Then you'll have to go back the way you came. There is no access beyond this point."

"But ... back that way, I'll have to travel into Scotland. PC Osborne needs immediate medical attention. She was attacked in the woods and ..." She stopped speaking. At the mention of the attack, heavy thudding broke out behind her, and the man drew a gun from beneath his tabard. Three of the five men ran to their cars.

Turning to the noise, she saw that Jenny was rocking to and fro inside the van. "She's in pain," she explained. As Javeen continued to plead to be let through Jenny smashed her face a rictus of pain. Running back to the van, Jenny tumbled out, staggering onto the road, her eyes bloodied, her teeth gnashing.

"She's infected!" a man called. "Fire!"

Shots fired, gravel sparked against the van, and bullets penetrated soft flesh. Jenny screamed, running in circles as Javeen sprinted to the other side of the van. The men lined up behind the barrier, and military grade rifles were trained on Jenny as she tore at her face, screamed, twisted, then launched herself towards them, dancing as the force of their bullets spent itself in her flesh. She dropped to the floor, dragging herself forward, teeth gnashing. How the woman was still alive, Javeen could not comprehend.

# CHAPTER TWENTY-NINE

Javeen swung the van back to face the village expecting a barrage of shots to pierce the metal panels. The bullets didn't come and, as the van's speed increased, she dared to look in the rearview mirror. The men were standing around what was left of Jenny, rifles still pointing at her inert body. Heart racing, pounding as though it would burst, she gripped the wheel and stared ahead at the road.

*What the hell just happened? What? Fuck!*

She slammed her fists on the steering wheel, her mind searching for understanding. "Fuuuuuuck!" she screamed.

Banging hands against the steering wheel, images of the carnage in the forest, of Ted, Mark, and the dog being torn to shreds seared her mind. The hanging bodies in the tree. The wolf-woman grinding her genitals over Sykes' hips. "What the fuck!" She couldn't think. Nothing made sense. *Calm it, Latimer. Calm-the-fuck-down!* The van powered forward as she accelerated. *Jenny!* The engine screamed. *Oh, Christ. What had happened to Jenny? She'd been bitten and ...* she swallowed hard as she remembered the woman's blood-filled eyes, the crazed look of absolute agony on her face as she smashed her cheek against the van's window again and again. She'd been infected by the bite—*like a fucking zombie.* Javeen's chest was so tight she could barely catch her breath, and she took shallow gulps of air as pain tore at her lungs.

Head pounding, she became aware of the engine, its revs way too high, and slipped it into fifth.

She checked the rear-view mirror. Nothing. She checked the side mirrors. Again, nothing. Ahead, the village sign came into view and then the Police Station. She pulled into the car park, stopped the van as close to the door as she could, checked for signs of 'them' through the mirrors and darted to the Station door. Keys in trembling hand, she unlocked the door and almost fell inside before slamming it shut and locking it tight then slamming the bolts across at top and bottom. The converted cottage was old, its door thick, its walls thicker, and the bolts were solid iron. As the final bolt slammed into place, she leant back against the door and sank to the floor.

She sat with head in hands, knees pulled up to her chest until the long shadows of late afternoon crept across the room and the cold of the floor made sitting uncomfortable. As her heartrate slowed, calm descended.

*She had to warn the village!*

With Stangton gone, it was up to her to protect them all.

*How in God's name was she supposed to do that?*

A knock rapped at the door then a shadow fell across the room. The curve of a palm pressed up to the glass, and a face peered in. The man noticed her, tapped at the window, and gestured to the door. The ordinariness of his gesture seemed surreal, and Javeen rose, unlocked the door, and allowed him in. With a furtive glance, she scanned the carpark and surrounding trees, then closed the door behind him, wishing his aged frame could move faster.

She had to remain calm. It was up to her now.

"PC Latimer."

She took a deep breath.

*Be normal. Be calm.* "Yes?"

The man looked flustered and out of breath. She resisted the urge to shout that she hadn't got time to deal with him and sat him down in one of the chairs pushed up against the wall—the station's paltry waiting room.

"We want to know what's going on, officer. What's being done about Jimbob and his daughter. They're still missing you know. And Doctor Anderson. Laura, his wife, is beside herself with worry. She's been having the most terrible nightmares.

*You want to know what's happened to Jimmy boy?* Javeen swallowed. *Jimbob and Anita hanging in a tree? K. I. S. S. I. N. G.*

The old man searched her eyes.

*And Max Anderson? Well, there's a story to give you nightmares.*

She suppressed the hysterical laughter that wanted to burst from her mouth. It would sound maniacal if she let it out.

Unable to speak, Javeen slumped in her chair.

"PC Latimer? Is everything alright."

*Get a grip, Jav. Just get a fucking grip. No, everything is not alright, and that's with a capital N.*

"Yes, Mr Pemberton. We have everything under control."

"Everything under control?" He frowned.

*Tell him everything is going to be OK. That's what they want to hear. They don't want the truth.*

She reverted to her training. "There's no cause for alarm. Nothing to be concerned about."

"PC Latimer?"

All efforts must be made to keep the public calm; any hint of danger could lead to mass hysteria, then tensions erupt etcetera, etcetera. She laughed, forced down the hysteria. She couldn't imagine the riot situations she'd been trained to deal with happening in Kielder, but tensions were high, and only likely to get higher.

"May I ask what is so funny?"

The door swung open. Javeen jolted. She hadn't locked it! Three figures stood as silhouettes against the lowering sun and Billy Oldfield entered followed by Jack Renwick and Simon Carter. Her attempt at a professional smile revealed itself as a grimace.

Simon huffed. "Old Pemberton beat us to it!"

The others made gruff rumbles of agreement. The group were dour, their usual barroom bravado gone.

"We've come to find out what's happening. Jimbob's still missing, and, from our count, there are more villagers unaccounted for, and Ken said that you think a girl who was out camping's gone missing too. The village is getting tetchy, Latimer."

"I was just asking her," Pemberton explained. "She seemed a little ... confused."

"The road's blocked at-"

"We're aware of that," Javeen interrupted, remembering Jenny's hideous last moments.

"You've seen it then? Up at Stannersburn?"

"Oh. No. It was down at t'other end where I saw the blockade."

"What the hell's going on, Latimer? That's both main roads out of the forest blocked.

"'Tweren't roadworks neither."

Javeen remembered the rifles so quickly and expertly utilised to destroy PC Osborne and shook her head in agreement. "No," she whispered.

"We can't find Stangton. Where's he gone?"

*No idea.*

Javeen's hands trembled. The tension in the room cranked up. She made one last effort to calm the situation and with the last of her energy, gathered herself. "Misters Oldfield, Pemberton, Renwick, and Carter. Rest assured that we are doing everything we can to deal with the ongoing situation." Mr Pemberton nodded, accepting her words. "My advice would be to go home-"

"But we wanted to help, you see. Kielder is such a small village, like family, and when one of us is lost, the others help to find them. We were-"

"No!" She jerked forward. "No. You mustn't go into the forest."

"Well, its-"

"We should at least go and look!" Carter blustered.

"No!" she repeated. *Think, Javeen!* "If Jim and his daughter are lost in the forest then we need a team to systematically search the area. It needs a concerted effort by a team of trained people."

"Like the ones that came this morning?"

"Yes, exactly."

"And where are they?"

"They've gone home for the day," she lied. "We'll be resuming the search tomorrow." She sat back. Mr Pemberton seemed to accept her explanation though the others were eyeing her warily. Oldfield narrowed his eyes as he searched her face. She hadn't got him fooled, but she just needed time to collect her thoughts. Once she had figured out the next step, he would forgive her lies—he'd have to.

"You're lying, Latimer."

The other men scrutinized her face. Mr Pemberton looked embarrassed for her. She closed her eyes and leant back in her chair. She was lying. Lying to buy herself time, to try and control this impossible situation. She could barely think straight after what happened, but she couldn't be honest about the slaughter in the forest. *Could she?* There was no way out of the village, they were trapped by whatever those creatures were in the forest and the men that guarded the escape routes.

"Well?" Oldfield prodded. "Well, Latimer?" His voice had an edge to it. "Why are you lying?"

She could think of nothing to say that was convincing enough to be a plausible explanation, so decided to brazen it out and tell the truth.

She locked her gaze to Oldfield's. "The truth is ... that there are wolfmen roaming through the woods. They've slaughtered the team of officers that came here to search for Doctor Anderson and Lois Maybank. And ... I think it was Anderson and Maybank that killed the team."

A snort of derision.

"Silly bitch."

Oldfield muttered darkly.

Mr Pemberton crossed himself and his thin frame quivered inside his overlarge jacket. "The Reverend warned me." His voice was reed-thin and went unnoticed by the other men.

Javeen continued. "Both roads out of the village are blocked by armed men. They won't allow us to pass. I tried earlier and they shot PC Jenny Osborne, fatally wounding her. She had herself been bitten by Lois Maybank and become infected."

"Infected!"

"We are trapped in the village."

"Do you really expect us to believe that shit?" Carter slammed his fist on her desk.

"You wanted the truth. I gave it to you."

"Silly cow! You must think we're stupid."

Oldfield muttered. "I did see it."

Her head thrummed as pain tightened across her scalp. Glancing at the window, the sun had dropped behind the trees. She stared back into Carter's glaring eyes and held his gaze. "It will be dark soon. Go home. Stay safe behind locked doors. Barricade yourselves in and don't come out until sunlight. If you have weapons, arm yourselves."

"Hang on, Latimer. You're going over the top now."

"She's right," Oldfield added.

Carter scoffed. "You were drunk!"

It was her turn to became angry. "Listen!" She banged her fist on the desk. "If you'd seen what I've seen this afternoon, how fast these creatures move, how quickly they can gut a human being and rip out its entrails, then you wouldn't be standing here ignoring my advice. Go home. Lock yourselves inside. And don't come out until daylight."

Carter searched her face. A flicker of recognition registered in his and he drew back. "I'll give you the benefit of the doubt, Latimer," he said more quietly. "Don't mean that I believe you, like. But I think you believe yourself. Like you say, it's getting dark. Tomorrow I'm leaving this village, blockade or not."

The others murmured their agreement, and she caught their tentative glances towards the forest beyond the carpark.

"Right," Carter said finally. "I'm off." He disappeared through the door and the room emptied.

# CHAPTER THIRTY

Javeen slumped back in her chair, head thumping, and ran her hands through her hair, the short fringe stuck up, then slowly flopped down. The smell of her own body odour rose to her nostrils, and she had a sudden yearning to feel the strength of Andy's embrace. Unable to think clearly, her heart still beating too hard against her ribs, she took a breath to ease the tension. Her priority had to be to protect the village. The others were dead. Certainly Osborne, Ted, and Callum had been savaged, and Jerry Sykes sure to be bitten and infected, if not dead. Perhaps Harry too. Is that what had happened to Max and Lois? It seemed fantastical, she wasn't given to a belief in the supernatural, or men changing into werewolves at the full moon, but the creatures she had seen resembled the missing doctor and student. The creatures looked human, but not. Had something happened in the laboratory? It was the only sensible explanation. Perhaps one of the dogs was infected and bit Dr. Anderson who then went on to infect Lois in turn? But did that explain their ability to run at seventy miles per hour and jump from tree to tree with superhuman agility? No. Her head throbbed. It was all too much. Perhaps she'd wake from this nightmare, and everything would be normal. *Perhaps it wasn't real and she'd imagined it all. She was losing the plot.* She took another calming breath. *Think!*

Tipping forward to the desk she took a pen and paper and listed the names of the people so far recorded as missing. Then listed all the people who had reported a sighting. One name sprung out. Max Anderson. If it was him that had vaulted his own wall, then perhaps he had infected Laura too. Switching on her monitor, she opened a document, and began to type:

A notice is hereby given that from immediate effect a curfew is in place for Kielder Village from the hours 3pm to 8am.

Beneath it she typed:

To discuss the recent unusual sightings and incidents in the village, a meeting is to be held on 9am at the Village Hall. It is advisable for all villagers to attend.

She printed off the notice and with a pile slipped into a folder, she locked the Station door, checked for movement among the trees, then sprinted to the van determined to deliver as many as she could before twilight and then pay a visit to Laura Anderson—if she could summon the courage.

AS JAVEEN FINISHED her interview with Laura and made her way back to the police van with bile rising in her throat, Carl McGuire tightened the last screw fixing the sign to the post. He stood back to admire his efforts as his colleague secured a length of wire mesh across the road. In the twilight, the white sign, with its extra-large red print, was still visible. It read: BIOLOGICAL HAZARD. CONTAMINATED LAND. ENTRY PROHIBITED.

MAX UNCURLED FROM BENEATH the workbench, and away from the warmth of Lois's body curled next to his. His breath billowed white in the early evening gloom and his belly ached with hunger. He salivated as his thoughts returned to the woman with the dark hair. Sinking his teeth into her throat would be an ecstasy. He nudged the woman at his side. An ache passed over his groin as he leered over her naked flesh. Later, he would fill her again, but now he needed food. He prodded at her shoulder. She grunted as she woke and snapped at him with a curling lip. He snarled in return and prodded harder, grasped for words, grunted, and pointed to the door. The noise from his throat rasped through his vocal chords.

At the door, he breathed in the forest air; rich and rotting loam mixed with the faeces of a thousand tiny mammals and birds. The reek of a deer's rotting corpse carried in a twirl of stinking particles. He needed fresh meat. Without waiting for the woman, he sprinted into the forest, leaving the shed door to bang against the slatted wood. The nearby cabin, once bright, was dark. Ignoring the small house, and with Lois close behind, he sprinted into the woods. Body alive with adrenaline, his legs powered him forward, lithely jumping over fallen trunks, easily moving between the trees and their low-hanging, scratching branches. The moon wasn't yet high, but his eyes saw through the growing shade. Lois ran parallel with him through the trees, her quick panting interspersed with dry cackles. He glanced at her and grinned, the red of her eyes sparkled in the moonlight. Aroused by her scent, he leaped to her side, tripping her to the dirt. They embraced and rolled among the rotting leaves, jaws snapping. Fangs sank into his neck, an ecstasy of pain as she wrapped her legs around his hips. She cackled and grunted as he thrust at her heat.

Finished, he tipped his head back, opened jaws wide, and howled. She grabbed his arm, pulling him towards the village and the prey that cowered there.

# CHAPTER THIRTY-ONE

Startled from sleep, Freddie's head throbbed, and he regretted staying up so late, although the time had been well spent. He glanced over to Hayley, blonde hair splayed across the pillow, bedsheet doing nothing to disguise her curves. With an ache of desire, he reached over to pull the cover – *there's no time Fred. Just a little look then.* Another howl filled the room, one so loud that it could have been called from beneath the bedroom window. He dropped the sheet as the hairs on his neck prickled and his scrotum shrivelled. *What the hell was going on in this village?* Hayley murmured in her sleep and pulled at the bedclothes. He crossed the room, kicking yesterday's jeans to the skirting, and stepped to the window. An orange haze from the single streetlight filled the road outside. Nothing moved. Across the village there were one or two windows filled with light.

Another howl ripped through the dark morning as Freddie stepped out of the warmth of the bedroom and onto the pitch-black landing. He shivered as he fumbled for the light switch and closed the door behind him, not wanting to wake Hayley. The radiators hadn't come on yet, and the stone-built cottage was quick to lose heat in the winter months. He scratched at his beard, walked down the stairs, shivered, and pulled the cord on his dressing gown a little tighter, already missing Hayley's warmth. The nights ahead on the rig would be lonely. He shivered again as cold brushed his neck and padded to the bottom of the stairs.

Moonlight brightened the dark hallway to grey where a white fold of paper sat bright on the doormat. Reaching down, he grabbed the leaflet, stepped into the kitchen, and flicked the light on. Toby, their liver and white Springer Spaniel, raised its head from its basket next to the radiator and eyed him for a moment, decided he was of no interest, and returned to sleep. The windows reflected the room, and he was suddenly aware that anyone could see inside. He dismissed the thought; apart from the fact that theirs was the last cottage on Church Lane before the road disappeared back into the forest, no one would be outside at this time in the morning. *There was only him dumb enough to be getting up this early.* Today was his first day back after a couple of weeks off from the grind. He checked the clock. Five-thirty am. If he didn't get a move on, he would miss the boat out to the rig. For once, he was anxious to get back. All the howling in the village was setting everyone's nerves on edge, and even Hayley, usually so laid back and unafraid of anything, was getting the creeps. He grabbed a bowl, filled it with muesli, sprinkled it with walnuts and almonds, then added some more, mindful of his mother's warning voice to get enough protein.

As he pushed in another mouthful of cereal, dripping milk onto the table, and, with nothing else to occupy him, he unfolded the leaflet. It was, no doubt another flyer about the village dance, or Marjorie Maybank on the warpath again about dog mess on the path. Freddie had been much more vigilant since she'd read him the riot act in front of Sid at the shop, and he'd faithfully scooped the poop since then. He gave the dog a baleful glance as he remembered the encounter, then read the red and black print writ large on the sheet.

"What the hell! Curfew? On your bike, lady!" There was no way he, Freddie Barnes, was going to be forced to stay in his house between sunrise and sunset. Silly cow was as bad as the others—getting spooked by things going bump in the night and some creature howling in the woods. Like Farmer Burdon had said, the Lynx Trust had done the dirty and freed the lynxes on the sly. What else would have killed his sheep unless it was a dog gone mad? He mused on that for a moment. If that were the case, then the rabies outbreak down in Whitby had perhaps travelled as far as Kielder. They said it was untreatable and virulent—a mutated form. The media were scaremongering there too – as per bloody usual – calling the outbreak a plague, likening it to the Spanish flu of 1918. People really needed to get things in perspective, but it sold papers and advertising space no doubt.

He took another spoonful of muesli, crunched down hard on a hazelnut, and shook his head as he read the remainder of the notice. 'To discuss the recent unusual sightings and incidents in the village, a meeting is to be held at 9am at the Village Hall'. *Sod that for a laugh!* Hayley could go. He'd be well on the way back to the rig by then, and she had another day off before getting back to work. He lay the notice by the side of the kettle and returned to the bathroom to dress.

By the time Freddie had washed, dressed, kissed Hayley goodbye, and pulled on his bike leathers it was six-fifteen am, but still dark. He wheeled the Kawasaki out of the driveway and cringed for a second as the bike's engine roared into life. They'd have to put up with the noise; a man had to get to work, and it wasn't that often he had to start so early, and they were on the outskirts of the village after all.

Freddie manoeuvred the bike in the direction of the village, took a quick glance back at the cottage, then released the clutch. The bike powered forward, gliding past Emily Carmichael's cottage where light and movement caught his attention; Kathy was already at work. She was a good soul—washing a ninety-odd-year old's backside day in, day out, wasn't something he would be able to stomach. He shifted up a gear, passed the church, turned onto Main Street then rode past the shop where Sid had witnessed Freddie's dressing down at the hands of Marjorie Maybank. The only light came from his headlight and the orange haze cast by the sparse streetlights.

Movement to the right, between two houses, caught his attention. He dismissed it; spotting the odd cat, fox, badger, or even deer, at this time of the morning wasn't unusual. With much of the village still asleep, he increased his speed, being careful not to rev the engine too hard. As he left the outskirts, passing the sign proclaiming 'Kielder Village England's most isolated village', a figure caught in the edge of his light then disappeared. He swerved, nearly running onto the verge. As his headlamp illuminated the edge of the road and the woodland beyond, yellow light flashed over a figure, highlighting its limbs and head. Arms rose to block out the glare, and its teeth bared in an angry snarl. *What the hell had he just seen?*

He changed up a gear, pulled down his visor, and opened the throttle. The Kawasaki powered forward. He checked the mirrors. Nothing was visible. He checked either side, swinging his head round to peer beyond the visor's limits. Nothing. He focused on the road ahead, processing the bizarre images now stamped into his memory. That each of the figures had been female was obvious from their bare, and freely moving, breasts. Both looked human but had been covered in – he grimaced – hair. It had been particularly thick between their legs but covered the rest of their bodies too, even their faces. *And what had happened to their faces!* The eyes had glinted in the dark, but when the light travelled across their bodies, the eyes were like dark pools of blood. *What the hell were those things?* The one that had raised its arms to cut out the bike's light had drawn back its lips in a grimace to reveal sharp incisors that resembled fangs.

*Someone was winding him up.* He wouldn't put it past Craig to pull a stunt like this. Craig knew what time Freddie had planned leave and he had also mentioned old Mrs Carmichael's tale of seeing a stark naked wolfman jumping over Max Anderson's wall. They'd laughed, said that it was the most action the old biddy had seen in decades, then got a little spooked when Hayley added that Kathy Oldfield had told her Billy had also seen one. They'd decided the whole village was getting over-excited, but now Freddie was seeing things too—unnatural things—things that shouldn't exist. His chest tightened. Get a grip, Freddie. It was just a trick of the light. *Yeah, two naked women running through the woods with their tits jiggling, snapping their fangs at him—just a trick of the light!* He snorted with derision; the image of the two 'women' strong in his mind. One was lithe and young with small, pert breasts, and dark hair. The other was obviously older, a natural blonde with larger breasts. Both were muscular though—*two bodybuilding, hairy as fuck, butt-naked werewolves.* Heart hammering, Freddie increased the distance between himself and the village, and whatever was running in the woods.

Pressure clamped down on his shoulder.

The bike swerved as he fought to keep it under control. He snapped his head round to look behind as a clawed hand disappeared into the gloom. *What the fuck!* The bike straightened and he pulled the throttle back and accelerated, forcing himself to focus on the road ahead, despite the pain in his shoulder. He checked the mirror and the blonde wolfman – *wolfwoman!* - dropped out of view.

Ahead, the rising sun was turning the sky from navy to thin grey, and the forest sat as a thick band of jagged black turrets across the horizon. He checked the mirror. Whatever had attacked him was nowhere to be seen. Heart pounding, his thoughts turned to the village and his gut began to twist. Whatever had attacked him could attack Hayley. Stomach knotted, he powered the bike forward, increasing its speed from ninety, and then to one hundred and twenty miles per hour. As the road disappeared into another bank of trees, he slowed and swung around. Behind, the forest loomed black, and the sky brightened. Before him was the road back to the village and whatever was crawling through the woods. He revved the engine and began the return journey, roaring past the village sign at one hundred and sixty miles per hour. *No hair-covered freak would stop him getting back home.*

LOIS SNAPPED AT KELLY as they left the road, leaving the wheels, noise, and man behind. *Too fast to claw and grab. Too fast to pull to the earth and sink her teeth into his throat.* Panting, Kelly bared her teeth as they ran side-by-side. She pushed against Lois. Rage flared and Lois jumped onto the woman's back. *The man was for her. Not Kelly-bitch.* The power of Lois' leap forced Kelly to the floor, and she sank her claws into flesh as she straddled her back. Blood seeped from the wounds. Kelly snarled, snapping her jaws as she twisted beneath Lois' weight. Lois bit down into her shoulder as Kelly twisted onto her back then sank fangs into her neck, pinning Kelly's head against a trunk. She bit hard, holding the woman in place. *The man had been hers. Kelly-bitch should have waited—waited for permission.* The woman quieted beneath Lois. She withdrew her fangs and sat back, staring down into Kelly's eyes and growled. *Mine. He was mine.* Blood dripped from her fangs, trickling to the skin through the light covering of hairs that swept across her chest.

# CHAPTER THIRTY-TWO

Freddie relayed his terrifying story to a disbelieving Hayley as Javeen waited for Doreen to unlock the door to the village hall. Their breath billowed as white clouds in the cold November air. Hands stuffed deep into her pockets, woollen hat pulled low, scarf wound tight around her neck and a thick, police-issue raincoat zipped with the poppers done up to the top, Javeen scanned the trees that once formed an enchanting, fairy tale-like border around the village but now only appeared dank and latent with terror. Despite the cold of the November morning, sweat had already made her underclothes damp. In her pocket was the sharpest kitchen knife she could find. She'd mulled over the weapon, knowing that carrying it would breach the law, but also knowing that leaving the house unarmed would make her far too vulnerable.

Sleep last night had been non-existent as she'd sat and listened to every creak of the branches from the trees surrounding her cottage. Images of PC Oldfield's snarling face smashing against the van's window, her eyes rimmed with blood, and then the men firing round after round into her body taunted her, along with Anita - poor, poor, Anita - disembowelled and hanging in the tree.

*Anita and Jim sitting in the tree. K. I. S. S. I. N. G.*

Javeen gritted her teeth. The damned rhyme just wouldn't stop repeating in her head. It was morbid, grotesque, a sign of the hysteria that she was trying so hard to hold back. Her hand gripped the handle of the hammer in her other pocket as she scanned the road, walls, cars, and trees for any sign of movement. *Come on, Doreen!*

With a shaking hand, Doreen unlocked the door and swung it open. A comforting waft of warmer air laden with the odour of cooking and floor polish wafted out as they entered. The door swung to a close.

"Could you lock it again, please, Doreen?"

Doreen gave a quick frown that flickered with concern and turned to lock the door then rubbed her gloved hands together. "I'll put the heating on. It's nippy in here and some of the older villagers will feel it."

"Thanks," she replied with pang of guilt; a large proportion of the village's population were pensioners, some still fit and full of energy, but a good number elderly. They would struggle to make it to the meeting. *What had she done? Calling the villagers out like this would make them all easy prey!* Her heart tapped a faster beat, her bowels suddenly queasy. *Get a grip! Stay in control.* She took a breath to calm herself, released some of the tension across her chest and walked to the rows of stacked chairs. Being busy, thinking of the meeting, and how she would deliver the 'news', would help her keep the horror of yesterday at bay.

As she finished setting out the chairs, a knock came at the door. Andy. She opened the door with relief.

"Morning, Jav." His usual smile had disappeared.

"Morning, Andy." It was as though they hadn't been intimate.

Through the doorway she could see other villagers making their way to the hall; they had about thirty seconds of privacy at most. *He'd gone off her!* "What's wrong?"

Jaw clenched, he shifted his gaze across the room, a frown settling between his brows.

"Andy? What is it?" Dealing with a mardy bloke was the last thing she needed. "I'm sorry I haven't been to see you, but yesterday was-"

"It's Topsy. She's missing. She never goes off." Javeen's relief was instant. "I let her out in the back garden last night. She was wary at first, but desperate, practically crossing her legs. I watched her disappear to the end of the garden. She's clean like that; doesn't like to do it in the garden, only right at the end. I trained her to go down there to do her business when she was a puppy. If we don't go out for a walk, then she goes down there." He was gabbling, obviously on edge. "I watched her go, Jav. She didn't come back."

A stone sank in Javeen's belly. Topsy was a beautiful Springer Spaniel that Andy treated as well as he would a precious child.

"This was last night?"

"Yes. About ten o'clock. I stood at the door waiting, but she didn't come back. I called her. Went down with a torch to find her. The garden backs onto the woods but there's a hedge at the bottom and a gate. She was nowhere, Jav. Do you think it was those lynxes?" His voice rose in pitch. "I'm not buying into the whole 'wolfman' hysteria. Do you think they could have attacked her like they did Thomas Burdon's sheep?"

"I-"

The figures of Billy Oldfield, Jack Renwick, and Simon Carter darkened the door's window. Javeen unlocked the door and asked them to take a seat.

"People are arriving, Andy ... Can we talk afterwards?" He nodded and took a seat as more villagers arrived. Low chatter filled the room, mingling with a hum of anxiety and tension. People smiled politely at one another, though no one laughed, and Javeen wondered what gossip had gotten around so far. Billy Oldfield had walked in with a new confidence, shoulders squared—a man vindicated. Beside him, Kathy helped the Reverend Baxter to sit.

By nine o'clock, the small village hall was full, although she estimated that at least half of the villagers had remained at home. She checked across the room, taking in the sea of faces. At some point it would be useful to take down their names, an inventory of sorts, in case anyone else went missing.

Moving to the front of the hall, the room fell silent. She coughed to clear her throat. "First of all, I'd like to thank you all for coming here this morning. I realise that my call for a meeting was short notice and likely to have caused a good deal of anxiety. I apologise for that." She scanned the room, shoulders back, making eye contact where possible, the voice of authority, despite the tremors that ran through her fingers and seemed to shoot up her arms. She took a breath. There was no point hiding the truth. She had thought hard about how to present the information to the villagers, she didn't want to frighten them, but they needed to realise just how much danger they were in. "There is no easy way to say this, but the exit routes out of the village appear to have been blocked off."

A murmur spread through the crowd.

"You called us here to tell us about roadworks?"

"Not just roadworks. There's something up in the woods."

"Yeah. Wild bloody animals that have no place in the forest. Lynx UK have dumped on us!"

She tried again. "The road to Stannersburn has been block-"

"You're not wrong. But why the hell you have to call a meeting about that-"

"Listen to the girl!"

"Pah! You listen. I tried to get through last night. I tried the old road as well. The same. It's just roadworks. I even talked to the workmen. They're doing it at night so as to cause the least amount of disruption."

The hall filled with noise as the villagers began to offer their opinion.

Javeen remained silent and looked out across the gathering. They had to be told. She stuffed trembling hands back down into her pockets, fingering the handle of the knife in her pocket. She held up a hand and the room grew quiet. "It's not just ... They're not roadworkers," she stated.

"Well, who the hell are they?"

"Two days ago," she scanned the room, cheeks burning. "Two days ago, I entered Kielder Forest, to the west of the village, with PC Stuart Stangton in order to commence search efforts for Lois Maybank and ... another missing girl."

"Two girls!"

A mumble shifted across the crowd then died to silence as she continued.

"One of the girls was found." A relieved murmur followed the information. "Unfortunately, the girl appeared to have been mauled to death and had died of her injuries." She held back the truth that poor Anita had been eviscerated, her entrails and organs missing.

The crowd gasped.

"It's them lynxes. Burdon lost three sheep—gutted they were."

The noise level in the room increased. Javeen held a hand up and it quietened once more.

"There is perhaps evidence to suggest that a lynx, perhaps more than one, has been set free within Kielder."

"Told you! I told you."

Javeen held her right arm up again. "However, there is something far more dangerous in the woods than a lynx. The girl PC Stangton and I found had been ... mutilated, and I believe it was by the same creature that killed Mr James Kendrick."

Another gasp. "Jim's dead?"

"What about his girl? His daughter's missing too. Is she dead?"

"I can only confirm that Mr Kendrick is dead. Killed by the same ... monster-"

"Monster!"

"Monsters! For crying out loud. What are you talking about?"

"She means a killer. Is there a serial killer out in the woods?"

Javeen took a deep breath. *Killers – plural – but not the type you're thinking of.* "I have reason to believe ..." *No, not reason to believe, you know!* She took another breath. *What she was about to tell them was beyond belief—they would think her a raving lunatic.* They might laugh at her. Dismiss her.

"I can confirm-"

The door swung open. Javeen flinched - *it should have been locked!* - but sighed with relief as Freddie Barnes stepped into the hall, clutching Hayley Wilson to his side.

# CHAPTER THIRTY-THREE

"Mr Barnes, could you please lock the door."
Without noticing Javeen's request, Freddie strode across the room clasping Hayley close to his body, his hand locked to hers, his frown a deep crevice.

She tried again. Louder this time. "Mr. Barnes. Could you lock the door behind you? Please?"

A murmur ran through the group.

"She's locking us in!"

"What the hell is going on?'

Freddie caught her gaze, nodded, pulled Hayley with him back to the door, and turned the keys in the lock.

The tightness across Javeen's shoulders bit as she waited for Freddie and Hayley to settle at the end of the first row of chairs before speaking once more. She took a breath and continued to address the villagers. "Yesterday, I entered Kielder Forest to the west of the village along with a team of police officers in order to locate the body of the murdered girl as well as to search for Doctor Max Anderson and Lois Maybank, both of whom had been reported as missing." She stopped to catch her breath and let the information sink in. The room was attentive, all chatter stopped. "The team consisted of four police officers and a police dog." She swallowed, forcing down the quiver rising in her throat. "I am the only one who returned alive."

The room gave a collective gasp then erupted with a barrage of questions.

"Who killed them?"

"What the hell killed that many people?"

Chairs scraped.

"Are we safe?"

"What the hell is going on?"

"Please ... Please. Let me speak. I can only answer your questions one at a time."

"Let her speak!" Billy Oldfield bellowed as he stood. "There are monsters up in the forest. I've seen one." The room grew quiet. "Nobody would believe me, and yes, I admit I was drunk, but I saw what I saw."

Kathy rose beside him. "Emily Carmichael's seen it too. And so has Reverend Baxter." She gestured to the elderly man in the seat beside her. "He's seen it up close. You have, haven't you Reverend." The room became silent.

With the help of Kathy at his elbow, Reverend Baxter stood and turned to face the villagers. "I saw two of them. They came into the churchyard and walked right up to me. They ... seemed to be to be human, but so much changed that you could no longer believe that they were."

"I told you! I told you!" Billy shouted.

"If they're not human, then what are they?"

"They ... I do believe the male was Max Anderson-"

A villager snorted in derision.

The reverend continued. "The woman looked," he swallowed, "though her face was distorted, the creature looked like Lois Maybank, Marjory's daughter."

The room erupted once more.

"If I could ask for quiet, please!" Javeen shouted above the noise then waited for quiet to return. "I understand that this all sounds ... fantastical-"

"A horror movie, more like."

Javeen continued. "I am able to corroborate the Reverend's experience with my own. The three creatures-"

"Three!"

"The three creatures that attacked the team of police officers in the woodland did bear striking similarities to Doctor Anderson and Lois Maybank."

"The other? You said three."

"The other, I now believe to be nurse Kelly Gray."

"Iain said she'd been bitten."

"Where is Iain."

"He went up to the cottage after we were in the police station yesterday."

"Did he come back?"

Fear rippled through the room.

"What do these creatures look like?"

"Well ..." Javeen hesitated. What she was about to say sounded ridiculous even to her own ears. "Well, they seem to be mutated-"

"Mutated! What the fuck are you talking about?"

"Please, PC Latimer. Ignore them. Explain what you mean by 'mutated'."

"Well, and I know how this sounds, it's hard to believe, even I struggle, and I've seen it with my own eyes."

"Get on with it!"

No matter how odd it sounded, she couldn't hold back. "They have fangs-"

"Fangs! She's really taking the piss now."

"And their eyes are ... God, their eyes are monstrous—filled with blood-"

"This is a joke! It has to be."

"And ... and they're covered with hair."

"Shut up, Latimer. You know this is bollocks, right? She's talking bollocks. It's a cover up. How much did they pay you Latimer? Hey?"

"Cover up? What are you talk-"

"The Lynx Trust? Huh? How much did they pay you to make up this cock-and-bull story? They killed my sheep, them lynxes did, and you're here trying to cover it up. They won't get away with it, I promise you."

"Mr. Burdon. I assure you-"

The room erupted. A woman began to cry and grabbed her husband's coat. He slipped his arm around her then turned to the room with a snarl, "Shut up, the lot of you."

*Chaos! The meeting was descending into chaos.* In all of her imaginings of how this would go, this was not a scenario she had imagined. Panic? Yes. Tears? Yes. Anger? Yes. Disbelief and being accused of lying, and worse, being part of a cover up? No.

"Honestly, Mr. Burdon, I-"

Freddie Barnes moved from his position against the wall, stepped next to Javeen, and faced the villagers. "She's telling the truth."

Despite the boom of his voice, the noise in the room was too loud, the people too concerned with voicing their opinions, to listen. He shouted louder this time, his voice a deep rumble. "She ... is telling ... the truth." The bickering and worried voices stopped, and all eyes turn to Freddie. "I saw them ... this morning. When I left for the rig, it was still dark, and I was followed out of the village by two ... creatures ... female creatures. One of them tried to pull me from my bike."

"Rubbish!"

Freddie shrugged his overcoat from his shoulders and turned his back to the crowd. Beneath the overcoat, his jacket flapped where the leather had been slashed.

"Followed *out* of the village?"

Javeen could hardly breathe.

"Fake! He's in on it too."

"Freddie would never lie about a thing like that!" Hayley shouted and stepped beside him.

"Oh, really? Him and his mate Craig are well known about the village for their pranks. He's the first to brag about the latest stunt they've pulled."

"Show them, Freddie! Show them what the monsters did to you."

Silence followed.

With Hayley's help, Freddie removed his leather jacket. Beneath it was an undamaged shirt.

"See! See, I told you. He's a fraud."

Freddie turned to face the crowd and began to unbutton his shirt. Javeen had the uncomfortable feeling of hysteria rising once more. The thought of this man, undressing as though for a striptease, in the village hall in front of the Reverend and a large collection of his godly congregation, made her want to squeal with laughter. She took a breath. Hysteria, it seemed, was an affliction that this new level of stress had birthed within her. As the final button was undone, a collective gasp, along with a titter from one of the older ladies, rose. The man was broad-shouldered, with abs you could run your fingers over. Freddie turned and shrugged the shirt from his shoulders, his very muscular and tanned shoulders. The room gasped. Beneath the shirt were long red welts scored across his back. In places, the flesh was sliced.

"Freddie, those wounds need-" A sudden thought rocked her sensed. "Freddie ... did they bite you?"

Their eyes locked and Javeen pushed down the urge to run out of the hall whilst simultaneously scanning his body and calculating the time between the attack and now. Jenny had turned so quickly. Freddie looked normal without any sign of blood in his eyes.

"No. Just scratched."

"Thank God!"

"More like thank Kawasaki."

"Huh?"

"My bike. It's fast—that's what saved me."

Freddie faced the villagers as he pulled his shirt back over his shoulders. "These creatures are real. I know it seems impossible—like something out of a film, but two creatures ran after me out of the village, tried to pull me off my bike. I was doing about forty-"

A snort. "Forty miles per hour? Nothing can go that fast."

"A leopard can."

"Perhaps one escaped from a zoo?"

"They weren't leopards. The only reason I got away was because the bike could go faster. I lost them at about sixty."

"Impossible!"

"Jesus Christ!"

"So, we're talking about ... werewolves?"

"I don't know if they were, but the women that chased me had fangs, and like PC Latimer said, their eyes were just black, and they were covered in hairs too."

"Naked?"

"Yes."

"So," a teenage boy raised his hand, "were they hairy ... down there?" He gestured to his groin.

"Kyle!" The boy's mother glared. He lowered his head, and sniggered into his chest, his shoulders heaving.

"Sorry!" the mother offered. "He's just immature." She glared once more at her son, then trained her eyes on Javeen, waiting for her to continue.

"I know how this sounds. But I believe we are all in grave danger from these ... these ..."

"Wolfmen." Kathy offered. "That's what Emily called them."

"They do look a bit wolfish."

"OK. Wolfmen."

"What do you suggest we do?" Conrad Shelby hugged his wife a little closer, concern etched on his face.

"The first thing we need to do is secure our properties—make them as safe as possible. Don't go out alone. Don't go out without some form of protection. Keep to the curfew."

"Is that it? That's your great plan to save us against these 'wolfmen' that you've admitted killed an entire team of police officers, savaged a poor, innocent girl to death, and ran at speeds no human could achieve when they tried to attack Freddie?"

Javeen shook her head. *Poor, poor Anita.* What else could they do? She searched for an answer.

"And don't forget Jimbob!"

"Yes, and they killed Jimbob."

"We need to get out of the village. Not sit here waiting to be attacked."

"We need to evacuate."

"But aren't the roads closed off?"

Chairs scraped against the floorboards.

"It's just roadworks."

People began to make their way to the doors.

"No!" Javeen shouted. "Please! Everyone, sit down." As more people headed for the door, her plea was drowned out by the excited, fearful chatter of the villagers. "They're not roadworkers. Please. Sit down." The hall emptied. Unheeded, Javeen ran fingers through hair that had been neither washed nor brushed.

Minutes later, only seven people remained; Billy and Kathy Oldfield, The Reverend Baxter, Freddie Barnes, Hayley Wilson, Andy, and herself.

"That went well."

Javeen sagged and sat down with a thud.

"What now?"

"I don't know. I just don't know."

# CHAPTER THIRTY-FOUR

Matilda 'Tilly' Stangton pushed out through the village hall doors into the cold November morning. *Where the hell was Stuart?* Javeen had assured her that he hadn't accompanied her into the woodlands where the other officers were killed – her knees buckled, and she leant up against the wall. She said he'd gone into town but not returned. Now, given what she'd heard in the village hall, how Freddie Barnes had been attacked as he'd tried to leave the village, she was certain something terrible had befallen her husband on his way to town. Her mind searched for an explanation. Unable to stomach any of them, she grew numb. One thing was for sure, she wasn't going to wait in the village for whatever lay in the woods to kill her too. She grabbed Barry Johnson's sleeve as he pushed past.

"Barry. What are you going to do?"

"We're leaving." Belinda, his wife, butted in, pulling her coat around her, slipping her arm through her husband's.

"Come with us, Tilly."

The wife frowned. She always had been a jealous woman. If she only knew what she and Barry had got up to when they were teenagers! Had he told her about their relationship? Is that why she was jealous? Did it matter?

"We'll leave at two pm," he said decisively. "That'll give us time to pack up a few things."

"We're going to stop with relatives in Newcastle until this all gets sorted out."

Barry rolled his eyes. "Let's just get out of the village. Susan may not have room for us. We can go to a hotel."

His wife nodded. "Or even go on holiday. I'll pack our passports." Her worried frown turned to a smile as she looked beyond Tilly's shoulder to the road ahead and their house. "We could do with a holiday."

"I'll follow you, then."

Allan Jenkins leant in from behind Belinda's shoulder. "Leaving at two, did you say?"

"That's the plan."

"Mind if I tag along?"

"No. Please do."

A small crowd gathered around Barry and Tilly and for the next ten minutes the villagers discussed the practicalities of leaving as a convoy. Some wanted to head north to the Scottish border, whilst others wanted to head south and onwards towards Newcastle and the midland counties. Allan Jenkins decided that an impromptu visit to his daughter in Spain was essential to relieve his wife's stress. She clung to his arm, jittery, her eyes flitting about the treeline.

As Tilly made her way home, twenty-five villagers had agreed to travel in convoy to the southern border, and she had decided to ask Mavis, who didn't drive and whose husband had died last year if she would like to accompany her. She couldn't leave the woman behind; she was family now. Living in the isolated village, raising their daughter without her own mother around - God rest her soul - it had been a godsend to be taken under Mavis' large and generous wing. She'd became a surrogate grandmother to her daughter and almost a mother to Tilly as well. Stuart hadn't bonded quite so well, but he was a taciturn old goat anyway and didn't even bother with his own mother. Not that she could blame him; Mrs Pamela Patricia Stangton was just as taciturn as he was, like mother, like son.

By two o'clock. Tilly had packed an overnight bag, complete with toiletries. She had also checked the oil and water levels in the car. There were sandwiches, biscuits, a flask of tea, and another with hot water, coffee, mugs, and all the fruit she'd bought last week. She had emptied the fridge and put all the perishables in the bin. The door was locked, the curtains drawn, and Mavis was in the front seat wrapped up and wearing her favourite woolly hat. In short, the car was ready for an escape. She pulled the door open and slid in behind the wheel.

Mavis was quick to speak.

"Kane Barley said that Kathy Oldfield had told him that the wolfman that attacked Jim Kendrick had fangs and dragged him off into the woods as though he were a ragdoll."

"Uhuh. Didn't she say it was Max Anderson?" She turned the ignition.

"And Emily said he was hung like a donkey."

Tilly snorted. "Emily said that?"

"Aye. She's getting a bit crude in her old age."

"Well, she is over eighty, perhaps nearly ninety. I'll forgive her."

Mavis pulled the blanket over her legs. "Do we have anything to defend ourselves with, if we get cornered by this well-endowed and hairy beast?"

Tilly couldn't help but burst out laughing. "Mavis!"

"Tree loppers perhaps."

"Mavis!" Tilly creased with laughter. "You make everything better. Do you know that?"

Mavis chuckled. "I try my best. If it was Max Anderson, no wonder Laura always had a smile on her face."

Tilly burst with laughter.

"But in all seriousness, if there is a maniac on the loose out there, well-endowed or not, we should have something to protect ourselves with."

Mavis was right. "Give me a minute." Tilly headed to the garage and returned five minutes later with a selection of Stuart's tools. He was fastidious about keeping his shed in order, and everything had a place. His obsession with its organisation had driven her nuts but, on this occasion, she was thankful; the tools were easy to find, clean, and very sharp.

As she slammed the door shut, having selected a weapon each for them to carry, and laying the remainder in the boot, Conrad Shelby, with Moira in the passenger seat, and then Amy Carmichael passed in their cars. Conrad's back seat was piled with what looked like duvets and pillows, whilst Amy's was filled with her children. Tilly slipped into gear and pulled out of the driveway, joining the small convoy as it left the village. Mavis looked to the trees nervously. She gripped Stuart's chisel tight and rubbed her thumb along its length.

"You alright, Mavis?"

"Yes, of course. Just hoping for a sighting."

Tilly laughed. "You're incorrigible, Mavis."

"I try my best."

The women laughed for a moment then fell silent. Tilly turned the radio on. The crackling of untuned radio waves filled the car. She attempted to tune it whilst keeping an eye on the road. Silence was interspersed with white noise. Mavis remained quiet as Tilly sighed, frustration mingling with an edge of fear; she really couldn't bear to be blocked from the outside world like this. The severing of communications, whether it was voices from across England on the radio, or the movement of images on the television had made her feel hemmed in—as though they were all trapped in a bubble. The feeling was only compounded by not being able to talk to her daughter; their daily chats were one of the highlights of her lonely days. The talk of the roads being blocked off had increased that sense of isolation and she had begun to appreciate the claustrophobic's anxiety at being shut in, even though there were wide-open spaces all around her.

She switched the radio off, biting back her unease. Ahead four cars led the way, with Conrad Shelby at the front. With him at the helm, she could rest a little easier; he was a true leader, a former Wing Commander in the Royal Air Force, and still carried himself with the innate confidence of a man of that position, despite having been retired for the past nineteen years. Tilly has a secret crush on him - fuelled by the man's uncanny resemblance to an older version of Cillian Murphy. That he shared a name with one of the actor's more intensely appealing characters was a joy that she hugged to herself. Behind, the convoy of cars had grown.

"Looks like most of the village is leaving!"

Mavis twisted to look. "There must be at least twenty cars behind us."

"Good! They'll have to let us pass the roadworks."

"They will. And if they won't let us past on the road, then we'll just have to go around them."

"I certainly hope so. I wouldn't want to have to go through them."

"Perhaps they've already finished the work on the roads. Afterall, there are only a few potholes on that stretch."

The women continued to chatter until the road seemed to disappear into a bank of trees as the road wound downwards. The car in front slowed, its brake lights burning red. Tilly slowed with a lurch, apologised as Mavis jerked forward, then stopped. The car in front had come to a standstill. Across the road was a barricade of steel panels that stretched from one side of the road to the other.

"What the very hell is that?"

"A ruddy great fence!"

The driver's door of the car in front swung open, and Conrad Shelby stood, hands on hips staring at the huge steel structure.

"Come on, Tilly. Let's go and find out what's happening."

"But, shouldn't we leave it to Conrad?" Tilly's innards were suddenly queasy.

"Not on your Nelly!" Mavis retorted. "I want to know exactly what's going on. You don't find that out by cowering in the car." Mavis was a resilient woman, becoming feistier with age. "Come on gal. Let's go."

# CHAPTER THIRTY-FIVE

Conrad scanned the forest and the road, checking for any sign of movement. All was quiet, seemingly normal, apart from a dirty great metal fence sitting across the road that stretched into the trees either side making an evacuation impossible. He wasn't convinced of the wolfman hypothesis – it was too outlandish to be true – but that there was someone, or a number of people, attacking and killing the villagers, he was in no doubt. PC Latimer's report of the destruction of the police team in the woods, and the further testimonies of attacks, had convinced him that he should lead the villagers out of the area until the police had apprehended the attackers. He had even mulled over the possibility of it being a peculiar terrorist attack; serial killers, after all, weren't known to work in groups, although it wasn't wholly unheard of.

"What on earth is this, Conrad?"

"It's a blockade."

"Obviously, but didn't Latimer say there were barriers with workmen?"

"She did."

"This isn't any kind of roadblock I've seen before and there are no workmen."

Conrad walked up to the fence. It reached for at least another seven feet above his six-foot three frame. He tapped.

Solid. Massive bolts held down the steel panels. He fingered them. It was not the first time he had seen such a structure; Nogales, Arizona, in 2015. He'd visited the US in his role as security consultant. After leaving the forces, he'd earned three times the money working in the private sector.

"Whoever put this up has no intention of letting us pass." He peered through to the road on the other side. More construction was taking place, but the workmen were temporarily absent.

"Who the hell put it here?"

*Someone with government backing, enormous influence, and perhaps military collusion.* "I don't know."

Tilly stepped beside him. "There's a sign bolted on the other side." She pointed to the edges of a white metal panel.

He pulled out his phone and swiped at the screen. That communications between the outside world and the village had been cut off for the past days was deeply concerning, but at least his expensive piece of technology wasn't completely redundant. He clicked the phone's camera on and held it, lens upwards, through the barrier, and clicked.

Pulling it back, his innards knotted.

"What does it say?"

He cleared his throat. *This was serious.* "It reads, 'Biological hazard. Contaminated land. Entry prohibited.'"

"What?"

Other villagers gathered around them.

"Biological hazard! What does that mean?"

"Contaminated land? Has there been an accident? Isn't that what they say when they find anthrax or something, or nuclear waste? We don't have that around here!"

"They found anthrax years ago further south. They took it out of the area at night by train, so no one knew."

"What? Here?"

"No. In the north midlands, a town near the Humber Bridge. They didn't put a sodding great wall up and trap people on the land though."

"We're trapped?"

"Looks like one of those border walls they put up to stop migrants."

"How can we be migrants? We live here."

"Tsk! We're not. I just said it looked like one."

Conrad blocked out the excited chatter, focusing on his next step. Something was dreadfully wrong. Someone was attacking and killing the villagers in a most savage manner, and they had, in effect, been imprisoned along with him, or her. He needed - they needed - to find out who was behind it but making sure the gathered evacuees were safe had to be his number one priority.

"Everyone back in your cars."

"But we're supposed to be evacuating!"

The sun had begun its descent, the trees casting longer shadows over the clearing, turning to black behind a lowering apricot sky. He checked his watch and noticed the marks in the road and adjacent grass. Bullet marks. He scanned the grass. Blood. Latimer had been telling the truth. Someone had been shot here. Shot perhaps wasn't the correct word. From the spray of bullets and the blood on the grass, the body must have been shredded. There was no evidence of a body though, and the area had been cleaned of debris. There were the marks of bullets but no casings, or remnants of flesh. He scanned the fence once more, thankful now that whoever erected it was no longer here, and moved back to his car.

Among the trees, a figure moved.

His heart began to thud. "Everybody back in your cars."

Tilly, still at his side, caught his glance towards the forest. A mewl caught in her throat, and she grabbed his sleeve. "Did you see it?"

"Tilly, would you please return to your vehicle?"

"But there was something in the trees. I saw it."

"Just a deer, I think. It's hard to see anything in the trees now."

"But-"

Sweat began to dampen his underarms. "We can't get through this way. It's best if we turn around."

"Back to the village?"

"Yes, back to the village."

As Tilly turned from him, Mavis guiding her towards the car, he scanned the forest. Another figure moved among the trees, and then another. He made an effort to focus in the diminishing light. Multiple figures seemed to flit among the dark trunks. He turned his attention back to the evacuees. Cars had pulled up politely, one behind another and many were too close for an easy, unimpeded, three-point turn and rapid escape. He made a quick calculation; getting them to turn around wouldn't be too difficult if the car at the end moved back first. He turned to the group, ushering them back to their cars, requesting that the cars at the back move first, as the creeping sensation of being watched crawled over his neck and across his shoulders.

From the other side of the fence, a vehicle came into view through its bars.

AMY CARMICHAEL TUGGED at her son's arm as she ushered him back to the car. Her daughter stood close to her side.

"I need a pee, Mum."

"You'll have to wait until we get back to the village."

"We're going back?" Her daughter's voice carried the pith of anxiety. She huffed. "There's no Wi-Fi there, Mum," she whined.

"Not now, Jasmine," her mother retorted and turned her attention back to her son. He tugged at her grip on his sleeve.

"Mum! I need to pee. Now!"

"There are no toilets here, Caleb."

"I can pee in the trees. You say to do that when we're on a walk."

Amy glanced at the crowds of people and the darkening treeline. "That's when we're on our own. There are a lot of people here."

"Do it behind the car," Jasmine offered.

"No way!" He turned to look at the gathering of villagers. "I don't want people seeing my tackle."

Jasmine snorted. "There's nothing to look at."

Caleb huffed. "I'll go to the trees."

Amy checked around. The villagers were either returning to their cars or standing in groups, some obviously riled, debating about what to do next. Karen Jenkins was in tears

– nothing new there – and Flight captain – or whatever – Conrad Shelby was standing with a smaller group pointing at the cars and giving commands. A few people seemed to be staring into the treeline fifty feet to the right. "OK," she relented. "Go over to those trees." She pointed to the other side of the road where the trees were about thirty feet away. "But be quick," she shouted to his back as he ran towards the large pines. "We'll be in the car."

Amy took another step closer to the car and was knocked against a front bumper as a woman ran blindly past. She grunted as dull pain moved through her thigh muscle. A hush descended. Instinctively casting a glance towards the villagers, she followed their gaze to the treeline. Among the trees, hugging the shadows, but easy to discern, were the distorted figures of numerous - *what in God's name were they?* - creatures. She peered for a second, squinting for a clearer view, her head spinning with confusion. She recognised one as a still curvaceous, but oddly deformed version of her beautiful friend Kelly. She swallowed. Kathy had said that Kelly had been bitten, but surely to goodness there was nothing on this earth that could cause such a hideous transmogrification so quickly. She'd seen hideous diseases that destroyed bodies, deformed their victims into monsters, but nothing that could act so quickly, they took years. The thing shifted and danced among the trees and ferns, hopping from foot to foot in agitation. *What was it waiting for? Caleb!* She twisted to see him relieving himself against the ferns then glanced back to the creatures among the trees. They *were* waiting—anxiously, excitedly, each one stepping in and out of the shadows, among the trees, squatting, hopping, cackling. Her skin crawled at the noise of their shrieking chatter. They were naked, or partially clothed with remnants of cloth, some with ripped t-shirts, or jeans that were nothing more than a waistband and a shred of denim. A thin layer of dark hair lay over their skin, very much thicker between their legs. Heart palpitating, she grabbed Jasmine's sleeve in a slow motion and urged her to step to the car.

These were the creatures that PC Latimer and Freddie Barnes had told them about. She hadn't really believed them, there were no such things as wolfmen, or zombies, or wendigos, they were all myth. Sure, there was something in the woods attacking them, but she'd thought it was only logical to believe that it was someone dressing up, a weirdo serial killer, or murderous cult perhaps, but not wolfmen.

She took another step towards the car, unsure whether to just pelt it down the road to reach it or walk slowly. *Stay calm! How the hell could she? There were monsters in the woods staring at her and her kids ... Caleb!* She swung around. Caleb had his back to them, oblivious of the wolfmen on the other side of the road.

"Caleb!" Her voice was thrown as a whisper that caught in her throat. Alternating between the monsters in the forest and her son, she called him again, keeping her voice low as he did his zipper up. "Caleb, come on!"

"Coming, Mum!"

*Too loud!*

The creatures shrieked as he called.

She beckoned him with rising panic. "Quick!"

There were three more cars to go before theirs. Caleb turned, pulling at his zipper. She panicked and motioned for him to be slow and steady, to be quiet as he walked to her. *No sudden movements!* In the forest the creatures hung back in the shadows, unafraid of being seen. Her stomach knotted. What were they waiting for? Javeen had talked of how she and the other police officers had been ambushed, how they had seemed to track them through the woods. Hadn't she said Max Anderson had been one of them? She scanned the trees. She couldn't see Max, but there were three women, a girl that could be Rachel, Jim Kendrick's daughter and two males, neither of which bore any resemblance to Max.

As Caleb joined them, she walked with a quicker step, making efforts to keep her movements smooth, desperate not to trigger the creatures into action. Caleb opened his mouth to speak and caught sight of the creatures among the trees. His mouth snapped shut. As Amy grabbed his arm with a firm grip and ushered him towards the car, movement caught her eye. A large figure stood among the trees. Amy's breath caught in her chest. The figure, a large male, stepped out from the trees only ten feet from where Caleb had relieved himself. It was Max Anderson. Amy tightened her grip around the car keys and pulled them from her pocket. They were surrounded. The man, the thing that had once been Max Anderson, locked its blood-red eyes on her, its lips pulled back over an elongated jaw. Incisors, bone-white and pointed, glistened with saliva as its head tipped back. "Run!" she hissed at Caleb and Jasmine. "Run!" She grabbed their sleeves and pushed them forward as the thing that had been Max howled.

"Run!"

Chaos erupted as the creatures broke from the shadows, and guttural, primal howls burst from open jaws. The monsters moved with incredible speed towards the convoy.

The air filled with screams, shouts, howls, and a dreadful insane snickering.

# CHAPTER THIRTY-SIX

Javeen peered out of the window as the first car pulled up. Amy Carmichael. The woman cornered with tyres screeching then rolled to an abrupt halt only feet from the front door, almost scratching Javeen's car. She opened the Station door, and Amy ushered her children from the car, pushing them over the threshold. Javeen slammed the heavy door behind them, quickly locking and bolting it.

As she waited for Amy to catch her breath, a second car passed the station, reversed, entered the car park, and screeched to a stop next to Amy's. Conrad Shelby jumped out followed by Tilly Stangton and his wife Moira. The woman's face and eyes were red with tears. Javeen unbolted the door to let them in as Amy pulled her children close, her sob heavy with relief.

"We were attacked," Conrad blurted as soon as the door shut behind him. Thick iron bolts slotted into place with a satisfying, and reassuring, clack.

Javeen offered Stuart's chair to Tilly, who appeared on the verge of collapse, then turned her attention to Conrad. "What happened?"

"The roads are blocked, as you said, but the barriers you spoke of at the village hall have been upgraded to impassable, twenty-foot high, steel girders."

"And the men?"

"There were no men, not at first, but as we were leaving, I saw a vehicle pull up on the other side and armed men get out."

"Police?"

"From the vehicle and their demeanour, I would say a private security firm, although one of military standard."

"What does that mean?" Amy butted in.

"My assessment of the situation is that whoever it is knows just how dangerous these creatures are and wants to keep the situation contained," explained Conrad.

"Contained?"

"One of them had a tranquiliser gun." Caleb added. "I watched him fire it at a werewolf."

"They're not werewolves!"

"How do you know it was a tranquiliser?"

"I saw it stick into the werewolf's neck—it had feathers on it like they do in the wildlife programmes. I saw one where they were shooting at elephants from a helicopter."

"Why would they tranquilise them? They should be killing them—to protect us!"

"Perhaps saving us isn't the main objective."

"How can that be so? If there are wild animals trying to kill us, shouldn't the military be coming in to try and rescue us."

"Perhaps they will."

Javeen's head throbbed. Their communications with the outside world, their ability to call for help, to report what was going on, had been blocked, as had their escape routes. Whoever was in control of this situation didn't want anyone knowing about it, of that she was certain.

"And take a look at this, Latimer." Conrad pulled his phone out of his pocket.

For one moment Javeen's hope flared. "You've got a signal?"

Conrad shook his head. "Sorry, Latimer. No. But I did get a photograph of the sign that had been bolted to the fence."

He pushed the mobile's screen into view. The knot in Javeen's stomach tightened as he scrolled back through the photographs, flickering past a scene that began with dark figures running from the woods to them lingering in the shadows, the rows of cars, and then several of the sign, all of differing quality. He clicked on the one that was most legible.

She read, "Biological Hazard. Contaminated Land. Entry Prohibited." Her mind flitted back to the meeting at the *Institute* on the morning Billy Oldfield had called them to oust the placard waving vegan activists from their gates, the small group of oddly incongruous men in Marta Steward's office, and Blake Dalton's shocked face when he'd received that call at the *Hound and Stars*.

"I heard him talking about 'staying calm' and 'seeing it as an opportunity'"

"Who, Latimer? And what 'opportunity'?"

"Blake Dalton."

"Who?"

"A colleague of Doctor Steward's from the *Institute*. He was armed."

"Why would a scientist be armed?"

"He wouldn't. I mean, he isn't."

"Armed?" Conrad's frown deepened.

"No, he's not a scientist and he was armed. I saw the gun strapped next to his ribs."

"So perhaps military?"

"I have no idea. The men at the fence who shot up PC Osborne looked as though they could be soldiers."

"Hmm."

Tilly Stangton erupted with a sob. "Mavis is dead!"

Moira walked across to Tilly and put an arm around the woman.

"Mavis is dead. Kelly ... Kelly Gray split her belly open like a packet of crisps and ate her insides!"

Jasmine began to cry.

"That thing – Kelly – she was going for me, but Mavis ... Mavis got in the way, and she ate her instead." Tilly dissolved into sobs.

Caleb put a protective arm across his sister's shoulder. He stared for a moment at Javeen, and then at Conrad, a frown creasing the brows of his young face. "I'll kill them monsters." His teeth bared as he spoke. "They'll not hurt my mum or my sister."

Amy managed a weak smile at her son. "We'll protect each other, love. Don't you worry."

Amy glanced beyond the window to the darkening sky. "We should go home. Before it gets dark."

"No!" Tilly blurted. "I don't want to be alone."

"You can come home with us," Conrad offered.

"What about us?" asked Caleb. "Can we come home with you too?"

"Caleb, we've got our own home to go to."

"Yes, but no man to protect us, Mum."

"Your dad will be back soon," she soothed. "Phil's out on the rig," she explained. "He's due back next week."

Javeen's hope flared. People would be trying to get into the village and Phil was bound to raise a stink if he couldn't get back to his wife and children. There was sure to be a rescue mission, there had to be.

Another car passed the Police Station, but this time didn't turn into the carpark.

"Hell!" Conrad blurted. "There were more than thirty cars in that convoy, Latimer. So far only three cars have made it back."

Javeen swallowed. Even if there was a rescue mission, at the rate the villagers were being killed, it would be too late.

# CHAPTER THIRTY-SEVEN

A ndy stepped back through the French doors at the rear of his house. He had spent the last few hours searching at the end of his garden, going into the woods, as far as he dared, to look for Topsy. With a bag of chicken flavoured treats in his pocket, he clicked the sliding doors shut with a sigh. The woods had been quiet, no sign of any 'beast', but no sign of Topsy either. He broke his shotgun over his arm, removed the cartridges, lay it on the dining room table then locked the doors and drew the curtains. The sun had dropped below the forest canopy leaving a jagged bank of trees black against a darkening sky. A single star shone bright.

A rapid series of knocks came at the front door. As he answered, Javeen practically fell into the hallway, her face flushed.

"What's wrong?"

"Close the door."

Closing the door, he locked it as she made her way to the kitchen. "What's wrong?"

"Everything!"

He flicked the kettle on.

"The convoy was attacked by the wolfmen. Only three cars made it back."

"Which convoy?"

"Conrad's."

"Hell!"

"Andy, he said the fences there were massive and that there was no way of getting through and the villagers were ambushed by the wolfmen and-"

"Slow down, Jav."

"There were at least ten of them."

"Wolfmen?"

"Yes!"

"I thought there was only Max Anderson and Lois Maybank."

"Tilly Stangton recognised Kelly Gray, and Conrad said there was a girl that could have been Jim Kendrick's daughter, and another woman that could have been Maria Konstapolis. Caleb Carmichael said there was another girl too, that could be her daughter. And there were two males that no one recognised, but ... but from the descriptions, I think they could have been Harry Pilkington and Jerry Sykes—the Police Officers attacked in the forest."

"So ... what we're talking about is a pack?"

"Yes! Conrad is sure that's what's happening. They're hunting in packs. They waited, Andy. They waited at the treeline until Max Anderson showed up. He appeared to give a signal for attack."

"Signal?"

"He howled. After that they charged. The villagers didn't stand a chance."

Andy remained silent with his thoughts. It was all so outlandish, would sound unbelievable to anyone who hadn't seen it.

"So ... so people are being bitten and becoming werewolves? Is that what we're saying?"

"... kind of."

His stomach knotted as realisation dawned. "So, they're being bitten and develop superhuman abilities and a desire to eat human flesh?"

"I think so."

"And we're trapped here with them ..."

"Yes."

"I went into the woods earlier. There was no sign of them."

"That was so dangerous, Andy!"

"I know, but I had to try and find Topsy."

"Did you?"

"No, not a sign of her."

The kettle boiled and Andy spooned coffee into two mugs, covered them with milk, and poured in the water. Javeen leant into him as she sipped her drink. Even though she was more than a foot shorter than him, he felt comforted by the arm that slipped around his back.

"Tilly said something odd. Kelly – the monster – sniffed at Conrad and then went for Tilly. She's only alive because Mavis tried to save her."

Andy took another sip of coffee as Javeen continued.

"It was like she smelt him and decided he was off or something."

"Maybe he's sick? It would make sense. They obviously see us as food—if the food's bad we can't stomach the smell so leave it. Didn't that happen to the Reverend too?"

"It did!"

"He's got pancreatic cancer."

"I didn't know."

"Billy told me. Kathy said he's terminal—only got a few months left."

As they stood in silence, holding each other, sipping their coffee, a howl erupted quickly followed by another.

"Sounds like playtime again."

Andy reached for the hammer on the kitchen table, walked across to the window, and nailed the last few wooden boards into place.

SQUATTING AT THE EDGE of the forest, the purple haze of twilight hung as a mist over the village. Lights flicked on, bright points of life against the dark. The pain of hunger stabbed at Lois' stomach, and she pulled in the sweet stench of the Screamers hiding in their light. The particles of their life-smell ... their meatiness ... their loving blood ... their intestines, their hearts, their livers – she groaned with pleasure – their slipping, dripping kidneys, hung in the air among the trees like tendrils of smoke. She raised her nose and sucked it in. Her mouth watered. A door banged somewhere among the lights. An engine started. A Screamer called, his voice distant but tapping at her eardrums. 'Topsy!' it called. 'Topsy!' Behind her the Others gathered, pushing their warmth against her. A Small clung to her side, wrapping its arm around her back. Sharp claws dug into her flesh as it anchored its hand. She growled but let it lay its head against her shoulder.

The One stepped to her side, kicking at the Small. It scurried to her other side and clung to her there. The One, the Max, grunted. She cackled as he pointed at the lights, the urge to tear warm, pulsing flesh riding her, making her jaw ache, and teeth gnash with anticipation. Kelly-Bitch, slid up beside him, her arm passed across his back. Lois sprang up, knocking the Small to the ground, and slapped at Kelly-Bitch's arm. She yelped and bared her teeth, but moved back, and Lois stood against Max, then squatted, looping her arms around his leg narrowing her eyes at the Kelly-Bitch. *Mine. The One, the Max, is mine. Only mine.* She stroked at the muscle of his thigh and waited. The Small crouched beside her. She grunted. *Later, Small, you will eat later.*

The One tipped his head back and howled.

With a bound, Lois sprang out from the treeline and ran. The One was ahead, Kelly-Bitch behind. The Small waited behind the trees. Lois' arms slid rhythmically at her side, powering her down the hill. She jumped with ease over rocks and fallen trunks. The air whistled as it passed her ears. Behind her were the pounding of feet, the breath of the Others that had joined them, the ones she curled with, warming her body as they slept.

Another light flicked on as she reached the village boundary. She ran to it, crouched beneath the window, then peered inside. A man sat in a chair, a fire burning in the hearth. For a moment, a sadness rode over Lois. Before ... her infected synapses poked at her memories ... tears pricked at her eyes ... A memory rose: a woman smiling at her, bending low to offer her a mug swirling with mist. The liquid inside was wet and sweet, warm as it ran down her throat. The woman passed the man a mug and another figure, smaller than the others, ran through the door. Lois' belly ached and saliva drooled from the corner of her mouth, catching on the hairs along her jaw. She grunted as Kelly-Bitch pushed up beside her. They both dropped beneath the sill as a figure pulled at the curtains and drew them together, blocking out the scene. Kelly-Bitch laughed then scurried around to the side of the house. Lois followed, pushing past Kelly-Bitch.

In the near distance a scream erupted. Lois licked her lips. The first kill. Memories of slashing and pulling and sinking of teeth transported her to past moments as she listened to the Screamer. She pushed down on the backdoor's handle. It moved with ease and the door swung open. Inside, a girl sat at the table, blonde hair pulled up on top of her head, skin honey-brown, dark lashes rimming a perfect circle of brown. Broad shoulders, lean body, swelling breasts. Her lips parted as her eyes widened and Lois pounced, reaching her within a second of opening the door.

Leaving the girl, as blood streaked across the whites of her eyes, Lois burst through to the living room. Kelly-Bitch straddled the man, holding his wrists down hard against the carpet. As he bucked, she lunged down, jaws snapping, and ripped at his throat.

A voice erupted behind her. "Lois! It's Lois Maybank!"

Lois turned to the woman with a flicker of recognition. The woman's lips were orange and the colour had leaked into the crevices of her ageing skin around her mouth. A memory of rage. A memory of – her cheeks began to sting – humiliation. *Dog's arsehole. She has a dog's arsehole for a mouth*. The woman's pulse beat at her throat as she held an iron poker high in the air.

"Don't take another step!" she threatened. "I'll smash you!"

Lois cackled and licked her lips. This one was flesh. This one was warm, dripping blood. The woman screamed as footsteps thundered down the stairs. The door slammed open, and a boy stood in its frame. In his hands he held a long iron rod.

As Lois turned to the boy-nearly-man, Dog's Arsehole screamed in rage. Lois staggered forward as pain ripped through her skull. Kelly-Bitch dragged the man into the kitchen. Dog's Arsehole screamed and launched herself at Lois as the boy sprang forward.

Kelly batted Dog's Arsehole away and pounced to meet Boy-Nearly-Man knocking the rod from his hands. He toppled backwards but fell before his head hit the wall, and she sank her teeth into his throat. Blood filled her mouth as they crashed to the floor, entwined as lovers. Dog's Arsehole staggered to her feet, raised the iron rod, and arced it down. Extracting her fangs from Boy-Nearly-Man, she jumped to her feet and with a swift twist kicked at the woman. She fell to the floor and Lois pounced, sinking her teeth into the soft pulse of her neck. The house fell silent as she crouched over the female. In her hand, the woman's heart beat for the last time as she bit down.

# CHAPTER THIRTY-EIGHT

The woman lay curled up beside the fireplace, the shadow of orange flames flickering on her cheeks. Max waited. His belly full, blood smeared his cheeks and dried among the hairs of his chin. Another of the pack dragged the body to the back door and through the forest for the Smalls to devour. The woman lay silent, her ribcage rising and falling with quick pants. She would be his. Later, among the trees, in the earth, with the soil and leaves, he would make her his. He stroked her cheek. She was beautiful. A memory pricked at him. A scene of her smiling, the bright pink of her fringe hanging above blue eyes, around them cages, inside the cages things moved, and Max was sad. The girl groaned, then jerked, bucking against the wall. Her eyes sprung open, the whites tracked with blood. She screamed as a spasm of agony took her. The house was empty but for She ... *Sally. Her name was Sally. Oh, no! Sally*. He stared into her reddening eyes with sadness punching at his heart and stroked at the blue veins threading across her pale skin.

*Laura. Laura. Laura.*

The name invaded his memory, an earworm that took him by surprise. *Laura*. Pain ripped through his chest. *Laura*.

The Sally curled into a tighter ball then ripped at her t-shirt, face contorting with pain. Max would return for the

Sally, but now it was only She, only Laura, that he wanted. He walked from the house to his own. Beyond the orange haze of the streetlight came the desperate cries, quickly silenced, of the Screamers. Max chuckled. They thought they could hide from him in their light, but there was nowhere to hide from Max.

Two minutes later he vaulted the front wall of his house and slipped down the driveway to the back. The garden stretched out to the forest and solar lights swung as bright globes in the old apple tree. He crouched behind the low wall that divided the lawn from the patio and watched. *Laura.* The kitchen light was on, and She moved there. As Laura walked up to the window, he crouched low, watching as she worked at the sink.

He waited. Listened to the tapping, running footsteps of the Others as they hunted, the quickly silenced screams, the low chuckles, and snickers as they played. White breath billowed in the cold air. The moon brightened the black sky to midnight blue. Lights disappeared until finally his bedroom lamp switched on. Max listened to the slow beat of his heart, each moment a torture of wanting. Wanting to touch her, feel her warm body close to his. Wanting to run his hands over her breasts and delve fingers within her dark spaces. One more time. Just one more time. Saliva drooled from his lips. He wanted to lick her flesh. Smell the heat between her legs, the soft, glistening flesh, wanted to lick it and – he salivated – bite it and rip it and devour her. He knocked his head on the dividing wall. *No! No, Max. Love She. You love She. Yes, but to love is to devour. To lick and bite and swallow is love.* Aroused at his thoughts of Laura's body, and seared by memories of their past unions, Max was tortured by the urge to fornicate. But the urge to rip at flesh and devour it, to fill his body with hers, consumed him. She would be his forever—a part of his body forever.

The lamplight in the bedroom disappeared. Max waited. When he was sure she was asleep, he took the key from its safe place – he snickered – *safe for me, safe for me to ... I'll huff and I'll puff, and I'll blow your house down*. He unlocked the door and stepped inside, sniffed at the familiar aromas, and took the stairs with quiet steps two at a time. On the landing he paused, taunting himself with the smells that caught in his nostrils, of her sweat and her sex. The door was open, the landing light on. He switched it off and stepped inside the bedroom. Moonlight fell onto the duvet, her hair laid out across the pillow, her face hidden. The bedclothes rose and fell with each breath.

The urge to jump across to the bed, pull back the duvet and sink his teeth into her throat was intense. He wanted her blood to ooze over his teeth, wanted to suck at her jugular and feel its metallic warmth slide over his tongue and down his throat. It would be an ecstasy.

"Max?" the voice was soft and questioning. He took a step back as she rolled over and her eyes locked on him. "Max?"

Taking a step forward, moonlight fell across his shoulders illuminating his face and torso with its light.

She remained silent, her eyes roaming over his nakedness, taking in his hardened desire, and pulled the bed covers up to her chin. "Max." Her voice carried a wave of sadness that settled over him. He took a step forward.

"It's me." His voice choked, the noise that vibrated over his vocal chords, a grunt. She pulled back the duvet and sat on the edge of the bed to face him. The smell of her sweat, her breath, her dark places, was intense and he inhaled it with each breath, holding it in his memory. He swallowed the lump in his throat, took a step forward and then knelt between her legs. Gripped by the urge to gnash at her throat he stiffened, pulled back. "Max," she repeated and slid a hand across his shoulder. He flinched. She repeated his name over and over with a sad lilt and pulled him to her chest. He closed his eyes, losing himself to the warmth, and with every cell in his body bit back the urge to dig at her flesh and sink fangs into her throat. Being with her was an ecstasy; being with her was a torture.

# CHAPTER THIRTY-NINE

Sleep was almost impossible for Freddie, but if he was honest, he hadn't even tried. He'd worked on his motorcycle, thankful for the integral garage, and sharpened his tools, then sat in the living room, fully dressed, freshly sharpened chisel in one hand, listening to the incessant howls. At one point, he had almost nodded off, until a howl split into his consciousness, a howl that seemed to be coming from outside the house. He'd stood with a start, moved quickly to the window, and peered through the edge of the curtain, making an effort not to move the fabric. He'd listened, heart palpitating, sure that something, not someone, was outside. He'd checked each window, moving from room to room, thankful for the double glazing he'd had installed last year, and the old, but very solid doors, he hadn't. The kitchen and living room held the rich aroma of engine oil from the array of tools on the table, including an old motorbike chain. He'd spent much of the night working on his Kawasaki Ninja, topping up the petrol, checking the oil, making sure everything was in perfect order.

After the news had reached him that of the large convoy of cars filled with villagers, only a fraction had returned, Freddie had determined to make sure that the bike was in perfect working order if he needed to get away from the monsters. The bike's speed and agility had saved him yesterday, it could do it again. The night had been full of their howls. When the howls had started, he could discern one 'voice', perhaps two at the most, but now the woods seemed to be full of them. How many of the creatures were out there now? He ran the number of people that had gone missing through his head, nearly forty at last count, and those were the ones he knew about. As the light of morning broke over the village, and the howls thinned to silence, he made a decision; he and Hayley would escape on his bike.

A pattern seemed to be establishing; attacks on the village happened at night and the howls disappeared during the day which seemed to suggest that the monsters, he balked at calling them wolfmen, were nocturnal. If he could get to the barricade during daylight, he could then get through the woods on his bike to the other side. There were plenty of well-laid tracks through the woods that he could easily run the bike along.

He made himself a cup of tea as an alternative to the too-strong coffee drunk throughout the night and listened. He checked his watch; six-thirty. The last howl had been nearly an hour ago. He sipped his tea, took himself upstairs and lay down fully clothed next to Hayley. Within five minutes he was fast asleep.

Wolfmen haunted his dreams, and he woke with a start to the sound of banging from downstairs. Swinging his feet to the floor, he knocked his knee against the bedside table, spilling the barely touched cup of tea, and leapt across the floor. What the hell was that noise?

Bang! Bang! Bang!

Running down the stairs, he raced to the living room and the source of the noise. Hayley! Dressed in jeans and t-shirt, hair pulled back in a severe ponytail, she was holding up a large panel of chipboard, nail between her lips, hammer stuffed into her back pocket.

"What're you doing?" He stepped forward to help with the wooden panel.

"Boarding this place up." Her voice was nasal.

"Have you been crying?"

She stopped and turned to him, her eyes puffy and bloodshot.

"What's happened?"

"I went round to see Tanya this morning-" A sob broke the flow of her words.

Dread sank like a stone in Freddie's belly. "Put the panel down, love. What happened?"

"Tanya and Guy didn't go with the convoy."

"I know. She decided to stay—same as us."

"The wolves-" She sobbed again. "Her back door was broken down ... There was blood in the kitchen."

Freddie ran his fingers through his hair, fear rising as anger. "Don't you ever do that again!" He grabbed her shoulder, digging fingers into her muscle just a little too hard, and held her gaze. "Don't ever go out without me again."

She winced and he released his grip. "You haven't heard the rest."

"Go on."

"I searched through the house. She wasn't there. Neither of them were."

"You could have been killed. What if those monsters were still in the house?"

"I wasn't, was I," she bit back. "I came straight back here. We've got to protect ourselves, Freddie. Something broke into their house and now they've gone."

"Even the kids?"

"I didn't dare go upstairs. I called for them, but there was no answer. I was too scared."

Freddie released her shoulder.

"Should we tell the Police?"

*What Police?* "I want to see it for myself first."

"I'm not lying, Freddie."

"No, of course you're not lying, but we should check for the kids. And anyway, what Police? We've only got PC Latimer and what use is that? We can't leave everything up to her to sort out."

"No, but-"

"The kids may be hiding somewhere, terrified. We'll go in and see."

A fine drizzle spattered Freddie's leathers as he walked up the driveway of his friend's house. Guy worked on the rigs alongside Freddie, they'd been in the same year at school, and joined the firm straight after leaving. Everything looked as it should as Freddie walked up the drive, Hayley by his side.

"It's the back door that's broken."

At the back of the house, a pushbike rested against the wall beneath the kitchen window and a small kennel sat pushed up against the fence. Freddie remembered Guy's dog, Eric, a snappy little Jack Russel Shiatzu cross with a penchant for ripping up trouser legs. 'He's just playing,' Guy would say as the dog snarled and anchored itself to Freddie's jeans. It was guaranteed that Freddie couldn't get through the door without the wretched dog snapping at him. This morning there was no snapping of tiny jaws and the house sat in silence.

Freddie looked about for the miniature menace. "Where's Eric?"

"Maybe he's run off?"

Stepping through the kitchen doorway, Freddie scanned the room. Tanya was fastidious about keeping the kitchen tidy and, despite two teenage children, the aluminium sink gleamed, and the black mock-granite worktops shone. The kitchen was immaculate bar the spatter of drying blood across the white floor tiles near the door to the living room.

"See!" Hayley prodded Freddie's shoulder. He grunted in return, checking around the room. Other than the splash of blood and splintered wood of the outer doorframe, nothing seemed amiss, but stepping through to the living room, Freddie was met by a scene of chaos. The flat-screen television lay in the middle of the floor, knocked from its stand. A large armchair was tipped and angular, its legs stabbing to the window. Long scratches ripped through wallpaper to the plaster below. An empty glass lay on the carpet, a red stain blossoming from beneath its curves across the cream fabric. The remains of another glass lay broken next to the hearth, its bowl crushed, its stem snapped. An arc of blood patterned the drawn curtains.

"Whoever broke in caught them unawares."

"What the hell were they doing drinking wine?" That Guy and Louise had been sitting drinking wine as though nothing was wrong angered Freddie. He'd warned Guy to make sure his house was secure—to lock the doors and windows. Freddie had kept a patrol throughout the night, making sure he had weapons at hand, that he was alert for any attacks, whilst Guy and Tanya had sat back drinking wine.

"Relaxing, I guess."

"Relaxing! How the very hell could they 'relax' when those monsters are out there?"

"Maybe drinking was the only way they could stay calm? Maybe it helped make it all easier to cope with?"

"Idiots!"

"Freddie! It's not their fault."

He slammed a hand against the wall; if only Guy had listened to him, he would still be alive.

"Whatever came in here, they didn't stand a chance. They're picking us off, Freddie." Her voice quivered. "This could have been us!"

"I stayed up. I watched."

"They're not here, Freddie. Let's go." She tugged at his sleeve. "We need to make sure our house is secure."

"We're leaving the village, Hayley."

"But, how? The roads are blocked. You heard what Javeen ..." Her voice died out as a noise from upstairs caught their attention.

Hayley broke the silence with a whisper. "Do you think someone's up there?"

The low thud repeated.

"Could be one of the kids?"

Freddie swallowed and nodded and took a tentative step towards the stairs. Hayley grabbed his sleeve.

"Stay here. I'll check."

He took the first riser, his light step silent against the carpet, and moved slowly up to the landing. Leading from the platform were three doors. The first was open and led to the bathroom. A quick glance confirmed that it was empty. Of the other two, one was ajar and the other closed. Freddie's heart tripped. Scuffling, and the sound of something moving, had come from behind the partly open door. Hayley's tight grip on his arm confirmed that she had heard it too. He held a finger to his lips and took a quiet step towards the open door.

Inside, the room was dingy with only a narrow band of light showing through the gap in the unopened curtains. Two beds, both unmade, sat side-by-side. Movement on the bed furthest from the window caught Freddie's eyes. A small and curled mound of tan and white fur. Eric! The dog looked up, stared at Freddie with blood-red eyes and snarled. Freddie quickly shut the door as the dog bounded from the bed with snapping jaws.

"Jesus! The dog's infected."

The dog's body thudding against the door was followed by scuffling and a snort from the next room. Eric's frenzied scratching made the door rattle.

"A fucking weredog! You've got to be kidding me."

The deep snore broke through the dog's snarling.

"That's got to be Guy. He snores like a drain. Do you remember when we all went camping-"

Freddie held a finger to his lips. Hayley stopped talking and they both listened to the snort coming from behind the closed door. Freddie grasped the handle, gave the door a polite, but barely audible tap, and opened it without waiting for a response. The view into the bedroom slowly widened. Hayley pushed up against Freddie to get a clear view, and gasped. Freddie's hands trembled.

The bedroom was darker than the previous one, being unlit by the morning sun, and the stench of human sweat and breath was muggy in its warmth. The bed was empty, but on the floor, curled in a tangle of legs and arms were four bodies. Freddie watched in deathly stillness as he took in the scene. All were fully clothed, the twin boys in their nightwear, Guy and Tanya still dressed in their usual jeans and tops. Though Guy was curled up next to his wife, what looked like bitemarks were visible on his shoulder through his torn shirt. Huge rents had been torn in Tanya's top and there were bite marks on her neck. He was unable to see any damage to the boys curled close to their parents. The scene was bizarre and reminded him of the packs of wolves he'd seen down at Beenham when a camera had been set up in the wolves' den and the animals would enter then curl together to sleep. The smell in the room clung to his nostrils.

"They're sleeping."

Unable to take his eyes off the sleeping forms, he checked each one in turn, watching the rise and fall of their ribcages as they inhaled and exhaled. One of the boys shifted. Hayley tugged at Freddie's his arm. "Come on, before they wake up."

"Didn't you see the bite marks on Guy and Tanya?"

"Yes, but let's come back later-when they're awake. We can help then."

"They've been bitten ..." He searched Hayley's eyes for understanding.

"They can get a rabies shot."

"If they've been bitten, Hayley. They could become one of them."

"Them?"

"The infected."

"Yes, but the doctor can help them."

A twin moved. The other began to murmur.

"Come on, before they wake up."

As Freddie watched the boys' movements, and noticed that Tanya had woken, the twins unfurled, and pushed themselves up to stare. Three pairs of eyes stared back at Freddie, three pairs of blood-filled eyes. Tanya snarled. Guy's eyes flicked open. Hayley screamed and Freddie slammed the door shut as Guy jumped to his feet and launched himself across the room.

"Run!"

# CHAPTER FORTY

Javeen had expected the night to be full of horror, but instead she'd drifted off to sleep at two am and not woken until daylight streamed in through the slatted boards Andy had nailed to the window's frame. She turned in the empty bed and listened to the clink of mugs in the kitchen and the unmistakable rush of the kettle boiling. The clock read nine-thirty am. *She was late. Didn't matter!* Stangton was not there to pass comment today. She ignored the nagging voice, showered, dressed then joined Andy in the kitchen.

"Why didn't you wake me?"

"Sorry, I thought you could do with the rest."

"I did. What time did you get up?"

"I haven't been to sleep."

A wave of guilt passed over her; she was the Police—she should be the one staying up all night on guard. He noticed her frown.

"Jav, it's alright. You can take the watch later and let me get some sleep."

"You make it sound like a war."

He didn't laugh. "I've been out already this morning. This far away from the village it's hard to know what's going on, but I heard a few noises in the night and wanted to check them out."

"And?"

"It's quiet."

"That's good, isn't it?"

"I'm not sure. The shop was still locked up half an hour ago."

Sid was never late to open the shop. "It's usually open by seven-thirty."

"I know."

Javeen spooned coffee into a mug, added another quarter, and covered it with milk. "Anything else unusual?"

"Some unopened curtains."

"I told everyone to barricade themselves in."

"Yes, it could be that."

"What are you saying?"

"I think we should check. Take a headcount of villagers. See who's still alive."

A stone dropped in her belly as she stirred the coffee. "Agreed."

They sat for the next twenty minutes listing the names of all the villagers they could remember. Andy drew up a rough map of the village, its shop, roads and lanes, the Castle, the bicycle hire place, the *Hound and Stars*, the library, along with each house. A cross had been placed on houses Javeen knew would be empty—those villagers who had left in the convoy and not returned.

"I'm amazed that you know all of the villagers."

"I've lived here all my life. It hasn't changed much and most of them come to me with their cars. It's like I said, we're more like family."

Javeen mourned for a second, remembering her own fractured family, the uncomfortable Christmases spent with relatives she didn't like, nodding in agreement as yet another distant cousin berated the poor job the police force were doing, the perennial 'they should try catching real thieves' and 'they make most of their money from the speed cameras'. "Hope they're not like my family then."

"I just meant that we're a tight-knit community, Jav. There are plenty that don't like each other, it's not a case of being one big happy family."

She took solace from that. "So how many villagers are there?"

Andy turned his attention back to the map and the list. The list had three columns: DEAD, MISSING, and ALIVE. "Counting those we know, or think, are alive then seventy-three."

Javeen finished the final dreg of cold coffee and reached for her jacket as Andy pulled on his own. Outside the day was drab and darker clouds hovered on the horizon. Jacket on, she reached for her waterproof and pulled on her gloves.

An hour later, rain spattering against her raincoat, Javeen knocked at another house. Her hand trembled, making the knock a limp thud. She took a breath, and rapped harder, taking furtive glances up and down the street, wary of movement. Andy had said that the howling became silent as the sun had risen, his theory being that the creatures were becoming nocturnal, but what they'd discovered this morning had made knocking on the doors a struggle. So far, they had found ten houses on the 'ALIVE' column of their list, empty. The owners had not answered their knocks despite the curtains being drawn shut and cars still being in the driveway. At the first house, the large kitchen window had been shattered and bloody footprints covered the tiled floor. At number fifteen Main Street, the head of Mr Bateman could be seen through the open doorway. Like poor Anita, his throat had been ripped out and his torso gutted. Andy had baulked at the scene, despite the distance, and vomited on the slabs. Javeen had put a red cross through the house on the map and they'd moved onto the next one. This time, the attacker had broken in through the backdoor. There was the sign of a struggle with upturned furniture and blood spattered across the chimney breast. Eight other 'inhabited' houses, so far, had also been broken into. In a further three, there were bodies, the remainder were empty.

Javeen knocked on the door and waited. Inside, slow footsteps made their way to the door. She breathed a sigh of relief. The door opened slowly, inch by inch, and a haggard face, peered out.

"Ben!" Andy pushed in front of Javeen, and the door widened. As Andy stepped up into the hallway, beckoned by the man's frail hand, Javeen noticed the tremor and realised that the man, despite his haggard look, couldn't be more than fifty. "Come in. Close the door," he said through rasping breaths. "She's in the kitchen."

"Who?"

"Kathy."

Andy grunted. "Kathy Oldfield. She's Ben's carer."

"Cancer," Ben added. "I'm riddled with it." He sagged against the wall. Javeen took hold of his arm to help steady him, and instantly wished that she hadn't. It was bone thin, and his entire body trembled. Cupping his elbow she helped him to stand. Andy walked ahead down the hallway and opened the door then turned with a frown, catching Javeen's eye.

"Can you help her?" Ben asked.

For a moment Andy didn't answer then he nodded. "Yes, but after we help you back upstairs."

Ben nodded. "Thanks. They came last night, two of them. Kathy heard them first, prowling around outside. She was scared, we both were, after what Billy had told her about the wolfmen. I told her not to be daft, but she said she didn't want to take any chances and went downstairs to lock the doors.

"And what happened?"

"They got in before she had a chance. I heard her scream but couldn't get out of bed quick enough to help her; yesterday was a bad day." He stopped, his face screwing up in pain, and leant heavily on Javeen's arm.

"Do you want to sit down?"

"Yes. In a minute." He drew air through clenched teeth. Javeen waited. "Perhaps ... before you go, you can help me with my medicine?"

"Yes, of course."

As the pain receded, Ben continued. "I heard her scream and then it went quiet. I thought maybe they'd gone, but ... they hadn't. First one came upstairs and then the other, and they both came into my bedroom. I couldn't move. I was that terrified that I couldn't move at all." He stalled.

"Ben, could you explain what happened, please?" Javeen asked.

"They came into my room. Hideous—just hideous." He grew quiet, screwed his eyes tight shut, and shuddered. "It was two females—I won't call them women although they had ... titties and ... well they just weren't women. They were naked and covered in hairs—most of their body, even on their faces, but it was their eyes ... they were filled with blood. One got up close, leant down to me. I thought she ... it, was going to tear my face. Its teeth were that sharp and she opened her jaws, spit dripped onto my face. Breath stank—like she'd been eating, excuse my French officer, but like she'd been eating shit."

Javeen remembered the similar tale the Reverend had told. "And she didn't bite you?"

"No, they both took a good sniff then left. I stayed in bed listening and when they'd gone, I came down here to find Kathy."

"And?"

"They'd attacked her. She was bleeding and unconscious. I tried to stop the bleeding, brought her a blanket, but she didn't wake up. She's still on the floor in the kitchen. I didn't know what else to do."

"Let me help you back upstairs, Ben."

"Will you help Kathy?"

"Yes, of course."

Ben scooped the man into his arms and, with a grunt, took him back upstairs. Javeen continued to the kitchen and opened the door. A blood-soaked blanket was strewn across the floor, but there was no sign of Kathy Oldfield.

# CHAPTER FORTY-ONE

Javeen returned to the car and rubbed at her shoulder as the tightness across the back of her head intensified. Pain thrummed at her temples. Hands trembling, she pushed the key into the ignition and took a final look at Ben's bedroom window. He'd asked her to give him his injection. It was the first thing Kathy did when she got there in the morning he'd said. He'd refused to have a cannula in his hand to help with the administration of 'Ben's buddy' as he called his medication, preferring the daily injections via syringe. Javeen had baulked at first but agreed when she'd realised the look in Ben's eyes had been fear, more fear than he'd shown when recounting the visit of the monsters in his bedroom last night. Fear was relative, and the pain Ben experienced from the cancer that riddled his body was more of a torment than the concern that wolfmen would rip him apart. It sounded absurd, but his tone, when he'd recounted that they hadn't bitten him, had been one of disappointment. He'd told her to fill the syringe to the top with the drug, and it wasn't until after she'd injected him with the full dose that she'd checked his paperwork. Each entry was carefully entered until last night at nine-thirty in Kathy's neat and very legible hand. Javeen had just administered more than triple that dose. When she'd pulled back the needle from Ben's flesh his smile of gratitude had made tears prick at her nose. She'd said nothing. It would be their secret.

Andy closed the door and joined her in the car. The banging of the door thudded in her ears and his voice grated at the pain in her head. She was heading for a migraine. Taking a packet from her pocket, she took a pill, and downed it with water.

"You shouldn't drink water that's been kept in your car. The plastic leaks poison."

"My head is leaking poison right now." She leant back against the headrest, the chalky pill bitter on her tongue, and took another swig. "Migraine," she explained.

"Let's just sit a minute. The past hour has been ... God, it has been unreal." Andy checked up and down the road.

"Sure." Javeen took another swig of water then took out Andy's map from her pocket and crossed out Kathy's name.

"Jav."

"Yep."

"If Kathy got up after being bitten and disappeared ... does that mean she's one of them now?"

Javeen's head throbbed. "Yes, I think it does. Here's my take on it. They're hunting—in packs. Some people they kill and drag off somewhere to eat, like Anita and Jimbob. Others they just bite, like Rachel Kendrick —I'm pretty sure it was her with Max Anderson and Lois Maybank in the woods, and Conrad said he thought one was Kelly Gray."

"What about the others—the ones they don't kill or bite?"

"Well, I think they don't attack them because they're sick. Reverend Baxter has cancer, and Ben is riddled with it too."

"Guess they can smell it or something."

"Dogs can. Even some humans can. Diabetics smell different. I remember my uncle Mike. He'd smell like he'd been drinking Jack Daniels even though he didn't touch a drop, but it was the sugar in his blood leaking out. He ended up losing a foot and going blind in one eye."

Andy remained silent, ran fingers through his hair. Infection and disease were smothering the village. Javeen released a long breath and her memory flitted back to the laboratory at *Kielder Institute* and the scene that had greeted Stangton and herself the morning after the activists had broken in and attempted to destroy Anderson's research. It dawned on her that Marta had lied. If the research assistant, Sally, had seen Dr. Anderson's car in the carpark, then she must have too. Her only reason to lie was to cover something up. An image of the dogs, both dead, one the result of 'blunt force trauma' (she remembered the phrase with sadness along with the frowning figure of PC Stuart Stangton as he'd stood over the mess), the other euthanised with the empty syringe sticking upright from its stiffening body.

"We should go to the *Institute*."

"What?"

"They've got drugs there that will kill them and-"

Javeen's reply was stifled as movement along the road caught her eye and a motorbike, complete with rider, passenger, and obviously full panniers, rolled out of a driveway further down the road. The bike was followed by another, also with full panniers and pillion passenger. *What on earth were they doing?* She checked along the treeline for movement - all was still - and opened the door. The noise from the engine thrummed at her already pounding head. She waved to catch the rider's attention. The engine revved and the bike moved closer then pulled to a stop beside her.

"Freddie, what are you doing?" She gestured to the panniers and Hayley in pillion.

"We're getting out of here." Hayley shouted above the sound of the bike's engine.

"I'm riding as far as the boundary and then taking the forest track out of here."

"It's too risky," Andy shouted.

Freddie's eyes flitted to Andy. "I can go faster than them. I can get there no problem, then it's just a mile through the woods. We can make it."

"Freddie, the forest is infested with them."

Judy, the pillion passenger behind Craig on the other bike looked from Javeen to the forest, her face pale inside the helmet.

"So is the village." He cast a wary gaze at the houses along the street. "The Armstrongs are all infected. We found them this morning—curled up in their bedroom, like rats in a lair."

"It was gross to see them, Andy. We only just made it back to the house."

"And Eric, their shitty little Jackshit, has been bitten."

"Jackshit?"

"One of them designer crossbreed fuckups. It's a Jack Russel crossed with a Shiatzu. It was out of its mind even before it was bitten. Fucking rat came at me like a hell hound. Red eyes and gnashing teeth-"

"So, we've got to fight weredogs now too?"

"Not us. We're out of here."

"The Armstrongs—they came after you?"

"We disturbed them. They came out of the house. I thought they'd chase us, but they went across the road and into the woods—just over there."

The close proximity made Javeen shudder.

Freddie looked to the sky. "Time we were off." He revved the engine, slipped it into gear, and with a final nod disappeared down the road and out of the village.

Javeen took out the paper and held her pen over the square that was Freddie's house. Andy grabbed her hand. "No, Jav. He'll make it."

*He won't.* "If he does, it will be a miracle."

"Then we have to believe in miracles."

# CHAPTER FORTY-TWO

F reddie powered the bike forward, passing through the village boundary, quickly gaining speed until the speedometer read one hundred and five miles per hour. When he'd escaped them before, he'd been doing over seventy so he felt confident that, even if they did try to chase him, that the bike would outrun them easily. As the miles passed, he grew in confidence. The journey to the edge of the forest, passing roads hugged by trees, and those with open grassland and streams either side, was a breeze. Their bikes were the only vehicles on the road, and they made good progress. By the time they got to the turn-off for the trail that would take them to the very edge of the forest, they had experienced no incidents, no attempts by naked and hairy beasts to run after the bike, and not a single sighting of the monsters that Javeen had insisted infested the forest. Their lair, he was sure, was close to the village. It would make sense for the creatures to stay close to their hunting ground. He shuddered at the thought; the village was a larder; the creatures' guaranteed supply of meat—free-range, though perhaps not strictly organic.

He turned off the main road, Hayley's arms hugging his waist, Craig and Judy close behind, and headed for the sign pointing out the trail. Much of it was tamped down so wouldn't be an issue for the bike. Only the last section, where they had to take one of the smaller tracks, could be a struggle. At that point, they would have to make it out on foot.

THE LIGHT FADED TO grey within the forest, and dark clouds blotted the bright November afternoon sun as rain fell on its canopy, dripping down to the damp earth. The air in the shed was warm, filled with the heat from them all ... their lair ... their flesh, curled together. She could smell each one: their odour, their sweat, their breath, their balls, their soft and salty lips, their dark places. Kelly snickered ... their deep, dark places. She leant into the One, taking in his scent, and an ache spread through her, a dull, delicious throb. Kelly shivered as the ache deepened. She wanted him to take the ache ... to ram at it, to bang at her, to thrust and to lick and to ... she groaned as her fingers slipped between her own legs. She was slippery, the place warm and swollen. She was ready. She needed him. Only him.

Kelly pushed closer to Max, pressing her naked flesh into his, fingers between her legs, fingering her bud, aroused, and driven to make him fill her, to fornicate, to thrust together until they howled in their ecstasy. She would claim him. She slipped an arm over Max's chest, let it slide down his belly, as her need pulsed, and stroked at the soft flesh between his legs. She curled her fingers through the hairs, stroking, teasing. He groaned in sleep, but the soft flesh began to harden. *Grow hard ... fill Kelly with your seed. Fuck Kelly ... Fuck Kelly hard.* She stroked the rod. Wanted his rod. Only his. The ache deepened between her legs, and she stroked harder, pulled at the rod.

Pain seared her shoulder. She yelped as sharp claws dug into her flesh, pulling her back, forcing a gap between herself and Max. Kelly twisted her head with a quick jerk, still holding Max, and snarled, teeth bared at the woman behind. Lois pulled up to a squat, snapped her jaws at Kelly, her snarl low and rumbling, a challenge. Max shifted next to her, growled in his half-sleep, and snorted. Lois continued to squat, legs apart, her genitals bared. She gnashed her teeth, shuffled closer to Max, and slipped a hand over Max's thigh, digging sharp nails into Kelly's wrist, drawing blood.

Kelly placed a hand on his shoulder. Lois bared her teeth, and, still squatting, moved a leg over his sleeping form, eyes locked to Kelly's. Ignoring Lois' claim, Kelly slid her arm across Max, hooking hers over his chest. He murmured in his sleep. His throaty grunt mingling with the inhale and exhale of the others. "Lauuura ... Lauuura." His teeth gnashed and his eyes flickered open. Eyes still locked to Kelly's, Lois smirked, bared her teeth, and pushed her hips along Max's thigh, forcing him to roll onto his back, squashing Kelly to the floor. She yelped. Lois snickered and rocked her hips, sliding her heat over Max's rod until he groaned. She rose, lowered herself down and rocked against him. He gasped, grabbed her breasts, lifted her into the air, and flipped her to face the shed floor. Fully erect, he took her from behind. Their grunts and moans filled the small, muggy space, waking the Others as Kelly scuffled to the corner. She watched as Max thrust into Lois and snarled as the woman giggled and gnashed, howling her triumph over Kelly. Rage grew within her, but she bit back the need to gnash and tear at the woman.

*Later, Max would be hers. Later, Lois would cower.*

As Lois and Max finished their rutting, Kelly stood and moved to the door. Max pounced, gnashed his teeth, and blocked her exit. She took a step back as he stood over her, teeth bared, and waited. The hunger in her belly was overwhelming. The drive to gnash and bite, to slice her teeth into soft, pulsing flesh, growing with each second. When Max gave the signal to leave, she burst out of the door, followed by the Others

A large male brushed past her. He was strong. She could bed with him, be his mate—if he was strong enough. She followed him to a hanging tree. Above, high in its branches, arms and legs dangled, and hollow torsos rested against the boughs. She clambered high, crouching on the branch, legs parted, and tore at the fabric covering the flesh. Her genitals gleamed pink at the Other waiting below. His rod grew. She snickered, locked her eyes to his, then bit at the buttock of the Hanging One. The flesh was cold, already with the stench of rot and poison. She jumped back down. Grunting at the Other. She needed fresh meat, fresh bleeding, throbbing flesh.

She pushed close to the Other, stroking her hand down his back, watching the reaction of He, Max, the Only One. She slid a hand down the Other's belly. He hardened and pushed her to the ground. The Only One leapt to them, pulling the Other from between her legs, throwing him to the forest floor. He snarled at the Other. It didn't growl back, but squatted, and cowered. Not strong enough.

Kelly bared her teeth as Max turned back to stare at her. His eyes gleamed hard and red in the forest gloom. Stepping forward, he raised his hand, and scratched talons down her arm. Blood seeped from split flesh, pain danced through her muscle, and she yelped, shuffled back, crouched beside the tree, eyes averted, waiting for the pain to stop, the flesh to heal. Lois snickered and Kelly's rage grew.

In the distance an engine roared. She recognised the sound, each revolution, each thrust of its pistons. The Uncaught. The rabbit ... she licked her lips ... the rabbit that had run away, that had bolted down its hole. Their eyes had met. She had wanted him then. Wanted him to take her. Wanted to be his. The strong one riding. *Ride Kelly. Take Kelly. Love Kelly. Fill her.* Her genitals throbbed, her pussy tightened. Her need was overwhelming. This time she would catch He. No more running, little rabbit. This time she would bite, sink her fangs into flesh, this one she would keep, make hers, and leave the Max, leave the Others. Make her own place ... hole ... lair. She snickered ... fill Kelly's hole. The Uncaught would be hers to keep, to fill her, hunt for her, make her swell with his seed.

As Max gave the order to run to where the lights burned, to where tender flesh and beating hearts hid, to where blood pulsed ready to be swallowed, Kelly's mouth watered and memories of the village, of hunting among the houses, danced in her mind. But a greater need filled her, and she darted to an upturned moss-covered ball of roots and crouched behind the thick ferns that grew from the upturned base. As the Others and The One ran down the slope and disappeared between the thick scratching trunks, and waving green leaves, Kelly listened to the engine, then turned to follow the sound. *Run rabbit, run, rabbit, run, run, run!*

# CHAPTER FORTY-THREE

As Kelly sprinted with ease through the forest, jumping roots, darting between trees, and vaulting across trickling streams towards the pulsing engine, Freddie led the group deeper into the forest. They reached a crossroads, and he slowed the bike to a stop, removing his helmet. The enclosed space, and the sweat of fear, had made his hair damp. Checking around, the space was silent, and he gestured to Hayley to dismount. Noticing Craig's frown, he gestured to the trees. "There's nothing here. Those things live closer to the village."

"How do you know that?" Craig scanned the trees, his frown making deep lines across his forehead.

"It makes sense for them to do that. The village is their hunting ground, why come out here," he gestured to the surrounding forest with its host of ramrod straight trunks, and fallen, rotting, moss-covered trees, "when it's empty? There's nothing in here but a few squirrels."

"He's right. How often have you seen anything living in the forest?"

"If there is anything it hides well." Judy scanned the forest, her cheeks pale though a red flush showed at her collar. "Can we just get out of here, please? The forest gave me the creeps anyway, but now I know it's infested with ... with wolfmen I-"

Her eyes darted to the trees where a branch quivered. From its boughs, a bird flapped its wings and launched into the sky. "Hell!" She patted her chest. "I thought that was one of them."

Freddie attempted a smile. "Don't worry, Judy. I told you, there's nothing at this end."

"Maybe, but I'll feel a whole lot better once we're on the other side."

"What if we get there and it's fenced off like PC Latimer said it was?"

"It's not just PC Latimer who's seen it. Conrad said there was a twenty-foot steel fence across the exit road."

"Yes, he did, Hayley, and it was at the barrier that the wolfmen attacked the convoy, so they do come over to this side."

Freddie swallowed. Another bird fluttered from the overhead branches and then another bolted into the air as though launched from a spring. Freddie watched as it flapped into the greying sky. Rain, filtered through a thousand pine needles, spattered against his cheeks and he blinked it from his lashes. A crack, deeper in the forest, pricked at his awareness and he turned his head to listen. The noise mingled with the flap of the bird's wings and seemed to fill the space as he waited.

"OK." Freddie turned a careful smile to Craig, Judy, and Hayley, sensing their need for his reassurance. "Let's go." He swung his leg back over the motorbike's seat and waited for Hayley to join him then turned the key in the ignition. The bike's engine roared, more birds burst from the canopy and hurtled into the sky. He waited for Craig's thumbs up, then manoeuvred the bike onto the path that would take them through the last, but most difficult, part of their journey to the edge of the forest.

They rode for five minutes, before a mass of worming roots rose across the path, Freddie slowed, moved to the edge of the track, ploughing through ferns, dodging felled boughs, and manoeuvred the bike to the other side. Here the track narrowed. Bowing fronds brushed against the motorcycle's wheels as he moved the bike forward. Achieving any kind of speed would be difficult, if not impossible here. He looked ahead, searching his memory of past hikes through the woods. If he was correct, they were nearly at the edge of the forest, and this track should lead them to open moorland where the going would be tough, particularly on these bikes, but not impossible. *What if there was a fence there, Freddie? Can't be. How could they fence an entire forest?* He rounded another corner, headed to a bank of ferns between a wide gap in the trees and jerked as the bike's front wheel lost contact with the ground. It spun in mid-air as the forest floor gave way to a steep bank, then crashed down, pulling the bike forwards. The bike wavered, the wheels spun, slipped, and then fell. He grasped the handlebars and leant into the bank. Hayley, used to riding pillion, did the same, and the bike stalled as it slid down the bank coming to a stop as the wheel caught against a thick sapling.

Heart pounding, he pulled his boot from beneath the tank. "You OK?" he shouted.

"Leg's caught!"

At the top of the slope, Craig dismounted, and Judy took side-steps towards them.

"Are you alright?" she called.

As Freddie called back, a figure flitted between the trees at the top of the slope and his startled expression alerted Judy.

"What is it?"

"Christ, no!"

Another figure jumped behind Craig.

"Craig, run!"

"There's two of them!"

Startled, Craig twisted to see, helmet impeding his peripheral vision. Behind him, two figures, almost camouflaged against the dark brown bark of the pine trees and the gathering gloom of the spaces in between, moved between the trunks. Craig froze. Freddie beckoned for Craig to move forward as he crouched and unbuckled the long bag of his hunting rifle. The creatures crept a little closer to Craig. Taking a step towards the slope, Freddie raised the rifle, and peered down the sights.

Before Freddie had left the house, he had loaded the rifle with bullets meant to obliterate vermin and small mammals. Apart from the pellets he kept for clay pigeon shooting, they were the only bullets he had that could do real damage. This thing, however, was the size of a woman, and muscular with it. The expanding tip of the bullet could do some serious damage, perhaps enough for them to escape. As he squeezed the trigger, he noticed the curves of the larger female and how the dark hair that spread across her chest thickened to a line past her bellybutton and ended in a curling mass of pubes. *Why had he expected it to be shaven?* His sights centred on the woman's temple, the thinnest part of her skull, the best place for the bullet to gain access to her raddled brain. He pulled the trigger just as the other thing pounced, intercepting the bullet's trajectory. The rifle kicked back against his shoulder. *Damn! That would have been a perfect shot!* The wounded beast dropped to the ground, dark hair covering its face, blood seeping from its throat. Freddie took aim again as it writhed. Craig stumbled down the steep bank, his feet trawling through the earth, losing his balance and slipping until his body jarred against a thin sapling.

The wounded beast shuffled backwards, a hand covering its damaged throat. Blood seeped through its fingers, its lips pulled back into a snarl, bare incisors an inch long. Freddie aligned his sights on the blonde once more. As he squeezed the trigger, it darted to the left, and disappeared behind a trunk. The bullet shot straight, and bark splintered.

KELLY SNARLED AS RAGE took her. Lois lurched to her feet, yowling as she disappeared into the woods. The Uncaught was there, down the hill. The pointing stick had his attention. She leapt from behind the tree and bounded beside the other male. She could smell his fear, and the scent of his underarms, and the musky delight of the soft places, his sex, his dark hole. Her mouth watered. She licked her lips. He was strong. Bigger than The One. The Uncaught one scrabbled on the ground, the long stick at his side as she leapt again. Close now, she could see the hairs on the back of the New One's neck, feel the heat of his body escaping from the collar of his jacket. She scanned the area, her senses finely tuned. Within seconds she had judged the situation. The woman stood behind the man with the shining stick. She passed him something from the forest floor, it caught the light as he took it. The stick lay broken, and he stuffed the silver thing inside. She feared the stick. The other woman, the one that belonged to the New One, was on her knees, her voice grated against Kelly's ears. In the forest, Lois chuntered and chafed as her flesh knitted. *Stupid bitch. Stay away stupid bitch. Go back to Max. They are mine.*

In the second that the Uncaught took the silver things from the woman, Kelly leapt. She pounced down the slope, clawed feet anchoring her to the forest floor, and grabbed the New One from behind. She was silent across the forest floor. Swift to embrace him. Her arm wrapped across his chest, and she hauled him to her breast, dragging him up the slope, digging her free hand into the soil, into bark, taking him with her into the dark places of the forest, the hidden places. He struggled. She liked his strength and ached for him to be hers. As they reached the top, she threw him to the floor and lunged at him, jaws open, saliva dripping to his pale, hairless flesh. Their eyes met as she bent to him, and he screamed as her fangs sank into the warmth of his neck. The pulse beat against her tongue, and she licked the blood as it seeped into her mouth.

The Uncaught appeared over the brow of the slope, his stick pointing, scanning the forest. He couldn't see them; hidden behind the bowing ferns, making their forever love. She looked down at the New One, her New One. Eyes rolled back, the red blood already seeping across the whites, his chest heaved. Her mouth watered, hunger growled, and the urge to gnash and tear at his flesh bit at her. She resisted. Keeping the Uncaught one in sight, she crouched and dragged the New One to the deeper wood, to wait and claim him. On the other side, Lois howled, called the Others and He.

THE RIFLE KICKED BACK against Freddie's shoulder. He cursed, aware that he was shooting blindly into the forest, shooting at something that howled, something that moved too fast among the growing dark, something that made his scrotum shrivel and his testicles retract. Judy's scream, muffled by his helmet, rang through the woods, then disappeared beneath the howls that filled them.

"Did you get it?" Hayley's breath came hard as she scrambled up the slope to stand beside him. "Did you?" Her voice was edged with despair. "Jesus, Freddie. What the hell happened? Let's go. Just go."

"He's gone!" It had all happened so fast. One second the creature was laid on the floor and then in a blur, Craig was gone. His scream had curdled Freddie's blood, but worse was the abrupt silence. The thing he'd shot had crawled back into the forest before he'd had time to reload and its screaming howl had turned his bowels to water. Hayley tugged at his sleeve.

"It's calling. The one you shot is calling."

"Calling?"

"Howls. That's what they are. Wolves howl to call the pack."

Freddie's eyes flitted among the ferns and trunks. The forest light was shifting to dark grey, further inside the forest the light had become shadow. "We'll have to get out on foot. There's no way we can escape this way on the bikes. They're too heavy."

Judy crouched against his bike, hugging her knees. If they were to survive, they had to gather their senses. He leant down to her, his face stern—now was not the time for kindness. "Judy. We have to get out of here." She pulled her arms tighter around her knees. "Judy! Get up. There could be more of them coming for us. We have to-"

"I can't ride that bike down there." She gestured to the steep slope.

"Neither can I. We're going on foot." She remained curled against the bike. He tugged at her sleeve. "Move it, Judy! We can't wait any longer."

"Judy." Hayley's voice was gentler. "Please. Get up."

Heart pounding and unwilling to wait, Freddie stepped away. "I'm going. If you stay here, you'll die. If you come with us, then you could survive."

Wind pushed through the trees, sending large drops of water pattering to the floor. Rain splashed against her cheek. She wiped at it then stood. With relief, Freddie moved away.

"What about our stuff?"

"Leave it. It's just stuff. We can always get more."

"He's right. It'll just weigh us down anyhow."

He took another step down the bank, gripping saplings then branches for support. Sure that Judy and Hayley were keeping up, he increased his pace and all three sidestepped at a run down the slope. In the distance, the too near distance, a howl carried through the woods. Another voice responded, one that could only be a call from the thing he had shot. A wave of cold washed over him along with the urge to open his bowels. He took a massive breath to release the tightness across his chest. *Don't shit your pants, Freddie-boy. Get a grip and run!*

# CHAPTER FORTY-FOUR

As Freddie, Judy and Hayley ran through the forest, Javeen steered the car up the road to the *Institute*. She was anxious to reach the building before the afternoon sun had the chance to begin its descent. The attacks seemed to have settled into a pattern, she wasn't superstitious, didn't believe that the wolfmen's appearance was linked to the moon's cycle, but the creatures seemed to have become nocturnal. No attacks had been reported as having taken place during the day; only in the haze-filled hours of twilight, during the night, or the earliest, still grey, morning. The howling faded to silence in the early hours. As she manoeuvred the car around yet another bend and moved into a lower gear to manage the incline, she didn't feel safe—not at all, but neither did she have the creeping sensation of being watched.

A chop, chop, chop nagged at the edge of her awareness as another bend loomed and she instinctively leant to the window and peered up to the sky. Andy leant forward too and grunted his surprise. In the near distance, hovering above the Gothic turrets of the *Institute*, was a helicopter. It swayed, turned ninety degrees, then lowered out of sight. Javeen pushed down on the accelerator.

"Slow down, Jav."

"But that's how we can get out of here." She took another bend, leaning into the door as stones scuttled beneath tyres. "They can help us evac-"

"Pull over."

She ignored him and shifted up a gear.

"Jav. Think for a minute. Whoever is in that helicopter, isn't our friend."

She slowed.

"They could be."

"You're right," he replied as she pulled the car to a stop. "But what if they're not. What if they're the ones who have fenced off the village. Whoever did that, knew what they were doing. Knew just how dangerous those things were."

Javeen sagged back in her seat. Andy was right. "We came up here to find out what was going on."

"Did you just expect to walk in and talk to the director?"

"Yes. No. I don't know. I guess I didn't think it through. I just knew I had to come up here and see if I could find out. Plus, I wanted as many of the vials of that drug they have for putting dogs down."

"What use is that?"

"Well, apart from maybe using it on them, if one of us got bitten, we could ... we could use it on ourselves."

Andy remained silent as he searched her eyes then shook his head. "It won't come to that Jav. We're going to survive this. We'll find a way out."

"But what if we don't?" The unrelenting horror of the morning's discoveries and realising that the villagers were being hunted even in their own homes, had chipped away at her reserves of fearlessness. She was strung out and tired, putting on a brave front, but being the stalwart local bobby for the villagers was wearing her down. "What if they," she jabbed a hand at the *Institute*, "won't let us out? And what if we can't escape from them?" She jabbed her finger at the forest. Javeen ran fingers through her hair. "I think we still need to go up there ... There's plenty of light left in the day. We'll go in on foot."

Andy shook his head and glanced at the trees with a flicker of apprehension.

"Maybe there's a phone in there that works," Javeen suggested. "We could call for help."

Andy blew out a massive breath. "Alright PC Latimer. Get as close as you can."

Javeen smiled, slipped the car into gear, took the rest of the hill at under ten miles per hour then pulled into a passing place. She checked her watch. They had at least three hours left before the afternoon drew to a close.

As they approached the gates, keeping out of sight of the main entrance, a figure stood beneath the stone arch of the main door. "That's not Sam Fletcher," Javeen said whilst comparing the gangly youth in his ill-fitting uniform and the thick-set man dressed in khaki combats with a matching shirt, and complementary black bullet-proof vest now stood at the door. A pair of binoculars hung around his neck and, from the way he held his rifle, he was ready for action. As Javeen looked on, three figures walked around the corner, followed by another two armed men, and disappeared into the *Institute*.

"Did you see them? That was Marta Steward and Blake Dalton."

"What about the other one?"

"No idea. I've never seen him before."

"Shh!" He pulled her back as one of the guards raised his rifle and stepped out towards them. They waited, listening to the crunch of gravel underfoot until the footsteps moved away and then the front door opened and clacked shut.

Andy peered around the stone pillar that secured the spiked iron gates. "We're not going to get in this way; the gates are padlocked and there's a guard at the door."

"We can go along the fence until it opens out into the forest. The gate is only for show, it's not fenced off all the way around the property."

"Go into the forest, you mean."

Javeen swallowed. "We just have to follow the fence until we find a gap. There are other doors at the back and sides of the *Institute*."

"Right." Andy didn't move.

Javeen's legs felt suddenly heavy as though her shoes were lead weights. "Right."

"You first then."

*Come on, Jav. Get a grip.* "OK." She glanced over the gravel track through to the forest that covered the hillside. Inside, despite the day's bright sunshine, the forms of rotted and moss-covered stumps sat in shade. All it needed was a bat to come flying down from one of the Gothic turrets and it would be the perfect setting for a classic horror; they already had the werewolves. Javeen pulled at her jacket, and stiffened her arms about her torso, instinctively making herself smaller. The entire forest floor was a sea of green mounds and hillocks.

The *Institute*'s stone wall ran from the tall pillar that supported its gate and disappeared into the forest. Her instinct was to turn around and run back to the car.

"Come on, Jav." Andy beckoned, already several feet ahead.

*Wait! Don't leave me.* She shuffled forward. *Calm it, Jav. They'll smell the fear a mile off!* She shuddered and glanced at the forest. *Perhaps they would smell her! Oh, God. Our Father ... Who art in Heaven ...*

Catching up with Andy, she stayed close. Adjacent to the house the wall ended, and a fence of horizontal wires took over. Large bay windows filled the ground floor, whilst smaller rectangular windows lined the upper floors.

"That's Marta Steward's office." Javeen pointed to a window on the second floor, the only one with a light on. A man walked past the window then disappeared from view.

"I thought you said there were doors here."

"At the back. There's one that leads into the café on the ground floor and another for the security and janitorial staff."

"They won't be open."

"We have to try."

The security guard from the front door appeared on the gravel, spoke into his radio, then walked back across the drive until he disappeared.

"Let's go."

Andy slipped a leg between two wires and began to manoeuvre himself through the fence. Two more guards appeared from the back of the building. He froze as they walked along the side of the building, until they too disappeared around the corner to the front of the building.

At the rear of the *Institute*, the gardens opened out to a wide expanse of expertly manicured terraces and then a lawn that ended where the forest claimed the land. On the lawn the helicopter sat empty. Attached to the building's imposing stone wall was a large, and ornate orangery arranged with huge potted plants, round tables, and expertly mismatched chairs. At one table, a prettily flowered and fluted teapot sat at its middle, two cups with saucers sat by its side. Marta Steward leant to reach for the cup and lifted it with a slim wrist to her lips.

"Steward. I thought I saw her upstairs."

"You did."

Marta jerked, tea spilled, and another figure walked into view.

"She's jumpy."

"So am I."

The man sat down with a thud next to her and ran his hands through his hair.

"Looks like he's on edge too."

"That's Blake Dalton."

"I recognise him. He was in the pub that night."

"Yeah, when Billy put a bet on me."

Andy nudged her with his elbow. "Not complaining, are you?"

"No. He's a cheeky bugger though."

As Marta lifted her hand, the cup visibly shook. She leant forward, took a sip, then rummaged in her bag before lighting a cigarette. The man talked at her, she threw her hands in the air and strode to the door, swinging it open, the smoke from her lit cigarette winding into the air as she stood, one arm clamped to her belly, the other rigid at her mouth.

"She's scared shitless."

"Yeah, bet she doesn't finish the fag." Javeen whispered.

As predicted, Marta took a couple of drags, dropped the cigarette to the floor, then closed the door. Within a minute both Marta and Blake Dalton left the orangery.

Bile swirled in Javeen's stomach and her back burned. *Why the hell had she suggested coming up here? They should be back in the village making preparations for the next assault.* She checked the sky; still bright enough to make her wince. She tugged at Andy's sleeve. "We go in or we go back to the car."

"Let's go in," he said then sprinted to the orangery.

Javeen followed him into the glass building. They ran with light steps across its tiled floor then into a hallway. The first door that Andy opened led into a room used as a pantry and they both slipped inside. It smelled of orange zest and cinnamon and was stacked with packets of tea, bags of coffee beans, mugs, cups, and plates.

"Bloody hell!" Andy's face broke into a smile.

Javeen took a breath, letting relief flood over her. They were inside. Safe. Away from the monsters in the forest. Now they just had to face the humans inside. Her heartbeat steadied. "I want those vials, Andy. They'll be in the laboratories on the first floor."

"Then we talk to Steward?"

"I'm not sure that would be a good idea. Since when does a researcher need an armed guard? She's hiding something and if she thinks we've found out what it is then it may be us they feed to the wolves." Whatever was going on at the *Institute* was funded by the government, one of its secretive agencies, or a corporation with deep pockets. Whichever it was, they had been ruthless enough to quarantine an entire village and let the population die, not just die, but be hunted to extinction.

Last year Javeen had discovered exactly how corrupting even a little power was, her 'disappearance' to Kielder at the command of Nigel 'bloody' Parker, was proof of that, but this was on an altogether different scale and potentially fatal to minions such as herself and Andy, given the military grade rifles the *Institute*'s guards were carrying.

"Andy, what if they created the wolfmen?"

He scoffed. "Don't be daft. That's just for films."

It was all bizarre and surreal, but it was happening. "The creatures exist. They shouldn't, but they do. Something created them. They're not exactly a new species that some explorer has discovered."

Silence fell between them.

"You're right," he said finally. "The whole thing is rotten to the core."

"I want to find out exactly what's going on."

He nodded. "We get the vials first."

"Agreed."

As they stepped out into the silence of the orangery, Javeen checked the sky. Still bright. Still safe.

It took them fifteen minutes to make their way through the *Institute* to the first laboratory. From the noises inside various rooms, there appeared to be a small number of people still working but the staff that walked the hallways were unfamiliar and their uniforms were of military style.

The first laboratory they checked in was Max Anderson's. There was no evidence of the attack; all traces of blood and gore had been cleaned away. On the table a folder lay open, a pen at its side. The steaming mug next to the folder indicated that someone was working and could be back at any moment.

Javeen headed straight for the chiller placed along the far wall. Inside were various glass bottles all neatly stacked. Each one was labelled with a neat hand; 'WLV1' or other variants. Not the euthanising drug she was looking for. She checked the cupboards as Andy did the same. The second cupboard was stacked with narrow cardboard boxes.

"Bingo!"

"Keep it down!" Andy whispered.

"I've found it." She removed a box and double checked the label. 'Beuthanasia D-Special. Contains pentobarbital and phenytoin. Warning: for canine euthanasia only.' "This is it." Reaching back in, she removed several more boxes. "We need syringes."

"Got them," Andy replied, pulling out a deep drawer.

Javeen searched the room for a suitable container then placed the vials in an empty wastepaper bin. Andy added the boxed syringes.

A low and familiar growl was followed by scuffling.

"Oh, Jesus!"

Both turned to the bank of cages that filled one wall of the laboratory.

A pair of blood-red eyes glared from behind the wire mesh. Bone-white teeth, with incisors at least an inch long, filled its snapping jaws.

"Oh, Jesus Christ in heaven. They've caught one."

Its fingers poked through the mesh, jaws gnashing. A red light pulsed next to the cage, and then an alarm sounded.

"It's a girl!"

Naked apart from a thick ring of black plastic around its neck it growled.

In the distance the banging of doors was accompanied by running footsteps.

"We have to hide!"

The thing howled as Andy grabbed her arm and pulled her in the direction of the door at the end of the row of cages. As the laboratory door swung open, they stepped into a walk-in cupboard and closed the door with a soft click. The laboratory filled with noise as men shouted, and the thing in the cage squawked and yapped. The distinctive tack, tack of a woman's high heels followed. The wolf-girl screamed then grew quiet before beginning to howl.

"For God's sake, electrocute it!" Marta demanded. "That's what the collar is for."

Another yap was cut short and then another before the noise stopped.

"Doctor Petrov, this thing needed tranquilising again." Marta Steward's heels tacked across the floor.

"There is no way to safely do that," said Dr. Petrov in a heavily accented voice.

"You were supposed to be keeping it sedated. How in the very hell is it awake?"

"I do not know. I gave dose calculated by Doctor Marston. It had enough to induce coma."

"You obviously didn't give it enough."

"It was recommended dose for ... girl her age."

"Imbecile! She ... it ... is not an ordinary girl."

It began to howl again.

"Shock it again. I cannot abide that noise."

A second yowl was cut short, halted by the electric shocks being administered by the collar.

"Get Chapman up here. He can shoot it."

Javeen sighed with relief; they were going to kill it.

"I thought you wanted it alive."

"Are you a total idiot, Doctor Petrov? Of course I want to keep it alive."

"I take offence Doctor Steward. I am not total id-"

"I care not one whit if you are offended, Petrov. Chapman can shoot it with a tranquiliser gun and then you can make sure it stays sedated—completely sedated." She tacked across the room. Her voice softened and Javeen pressed her ear to the door. "These ... *things* ... are absolutely deadly. If you make another mistake, we could all end up gutted like Walton. You saw the video."

"Yes, Steward. I did."

A man's voice added to the conversation. "When can we begin trials?"

"When Doctors Marston and Petrov have figured out how to keep them sedated for long enough, and *you* have supplied us with a suitable receptacle to keep them in. These cages are meant for dogs, not monsters."

"Them!" Javeen whispered. "Did you hear that? They've got more than one."

"Or getting more," Andy replied.

Marta tacked across the floor and the lab door opened then banged to a close.

Minutes passed as the scientists continued their work and Javeen continued to listen. What she heard made her realise that no one was coming to their rescue.

# CHAPTER FORTY-FIVE

Marta scanned the treeline. Nothing moved although she knew, without doubt, that there were monsters waiting deeper inside the forest. The black outline of the trees were a sharp contrast to the fading blue horizon. She shuddered. Despite the security *Titan Blane Industries* had provided, her heart hammered several beats faster every time she caught a glimpse of the trees and the darkness that festered between them. The *Institute* was surrounded by the forest, a forest where the creatures - she couldn't bring herself to say 'werewolves' although that was how Blake Dalton had at first laughingly referred to Max and Lois - now reigned supreme.

Over the past few days she had watched the activities in the woods with horror, and a growing fascination, listened with greedy interest to Dalton's plans for the creatures, and put her not inconsiderable scientific talents into designing further trials. Dalton had called her proposed modifications 'genius' and was sure that they would be of interest to *Titan Blane*'s demanding, ruthless, and grotesquely well-funded customers. That their use of the monsters she would create would be unethical made not one scratch on her conscience.

Blake eased himself down into the leather sofa and peered out of the window before picking up the binoculars and scanning the treeline. He didn't appear to share the same apprehension – let's be honest – the same shit-your-pants, yet thrilling, fear that Marta was experiencing. He lay the binoculars on the table beside the sofa and huffed a dissatisfied sigh and walked across to the monitor. He clicked a key and the black screen brightened with lines of green, and multiple red dots.

Outside, the heavy chop, chop of the helicopter began to whir and the windows vibrated. Marta joined Blake at the desk, pushing her hip against his shoulder. "Have they got him yet?"

"Max? No. Not yet. He's been sighted twice, at least Staines thought the werewolf he saw was Max."

"Don't call him that!"

"Pah! What do you want me to call the freak? Huh? He's covered in hairs, has fangs, eats people, and seems to be immortal. Add that he was infected by a mutated rabies virus and-"

"Calling him a werewolf is just stupid. It made it all ridiculous. What next? Vampires?"

"Well, he does appear to be immortal."

Marta scoffed. "Of course he's not immortal. The dog he was bitten by was part of a trial exploring the regenerative capabilities of stem cells. His body has somehow, miraculously, adapted after being infected."

A beep sounded and a red dot flashed on the screen. She leant against Blake and peered at the monitor. "What is it doing?"

Blake tapped a key and the screen changed to a live-action feed. Martha grimaced as one of the creatures walked across the screen, scurried across to a tree, and shimmied into its branches.

"Follow it!"

"I will."

Blake's tone had an edge to it and Marta pushed down her desire to snap back. She was tired and edgy, but the last thing she wanted was a surly, and uncooperative, Blake Dalton. He manoeuvred the camera to follow the creature. It sat in a higher branch, pulling at something. Blake zoomed in. Marta gagged. In its hand it held a lower leg, a lower leg still attached to a body. It lifted the leg to its mouth and clamped its jaws around the calf. Marta looked away. "Why do they have to be so disgusting?"

"They're fascinating."

She agreed; they were fascinating, but utterly horrifying too. Pulling away from the screen, she wiped damp palms against her skirt, reached for the bottle of wine, and poured the last of it into her glass. Damn! Another bottle already empty. Blake would have to get another one from the storeroom, or at least come with her; going anywhere near the back of the *Institute* with its ridiculously fragile orangery made her knees weak. Blake may think the *Institute* was safe with its armed guards, but as soon as enough specimens were collected and the rest tagged, she was leaving. She took a gulp. At least the alcohol soothed the edges, her nerves were like pieces of sandpaper rubbing together.

"Look at how it jumped down!"

Marta caught a glimpse of the figure as it darted off screen.

"They're incredible. Do you see how honed their muscles are?" The camera caught up with the figure once more before it disappeared.

*Hairy, muscle-bound monsters!* "How many have your men tagged so far?"

"Two?"

"And how many are there now?"

"At last count, twenty-three confirmed individuals."

Marta took the final mouthful of wine and paced the floor, her gut twisting. There had been two creatures—Max and Lois, and now there were twenty-three, possibly more! Pain spiked at her innards. Blake continued to scrutinise the screen, a smile stuck to his lips. How the hell could he sit there and smile, as though it were some sort of game?

"That's not a great success rate, Blake. In the past two days you've only managed to capture one and chip two."

He twisted the chair to face her. "These creatures are the ultimate apex predator, Marta. What they're capable of is quite incredible. You saw what Max did to Walton. I'm prepared to take some risks, but I'm not sending lambs to the slaughter. We'll get more. We just have to be patient. Tracking them in the forest is too dangerous. We're waiting for them to go to the village."

She huffed, her guts twisting. The last thing she wanted was to stay here any longer.

"Why don't you get on with what you're good at? Huh? Leave me to organise my men."

She pulled her lips back against her teeth. If she could walk away from this right now, she would, but she was in way too deep, she knew way too much for them to let her just walk away, and besides, if she could hold her nerve, she would never have to worry about money again—ever.

Blake eyed her and placed both hands on her shoulders. "I know this is terrifying. You don't think I worry about that too? But we've got to trust in the guys down there." He motioned out of the window towards the lawn where the patrol kept guard. "And get on with our part of the plan. The potential here is enormous. Corbeur has said that he's had expression of interest from the Saudis, the Russians, and the North Koreans, as well as the US. Only one will get what we have to offer. They're going to be chewing their hands off to get our product. These creatures are incredible predators, they can hunt and rip a man to shreds before he even has a chance to realise anything is there. They're the next step in biological warfare. Can you imagine what carnage a pack of these could do?"

She grimaced. "I've seen what they can do."

"They can be a force for good."

"How the hell do you figure that?"

"Right, so, ISIS. We're both agreed that they're monsters—one of the most brutal and disgusting terror groups that has ever existed, right?"

"Right."

"They hide among civilians. When soldiers go in to ferret them out, there's always the possibility that they'll be the next victim. These," Blake motioned to the screen, "are apex predators that could sniff them out and kill them before they've even had a chance to realize they're in the same room. If we can control them, then they'll be a new biological weapon to be used against terrorists. Plus, the wolfmen are expendable. No one would care if they're killed in action. They're just another weapon that has been utilised. No harm done." Blake's eyes gleamed. "And ... and this is the amazing part, if they pro-create, we can train them from being pups."

"Jesus!"

He laughed. "We are all God's creation."

"These aren't."

He laughed again. "True. These are yours and Max Anderson's babies."

She shook her head. The idea was ... disgusting. The idea was brilliant. Any country that had a pack of these monsters would be feared—the regimes *Titan Blane Industries* peddled their wares to would snap their hands off to gain them, the bidding war would be beyond her wildest dreams. She snorted. "You may get your wish, Blake. They're constantly shagging, perhaps they'll even have litters."

His eyes widened with a greedy glimmer. "I knew there was a reason I liked you, Marta."

She leant into him. "Only one, Blake?"

# CHAPTER FORTY-SIX

The pain down Freddie's side was excruciating, a stitch he hadn't experienced since high school. Sweat beaded at his temples and trickled down to his sideburns. He knew with certainty that if the things caught up with them, there was no way on God's earth that they could outrun them. He has pushed himself hard, pushed Hayley and Jude too, encouraging them to move faster, always faster. Judy was the slowest, but none of them were in peak fitness. He wished now he'd listened to Hayley, and joined her morning run, or used the gym on the rig. Instead, he'd sat with the blokes, drinking a beer after his shift, playing cards, or just chewing the fat. Now, it was Hayley who was keeping a good pace and, despite her heavy breaths, they were not gasping ones like his, and her face wasn't puce. "Stop! Just for a minute." He bent over, hands on knees, catching his breath, then stood, fingers digging at the stitch in his side. Judy caught up.

Beyond, as the crow flew to the south, was the edge of the forest. To their right was the river that led off Kielder Lake. Jake down at the sailing club was fond of boasting that it was the biggest man-made lake in Europe. Now it sat as a silent expanse of black glass in the far distance whipped by the wind into wavelets and spattered with rain. Another gust of wind blew, and icy water spattered against Freddie's cheeks. He welcomed the chill against his burning cheeks and took another drag of cold air.

"Have you noticed how the howling has stopped?"

"Yeah."

"Last time they seemed further away."

Freddie disagreed. To him they had sounded even closer, but he didn't contradict Judy; he needed her to stay calm. He nodded. "Could be."

She sighed, blowing out a great breath, shoulders sagging. "I can see the edge of the forest." She jabbed a hand to where the line of trees came to an abrupt halt. Beyond that a large swathe of land had been logged, and stumpy orange-brown trunks littered the area. In the distance was movement, slabs of grey rolling along the winding hillside roads.

"What if they follow us?"

The prospect of the creatures following them out of the forest wasn't something that Freddie had considered. His whole thought process, all his energy, had been geared towards reaching the edge; that was their escape point—that was safety. "They won't." He snapped back. "Sorry! I didn't mean to snap. What I meant to say was that-" She wasn't listening, and Freddie followed her concerned gaze. The trees seemed to undulate, their trunks fluid, until Freddie realised that the movement didn't belong to the woods. Figures stepped out from behind the trunks, naked bodies that blended with the brown of the trees and the forest floor. He swallowed hard as his eyes flitted from face to face, chests to navels, to naked thighs, genitals, and buttocks. He swallowed again as he recognised their faces. The small one behind the leader was Rachel Kendrick.

He quickly shifted his eyes from her to the large male standing out in the open. Max Anderson. He remembered him as a friendly, bespectacled studious type, obviously in love with his new wife. He'd even attended their evening wedding reception. He scanned the others. Another child—this one a male—Jake Ashton's boy. And Lois Maybank! But it couldn't be! He'd shot her through the neck, and this creature's throat, though still smeared with blood, seemed undamaged. He'd seen the wound, the gaping hole left by the bullet, bullets that were meant to expand and explode inside rats and mammals. How could she still be alive? Ridiculously, her hair, though matted, was still hanging in a side plait, a pink bow dangling at her ear. Some of the others he didn't recognise, their features too corrupted to tell. He attempted to swallow but his mouth was completely dry. There were at least thirty monsters, all staring back at him with blood-filled eyes, jaws opening and snapping shut. His gut twisted. Hayley's fingernails dug into his forearm.

The biggest, the one at the front, Max Anderson, tipped his head back. In that second, Freddie realised that he was sounding a charge. "Run!" he yelled and grabbed Hayley's arm. "Down the hill!"

Max Anderson howled, the noise bellowing from his chest, carrying across the air, and filling Freddie's ears. All other sound disappeared.

He charged down the hill whilst behind him the air filled with the thunder of yaps, yowls, and thudding feet crashing over the forest floor. His pulse pounded in his head, his breath rasped, Hayley gained on him. Judy screamed.

Freddie turned to the scream. Judy was surrounded, forced to the floor by the creatures, her arms visible as she punched out. The largest male lunged down and her scream stopped.

Pain seared his shoulder and old wounds opened as the tip of a claw ripped at his back. He powered forward. No thoughts passed, only the desperate need to gain distance between himself and the creature at his heels. Below him, Hayley jumped down to the river's bank and waded into the water.

Breath blew hot on Freddie's cheek. Teeth gnashed, brushing against his skin. His nostrils filled with the stench of stagnant water.

He stumbled, his foot catching on a root, and he became airborne. Arms flailing, he landed with a thud. A dull and heavy pain broke through his body and somewhere at the edge of his awareness Hayley screamed. Then he was being dragged. Ice cold water lapped over his face, and he spluttered, scrabbling against watery ground. Cold wrapped around his feet, legs, and belly, and his mouth filled with water. A hand cupped his chin, lifting his head to the surface, he gasped, pulled air into his lungs, and caught sight of the bank. The creatures stood along the edge their yowls and yaps filling the air.

They stood in a huddle, some running backwards then forwards, others twisting in circles yapping and snarling. Hayley pulled at Freddie's arm, dragging him to deeper water. A female ran across the pebbles, staring straight at him, knocking into another. She turned and gnashed her teeth. In the next second, the larger female attacked, biting down on the smaller one, scratching at her arms, ripping gashes in her back. The smaller female retreated, making herself small, then scurried to the back of the group.

"They're not coming in."

The large male that stood at its centre of the chaotic group, steadfast as the others yapped, snarled, and ran along the bank.

"Freddie! Come on." Hayley tugged at his arm.

He broke away from Max's blood-filled eyes and scanned the river and its banks. Only fifteen feet stood between them and the ravenous horde of monsters. There was another ten feet to the other bank.

"Which way?"

"If we follow the river we can get out of the forest. If we go back upriver, then we can get back to the lake and the village."

A howl erupted from the large male and the hairs on Freddie's arm prickled, painful on his cooling skin. The water pushed against his legs, his toes already becoming numb.

"If we follow the river out of here, we'll be safe."

The figures on the bank clustered around the male then, as a pack, ran back up the steep bank and disappeared into the forest. Only two remained.

"Come on, Hayley." Freddie took the first steps upriver. The creatures mirrored his steps.

"They're following us."

Freddie turned, waded upriver for ten feet. The creatures followed.

"Jesus!

Grabbing a stone from the riverbed, Hayley lobbed it. "Fuck off!" It landed with a thud, several feet from the target. The larger male barked and darted towards the river, then pulled back.

"Damned monsters, why can't they just fuck off!"

"They're fucking demented." Her voice cracked. "Fuck ... Off!" She screamed and this time grabbed a handful of stones from the riverbed, lobbing them in rapid succession at the hideous creatures. One hit home, bouncing off the smaller male's temple. He growled at her, gnashing his teeth.

Following the flow of the river, they waded towards the forest boundary.

THE SCENE WAS TERRIFYING, but utterly fascinating. Marta kneaded Blake's shoulder as the drama played out on the screen. It was like watching one of those found footage horror films, only far more absorbing. This was real. This was happening within the forest, the now black and utterly terrifying forest that surrounded her as she watched. Another bottle of wine sat on the desk, half empty, but Marta remained stone cold sober. Blake's hand squeezed her arse cheeks as he leant forward, his running commentary barely noticed as Marta continued to watch. In the room three more screens had been set up to relay back the live feed from the drones. Two had followed the pack and the other bikers as they made their bid for freedom. Marta's pulse throbbed with a dull, but rapid thud at the base of her neck; she'd watched with fascination as the two females fought. What was truly fascinating was the way in which the creatures were now interacting.

Marta had barely been able to watch as the heavier set blonde had dragged the biker into the ferns, but instead of tearing him apart, eviscerating him as she'd expected, the woman had bitten his shoulder then dragged him away. She'd ordered the drone to follow them and to her surprise the woman hadn't killed him. The creature had watched the man buck and twist, his face contorted in agony, and then guarded him when the others arrived. That too was a twist Marta hadn't expected. Lois had howled and less than ten minutes later a whole horde had arrived. That group had then followed the survivors to the river.

Back in the forest, Max had appeared, circled the well-endowed blonde with her infected biker. Both had snapped and snarled. The woman had been fierce, taking great swipes from Max that had sliced the flesh of her stomach, but hadn't backed down. She'd torn into him, then run back to the still writhing biker, hovered over him, pulled him into her arms, and gnashed her teeth at Max. What she'd watched, she felt sure, was the woman claiming a new mate. Certainly, the woman hadn't gone on with the rest of the pack.

"Blake. I want these two targeting for tracking." She pointed at the screen.

His attention was on the scene at the river. "Why?"

"Because I think they're forming a new pack."

He grunted, his attention absorbed by the other drama.

"It's fascinating, Blake. We could develop entire squads of ... dog soldiers."

He grunted again and tapped at the screen. "We may have a problem."

Irked at his indifference, she snapped. "What?"

"They're afraid of water."

His words were sandpaper. "Shit!"

# CHAPTER FORTY-SEVEN

Freddie and Hayley reached the edge of the forest as the sun reached its final decline. Still parallel, along the bank, were the two creatures. Twice they had disappeared. Twice Freddie had let his hopes that they had finally given up hunting them rise. Twice he had been disappointed. Now, as he stared at the point where the river left the forest he was crushed. The river narrowed before disappearing underground. In itself, this was a disaster, the creatures would attack as soon as he and Hayley set foot on dry land. Worse was the fence of narrow rods that lay across it.

"It's a dead end."

"What's the fence for?"

Freddie took another step forward. The creatures moved closer. The narrow rods were threaded with wire.

"It doesn't look like the one Conrad Shelby described. He said that had thick panels twenty feet high." Hayley took a step forward, peering over Freddie's shoulder. The creatures yelped with excitement. One rushed towards the fence.

"Maybe he exaggerated. He's known to be a bit of a bullshitter."

"Conrad? He's alright. A bit posh-"

Hayley's defence of Conrad came to an abrupt halt as the creature reached out to touch the 'fence' and was instantly thrown back, landing in the trickling water. It lay inert, water lapping at its head, as the other began an agitated dance.

"It's not moving. What should we do?"

"Do? Bloody nothing. I'm not going to help it! It's not some injured animal you've found at the roadside."

Hayley remained silent and he regretted his barbed response. He got it though - that reflex - to help something that was hurt.

"It's an electric fence."

"Maybe for the sheep?"

"Sheep?"

"Yeah, to keep them in."

"It looks new."

They both considered the fence as the creature on the bank ran in circles whilst the other lay deathly quiet in the water.

Freddie watched its ribcage, waiting for the rise and fall. It remained still. "It's dead."

"Yes!" Hayley fist-pumped the air then tugged at Freddie's sleeve. "If we can't get back this way, then we'll have to go upriver."

"But the dam's that way."

"Yes, and so are the lake and the village. If we can't get out, Freddie, we need to get back."

He grunted. It would be a long and freezing journey back, but at least they could share what they'd discovered with PC Latimer and the others.

AS THE MINUTES PASSED to hours, the ache in Javeen's limbs and joints became unbearable as she sat cramped next to Andy in the tiny cupboard. Footsteps had come dangerously close to their hiding place numerous times and each time Javeen had steeled herself to jump up and wrestle whoever was on the other side to the floor. As time passed, the voices in the room grew fewer and eventually only one pair of shoes could be heard tapping about the floor. When the door of the lab opened and clicked shut for a final time, Javeen was woken from her half-sleep by Andy. He nudged her arm.

"Wake up Sleeping Beauty."

She made a soft grunt. "Have they gone?"

"Sounds like it."

He eased the door open to a dark room. Outside the sun was making its final descent behind the trees. Only their outlines, black and jagged, were visible, the sky a ribbon of pale orange topped by a bright, but darkening blue.

"Looks like we're stuck here for the night."

"Hell!"

"Well, there's no way I'm risking going out in the dark."

Javeen let out a dissatisfied, bordering on angry, sigh.

"It's not my fault!"

"No, of course it's not. I'm just gutted that we couldn't get back." The strain of the day bubbled to the surface and tears pricked at her eyes. "I wanted to get back to the village. Now they're all down there—just sitting ducks for those monsters."

"What could you have done, Jav? I mean seriously, what could you have done? This situation needs some serious military intervention, and from what we've heard, that's the last thing that is going to happen."

Javeen swallowed, sickness swirling in her belly. He was right. Absolutely right.

"They've fenced us in with them, Jav. Fenced us in to protect *them*, not us. They don't care who dies in the process."

She glanced across the greyed-out and darkening room to the bank of cages. A green light shone at the side of the one with the girl. She snorted in her drugged sleep. Javeen grimaced. "Poor thing."

"Poor thing?"

"It's not her fault is it. She can't help being like that."

"A monster?"

"Yes, a monster." She took another step closer. The girl shifted in her sleep. "I think I recognise her."

Andy stepped beside her, peering into the cage. "Me too. Is it Wendy, Zena's daughter?"

"I think so. Zena and Alex were in the convoy that followed Conrad to the blockade. They have three girls."

"She's only eight."

"Was. You can't think of them as human anymore, Jav. She would kill you in an instant if she had the chance." He pointed to the clear plastic container now sitting on the desk. "That could be her dinner."

Inside was a mass of reddish-brown flesh, a mixture of heart, intestines, kidneys, and liver. "Gross! What the hell is that from?"

"Too small to be human-"

"Surely to God, they wouldn't feed her human meat!"

"Who knows. If they're willing to fence us in here, then maybe so."

Outside a howl carried to the windows and vibrated in the room. Javeen's heart thumped and the stench of her own fear, harsh and sour, rose to her nostrils. "I know we're stuck here for the night, but there is no way on God's earth that I'm having a sleepover with a werewolf!"

THE JOURNEY BACK UP the river had led Freddie and Hayley to the dam. They'd managed to clamber up its concrete sides then down into the lake. The creature that had followed them had disappeared with the dark and there had been no sight of it since. Even with the moon at its brightest, Freddie hadn't been able to discern movement along the shore. Exhausted, but too afraid to make their way to the village, they'd decided to wade along the lake's shore towards the marina and then swim out to one of the boats anchored at a safe distance from land and inaccessible to the monsters that prowled the forest. The boat had a cabin in its hull and was stocked with a few packets of biscuits, squash, and a six-pack of bottled water.

Freddie slumped down on the couch-cum-bed as Hayley opened a packet of Jaffa Cakes. He took one with gratitude, his bare legs resting against the opposite seat and bit down. "Never in my life has a Jaffa Cake tasted so good!"

Hayley bit down on her own biscuit, her bare legs matching his across the walkway. "You're not wrong."

The gaslight of the tiny stove burned blue. A bright LED hung between them, illuminating the cabin. Wet jeans hung over the railings, crystals of frost already creeping across their threads. Hayley shivered and wriggled her toes. Freddie took her foot and rubbed, gesturing to his own with a nod of his head. She laughed and cradled his foot on her lap and rubbed. Though cold in the cabin, it was warmer than the freezing lake, and the stove, with its burning gas combined with their body heat, was bringing it from uncomfortable to cosy. Freddie's cheeks burned as his body temperature rose.

After sharing the packet of biscuits and drinking a cup of black tea, they searched the cabin for other supplies. Among the ropes, wellies, and tools was a box for emergencies. Hayley grabbed a tube and held it up. "Is this a flare?"

Freddie peered down. "Looks like it."

She put it back. "No point using that. There's no one coming to rescue us."

"Nope." Freddie pulled the blanket tighter around his shoulders.

"We're on our own." Another howl split the night and Hayley pulled at her own blanket. "Let's stay here, Freddie. On the boat. I don't want to go back ashore."

A howl was accompanied by a scream whilst in the distance the chopping blades of a helicopter hummed.

# CHAPTER FORTY-EIGHT

The helicopter swung over the trees, the cameras picking up nothing but black in this part of the woods. Marv Chapman glanced down to the forest below where the high intensity beam exposed grey trees beneath the blanket of black. This had to be the strangest, and potentially most terrifying, job he'd ever been assigned to. Blake Dalton hadn't exactly been honest when he'd first contacted him to set up the mission, but he couldn't really blame the man, the truth would have sounded insane. Even now, Marv wasn't sure he hadn't imagined the creatures pictured on the drones' video recordings. That there were large, fast-moving creatures down in the woods was undeniable, the thermal camera had picked them up, and whatever they were, they moved with incredible speed and agility.

"Gotcha!" Ryan McPherson, one of the other members of the group, blurted with undisguised excitement.

Marv turned back to the camera where untidy orange dots moved across the screen.

"Ah! Wait. No. That must be a herd of deer; they're moving all wrong."

"Let's take a look." From his vantage point Marv could see nothing. "Swing left, Archie."

The pilot manoeuvred the helicopter and a beam of light shone down to the area of open grassland where the forest gave way to a clearing. At its centre, a herd of deer galloped into the forest where the thermal camera picked them up winding between the trees.

"Confirmed. Let's head to the village."

Two minutes later the thermal camera picked up heat. The village streetlights cast a dull orange haze and several houses glowed.

"Must be some survivors down there?"

"Dunno. You've seen the videos. Does anything stand a chance against those monsters?"

Marv had heard the talk, listened to Blake brag about the superhuman agility of the 'werewolves', and watched the videos. They had made his stomach churn. He couldn't bring himself to call the infected and deformed monsters that now infested the forest and preyed on the people left in the village, 'werewolves', but that they were lethal predators with incredible speed and strength was not in doubt. They also seemed to have astounding regenerative capabilities. Marv had never seen anything like them. His best guess was that the *Institute* had been carrying out some possibly illegal, definitely unethical, drug tests that had gone wrong. Now the 'patients' had gone AWOL and were rampaging through the town and it was Marv's job to bring them back in. The fence that was being constructed 24/7 around the village made him uneasy. It took real money, deep state kind of money, billionaire kind of money, to put up a thing like that. There had been a total media blackout about it too. He'd checked online, snooped around, and there was nothing. Nada. Zilch.

Thermal outlines of moving shapes appeared on the camera's screen. "Got some!"

"Let's get a look at these beasts then."

Marv reached into his bag and pulled out the tranquiliser gun. Marston had assured him that there were enough drugs in a single shot to floor an elephant.

"Going down."

Two figures bounded along the road then scuttled to the left. Marv fired a shot. The beast dropped to the floor. "Got it!"

"We need two."

Marv reloaded as the creature's companion stopped. O'Keefe fired. The second orange outline stopped moving.

"Job done!"

The helicopter landed though the blades continued to rotate.

Marv jumped to the tarmac, scanning the area, the torch on his helmet flooding the scene ahead. The two monsters lay fifty feet up the road. "O'Keefe. Let's haul them in." Marv was under no illusion; for the next few seconds they were vulnerable. McPherson jumped to his side, scanning the area, ready to fire at anything that moved.

"Go!"

Senses heightened, alert for any movement among the houses, or in the front gardens, Marv made his way to the bodies. Deep in the forest a howl erupted, carried on the wind, and made the hairs on his neck tingle though it was too far away to be of concern. He ran to the prone bodies. This was first contact, and he was eager to get a close inspection of the creatures he'd only seen in grainy video footage.

The first thing that struck him was the smell. His nose wrinkled. "God that hums!"

O'Keefe grunted as he shone light on the first body. "Take a look at this, Sarge."

Marv leant in, nose wrinkling, a deep and questioning frown across his brow. "What in the very name of God is it?"

"It's a woman, Sarge."

O'Keefe put out a tentative hand, then pushed at the creature's leg, rolling it over onto its back, the tranquilising dart sticking out from its neck.

"That is one hairy beast." O'Keefe snorted as he pointed a finger at the creature's genitals. Thick and curling hair spreads over the rising mound, spreading across its belly and down its legs.

"Tits could do with a Brazilian too."

McPherson snorted.

Scanning its body, the lean muscles, the curve of its belly and hips, the breasts full and rounded, it appeared athletic, and young. Marv crouched, inching closer for a better view. The woman's – no, female's – face was threaded with blue veins, and dark hair had grown over its top lip, cheeks, and forehead. Its mouth hung open as it lay unconscious. Incisors at least an inch long hung down from its upper jaw, those on the bottom jaw were shorter, but no less sharp.

"It looks like some fucked-up dog/human mutant."

"Sarge, do you think those sick bastards at the *Institute* did this?"

*Yes, I fucking do.* Marv held his tongue. Whatever, whoever, was behind this wasn't someone he wanted to cross. "We're here to do a job, so let's do it." He stood, slipped the torch back in its holder and unzipped his bag, pulled out the cable ties and passed them to McPherson. O'Keefe lowered the stretcher next to the unconscious creature. "Secure the subject and get it on board." As he made his way to the next body. A howl split the air. A howl that sounded much closer than the last. Grabbing a handful of cable ties, he bound the hands and ankles of the male's feet. It twitched as he grabbed its wrists and crossed them. Marv flinched and scanned its face for signs of waking. The black eyes were half open but didn't appear to see him. A pulse throbbed steadily at its throat. He slipped the thick black plastic tie around its wrist and then tied its ankles, grunting with relief as the thing was secured and sedated, and showed no sign of waking. Although he had been reassured that the effects of the tranquiliser would last long enough for them to bring it back to the *Institute*, sweat beaded at his brow, the cloth under his arms damp.

"Get these fuckers on board and let's get the hell out of here."

*Take it easy, Marv. Just take it easy.* He took a breath and wished he hadn't. Despite easing the tension across his chest, his nose filled with particles of the creature's stench, a revolting aroma like his grandfather's old gundog. Grandad would always put the dog, a very friendly, but sadly odorous, English Springer Spaniel, in the back-place after a day's shooting. The dog would have mud up to its knees, black marsh mud that clung in thick lumps to its fur, and it stank.

With the first body hauled into the helicopter, and dumped on its bare metal floor, the stretcher returned for the male. Grabbing the monster beneath its armpits Marv hauled it across. The thing twitched, then snorted. Marv scanned its face, heart pounding. There was no sign of it being conscious, but Marston had promised that it would be in a state of complete paralysis, which meant that it should not be bloody twitching. For a moment he considered leaving it on the ground. If it woke during the flight ... *Just get back to base and offload the thing!* "Let's get it to the helicopter. O'Keefe, keep this one next to the door and a shot ready."

"Yes, Sir."

A screech split the air. The skin of Marv's scalp tightened.

"That was too fucking close!"

"Get in!"

At the open door of the helicopter, Marv jumped in, and kicked at the female's thigh. When it made no response he gestured for McPherson and O'Keefe to lift the male on board.

The screech was followed by a howl. The noise was close, could be coming from one of the nearby gardens.

Startled, O'Keefe stumbled. One side of the stretcher slipped from his grip. The creature slid to the ground, knocking its head on the tarmac with a grunt.

"For fuck's sake!"

"Sorry! It's those fucking howls. They shit me up."

"Just haul the fucker up. Grab its wrists and ankles and throw it in."

The men bent to grab its ankles and wrists but as they straightened, grunting with the burden, movement caught in Marv's peripheral vision. He snapped his head to see a figure stepping out from behind the brick pillar of a garden wall. More movement, this time to his left, and then another creature, its features contorted by the streetlight's orange haze, jumped across the bonnet of a parked car.

"Drop the body," Marv commanded. "And get in!"

Breath caught in Marv's chest as the men released the creature. It thudded once more to the tarmac, a spasm rocking its body. Eyes flicked opened, teeth instantly bared.

"In! In! In!"

He scrambled back as his men hauled themselves into the helicopter. "Go! Take off! Take off! Take off!"

The creatures sprinted. Marv's heart thudded and as the helicopter lifted from the ground, angry grunts and yelps filled the air. Teeth bared, the screeching grunts of the animals running towards them pierced Marv's ear.

As McPherson reached up to pull himself inside the helicopter a clawed hand grabbed his shoulder. Unbalanced, he fell back. Marv fired, hitting the creature in the shoulder. Punched by the force, it staggered back. McPherson scrambled to stand and began to pull himself into the cabin.

The blades thwacked in a steady monotony as the helicopter began to lift. A clawed hand slammed down on McPherson's back. McPherson screamed and the helicopter swayed as a creature jumped onto his back, locking his head in its arm. Once again, Marv aimed his rifle, shooting at the creature. It fell back as the bullet obliterated the back of its skull, but as it released McPherson, a third creature sprinted forward and with one enormous leap landed on McPherson's back. Teeth snapped only inches from Marv's face and the weight of the creature broke McPherson's grip, and the man fell from the helicopter.

"No!"

The helicopter rose above the road as McPherson disappeared beneath a frenzy of biting jaws and grabbing hands. His screamed pierced Marv's soul. Aiming his rifle, he pulled the trigger. The bullet hit home, passing through a monster's open jaw and hitting McPherson immediately above the bridge of his nose. It was the only humane thing to do.

As the helicopter lifted above the cottages and turned in the direction of the *Institute*, the female moved. Marston had assured him it would be completely paralysed—comatose for hours! Still reeling from the death of McPherson, he grabbed the case strapped behind O'Keefe's head. He grunted as Marv fumbled with the straps, but didn't complain, his eyes fixed on the jerking creature on the floor.

The spasm could be involuntary, but Marv was not taking any chances. He ripped open the case and grabbed one of the pre-prepared syringes. Marston had told him exactly what to do in this eventuality; instructions that Marv now suspected were a back-up for Marston's guesstimate on how long the sedative would work on the monsters. *Not as bloody long as you calculated, Marston. Nowhere near.* 'An intramuscular injection at the ventrogluteal site is the best option for a rapid absorption of the drug. Use the Z-track technique, so pull the skin laterally away from the injection

site, inject the medication, withdraw the needle, and release
the skin. Using this site allowed us to use a longer needle
with a larger gauge therefore penetrating deeper into the
muscle with a larger dose'. Translated this meant, stab the
fucker in the arse with a big dose of poison to close it down.
Marv rolled the monster to its side, repulsed by the hairs on
the woman's hips and buttocks. He stabbed the long needle
into its rump then pushed the plunger down until all the
medication had been absorbed into its body and withdrew
the needle.

Within two seconds, the jerking and spasms stopped,
and the creature lay still but for the pulsing throb at its
throat.

"Jesus, it stinks."

Marv stared down at it, gritted his teeth, and clenched
his jaw. Every ounce of his being wanted to take his gun
and blow its head off. Every rational, sane, instinctive desire
wanted to destroy it. He gripped the gun in his hand and
pointed the barrel.

"Chapman, put the gun down."

"It's unnatural. Obscene. Things like that shouldn't be
alive."

"Yeah, but it is, and it is our job to bring it in."

He glared at the monster laid out across the floor—a
repulsive parody of a woman. Something glinted in its hair,
and he bent to retrieve it.

"What is it?"

He plucked the metal from the lock of hair. "It's a
hairgrip." He held it up for inspection, a prong of softly
zig-zagged metal sat between his thumbs.

"My sister uses those." O'Keefe gently moved the creature's black hair to the side to reveal its ears. A stud of gold sat at the centre of its lobe. "What the hell have they been doing at that laboratory? This is ... was ... a woman."

Marv sat back hard against his seat. "Something fucking evil."

# CHAPTER FORTY-NINE

The night had been uncomfortable. The sound of the helicopter taking off, along with the haunting noise of the wolfmen's howling, had penetrated the confines of the canteen's food store. Sleep had been broken and shallow as they took it in turns to listen for the sound of approaching footsteps, or, Javeen's worst fear, the breaking of the orangery's glass walls. Her heart had palpitated as they'd stepped inside the cupboard, and she had realised just how vulnerable the glass structure made them. If one of *them* got in, it would be goodbye cruel world, hello a savage death or, perhaps worse, a walking death. Either way, it wasn't good. To her relief, as the grey light of morning filtered in through the small window, the glass hadn't been shattered, and she hadn't been savaged to death by a stinking and hairy beast. Their stink was one of the abiding details of Ben's story of the two females' visit to his bedroom. 'Stank like shit, it did—their breath. Shit and wet dog.' Strange how that detail seemed more repellent than the knowledge that they'd rip out your innards and eat your kidneys.

Andy pulled a packet of biscuits from the shelf, tore at the packaging, and offered it to Javeen. She took one and followed it with a sip of water. If they had to hide out somewhere, then the store cupboard would at least help them stay alive. "Shame we can't take this lot with us." She

330

gestured to the stocks of biscuits, bread, crumpets, teacakes, water, tea, and coffee. It hadn't crossed her mind until now that if the village was fenced off then there would be no trips to the supermarket in the next town and no food deliveries to the shop. She, Andy, and the remaining villagers, once they'd munched through their stores at home, would begin to starve. She huffed. If there were any villagers left today. *Please let them be alive!*

"We *can* take some. There are bags over there." Andy proceeded to fill a couple of bags with supplies as Javeen brushed off biscuit crumbs and leant an ear to the door. All was silent. By the light seeping in through the window, given the time of year, it must be getting on for eight o'clock. They hadn't heard a howl for the last hour. "Time to go, Andy."

She eased the door open then checked across the room. "Clear," she whispered and took a tentative step out of the storeroom before running to the glass door. Beyond, the mist lay heavy across the grass, hiding the helicopter's landing gear. Its position had moved, confirming the noise last night had been the helicopter taking off.

Andy nudged her, and they both sprinted across the back of the *Institute*, racing across the dew-sodden grass, and slipping through the wires to the other side. Javeen's breath billowed as white clouds. They ran together back to the car and fell inside. Javeen clicked the central-locking and dropped back against the seat. The relief was huge. Without waiting for the condensation to clear, Javeen turned the car to face home whilst Andy wiped at the windscreen.

As they approached the village, dread settled like a damp cloth. What carnage had night brought to their tiny, and rapidly shrinking, community. First stop would be home to freshen up, then she would make the rounds with the map and pen. She dreaded having to put a red cross against a single home.

As the car passed over the village threshold, and then moved past the first houses, the roads were empty. In the distance black smoke twined into grey drizzle. Smoke rising from chimneys was not unusual, most of the houses still had coal-burning fires or log burners, but the smoke that was visible on one of the village's easterly roads was more like a bonfire. Andy mirrored her unease.

"Who'd have a bonfire at this time of day? There's something not right over there, Jav."

Despite her desperate need to go home and freshen-up, she accelerated and turned to the smoke.

"Looks like it's coming from Conrad's place."

Ahead, the smoke rose above a small cottage sat in grounds surrounded by trees. As they drew close, the source of the smoke became obvious. Javeen had expected to see the burned-out shell of the cottage, instead the remains of two cars sat charred and smoking on the driveway.

"What the hell happened here?"

Apart from the two cars, which had been parked about ten feet across the front of the cottage, there were the remains of other burning objects including a chest of drawers. The charcoaled remains and ashes circled the house.

"Andy, what does this look like to you?"

"Well." He rubbed at the stubble on his chin. "I reckon Conrad put a barricade around the cottage and set it on fire."

"That's what I thought." Her chest tightened. "Something very bad happened here last night." Movement at the window caught her attention, and then a hand waved. Her relief was undisguised. "Conrad!"

Within seconds, the front door swung open and Conrad, face pale, eyes puffy and red-rimmed, stood with his rifle in hand. Behind him stood Moira, her blonde hair pulled back in a functional ponytail. She looked tired but defiant.

"Come on in," she beckoned.

Javeen jumped across a narrow section of the dying bonfire.

"Sorry about that." Conrad took a firm grip of her elbow and guided her through the front door. Andy followed. "Good to see you, PC Latimer, and you too, Blackwell."

The door clicked behind them, and Moira gave a sigh of relief. "Sorry to pull at you like that, but after the night we've had, we're both a little jumpy."

"What happened here, Mr Shelby?"

"Moira, let's get that kettle on," he said as she stepped through to the kitchen.

"Already on it, love."

"Come through." Conrad led them through to the kitchen, asked them to take a seat, and then began his story. "After it became obvious that we weren't going to be able to leave the village, we decided that we should make this place a fortress." He motioned to the panel of wood that sat propped against the kitchen cabinets. Javeen noticed the screw holes in the wooden frame of the window above the sink. "I've taken this one off this morning to let some light in, but the other windows are all blocked in."

"I hate it being so dingey," Moira said.

"You don't mind it keeping us safe."

"No, of course not, love." Moira dropped teabags into the teapot and reached for the cupboard. Javeen noticed the quick frown that passed over Conrad's face. Moira tightened her lips but let her hand drop. She took the exchange as evidence that Conrad was also aware of their predicament; no deliveries would be made to the village which meant food supplies would soon run short, so no biscuits to be offered with the tea.

"I did the same at mine," Andy added.

"Good man."

"I hate it though," Moira added as the kettle boiled. "It made me feel trapped."

"That's exactly how I felt," Javeen replied. Andy's house had quickly become claustrophobic as each window had been blocked up. "I hated not being able to see outside."

"You can't see if they're on the attack," Moira said.

"Precisely."

"We have CCTV so we could see what was coming for us."

"And they did," Moira added.

Tea was poured and handed round as Conrad described the attack. After the previous night, when many of the villagers had been attacked in their own homes, he'd decided that the only way they would survive was to be prepared, so the windows were blocked, his rifle cleaned and loaded, and the garden booby-trapped. Every piece of old furniture and wood he had was laid out as a bonfire around the house. He'd sloshed it with lighter fuel and petrol, and waited, watching for any sign on the CCTV monitor. He'd waited all night and was almost ready to give up and go to bed when the first one arrived. It had tipped its head and howled.

As they gathered in the driveway, he'd thrown the first Molotov cocktail at the petrol-soaked driveway beyond the wooden blockade. The driveway had burst into flames, the fuel quickly used up, but it gave him time to set the blockade alight. Moira, who was an experienced clay pigeon shooter had covered him whilst he set it ablaze.

"I shot them. I shot five of them, but they just got back up, kept dancing around the house, screeching and snarling. I could see them through the flames, demented, howling beasts. They were furious they couldn't get through."

"How did you keep them at bay? The furniture must have burned quite quickly."

"It did. I'd parked the cars there too. Sadly, they had to be sacrificed. Went with quite a bang did my old Nissan."

"We had a stash of Molotovs too, at the side of the door."

"They didn't leave until the sun came up."

Javeen sipped her tea. Conrad's efforts to keep himself and Moira safe during the night had been immense, heroic, but it was only one night. Their efforts hadn't destroyed a single creature and tonight, they would return.

She took another sip of tea. "Mr. Shelby-"

"Conrad."

"Conrad. How will you protect yourself tonight?"

Conrad slipped an arm around Moira's shoulder. His face drained of colour. "We're going to spend the day making the cottage safer, setting more traps."

Moira bit her bottom lip and glanced to the window. "We'll fight them to the end."

Javeen doubted they would get through another night, and if these creatures were hunting in packs, then perhaps neither would she and Andy. "There's another option."

All eyes turned to her.

"We all go to the castle."

Conrad sat up straight. Moira looked confused.

"The castle?"

"Yes. It's the safest place I can think of. It has thick walls, narrow windows, heavy doors."

"It was never built as a defensive structure, Latimer. It's really only a castle by name."

"You're right, but we can make it a fortress against them. There's nowhere else that can offer us that kind of protection. It has a wall and gates."

"Yes." Moira's eyes brightened. "And there are cellars, and a kitchen, and a café, and toilets."

"Café and toilets?"

"Yes. What I mean is, that there are the amenities to house quite a few of the villagers. Enough rooms, and dining space. Don't you remember too, that all of the windows have their own shutters."

"She's right."

Conrad nodded. "I have to agree. Despite our best efforts, given the strength, ferocity, and cunning of these beasts, I don't think that we will survive here tonight."

Moira shuddered and Conrad pulled her close.

"That's settled then. We're going to move the villagers up to the castle."

# CHAPTER FIFTY

Marta clicked the office door shut for the last time. The helicopter's blades pulsed as she lugged the heavy bag over her shoulder. "Marvin. Take this please." She handed him the bag. He took it without question and led the way down the stairs and out to the waiting helicopter. Marta's hair swirled in the blades' turbulence. Blake Dalton was already inside. She slid into her seat and buckled the belt.

"Where's Marston?"

"He's finishing his work in the lab. I gave him instructions to ... eliminate the test subjects."

"He'd better hurry up. I need to get back to the office. I have a meeting with Corbeur scheduled for tomorrow and can't miss my flight."

Marta clenched her teeth. The first sign of a problem and Dalton had bailed. So what if the creatures were afraid of water, surely that was something that could be overcome? A wave of grief for the swollen bank account that she would no longer have, rolled over her.

"This isn't necessary, Dalton."

"I spoke to Corbeur. We agreed. The water issue is a fatal flaw."

"That we could have overcome!"

"Listen." He turned to her with gritted teeth. "The situation here is out of control. Those beasts are monsters. They've wiped out the entire village-"

"Neither you, nor Corbeur, cared about that when you thought you could use them."

"It's a pest control operation now, Steward."

A figure appeared at the glass door of the orangery.

"Here's Marston."

The scientist ran across the grass towards the helicopter, a large satchel slung over his shoulder, a laptop under his arm. The irritated air played with his greying hair, making it dance around his head. He pulled himself into the helicopter with a grunt.

"Is it done?"

He pursed his lips. Getting him to stay on board with the project had been a battle, but everyone had their price, and for Marston it hadn't just been about the money.

"Both have been ... put to sleep, Steward." He turned and locked his eyes to hers with a steel gaze. "If our involvement in this ever gets out-"

"It won't!"

"Then we're finished. They'll lock us away for life."

Dalton leant forward, placed spread fingers over Marston's knee, and squeezed. Marston grimaced. "*They* will never let that happen, Marston."

"They?"

Marta looked out of the window ignoring Marston's pained frown.

"Yes, they."

The helicopter lifted from the ground and Marta's breath caught in her throat, her heart tripping a hard beat. At the treeline stood the distorted figure of Max Anderson. Around him, smaller creatures hopped and jigged as though impatient, whilst larger males and females gathered behind. He lifted his head to howl.

A gunshot rang out and a small creature dropped to the floor.

"Jesus Christ!"

As Max's howl broke through the constant chop, chop of the helicopter's blades, the pack bounded across the lawn towards the *Institute*.

"Get us off the ground!"

The helicopter lifted, swung away from the scene, and Marta watched Marv Chapman fire another shot then retreat at a sprint to the orangery. She screwed her eyes tight shut as Max swiped a clawed hand down onto Marv's shoulder.

THE DOOR CLICKED SHUT behind Javeen. Everything she needed, her clothes, toiletries, and bedding, had been packed into bags and stacked into the car's boot along with every morsel of food from her kitchen cupboards. She checked the sky, and her heart skipped a beat; the sun was beginning its decline. She scanned the trees that bordered the cottage garden. All was still, but that they were infested with the infected 'wolfmen' she was certain. After leaving Conrad and Moira that morning, Javeen, desperate to shower and change her clothes, had made a quick stop at home, and then visited each house without a cross on her list.

As she pulled out of the drive, the list sat on the passenger seat. Red crosses were struck through most of the houses. Of the one hundred and twenty residents of the village that she and Andy had listed, only twenty-eight remained, the rest presumed dead or infected and now lost to the pack. That was how she thought of them now, the infected monsters, as a pack. As she'd made her way around the village, to find the survivors and encourage them to join her at the castle, the same pattern had emerged: broken doors and windows, and inside signs of struggle. In a few, the monsters had left the remains of their feast. Other houses were simply empty, their occupants either dragged off like Jim Kendrick and hung from a tree to be consumed at a later date or bitten and infected. In three, there were villagers who had experienced close encounters. Mrs Simpson was still gibbering about the monsters that had broken into her house. The poor woman had woken up in the middle of the night to find them poring over her, sniffing at her neck and armpits. They'd left her a quivering wreck, but unhurt. As she'd relayed this story, another of Javeen's theories had been confirmed. They didn't attack the sick. Mrs Simpson had breast cancer, recently diagnosed, but virulent and terminal. It made sense. If they were hunting to feed, they wouldn't want to eat poisoned meat. In total, to Javeen's knowledge, there were three villagers with immunity from the beasts: the Reverend, Ben Carter, and Emma Simpson. Sadly, they were terminally ill and very weak, Ben presumed deceased.

As Javeen drove through the village the church came into view and she was reminded of Emily Carmichael, the first witness to what had become a living nightmare. She took a left onto Church Street and pulled up in front of Emily's house. As she knocked on the front door, having glimpsed Emily lying on her sick bed in the living room, the Reverend Baxter walked slowly, leaning heavily on his stick, towards the church. He grimaced as he raised his hand to wave. Javeen knocked again on the door and leant back to wave at Emily through the window. The elderly woman pulled the oxygen mask from her face and mouthed 'come in' as she gestured to Javeen with a gnarled hand.

At the back of the house she checked under the door mat, then under various pots of dormant bulbs and browning lavender shrubs clustered around the doorway, until she found the backdoor key and made her way through to the downstairs bedroom where Emily lay on the hospital-style bed with its clinically white and tubular frame complete with side guards and foot pedal to adjust the height. The woman lay deep in her pillow, her face wan. The room was stuffy and had a stagnant air despite a window kept ajar. The skin of Emily's face looked even more tissue-like than on Javeen's last visit.

Javeen held back the urge to wrinkle her nose. "Mrs Carmichael."

"Emily," she rasped, her voice dry.

"Emily. Would you like some water?"

She nodded.

Javeen refreshed the water in the jug at her bedside and poured some into a clean glass then helped Emily to take a sip. She drank then lay back on the pillow exhausted.

"Kathy? Where is Kathy?"

"She can't come in today, Emily."

"Did they get her?"

"I ..." Javeen didn't want to scare the woman but patronising her by lying was perhaps worse. She was elderly, not a fool. "I'm not sure, Emily, but I think that perhaps they did."

"I've been watching them. Running up and down. Every night there's more of them."

"I'm taking the villagers up to the castle. We'll be safer up there."

"He's been back you know." Emily raised her arm and pointed out through the window.

"Who?"

"Max. He's been back to see her."

Javeen remembered Laura's terrified eyes when she'd visited her after the police team were attacked in the woods, the first day she realised they were trapped with the monsters. The woman had hardly been able to speak, almost catatonic from the terrible nightmares she'd been having. Sweat had trickled down Javeen's temples as Laura had described her terrifying dreams. Javeen had baulked at telling Laura that the dreams were perhaps memories. In her dream, and it had to be a dream she'd insisted, although it had seemed so real, Max was transformed into a monster with fangs, and eyes filled with blood, but it was still him, her husband. He'd pulled back the bed covers and ... She'd stopped then, her pale skin tinged red. 'It was just a dream though. It had to be.'

Emily lay back on the pillow exhausted, her chest heaving. Javeen reached for the oxygen mask and placed it over the woman's mouth. She sucked at the gas greedily.

"Doesn't matter how much I suck, I just can't get enough breath in me."

Javeen's chest tightened in sympathy. "Emily, I'm helping everyone I can to move up to the castle. I'll come back for you later."

"Me, love?"

"Yes. I can't leave you here. They'll be back tonight, and ... you won't be safe."

"Not me love. I'll stay here." She took another massive suck of oxygen.

"But, there's no one to look after you now. Kathy's gone and-"

"No, love. Cyril won't know where to find me, and I've promised him that I'm coming. Don't worry. I won't be alone. Reverend Baxter is coming to sit with me later."

Javeen remembered Emily's insistence that Cyril had told her not to be long, to hurry up and join him on the other side. She glanced from Emily's pallid face to Max Anderson's house opposite.

"I'll be back to collect you later, Mrs-" The woman's snores cut through Javeen's words. She stroked the paper-thin back of Emily's hand. "I'm sorry, Emily, but I can't leave you here. I'll be back later to collect you." As another snore rumbled at the back of Emily's throat and her lungs rattled, Javeen locked the backdoor, slipped the key under the pot, then made her way across the road to Max Anderson's home.

Laura opened the door though seemed in a trance, still in her nightwear and with hair unbrushed. "Mrs Anderson, can I come in for a moment?"

Laura widened the door without speaking and Javeen squeezed through. She noticed her almost furtive glance outside and quick close of the door. As she stepped away, Laura rubbed a hand across her stomach and grasped a chair, her knuckles whitening as she gripped it. "Sit down, Mrs Anderson. You look exhausted. Can I get you a glass of water?"

She seemed confused, but nodded, gulped down the water and asked for more.

"Mrs Anderson," Javeen continued as the second glass disappeared, "the village has become unsafe." Laura stared at her. "We're currently evacuating all surv- ... all remaining villagers up to the castle." Laura nodded. "Are you able to pack some essential items? We're taking clothes, toiletries, and bedding, along with as much food as possible. If you have any camping beds that would be ideal. We do have cooking and washing facilities-"

"Max ..."

Javeen caught her breath.

"Max will want me here."

"I'm not sure what you mean, Mrs Anderson. Do you know where Max is?"

"He's here."

Javeen's heart thumped, and she pushed the chair from the table, scraping it across the floor, spinning to look around the kitchen.

"Not now."

"Jesus! Sorry." Javeen sat back down. *Calm it, Latimer. Stay in control.*

"He's been back."

"He has?" Javeen's skin crawled as she remembered her last sighting of Max Anderson; his fangs and blood-red eyes were terrifying even from a distance.

"He visits at night."

Sickness swelled in Javeen's belly. "He does?" *Such incisive questioning, Latimer!* "Could you ... could you tell me what happens when he visits, Mrs Anderson?"

"He lays with me."

"Lays?"

"Yes. I think he misses me."

"Does ... You must have heard what is happening in the village—to the villagers. Don't you feel afraid?"

"No ... yes ... I think he ... Max is different, but he's still in there."

Javeen remembered the glimmer of insanity raging through Jenny Oldfield's eyes as she'd thrashed with agony after being bitten. How much of the victim did the infection leave?

"He doesn't try to hurt you?"

"I think the part that loves me is keeping him from killing me."

"It's not safe for you to stay here."

Laura grunted then curled forward.

"Are you in pain."

"Just a stomach ache." Her frown smoothed. "There. Gone now. Maybe just time of the month."

"Paracetamol and a hot water bottle?"

Laura grimaced.

"Do you drive?"

"Yes, my car is parked in the driveway."

"Good, then pack what you need and drive up to the castle. We're locking the gates at three-thirty pm."

"Three-thirty?"

"We want everyone in before twilight. We believe they're becoming nocturnal, and twilight is when they become active."

Laura nodded. "I'll be there."

# CHAPTER FIFTY-ONE

Javeen checked her watch. Three-twenty-five pm. There were only five minutes before the gates closed and were locked for the night. Laura Anderson still hadn't arrived. She pulled the door open to let another survivor pass through and directed him to Moira who was busy organising sleeping arrangements whilst Andy and Conrad drew up their defensive plans. She checked her watch again. Three-thirty. She would have to bring Laura in herself.

Rain spattered her cheek as she walked to her car. With an overcast sky, the day already seemed at an end. Her belly gave a watery roll.

At the back of the Anderson's house, Javeen rapped at the door. Her hand trembled and she stuffed it deep into her pocket as Laura answered the knock. On the kitchen table were two large bags and a washbag.

"Do you need any help, Mrs Anderson? It's gone three-thirty."

"Oh, hell! I didn't realise it was so late. I just have something to sort out upstairs." She turned, strode out of the room, and disappeared.

A howl pierced the air and Javeen's guts twisted as her heart hammered painfully against her ribs. *They can't be here! Not yet!* "I'll load the car!"

As she lugged the overly filled bags outside, another howl broke from deep within the forest. Opening the boot, Javeen threw the bags in with a grunt. Across the road, Emily Carmichael lay on her bed, the glow of her bedside lamp illuminated the scene and Javeen took comfort from it. The Reverend sat at her side, his hand holding hers, whilst in the other he held a small book, presumably the bible, his lips moving as he read from its pages.

Leaving the boot open, Javeen returned to the empty kitchen. Another howl cut through the air.

"Laura!"

"Coming!"

"Meet me at the car!" Javeen called, grabbing the final bag.

As she stepped out of the door, Laura returned to the kitchen and the howl repeated. This time the ungodly noise was in the village.

"They're here!" Laura's voice was hoarse.

"Not yet." *Stay calm.* "We'll take my car. It's parked outside."

An icy blast of wind-driven rain spattered Javeen's cheeks as they ran down the drive The sky was a dark and mottled grey.

"I thought you said they only come out at night!"

"That's what I thought. Perhaps it's just the light they don't like. It's so overcast now it might as well be twilight."

As they reached the end of the drive, the sight at the end of the road sent shockwaves coursing through her body and she stumbled. A large group had gathered at the corner. Javeen froze and Laura knocked against her back, sending

Javeen staggering forward. She dropped to a crouch, eyes trained on the pack. "Get back," she hissed. Heads turned towards their position. Laura whimpered but stepped back.

"Now what?"

A heckle. A cackle. The clacking of claws on tarmac.

Javeen took a deep breath. *Stay calm. Got to stay calm. Think.* Going back into the house would be suicide. "Get in the car!"

In the next second, she leapt out from behind the brick column and sprinted for the car. The creatures spotted her, screeched, and sprinted forward. Thigh muscles rippled as lips pared back and they bounded forward. Javeen pulled the car door shut as a body thudded against it. Laura slammed her door shut as Javeen slipped the key into the ignition.

"Jesus! Jesus! Jesus!"

A creature jumped onto the car, its face hideously distorted as it snarled and gnashed its teeth. A thud came from the roof and metal scraped.

"They're cutting the roof open!"

Javeen twisted the key in the ignition. It turned but didn't start. *Calm down, Jav. Just calm the fuck down!* She tried again. The ignition caught. Lights illuminated the creatures as she shifted into first and released the clutch. The car jerked forward and stalled. "Shit! Fucking shit!"

Laura placed a firm hand on Javeen's shoulder. "Stay calm. Breathe."

The Reverend appeared at Emily Carmichael's window and began to bang on the glass with his bible. The screeching of metal stopped and the creature on the front of the car twisted its head to look across the road. The engine burst into life and the car jolted forward as Javeen crunched the gears.

The pack bounded across the road.

Javeen slammed the accelerator to the floor speeding past the horde as they swarmed into Emily's garden and the car's boot clicked shut.

# CHAPTER FIFTY-TWO

Reverend Baxter's breath caught in his chest as the monsters lurched across the road, jumped Emily's wall, and slammed against the window. Great trails of slather swirled over the glass.

Thud!

A clawed fist slammed against the glass.

Thud!

Another fist slammed, and then another. The entire window rattled, and plaster cracked around the frame. The room darkened as bodies pushed against the glass, each forcing themselves in front of the other. On the bed, Emily took great sucks of oxygen, her bony hands holding the mask tight to her face. The last two hours had been spent reading to her. She'd requested some favourite passages, some of the most beautiful in the English language that she had to hear for the last time. Like him, her time was near, and she'd confided in him, with tears welling, that she didn't think she'd get to see the peonies beneath the lilac next spring. She didn't mind though because Cyril was waiting for her. He'd taken her hand then, placed his other with a gentle touch across her paper-thin brow and told her the truth—that this life was merely the journey, beyond its final gate was their true home, with the Almighty, in the loving light of His Son. She'd smiled, closed her eyes, and asked him to read.

He'd attended many deathbeds, soothed the desperate, given them succour in their time of need, and accompanied those who embraced it, and he had developed a sense for when their time for passing was near. Emily's time was close, perhaps this afternoon, or early evening.

Thud!

Faces pressed up against the pane, incisors scratched against the glass, and eyes, pooled with blood, stared madly into the room. The car disappeared past the church, and he stepped back to Emily's bedside and sat back down. With a shaking hand he opened the book and read aloud.

"The Lord is my shepherd; I shall not-"

The chattering, screeching and gnashing intensified, drowning out the Reverend's voice. He raised it. "He restoreth my soul: he leadeth me in the paths of righteousness ..." The chattering subsided, the horde of creatures thinned, and grey light returned to the room. At the back of the house the door handle creaked. *He hadn't locked it!* Heart palpitating, he turned to Emily. She lay deep in her pillow, eyes closed, chest heaving despite the oxygen mask. He removed it. The door slammed open. His hand visibly shook as he took hold of hers. "It's time to go now, Emily. Cyril is waiting. The Lord is waiting." She took a great rattling breath as the cackling from the kitchen rose to a crescendo and the bedroom door slammed open.

The Reverend stroked her hand with his, resting his shaking hand on her belly. "I commend you, my dear sister, to almighty God ..." The room filled with their stench. "And entrust you to your Creator." Teeth gnashed. One pushed from behind the others. A screech rose and jaws snapped.

"May you return to Him." Emily's eyes flickered open. She pulled her hand from his and flung her arms out as though in an embrace and lifted her head from the pillow.

Hot breath, sour and rank, brushed against the Reverend's cheek. The room had filled with monsters, the small space claustrophobic. He continued. "...who formed you from the dust of the earth."

The heat and stench of their bodies filled the room. A large female bent to his neck and sniffed, growled, snapped, then pulled back. The noise of their snapping and snarling drowned out his voice. He shouted the prayer as they closed in around Emily's bed. "May holy Mary, the angels, and all the saints come to meet you as you go forth from this life." Emily remained silent with her eyes closed. She exhaled but did not inhale. Talons dug deep into the muscle of his shoulder, and he sank beneath the pressure, his old knees unable to resist. "May Christ," he shouted as the pain intensified and Emily disappeared beneath the horde, "who was crucified for you, bring you freedom and peace. Amen." Emily made no sound as the creatures fell upon her.

THE CAR'S TYRES SQUEALED as it careened from the road onto the castle's driveway. Picnic tables disappeared in a blur and the heavy double gates of the arched entrance loomed. To her relief, they opened as she drew close. She parked as Andy closed and locked the gates.

"What the hell are you doing?" Andy asked as she stumbled from the car. "We were all supposed to be here! Jesus, Jav! When I couldn't find you-"

"I had to get Laura," she said gesturing to the woman in the passenger seat. "Andy, they were there, at the house, the Reverend saved us."

"Jesus!" The frown of disapproval deepened. "You idiot! You absolute idiot!"

"Thanks."

"Jav, you could have died."

"Well, I didn't," she threw back.

"What happened to the Reverend?"

"He ... he distracted them."

Andy shook his head. "Was he with Emily?"

Javeen nodded. "He knocked on the window to distract them. He saved us!"

"So they ..." A pained frown passed over Andy's face. "So ... they attacked him and Emily instead."

Javeen swallowed, suddenly overcome with shame; if she hadn't gone to fetch Laura, the Reverend and Emily would still be alive.

"I didn't think they'd come out this early. I thought they were nocturnal."

"You were wrong."

"I think it's just the light they don't like."

"Werewolves only come out on the full moon in the movies, Jav," he said. He gestured to Laura. "She should have been here by three-thirty. You've put us all at risk by going out and coming back the way you did. What if they'd gotten in? If we're going to survive this ... this ... their attacks, then we've got to follow the rules."

"I didn't know there were rules."

"There are going to have to be rules. We're all going to die otherwise."

She sagged, weary after the shock of adrenaline. "I'm sorry, I just couldn't leave Laura out there."

Andy shook his head although his frown softened. "I get it."

A creature howled, another answered, and Javeen sank against Andy's chest as the cacophony reached a crescendo then faded. Yaps and snarls carried on the wind.

"Bring her inside," he said with a glance to the woman still in the passenger seat. "Moira can take care of her. She's been allocated a room in the east wing; it's on the plan."

As Andy disappeared inside, and Laura pulled her bag from the back seat, a clawed hand ripped at the bags inside the car's boot.

THE SUN SET ACROSS the village, long shadows growing until the only light was the orange haze from the streetlights. Jim Kendrick's cat dashed across the road, chasing a scurrying rat. At Seven Main Street, Kathy Oldfield's Jack Russell scratted at the back door and barked at the noise of galloping feet in the garden. Further along the road, at number Twenty-Three Mary Barker's Bassett Hound howled a lament, its stomach aching with hunger as it padded around and around the kitchen, stepping in its own urine and faeces. A face pushed up to the window. It wagged its tail, jumped up at the door leaving a stinking smear of shit on the white paintwork, then barked as the glass smashed, snarled as the thing broke through the door, and yelped as teeth sank into its neck. As it died, the air filled with chattering, snickering, incomprehensible voices, and the patter of dozens of feet on the tarmac.

# CHAPTER FIFTY-THREE

Javeen ticked off the names on her list as she took a head count of the villagers that had made it to the castle. Only nineteen people remained. *All of them dead or infected. All of them.* Nineteen out of more than one hundred! The paper in her hand was covered in red lines, and almost every house on the map Andy had drawn of the village had a red cross through it.

"PC Latimer."

She stared at the paper, unaware of Moira's voice.

*All of them dead or infected. All of them.*

"PC Latimer!"

*All of them.*

Javeen flinched as a hand landed on her shoulder. "I've made you a sandwich. Why don't you come and sit down? I'll get you a cup of tea."

"Sorry, Moira. Thanks, I will."

Following Moira to the table she sat and stared at the sandwich. The bread was stale.

*All of them dead or infected. All of them.*

Andy sat down beside her, leant a large axe against the wall, and took a cup of steaming tea from Moira's hands.

Javeen scanned the group. There were no children. None! What happened to Amy and her children? Her stomach griped. Apart from herself, Andy, Freddie, and

Hayley, the other survivors – her belly rolled again – were older and two were at least eighty. Conrad would be useful, of course, given his background, and his wife Moira was a force to be reckoned with, but although Laura was in her early thirties, half the time she seemed to be lost in her thoughts, and the other sleeping. Even now, with mug of tea in hand, she was curled up on the large sofa that Andy had pulled up to the open fire and seemed to be nodding off. For Javeen, sleep was impossible, her senses on overload. Andy slipped an arm across her shoulder. She shuddered at his touch. He pulled his arm away with a quick movement.

"Gone off me already?"

"What? No. I'm on edge that's all."

The subdued chatter in the room grew quiet and she lowered her voice to a whisper as she pushed the list of names across the table, each red line a painful reminder of a face, a wave, a smile, now gone. "They've all gone. We're all that's left of the village."

"Whispering, Latimer?" Conrad stepped up to their table. "If you've got something to say, we should all hear it."

Javeen swallowed, blinked back the tear that threatened to spill over her lashes, and pushed the paper towards him.

"Damn!"

"We're all that's left, Conrad. Just nineteen of us. And no children. In a few days they've decimated the population of this village."

"They're ravenous, that's for sure."

"The ultimate apex predator."

Conrad grunted. "Well, I-"

"They're monsters. Within a few days they've destroyed an entire village; either hunted us down or infected us to become like them."

"I think they're deliberately strengthening their packs."

"And we're trapped in here with them."

"Sitting ducks."

"They've left us here to die."

"Marta Steward has left us here to die. The programme that created these monsters is under her direction."

"Are you saying this is deliberate?"

"Are we part of an experiment?"

"We are now. Steward and Dalton want to capture the 'wolfmen' and use them as weapons."

"That's ridiculous, Latimer. What are you saying? That they're going to capture them and train them as soldiers?"

"Something like that."

"Science fiction! Nonsense!" Conrad scoffed. "Never heard anything so ridiculous in all my life."

"It is ridiculous, but so is the existence of wolfmen, yet they're out there, hunting us down."

"They're not werewolves. That's just fantasy. Certainly, they've been infected with some dreadful virus-"

A howl split the air and silence fell upon the room.

"That was close," said Moira with a fearful look towards the shuttered window.

"We're safe in here." Andy slipped a comforting arm across Javeen's shoulder.

"The fence-"

"Whoever put that up should be imprisoned. They've signed our death warrant."

"Why would they do that? If they knew what these creatures were capable of, why didn't they evacuate us before it was too late?"

Javeen didn't have an answer.

"If they ever get beyond the fence, they'll hunt humans to extinction."

Freddie caught her gaze.

"We have to stop them."

"How? They've killed everything they've found so far, killed it or bitten it, and made it one of them."

"Conniving bastards."

"It's time to turn the tables. Let the hunted became the hunter."

"How do you suggest we do that? It would be suicide to go into the woods."

"We set traps—here in the village."

MAX SPRUNG WITH EASE to the wall and vaulted over, landing with a soft thud on the grass. It crunched beneath his feet, its iciness in this first frost of winter, sharp against his bare toes. The house sat in darkness; the curtains drawn. Something was different. He walked to the back of the house and pushed down the door handle. It opened to the silence of an empty house. He strode through the kitchen to the living room and then took the stairs two at a time, inhaling the scent of orange zest, oatmeal soap, Chanel No. 5, and the intense particles of Laura's sweat and the sweet scent of her dark places. The air in their bedroom was cold, her scent stale. She was gone. Rage swirled. He tipped his head back and howled, "Lauurraaaa!"

Within ten seconds he was out of the house and sprinting past the church. The streets were silent, the houses dark. To his left came snickering and tapping feet. The monsters ... his monsters ... ran parallel. From the distance came a howl—a call for the hunt. A thrill shuddered along his spine, and he pumped his arms harder, easily outpacing the strongest among the others. He followed the howl as it rose again, running along the empty roads. Light shone from the dark, a tiny slither that became two then three as he rounded the corner. He cackled, his mouth watering; the Screamers were hiding in their light. Ahead, the castle sat as a wide block on its hill. Slithers of light were patterned as stripes on its walls. *Come out, come out, little piggies.*

# CHAPTER FIFTY-FOUR

The chair made tracks in the carpet as Javeen dragged it closer to the fire. The glow and flicker of its orange flames danced on the hearth's tiles. Laura caught her glance, smiled, then moved to stand.

"My bags are in the boot of your car. Is it open?"

"Yep. I didn't lock it."

Laura smiled again. The door opened and Conrad walked in, his face flushed from the cold night air.

"The front seemed clear. I've checked all windows and doors. We've pushed as many cupboards and chairs up against the outside doors as we can find."

Laura waited patiently as Conrad relayed his message. "Excuse me, Conrad. Could you let me through, please?"

His usual smiling ease was replaced with a frown. "Where are you going?"

"Well, I just need to get my bag from the car."

"We've locked everything down now, Mrs Anderson. Can't it wait until morning?"

"Oh, but it has my toiletries in it ..."

The flush on Conrad's face deepened. "Well ..."

"There are things in there I *need*."

"... Ah. Well, alright ... but ... I'll come with you. You won't be able to move the furniture on your own."

As they disappeared through the door and out into the hallway, Javeen rose from the warmth of the fireside and followed them. The cold air was a shock to her warmed skin, and she shivered, pulling her jacket tight to her body. If the night got much colder, getting any sleep would be unlikely. It would be tough getting to sleep in the large, unheated rooms of the castle with only a makeshift bed. Perhaps they should all make their beds in the room with the fire instead, and forget about their privacy? The thought brought its own relief—there was safety in numbers.

She caught up with Conrad as he stepped outside where sharp drizzle had become driving sleet. Laura ran to the car as Conrad shone his torch to light the way.

"Just a thought, Conrad, but instead of us all having separate sleeping areas in the castle, would it be better for us all to be in one room?"

"I'm not sure Moira would like that. However, it does make sense. If we're all in one room, then we don't have to worry about each other as much. I won't be sleeping tonight though. I've drawn up the rota for a patrol—my watch is first. There are to be two of us awake at all times. We'll share the duties throughout the night."

The tension across Javeen's shoulders eased a little; having Conrad in charge was a godsend.

Sleet spiked Javeen's cheeks as she checked the courtyard and the rooftops for signs of movement and followed Laura to the car. As Conrad shone light on the boot, Laura fumbled beneath its door.

"It's locked PC Latimer."

"I'm sure I didn't lock it," replied Javeen and slid her fingers to the catch. The latch released. "There you go." As she spoke movement caught in her peripheral vision. She turned to see Max Anderson squatting on the roof. He snarled as the boot's lid lifted, Scuffling from within startled Javeen, and Laura screamed as a figure sprang from the recess, pushing them to the floor. Pain flared in her ankle. Max roared, distracting the creature.

Javeen pulled herself from beneath Laura, flinching as sharp pain shot through her ankle.

With terrifying and primal strength, the creature grabbed Laura, threw her to the floor then straddled her. A roar filled the space and in the next moment Max Anderson grabbed the creature throwing it from Laura. She lay inert as the males circled one another, lips drawn back from razor-sharp fangs, growling from the depths of their bellies. Javeen dragged herself towards the car, gasping at the pain in her ankle as it caught on the cobbled stones.

Max bared his teeth and snapped at the other male as they continued to circle, fists clenching, deep growls filling the air, eyes locked. Max pounced, knocking the male to the floor, sinking his fangs into its jaws, and pinning it to the cobbles. The male thrashed, but Max held him down, digging his claws into its shoulders. Minutes passed as the male bucked and growled until he submitted. Max retracted his incisors and the defeated male scurried across the cobbles. Max turned his attention to Javeen.

Across the courtyard, Conrad screamed as the inferior male attacked, dragging him into the shadows.

Javeen scrabbled back as Max advanced, spikes of pain running through her ankle and up her shin. He towered above her as Conrad's strangled cry was silenced.

Laura staggered against the car. "Max! No!"

Max grunted but took another step to Javeen.

"No! Don't hurt her."

He faltered and with a final growl turned to his wife. As Javeen dragged herself inside and locked the doors, Max Anderson wrapped his arms around Laura and sank his teeth into her neck. With her head lolling, eyes rolled back to white, he carried her to the gates, lifted the bar that secured them and threw it across the cobbles. He pushed them open to the night and the ravenous horde.

Chattering, cackles, and excited howls mingled with the tack, tack of clawed feet across the cobbles as they streamed across the courtyard. Javeen slipped into the footwell of the backseat and lay still as the creatures disappeared inside.

Time passed and she grew cold.

Pulling herself up from the footwell, she peered into the courtyard. The driving sleet had lightened to drizzle, and the cobbles gleamed in the moonlight. Conrad lay curled in grotesque, foetal parody against the far wall. The monster that had slashed his throat had gone, and there was no sign of Laura or Max Anderson.

She sagged against the door, forehead pushing up against the glass with an overwhelming dread, realising that the horde of monsters that filled the courtyard was now inside the castle. The survivors didn't stand a chance.

"Andy!" Her whisper was pained. "Andy."

Her mind was numb. Instinctively, she knew that survival meant staying put, being small, invisible. She sank back into the footwell with a sense of failure and crushing inadequacy biting into her. Her ankle throbbed and the windows grew opaque. The car became a cocoon, but her thoughts brought a new torture. *What if they noticed? What if one of them was still conscious enough – still human enough – to realise that something warm, something living, something with a beating heart, and pumping blood, warm and sticky, ready to be swallowed, hid inside? What if -* she swallowed *- what if they could smell her? Calm down, Latimer! Get a grip.* She took a deep breath to calm herself, but it did little to ease the tension. The fogged-up car offered a hiding place away from prying eyes, but it trapped her too. *Andy! Please be safe. Please be alive.*

Rubbing a small hole in the misted glass she squinted through. The courtyard was empty.

She reached for the doorhandle but released it as though scorched as the courtyard filled with chattering, cackles, and excited yips as creatures swarmed from the castle. Watching through the misted circle, she hardly dared to breath.

A female passed, and then two males, one with a body slung across its shoulder. As it jogged past, she realised the body was Moira Shelby, Conrad's wife.

Despite its contorted face, deformed with a snarl and bone white fangs, Javeen recognised the carrier as Thomas Burdon, the farmer who had chewed her ear off about the lynx conservation project.

The creatures appeared in small groups, some with the harvest of their hunt slung across their shoulders. As each passed, she searched for Andy. Eventually the flow thinned to a few stragglers and then nothing. She waited, counting the seconds and, after ten minutes without sight of a creature, she opened the door. Freezing air blasted her cheeks.

Movement in the castle doorway trapped air in her chest and a figure appeared. It staggered against the door's frame then stumbled out into the courtyard. *Andy!*

As he sank to his knees, she stumbled out of the car, her ankle an agony, then limped to him. His shirt was torn, the ripped fabric soaked with blood.

"It bit me," he rasped. "Help me, Jav. Help me." Overwhelmed with pain his body jerked with stiff movements. "Please!" He forced the words through clenched teeth.

Face contorted by pain, ugly in the harsh shadows of the outside light, he sagged as the agonising spasm subsided

"Jav. The vials. Get the vials. End it!"

"They're in the car," she replied.

"Get them," he grunted.

Javeen limped to the car and retrieved vials and syringes. As she returned another wave of pain hit him and he jerked, in a backwards arc. His pale skin glowed, highlighting the criss-cross of blue veins across his cheeks. Another spasm controlled him, and his head thrashed against the cobbles.

"Stop! Oh, God. Stop!"

Blood trickled over the stones.

Kneeling behind him, Javeen prepared the poison injection, drawing fluid into the syringe. She filled three vials, placed them on the cobbles beside her, then pulled him to lay across her lap. Rain bounced from the stones as she stroked his forehead, holding him as another spasm wracked his body.

"Please ... please ..." He jerked again and growled. The bones of his jaw dislocated, and his eyes rolled, blood filling the whites.

Javeen reached for a syringe.

*How much should she give him? It was meant for dogs. It had killed the beagle at the Institute, but would it kill him?*

*Kill him! Kill Andy?*

She had never killed a man. As part of her training she had been taught to shoot, and to fight, but it was all defensive stuff. No part of her being had ever considered actually killing a man. Andy bucked and groaned, his eyes locking to the syringe. *How could she kill a man that she loved?*

"Do it!"

She sobbed, her heart breaking as their eyes met. His were almost entirely black, the white replaced with blood, the pupils huge. With trembling hands she pointed the needle against his throat. From the distance came a howl.

*How had this all happened? How had the entire village been destroyed in the space of a few days?*

She was entirely alone. What chance had she of survival? Every avenue of escape had been closed. The woods were infested, her theory about them being nocturnal wrong. So far, all efforts at escape had ended in disaster. She was the last survivor. But for how long? How long before she was torn to shreds, disembowelled, her innards feasted upon? Bile rose in her throat. How long? A week? A day? Through this night? One more hour? Andy groaned and writhed against her, and she held his head close to her belly, keeping him still as another fit overwhelmed him.

In a moment of clarity, she threw the syringe to the cobbles and waited for his bite.

THE END

**READ THE NEXT IN SERIES:**

The next in series is: *The Alaska Strain* – read the prologue below.

**What to read next:**

If you enjoyed this novel, try *Feeders*.

# THE ALASKA STRAIN: PROLOGUE

*International Institute of Bio-Tech Advancement,*
*Volkolak Island, Southwest Alaska*

From her office at the heart of the research facility, Dr. Marta Steward watched the live feed with anticipation. As director of the programme she had ordered the team to procure a higher quality female and they hadn't disappointed. The woman was young and attractive, with slim waist, rounded buttocks, large breasts, and a pretty face, but she looked unwell, as though recovering from a bad hangover, or perhaps suffering drug withdrawal symptoms. Marta made a note to request that a 'clean' specimen be procured next time, then returned her attention to the screen.

Breath caught in her chest as the door opened and Max, or at least what had been Max, stepped into the cell. For several moments he hung back, sniffing at the air, then began his approach to the woman. Her screams weren't audible, but from the way she cowered in the corner, hiding behind the thin mattress, the only object of comfort in the cell, her terror was obvious.

"Put it down woman!" Marta hissed, frustrated as the woman remained out of sight. She made another note to tell Kendrick to remove the mattress next time; the woman's reactions were just as important to note as Max's.

Marta gave an exasperated sigh; something in Max's gait, the way he held himself, indicated failure. After another minute Marta was certain and cut the live feed to dead with an irritated prod at the keyboard; she had no stomach to watch the carnage that would follow yet another failed introduction. The screen returned to an image of herself, Peter Marston, Katarina Petrov, and Max Anderson against the backdrop of the Gothic façade of Kielder Institute. Taken on their first day at the newly refurbished building, their smiles were bright and hopeful. A moment of sadness, quickly extinguished, flickered within Marta. Max stood smiling, innocent, unaware of the terrible fate that awaited him, and she was struck by the realisation of how our lives progress, the incidents that make up who we are, and what path our life would follow, were totally random, inexplicable, and sometimes just bloody bizarre.

"Poor Max." Her focus moved to the Institute's portal on the screen. "But it won't have all been for nothing. I can promise you that. Peter will know what to do." She entered a password and accessed the hidden files labelled 'Project Kielder' then began to read through the notes before booking a flight back to England.

# Never Miss Another Book

J oin me for more early access to novels, to be notified of publication days, novel updates, and fan discounts: https://deadcitychronicles.substack.com/

# About the Author

An English author, Rebecca lives with her children among the flatlands of the Humber estuary where Vikings and Anglo-Saxons once fought. Sometimes, on foggy mornings, the sounds of clashing swords can still be heard.

She writes dystopian and post-apocalyptic thrillers and novels of horror.